Plato's Quest:
Atlantis and the Emerald Tablet

By J.D. Blondin

ISBN: 979-8-218-48110-0

First Edition

Published by: Creative Synergy LLC

Cover design by Jayson Blondin

Printed in the United States of America

This tale is woven with threads of love and sacrifice, a tribute to the one whose unwavering strength and grace brought light to my darkest hours. To my mother, who raised me with boundless courage and saved my life with her enduring love, I dedicate this journey. And with deepest gratitude to God the Father, Son, and Holy Spirit, whose divine guidance, mercy, and love have been my constant source of strength and inspiration, I offer this work as a testament to His everlasting grace.

"This is the tale I pray the divine Muse to unfold to us.
Begin it, goddess, at whatever point you will."
— The Odyssey of Homer

"Like the generations of leaves, the lives of mortal men. Now the
wind scatters the old leaves across the earth, now the living timber
bursts with the new buds and spring comes round again. And so
with men: as one generation comes to life, another dies away."
— The Iliad

PROLOGUE

The soft glow of moonlight seeped through the window, mingling with the candlelight, casting an ethereal glow upon the mural that adorned the walls. Critaeus marveled at his creation— an intricately painted tableau depicting the mysterious tale of Atlantis. The mural breathed life, shadows flickering with the dance of candlelight, as if the ancient city beckoned you into its depths.

As the last stroke of his brush dried, he turned his attention to his nephew, who was tucked snuggly under his covers, eyes wide with anticipation. It was finally time for the bedtime story, a tale that had been passed down through their family for generations.

"Plato, my dear boy," he began, his voice tender and rich with anticipation. "Today is your seventh birthday. You're well on you way to becoming a man. The story I am about to tell was told to your father and I from our grandfather, who was told by his grandfather, Solon. Your great-grandfather is no longer with us, but I promised him that I would keep this story alive in you once you came of age. Now, is that time. Look upon the mural and let the whispers of Atlantis guide us through the veils of time."

Plato's gaze was fixed upon the mesmerizing mural, where moonlit hues mingled with the vibrant colors of the painted city. Shadows cavorted across the walls, casting an air of mystique, as if Atlantis itself stirred in the dreamscape of their room.

"Do you see?" He encouraged, gesturing towards the mural. "This is the ancient city of Atlantis, lost in the mists of time, yet forever imprinted upon our family's heritage."

Plato's eyes widened, drinking in the details woven within the mural's brushstrokes. Ivory towers stood proud, kissed by the moon's gentle radiance, while crystalline canals weaved through the streets like liquid veins.

"Atlantis," the boy murmured, his voice barely above a whisper.

His uncle nodded, a smile of reverence gracing his lips. "Indeed, boy. Atlantis was a city of unparalleled splendor, a marvel of advanced knowledge and civilization."

As he spoke, the shadows from the mural danced upon the wall, creating a mesmerizing interplay of light and dark. It was as if the spirits of Atlantis themselves stirred within the room, eager to reveal their secrets.

"10,000 years ago, Atlantis thrived in a great golden age," he began, his voice carrying the weight of the tale. "The Atlanteans were a prosperous and enlightened people, guided by the gods' favor."

Plato sat up, clutching his quilt and leaned forward, captivated by his uncle's words, his eyes reflecting the flickering candlelight.

"But their prosperity bred arrogance and a desire for power," he continued. "In their hubris, the Atlanteans waged war against the neighboring lands of all of the world, including our ancient Athenian brothers and sisters, seeking to conquer and dominate."

The mural's shadows shifted, casting dark figures upon the walls, depicting the war and the strife that plagued Atlantis.

"The gods, displeased with this lust for power, favored Athens and decided to teach the Atlantean's a lesson," he continued, his voice tinged with sorrow. "They unleashed their fury upon the city, causing the earth to tremble and the seas to rise in a great cataclysmic event."

Plato's eyes widened, his heart quickening as he envisioned the wrath of the gods and the catastrophic fate of Atlantis.

"The city, with all its grandeur and knowledge, was swallowed by the relentless waves," he concluded, his voice softening. "And Atlantis sank beneath the ocean depths, lost forever."

Plato felt a mixture of awe and sorrow, his young mind grappling with the magnitude of the story he had just heard. He looked once again at the mural, where the city now lay submerged beneath the painted sea.

"Remember, Plato," his uncle said, his voice filled with a gentle admonition and wisdom, "let the tale of Atlantis serve as a cautionary reminder. It reminds us of the consequences of arrogance and the importance of maintaining a harmonious balance with nature and our fellow beings," He paused, "as well as a reminder of the perils of crossing our great city-state, Athens, who are loved by the gods above all others."

Plato nodded, his young mind absorbing the profound lessons embedded within the story. He traced the outlines of the submerged city on the mural, contemplating the intricate connections between Atlantis and their beloved Athens. "Just as Atlantis met its tragic fate," Critaeus went on, "we must recognize the fragility of our own existence and strive for humility and wisdom. Atlantis's downfall serves as a call to nurture the gifts bestowed upon us by the gods and to preserve the harmony of society."

Plato's gaze shifted from the mural to his uncle, a newfound understanding blossoming within him. He recognized the significance of his family's tale, intertwining the ancient city's story with the values cherished by Athens.

"Thank you, Uncle," Plato whispered, gratitude and wonder blending in his voice. "One day, I will find the lost island, and reignite the partnership between Athens and Atlantis." Claimed young Plato, with a child-like sense of wonder.

Critaeus leaned closer, his eyes filled with affection. "Ah, if only we could. The island is long gone by now, my boy; forever lost in the sands of time. All we have left are our stories; and keep them in our hearts we must. Sleep well, dear Plato, and may the dreams of Atlantis guide you towards enlightenment and inspire your own intellectual pursuits."

As Plato closed his eyes, the moonlight continued to cast its enchanting glow upon the mural, while the shadows danced, weaving tales of lost civilizations and eternal wisdom. In his slumber, Plato embarked on a journey of imagination and knowledge, carrying with him the legacy of Atlantis and the profound teachings it held.

Act 1: Separation

"Every journey begins with a departure from the familiar, a step into the unknown, and the courage to seek beyond the horizon."

In the cradle of the dawn,
A seeker sets his gaze,
Beyond the comfort of the known,
To where the new light plays.

Chapter 1

The Oracle's Whisper

He could hear the terrorizing screams of the people, their cries for help echoing in his mind. The sound of crashing waves and destruction were deafening, as he lifted in the air, soaring fast and high above the earth, the wind whipping past them as he flew towards an unknown destination. Below, the world was being consumed in a great and terrible flood, the water rising higher and higher, drowning everything in its path. He could see ancient temples and towering cities sinking beneath the waves, their grandeur and majesty reduced to nothing more than a memory.

In the distance, he spotted a massive central temple, its spires reaching towards the sky, but as he flew closer, he saw that it too was sinking, its walls collapsing as the waves crashed against them.

He tried to reach the temple, to save those in need, but no matter how fast he flew, it seemed to always be just out of reach. And then, suddenly, the temple was gone and he was falling, tumbling towards the water below.

Plato awoke with a start, feeling water splash on his face. For a moment, the dream lingered, and he felt a sudden jolt as he crashed into the water in his dream, as if reality itself had intruded upon the realm of his subconscious. He bolted upright, his eyes wide and disoriented, only to find himself face to face with the flickering

morning light through the window and the figures of an Athenian priestess standing beside the statue of Hermes.

The Priestess, adorned in her sacred robes, was pouring water from a jug, the clear liquid cascading onto the ground at the feet of the statue. The gentle sound of water mingled with the rustling leaves outside the window, created a soothing symphony that slowly brought him back to his senses.

"Apologies, esteemed Plato," the priestess said, her voice carrying a hint of mischief and familiarity. "I didn't mean to startle you. It's time to wake and prepare for the second day of the Hermaea Festival."

Plato blinked, his mind still clouded with the remnants of his dream. As he focused on the priestess, recognition flickered in his eyes. It was she — the enchanting priestess with whom he had shared a night of revelry and laughter.

A bashful smile tugged at the corners of her lips, her cheeks tinged with a rosy blush. She leaned closer, her voice barely above a whisper. "I trust you slept well, Plato. It seems our evening together has left its mark."

His heart skipped a beat, and a mischievous glimmer danced in his eyes. "Ahh, the night we shared, a memory that still lingers like a haunting melody. I must admit, dear priestess, your presence has made quite the impression."

She chuckled softly, a twinkle of desire sparkling in her gaze. "Let us be discreet, for we tread a delicate line between the gods and our mortal desires. But I cannot deny my eagerness to see you again, to explore what lies beyond this vestal haze."

His mind whirled with conflicting thoughts, torn between his philosophical pursuits and the allure of this intoxicating connection. He knew the boundaries that bound them, the expectations placed upon a godly temple priestess, but the temptation whispered to him in the soft morning breeze.

With a teasing smile, the priestess added, "And may I say, Plato, your name, like your prowess, carries a breadth that extends beyond mere words. It seems you truly embody the essence of '*Platos*' in more ways than one."

A blush crept across his cheeks, his pulse quickening at her innuendo. He was both captivated and torn, caught between his desires and the weight of their respective roles.

Before he could respond, the priestess held up a finger, a playful glint in her eyes. "But, my dear Plato, time waits for no one. If you wish to catch the grand procession and prepare for your wrestling match in honor of Hermes, I suggest you hurry and sober up. The day holds much in store for you, my philosopher-wrestler."

He nodded, the gravity of the day's events settling upon him. With a final, lingering gaze, he rose form his slumber and set himself on a path that would intertwine the realms of thought and action, passion and reason, and perhaps, reveal the truths that lay hidden within his recurring dreams.

Plato walked briskly along the bustling streets of Athens, his mind preoccupied with the hazy remnants of the previous night. The vestal tryst with the temple priestess, and the vivid dream that followed had left him in a contemplative state. His footsteps rhythmically clacking against the uneven surface of the cobblestones as he made his way from the temple of Hermes toward the stadium for his wrestling match in honor of the god.

As he passed by a group of beggars seeking solace in the shadows of the buildings, Plato couldn't help but feel the tug of emotions. Their presence stirred his philosophical beliefs, prompting thoughts of personal responsibility and the importance of striving for a better life. He believed that hard work and intellect should guide one toward prosperity, and he often struggled to comprehend those who found themselves destitute, and thought they should accept their lower status and get employed as a servant to an elite family instead of

embarrassing themselves on the side of the street by begging. They should have some standards and self respect, he thought.

However, this time was different. Where he would normally be agitated at their presence, this time he found himself questioning his own thoughts and reasoning behind his feelings. Then unexpectedly, his attention was drawn to a most peculiar sight: a large, vibrant butterfly dancing gracefully between him and one of the beggars sitting against the wall. It's colorful fluttering wings seemed to carry a mysterious message of beauty and transformation, he thought, as a sense of wonder enveloped him. His curiosity of the beauty of the butterfly's fleeting nature of existence was interrupted as the beggar extended out his hand to request an offering, startling the butterfly to fly away and out of sight, over the building. Agitated, Plato pushed the beggars hand away in a scolding fashion.

Continuing on his path, the city was alive with excitement as the Hermaea festival sports approached. Plato's gaze was again arrested by another peculiar sight. Perched atop a nearby tree, an owl stared directly at him; its piercing eyes seemingly filled with ancient wisdom. The presence of the nocturnal creature during the daylight was a rarity, and Plato couldn't help but feel a sense of significance in this encounter. The owl's gaze penetrated deep into his soul, urging him to seek understanding beyond the confines of his usual intellectual pursuits.

At the stadium, Plato, clad in his wrestling tunic, made his way toward the wrestling area. He exchanged nods and greetings with fellow wrestlers, each displaying a mix of confidence and anticipation.

"Good luck to you all today. May Hermes favor us in our matches. I trust you all have prepared yourselves for an honorable defeat," boasted, Plato, confidently as he adjusted his wrestling tunic.

"Confident as always, Plato," chuckled Euclides. "I'll make sure to show you how real wrestlers compete. You can't think yourself out of these arms," he said as he flexed.

"You may have luck on your side today, Plato, but I'll make sure you regret underestimating me," exclaimed Pericles.

"We'll see who stands tall in the ring, my friends. Prepare to be humbled." Plato said, smirking.

As the wrestlers gathered near the edge of the wrestling area, they applied oil to their bodies and began stretching. The noise of the crowd grew louder, eager to witness the forthcoming matches. The referee, an elderly man with a stern demeanor, stepped forward, raising his staff to command attention.

"Wrestlers, it's time to prepare for your matches. Line up and await your turn," shouted the referee.

Plato and the other wrestlers formed a line, awaiting their matches. The crowd roared with anticipation as the previous bout concluded. The wrestlers entered the arena one by one, accompanied by the cheers and applause of the spectators. Plato found himself face-to-face with a formidable opponent, Lycon, a strong and experienced wrestler.

"So you're the young one they call, Plato?" Lycon said, smirking. "Let's see what you're made of."

I may be young, but I've trained diligently for this day. Prepare yourself, Lycon," assured Plato.

The referee blew his whistle, commencing the match. Plato and Lycon circled each other, their muscles tense with anticipation. Plato launched forward, attempting to grab Lycon's arm, but Lycon swiftly evaded his grasp. The crowd gasped, acknowledging Lycon's skill.

Plato adjusted his strategy, adopting a more defensive stance. He bided his time, waiting for an opening. Suddenly, Lycon lunged forward, aiming to overpower Plato with his sheer strength. However, Plato skillfully sidestepped, using Lycon's momentum against him. With a deft maneuver, Plato seized the opportunity, executing a perfectly timed throw.

The stadium erupted in a mix of cheers and applause as Plato triumphed over Lycon. The referee raised Plato's hand in victory, and the crowd's admiration was palpable.

"Plato, son of Ariston, emerges victorious! Well done!" announces the referee loudly.

Plato, exhausted, yet, exhilarated, bowed to the crowd, acknowledging their support. As he exited the wrestling area, he caught sight of Socrates, his mentor and teacher, smiling proudly.

"Well done, my young friend! Your prowess in the wrestling ring is matched only by your wisdom," grinned Socrates.

"Thank you, Socrates. Your guidance has been invaluable," said Plato gratefully.

With the second day of the Hermaea festival in full swing, Plato's victory became a memorable moment, inspiring the countless conversations and philosophical Musings in the days to come. The spirit of the competition merged with the intellectual pursuits of Athens, and Plato's journey continued to unfold.

That evening found Plato relishing in the day's victories and losses. The sun had set over the vibrant city of Athens, casting an orange glow on the agora as the second day of the Hermaea festival came to a close. Plato, still buzzing with excitement of the day's tournament, found himself surrounded by a lively group of fellow celebrants. Merriment and boisterous banter filled the air as they raised their cups, toasting to the victories and defeats of the matches.

Plato, his cheeks flushed with pride and wine, regaled the group with animated tales of his triumphs. "You should have seen it! I wrestled with the strength of Hermes himself, tossing opponents left and right!" he boasted, a glint of arrogance in his eyes. "Though I may not have won the tournament, I fought valiantly and made a definite mark."

Laughter erupted from the group as they clinked their cups together, relishing in the jovial atmosphere. Amidst the revelry, Plato's attention was caught by a familiar voice. It was Socrates, standing on the outskirts of the celebration, engaged in a philosophical discussion with a small group of children who had gathered around him.

Plato's curiosity piqued, he wobbled his way toward the group, his steps uneven from the effects of the wine. While leaning against a nearby pillar, he strained to listen to Socrates' words of wisdom. The aged philosopher's voice carried a gentle yet commanding tone, captivating the young minds before him.

"My young friends, today I want us to explore the notion of truth and wisdom. Many in our society look to the gods and the city's authorities as the ultimate sources of knowledge. But I propose that we must not accept anything blindly. Instead, we should question and scrutinize all ideas, even those that come from divine beings."

"But, Socrates, isn't that sacrilegious?" asked one of the youths in the back of the group. "The gods are all-knowing, and their wisdom guides us."

"Ah, an excellent point. But, what if the gods' wisdom is not beyond scrutiny? What if they provide us with opportunities to think critically and make choices based on our understanding?" Socrates rebutted.

"So, are you saying we should doubt everything, even our beliefs in the gods?" questioned a short teenager close by in front of his friends.

"Precisely!" exclaimed Socrates. "Doubt is the gateway to knowledge. It is through questioning and challenging our beliefs that we can discern truth from mere illusion. Blind faith can lead to dogma and stagnation of the mind."

"But, Socrates, how do we find the truth if we question everything? Won't we be lost in uncertainty?" asked another student.

"A valid concern, my friend. The journey to truth may indeed be challenging, but it is a journey worth taking. We must have the courage to confront uncertainty and embrace the pursuit of wisdom.

For it is only through doubt and questioning that we can truly think for ourselves."

"What about the city's laws and authority? Should we question them, too?" mouthed a particular youth of questionable intentions.

"Absolutely! Our society's laws are created by fallible humans, not infallible gods. Questioning them allows us to discern between just laws and unjust ones. It is the duty of a thoughtful citizen to engage in critical reflection on the laws that govern us."

"This seems like a radical idea, Socrates. Won't it lead to chaos?" the questionable youth replied.

"On the contrary, my young friend." replied Socrates with a wide smile across his face. "It will lead to a more enlightened society. By challenging the authority and seeking truth, we can collectively strive for justice and a more harmonious existence."

Plato's brow frowned, a mixture of concern and admiration washing over him. He knew Socrates had a penchant for stirring up trouble with his unconventional ideas, but, tonight, with a parent of one of the children he was preaching to being a prominent state senator, Plato sensed potential danger.

"…Always remember, my young friends," Socrates said, his eyes shining with fervor, "never be afraid to question any authority. Think for yourselves; seek truth, and challenge the status quo. The government, the aristocracy — they may hold power, but, it is your duty as citizens to examine, analyze, and form your own conclusions, and if necessary, to even question the gods themselves!"

With a hushed voice, Plato approached Socrates, nudging him gently. "Socrates, my friend," he slurred slightly, "be cautious. One of these children's parents holds great sway in the senate. Teaching them to question authority may not sit well with them."

Socrates turned his gaze toward Plato, his eyes gleaming with an unwavering resolve. "Plato, my dear pupil," he replied, his voice calm yet resolute, "the pursuit of truth and the dissemination of knowledge are of the utmost importance. While caution is always wise, we cannot let fear deter us from enlightening young minds and fostering critical thinking in our youth. It is through such questioning that progress is made. Plato, my boy, he who holds no principles, even in the face of persecution, will succumb to any persuasion. If we do not stand firm in our beliefs, society itself would soon collapse. It is through questioning authority and seeking truth that we build a strong and healthy community. Toning down our pursuit of wisdom, even for the safety of influential individuals, would betray the very foundation upon which a just society is built."

Plato nodded, his intoxicated state allowing a momentary glimpse of the profound wisdom within him. He respected Socrates' unwavering commitment to his beliefs, even if it meant facing potential repercussions. With a somber expression, Plato offered his support. "Very well, Socrates. But tread carefully. The path you walk is fraught with peril, even within the shadows of celebration."

Plato and Socrates shared a lingering gaze, an unspoken understanding passing between them. In the background, the sounds of merriment and revelry continued, oblivious to the weighty conversation that had transpired. Their philosophical journey, filled with it's triumphs and challenges, would persist, even as the festivities carried on around them.

As Plato made his way back to the crowd, he could sense his mind wandering back to the festivities, when, all-of-a-sudden, his attention was gripped by the glowing stare of two yellow eyes gazing at him out of a shadow, perched atop the roof of the portico. It was the owl he saw earlier, he thought. He felt a strange connection with this owl, as if it had something important to tell him. Plato was so fixated by the owl's gaze, that he hadn't realized that he had stopped walking, until he was aroused out of his shared trance with the owl by the calling of his friend, Demos, to hurry back to the festivities with the group. Immediately his mind flashed with the image of the butterfly from earlier that morning. In his mind he could see it's large, vibrant, blue, yellow and black colored wings flapping as vividly as if it were right there in front of him. The textures of the wings were so detailed and geometric, with it's wings fluttering almost rhythmically as if in a pattern. The most beautiful melody he had ever seen reverberated from it's wings in the air around him. Such splendor; Plato was captivated and in awe by this wonderful site.

"Plato!" shouted, Demos as he shook Plato by his shoulders. "Can't you hear me? I've been calling you now for some time, my friend. It's as if you are frozen stiff, just standing in the middle of the street, like a madman. What are you staring at?" Demos asked as he looked down to see what Plato's eyes were fixated on.

"What?" asked Plato, still confused and in between the here and there of his thoughts, not realizing that such a divide between realities could even exist.

"Oh, nothing, just admiring that large butterfly, did you not see it?" Plato asked. He knew the butterfly was in his mind, but for some reason he found himself at a loss of what to say, his thought still in a haze and bridging a right between two worlds. Somehow, his reality, with his friend, Demos standing in front of him, seemed far less tangible than the one he just witnessed in his mind.

"Come," ordered, Plato as he brushed off his thoughts and directed Demos by the shoulder, "we still have much wine left that needs our undivided attention. Let's hear about that match you had today."

As the two made their way back to the group, Plato instinctively looked up to where the owl was, just as it lifted up off of the roof. It swooped down, out of the shadows, and flew in front of them and over the gathering as if leading him back to reality.

"How wonderful," said Plato, not realizing he was speaking out loud.

"It was a great throw," Demos responded, not realizing that Plato was not speaking to him. Oblivious, Demos continued on with his story as the two ventured back to the wine and revelries of the Hermaea festival...

Chapter 2

Fated to Wander

*S*omething about the weather was enchanting, as he found himself basking in the embrace of a serene outdoor setting. A symphony of natural wonders surrounded him, painting a dreamy tapestry of colors and scents that filled the air. Despite the absence of discernible faces, the laughter and joy of everyone sharing the picnic table resonated all around him. The atmosphere was charged with an unspoken connection, an unbreakable bond forged through shared experiences. It was a moment of perfect harmony and bliss; of perfect love.

His attention was drawn to the table, laden with an array of sumptuous dishes that seemed to beckon him. Platters of roasted meats, fragrant breads, and bowls overflowing with ripe fruits and honey glistened under the sunlight. Each dish was more enticing than the last, their aromas mingling into a heady perfume that made his mouth water. Among them, a particularly exotic dish caught his eye — a lion's paw, still wrapped in its majestic fur. There was an odd absence of blood, with only a solitary fly drifting near the enigmatic offering.

Driven by an unthinkable impulse, he naturally grasped the lion paw, marveling at its weight and texture. Without a moment's hesitation, he raised it to his lips, preparing to savor the taste of this extraordinary delicacy. Just as the fur brushed against his lips, a peculiar realization dawned upon him — a vivid awareness that he

was dreaming, a fleeting glimpse into the realm of his own subconscious.

With a jolt, he wrenched up from the dream's embrace. His eyes opened wide, adjusting to the stark reality that awaited him. The echoes of the dream lingered, leaving behind a trail of sensations and emotions. As he lay there, contemplating the enigmatic dream, the world outside his slumber beckoned, awaiting his return. His room was dark. It must still be night, he surmised.

He was lying on his back in his bed, with only a sliver of moonlight shining through the window at his feet, and wrapping around the shadow of an owl perched on his legs. Still hazy from his deep slumber, and longing to return, he didn't think much about it before rolling over on his side to return to sleep. Only, his body seemed to be split in two exact copies of each other. One of his bodies rolled over as planned, but the other was still lying on his back with the shadow owl still perched on his legs. *Why didn't it fly away when I rolled over?* he thought hazily. Before he could get another thought in, his mind quickened, and came to its senses and he awoke, startled, jolting upright in his bed. It was daytime with fresh morning sunlight shining through the window, and the sound of birdsong rushing to his ears. Squinting and confused, he rolled out of bed and sat on the edge. *What just happened?* he thought, wiping the sleep from his eyes. This was the first night in weeks that he didn't have the dream about the great flood, which he thought was most curious.

Most dreams faded from memory as he woke throughout his life, ever since childhood. That, he thought, was commonplace among men. But something about these dreams lingered and stuck to his memory. These dreams were different. The most peculiar part was the vivid nature of the visions themselves. There was so much detail that they strangely felt even more real and tangible than his waking life. But how could that be?

As he tried to hold on to the dream, he sat up in the bed and closed his eyes. He took a deep, long breath in through his nose and slowly exhaled. With each breath becoming more rhythmic and focused, more and more details from his dream started to become clear. As his rhythmic breathing continued, a strange tingling sensation began to rise up his spine, filling his head with his in-breath, and then falling back down to his tailbone on the exhale. Soon his thoughts were focused and centered on his breathing only, and forgotten were his dreams. He could feel a certain connectivity with everything around him in a way he never had before. Time seemed non-existent. Every cell in his body seemed to be alive and singing for the first time in his life. He could've stayed in this hypnotic state forever if not for the distant music he heard outside of his window. He remembered that today was the final day of the Hermaea festival. There was a play he was to attend soon, he remembered, and a poetry reading in the evening. He felt a sudden sense of complete and utter appreciation for his life; for the very air in his lungs; the beating of his heart. How wonderful it was to be alive, he felt. As he meditated on that feeling, his name was called from off in the distance of his mind… "Plato… Plato…" Instantly, he was called back to attention, back to the present moment.

"Plato!" shouted Melitta, her voice disturbing the distant music and song in Plato's mind, her voice getting louder as she approached closer to his room. "Plato! What are you doing still in bed, boy? Get up. You bring dishonor to Hermes with your laziness. Your uncle is looking for you in the vineyard."

As he slowly came back to reality, following the sound of Melitta's voice, a sweet smell filled his nose. It was the scent of sykites, those fig-filled pastries he loved so much, reminding him of his other five senses that he somehow managed to lose his grip of while deep in his meditation. His stomach growled loudly, the lingering taste of honey and figs from the dream teasing his senses.

"Come on, boy," Melitta ordered as she barged into the room, immediately grabbing and pulling the sheets off the bed in order to clean them. "Go and get yourself some pastries from Phaedra and meet your uncle in the orchard before you miss the rest of the festival. Today is the last day of the Hermaea, and everyone is expecting you and Socrates at the poetry readings."

Plato's mind wandered to the thought of the pastries, his mouth watering at the mere thought. He imagined the sweetness of the figs and the crispiness of the pastry, feeling a pang of longing. He had always had a weakness for such delicacies, often finding himself indulging in them far more than he should. This morning was no different, as the promise of the sykites drove him from his bed and towards the kitchen, his hunger overpowering any lingering curiosity about the strange dream.

Plato made his way through the family olive orchard, guided by the familiar rustle of leaves and the scent of fresh brine and earth. The soft breeze carried a hint of anticipation, mingling with the fragrance of blooming flowers. Melitta, the house servant, had informed him that his uncle, Critaeus, awaited him here, adding a note of mystery to his otherwise joyous day. With his dream still lingering in his mind, he felt as if he was floating through the trees. It was almost as if everything was vibrating and he was resonating in synch with his surroundings, and a newfound enchantment washed over him. It was as if a veil had been lifted, revealing a world of exquisite beauty that had previously eluded his perception. His eyes widened in awe at the kaleidoscope of color that unfolded before him.

Butterflies, their delicate wings adorned with a myriad of hues, fluttered gracefully through the air, their presence transforming the orchard into a living tapestry of vibrant splendor. Plato marveled at this newfound symphony of nature, the trees serving as the backdrop to a breathtaking ballet of dancing flowers and graceful insects.

In that moment, the world seemed alive with an ethereal glow, as if nature herself had conspired to paint a masterpiece in celebration of his arrival. He had never noticed such abundance and beauty before, and it stirred something deep within him. Mesmerized, he stepped forward, his senses overwhelmed by the sight and scent of blossoms and the gentle touch of butterfly wings brushing against his skin. It was a transformative experience, an invitation to see the world with fresh eyes and embrace the wonders that had previously eluded his awareness.

With each step, he found himself immersed in this newfound realm of enchantment. He couldn't help but smile, captivated by the harmonious dance of colors and the delicate elegance of the butterflies. It was as if they had been waiting for him, beckoning him to unlock a deeper appreciation for the beauty that surrounded him.

In the orchard's embrace, Plato felt a profound connection to the natural world, and an understanding dawned within him. Life, like the butterflies and flowers, possessed a remarkable capacity for transformation and beauty. It was a reminder that even in the most ordinary of places, hidden wonders could be discovered, if one took the time to truly see behind the veil of the illusion of human senses and emotion.

And so, Plato reveled in the enchantment of the orchard, a witness to nature's magnificent display. With a heart brimming with a newfound awe, he ventured deeper into the tapestry of color, allowing the butterflies to guide his path and illuminate his journey of discovery.

As he neared a clearing, Plato spotted his uncle seated on a stone bench, his eyes lost in contemplation. Plato approached with a cheerful stride, his excitement barely contained.

"Uncle!" Plato called out, his voice filled with warmth.

Critaeus turned his gaze toward his nephew, offering a half-hearted smile. The lines on his face seemed etched with concern,

casting a somber shadow over his countenance. Plato sensed a heaviness in the air, contrasting sharply with the festive atmosphere surrounding him.

"Plato, my dear boy," Critaeus replied, his voice carrying a hint of caution. "I'm glad you've come. I wanted to speak with you"

Plato's enthusiasm flickered momentarily, his brow furrowing with curiosity. "Of course, Uncle. You have my full attention. What troubles you?"

Critaeus hesitated, his eyes scanning the orchard as if unsure if they were alone. He leaned in closer, lowering his voice to a hushed tone.

"Plato, my nephew," Critaeus began, his words measured and careful, "I've heard whispers, rumors if you will. They speak of turbulent times ahead; of potential dangers that loom over those who dare to challenge authority."

Plato's eyes widened in surprise, his mind grappling to comprehend the gravity of his uncle's words. He leaned forward, his voice barely a whisper. "What do you mean, Uncle? What dangers?"

Critaeus sighed, a mix of concern and frustration etching his features. "I cannot divulge more, Plato. I am bound by an oath of secrecy, and I've already said too much, but know that your association with Socrates, may attract unwanted attention to yourself. You must exercise caution, my boy."

Plato's heart sank, conflicting emotions swirling within him. The weight of his uncle's warning clashed with his own excitement for the day's events, the final day of the Hermaea festival and the upcoming poetry performance with Socrates.

"But, Uncle, today, Socrates and I are set to perform on stage; I must be there."

"Plato," Critaeus spoke softly, "I understand your passion, but sometimes the greatest wisdom lies in knowing when to step back, when to protect one's self and those we hold dear. I implore you, at

least for the next few days, distance yourself from Socrates, as difficult as it may be."

Plato's gaze dropped to the ground, a swirl of conflicting emotions overwhelming him.

"Oh, Uncle, I think that you are indeed exaggerating. Socrates is just an old street philosopher. He is no danger to anyone. We will only be performing poetry. What harm can there possibly be in that? I promised him that I'd be there. I can't abandon him. We stand together, come what may."

Critaeus sighed, realizing the depths of Plato's commitment. "Very well, nephew. You are your own man, I cannot sway you, but promise me you will be vigilant, exercise caution, and stay alert to the dangers that lie ahead."

Plato nodded, gratitude mingled with determination shining in his eyes. "I hear your words, Uncle. I will remain cautious, but I cannot let fear dictate my path."

Critaeus' expression softened, pride and concern intermingling. He knew he could not dissuade Plato from his chosen course, but he hoped his nephew would tread carefully in the uncertain times that lay ahead.

As they left the orchard, Plato noticed up in the tree the same white owl from the night before; it's large black, oval eyes locked on his, drawing him back inward, causing his surroundings to narrow within. *How wonderful,* he thought. Yet, the weight of his uncle's words lingered. With that thought, the owl lifted off of his perch and flew away in the direction Plato was heading, toward the agora.

The vibrant agora awaited, buzzing with the excitement of the final day of the Hermaea festival. Amidst the revelry, Plato and Socrates would share their wisdom with the crowd, their words echoing through the hearts and minds of any willing to listen. The thought of the poetry performance with his mentor fueled his spirit, and his steps quickened, his resolve solidifying. He would embrace the

festival, the poetry and the spirit of intellectual freedom, while keeping a watchful eye out for his uncle's shadows.

Plato's heart raced with excitement as he approached the bustling agora, the central marketplace of Athens. The warm sun cast a golden glow over the vibrant scene, and the lively sounds of vendors, philosophers and citizens filled the air. The vibrant colors of the celebratory banners and garlands still adorned the surrounding buildings, remnants of the grand parades that had taken place earlier. The joyous spirit of the festivities infused the atmosphere. It was a perfect day, and Plato could hardly contain his eagerness to see his revered mentor, Socrates.

As Plato made his way through the crowds, his eyes caught sight of a gathering near the fountain. A mixture of children and teenagers had gathered around Socrates, who stood at the center, passionately engaged in a speech. The philosopher's animated gestures and piercing gaze captivated his audience.

Drawing closer, Plato strained to catch snippets of Socrates' words, his excitement growing with each passing moment. Finally, he reached the edge of the crowd, and his gaze, for just a moment, met Socrates' wise eyes.

"Socrates!" Plato called out; his eyes widened and a broad smile spread across his face.

As Plato approached the gathering where Socrates held the attention of the young audience, he couldn't help but notice a group of senators lingering nearby, their expressions filled with suspicion and unease. A shiver of worry coursed through his being the moment he recognized some of them as highly influential figures within the Athenian government.

Plato's eyes darted between Socrates and the secretive group. The crowd surrounding Socrates included children and teenagers, and the offspring of prominent senators and influential leaders. Plato's concern for Socrates' safety grew with each passing moment.

His gaze shifted back to the senators, their hushed whispers and exchanged glances betraying their clandestine intentions.

Plato took a step closer. "Socrates!" He called out again. This time Socrates turned his attention to his beloved pupil, a warm smile forming on his aged face. Curiosity piqued, Plato listened intently as Socrates continued his speech, his voice carrying over the crowd.

"Let us reflect on the recent upheaval caused by the Peloponnesian War, for instance," Socrates proclaimed, his voice carrying higher with an air of conviction. "Athens, a beacon of democracy, has suffered greatly, and it's people have witnessed the consequences of blind adherence to authority."

Plato's brow furrowed, as he leaned closer, eager to absorb Socrates's wisdom.

"You see, my young friends, "Socrates continued, addressing the attentive youth before him, "the government, with it's power, control and personal agendas, can lead us astray. It is our duty, as citizens, to question, to challenge, and to think critically about the decisions made on our behalf."

A murmur of agreement and curiosity spread through the crowd as Socrates paused for a moment before resuming his speech, his voice carrying a tinge of urgency.

"Take, for example, the recent policies imposed by our rulers," Socrates said, gesturing toward the crumbling buildings that still bore the scars of war. "They claimed it was for the greater good, but look at the destruction it has wrought. The authorities, though well-intentioned, may not always have the answers. It is our responsibility to seek truth, to examine and to use reason, in order to determine what is truly beneficial for our society as a whole."

Plato's mind raced. The implications of Socrates' words reverberated within him. He marveled at the relevance and timeless wisdom of his mentor's teachings. This was the essence of philosophy,

of questioning and seeking truth in a world clouded by uncertainty and blind conviction.

As Socrates concluded his speech, the crowd erupted in applause and eager discussions. Plato stepped forward, meeting Socrates' gaze once more. Plato felt an unwavering sense of purpose. He raised his hand to wave Socrates down and call his name once more, but before he could, just as Plato was about to push forward, a strong hand grasped his arm, bringing him to an abrupt halt. He turned to face a prominent senator, his presence exuding an air of authority and concern.

"Plato," the senator said, his voice soft and persuasive, "your uncle has sent me to find you. He fears for your safety, especially in light of recent events. It would be best if you did not go any further."

Plato's brow furrowed in confusion, his trust in his uncle making him hesitant to question the senator's motives. "But... Socrates; I need to reach him. Something doesn't feel right."

Plato's heart raced as he watched his mentor, Socrates, deliver his thought-provoking speech on the grand stage in Athens. The crowd was captivated, hanging onto Socrates' every word. But suddenly, the atmosphere shifted as city guards surrounded the philosopher, their stern faces betraying no emotion.

"What's happening?" Plato's voice trembled with anxiety as he turned to the man beside him. It was Senator Marcus, a family friend, and a respected figure in Athens.

"We must leave this place at once, Plato," Senator Marcus said, his voice urgent. "It's not safe for you here."

"But I can't just abandon Socrates in his time of need," Plato protested, torn between staying and defending his mentor.

"No, Plato, listen to me," Senator Marcus held Plato's shoulder firmly. "Going on stage might only make things worse for both of you. We need to regroup and think carefully about our next steps."

The senators expression softened, his eyes conveying an understanding that seemed genuine. "Plato, I assure you, I'm here to help. Your uncle is concerned for both your well being and that of Socrates. We have information that the authorities seek not only Socrates, but also his known associates. If you cooperate with me, then we can assure both his safety and yours."

Plato's mind whirled with conflicting emotions, the desire to reach Socrates clashed with the senator's seemingly genuine concern and offer of assistance. It was a difficult decision, but the weight of the situation pressed upon him.

"His safety!? Why is he in danger, and from whom? What would I need to do?" Plato asked, his voice tinged with resignation. "How can I help Socrates?"

The senators smile widened, his charm veiling his true intentions. "Plato, my boy, answer a few questions for me. Provide me with any information you have regarding Socrates and his activities. In return, I promise you safe passage and assistance in helping him once we have him released. But, time is of the essence."

Plato's heart sank, realizing that his dreams of performing poetry on stage with Socrates would remain unfulfilled. Yet, a flicker of hope ignited within him, the possibility of aiding his mentor and ensuring his safety.

"I... Yes, I agree," Plato finally conceded, his voice tinged with a mix of determination and disappointment. "Help me protect Socrates, and I will provide you with the information you seek. Let us ensure his release and safety."

The senator nodded approvingly, his grip on Plato's arm tightening subtly. "Wise decision. Come with me now; we must act swiftly."

As they began to navigate through the dispersing crowd, Plato couldn't help but steal one last glance toward the stage, where he and Socrates were to perform. Their eyes met just as the authorities got on

stage and surrounded him, stopping the show and taking Socrates into custody.

Plato swallowed the bitter pill of disappointment, knowing that his sacrifice was for the greater cause of Socrates' freedom and safety. The journey ahead was uncertain, and the senator's true intentions remained veiled, but Plato resolved to play his part, hoping that his actions would lead to the liberation of his beloved mentor.

And so, they slipped away from the agora, leaving behind the anticipation and applause; their path now intertwined with secrets, uncertainties, and the shared objective of securing Socrates' release.

As they retreated from the crowds, the two made their way toward the Oracle's Haven, a hidden gem nestled in the labyrinthine alleys of Athens. The tavern's weathered, wooden sign depicted an ancient oracle, veiled and mysterious, casting an enigmatic allure to those passing by. The entrance was unassuming, with a heavy wooden door that creaked as it swung open, revealing the dimly lit interior, and its inhabitants.

Upon entering, they were greeted by the warmth of flickering oil lamps hanging from the timber-beamed ceilings. The walls were adorned with faded frescoes depicting scenes of ancient gods and mythical heroes and creatures, imparting an ambiance of both reverence and intrigue. The aroma of spiced wine and savory dishes wafted through the air, inviting patrons to partake in the pleasures of the tavern. A diverse mix of scholars, artists, travelers ad locals, gathered around low, wooden tables, engaged in spirited debates and laughter.

In one corner, a musician strummed his lyre, filling the air with enchanting melodies of ancient ballads. Nearby, a group of philosophers engaged in deep discussions, their animated gestures filling the room's atmosphere with intellectual fervor.

The haven was something different for everyone. To philosophers it was a haven for seekers of knowledge and truth, a

place where minds could wander, ideas could blossom, and secrets could be shared under the guise of camaraderie. It was a place where patrons could escape the prying eyes of the city and immerse themselves in spirited discussions, exploring concepts that challenged the conventional wisdom of Athens.

Beneath the surface, the haven was a harbor for dark and secretive elements, attracting individuals with hidden motives and agendas. The haven was a hub for closed-door, backroom negotiations for the elite. Senators were known to exploit the tavern's reputation as a sanctuary to conduct secret transactions, trade forbidden knowledge, or engage in activities that straddled legality. Hidden within the tavern's shadowy corners, discreet traders and sellers found a secret safe-haven for a black market of rare and forbidden goods and services, enabling the tavern's reputation for anonymity and the discreet nature of much of it's clientele. With the gravity of their need for safety and secrecy, it was no wonder that this was the place the senator brought Plato to.

Seated at a corner table, Plato's mind was in turmoil, still unable to process the events that had unfolded. "I can't believe they arrested him," he said, his voice choked with emotion. "He only sought to enlighten the people."

Senator Marcus poured a drink for Plato, his face grave with concern. "I understand your frustration, Plato. Socrates' teachings were thought-provoking, but they also brought him enemies. We must be cautious in how we approach this situation."

Plato took a sip of the drink, trying to calm his nerves. "What can we do? How can we help him?"

"Right now, we must focus on your safety, too," Senator Marcus said reassuringly. "I am here to support you, and ensure you don't get into trouble, as well."

"Yes, you're right," Plato replied, feeling a sense of relief knowing he had someone to rely on. "I don't want to bring harm to myself or Socrates."

"Exactly," Senator Marcus nodded, feigning empathy. "Now, tell me more about Socrates' beliefs. What did he teach you?"

"Socrates... he always challenged the traditional beliefs about the gods and the authority in Athens. He questioned their wisdom and claimed that he had a divine calling to pursue the truth."

"Really?" The senator feigning curiosity." That's quite intriguing, Plato. And how did you feel about his claims?"

"At first, I was taken aback. But then, I saw the passion in his eyes, the sincerity in his voice. He believed he was guided by a higher power to uncover the truth hidden from the masses."

"Fascinating," replied senator Marcus while smiling internally. "It sounds like Socrates has quite the rebellious spirit."

"Yes, he does. But he never sought to overthrow the city or it's gods. He merely wanted to enlighten the people and help them find wisdom within themselves," Slurred Plato.

"I see. It must have been quite the dilemma for you, knowing that Socrates' beliefs went against the very fabric of our society," retorted the senator.

"It was. But I also admired his courage. He had no fear of the consequences, for he believed in the righteousness of his cause."

"Thank you, Plato. Your honesty is commendable," assured the senator with a malicious smile. "I promise this conversation will remain between us. You have nothing to worry about."

As the conversation flowed, the drinks kept coming, and Plato found himself more and more intoxicated. "Socrates always encouraged us to question everything," he said, slurring his words, "... including the gods and the authorities. He said that through doubt, we find truth, and through questioning, we learn to think for ourselves."

Senator Marcus listened intently, concealing a sinister smile. "Fascinating. Socrates' ideas are indeed intriguing, but they might be misunderstood by the jurors. I hope you understand why it's crucial not to speak openly about this to anyone."

Plato, trusting and naive, nodded eagerly. "Of course, I trust you. You're a true friend, looking out for us like this."

"Thank you, Plato. Your trust means a lot to me," Senator Marcus said, masking his deceit. "Let's keep this conversation between us, and I promise to do everything in my power to help Socrates and to protect you."

As the night deepened and the tavern's activity slowly waned, Senator Marcus leaned in closer to Plato, his expression shifting to one of solemnity. "I understand how much Socrates means to you," he said softly. "Tomorrow morning, I will take you to see him in his jail cell before the trial. You have my word." With those final words, Marcus's promise hung in the air, offering a glimmer of hope to Plato, who clung to the belief that his mentor might still be saved.

Plato nodded, feeling a mix of relief and lingering doubt. The senator's words were reassuring, but a small voice inside him warned of hidden motives. As Marcus rose to leave, he placed a firm hand on Plato's shoulder. "The hour is late, and the streets are not safe at night. Stay at my home, Plato. It is close by and you will be safe there."

Too weary to argue and reassured by the senator's hospitality, Plato agreed. He followed Marcus through the winding streets to a grand residence, where he was shown to a comfortable guest room. As he lay down, the events of the evening played over in his mind, his thoughts a tangled web of trust and suspicion.

As Plato drifted into an uneasy sleep, the senator's shadow seemed to stretch ominously across the room, merging with the darkness. Plato shivered, a chill running down his spine. The promise of seeing Socrates filled him with both hope and dread, but little did he

know, the events of the next day would test his loyalties in ways he could never have anticipated.

Chapter 3

The Price of Ambition

The morning light filtered through the curtains of the senator's lavish guest room, gently rousing Plato from his sleep. He rubbed his eyes, trying to shake off the remnants of the previous night's wine and conversation. The events at the tavern seemed hazy, and a sense of unease lingered in the back of his mind. In their inebriated state, staying at the senator's house had been the only option.

Senator Marcus entered the room with a warm smile. "Good morning, Plato. I trust you slept well," he said, his tone as inviting as ever. "Before we go to see Socrates, there's something I wish to discuss with you."

Plato nodded, still trying to piece together his thoughts. "What is it, Senator?"

Marcus leaned in slightly, his demeanor turning more serious. "Plato, I must admit, there is more I can offer you than just my support for Socrates," he began, his voice low and inviting. "You are a man of great intellect and potential. Imagine what you could achieve with the right resources at your disposal." He paused, letting his words sink in before continuing. "I have connections with influential patrons who appreciate the arts and philosophy. They are always looking for promising minds to support financially. A generous endowment for your work could be arranged, allowing you to pursue your studies without any financial burden."

Plato's eyes widened slightly at the mention of patronage. The thought of having the means to further his philosophical inquiries and establish his own academy was tempting. He had always dreamed of creating a space where ideas could flourish freely, unrestrained by monetary concerns. "Your work could have a profound impact on future generations," Marcus continued, sensing Plato's interest. "All I ask is for your cooperation in this matter, and in return, I promise to facilitate this support. Think of the good you could do, the legacy you could build. Socrates himself would understand the necessity of such a sacrifice for the greater good."

The senator's words were reassuring, but a small voice inside him warned of hidden motives. As Marcus rose to leave, he placed a firm hand on Plato's shoulder. "Let us enjoy a hearty breakfast before we go. You need your strength for the day ahead."

Too weary to argue and reassured by the senator's hospitality, Plato agreed. He followed Marcus through the winding halls of the grand residence, his mind a whirl of conflicting thoughts. As they entered the dining area, Plato's senses were immediately assaulted by the tantalizing aromas of a lavish breakfast spread.

The table was laden with an array of delicacies: fresh fruits, warm bread, honey, and various meats. But what caught Plato's eye were the sykites, the fig-filled pastries he had enjoyed the morning before. His stomach growled, and without thinking, he reached for one.

"Please, help yourself," Marcus encouraged, a knowing smile playing on his lips. "You must keep your strength up for today."

Plato bit into the pastry, savoring the sweetness of the figs and the flaky crust. As he ate, the senator continued to speak, weaving visions of future success and academic freedom. Plato listened, feeling a strange mix of excitement and guilt. The food and the senator's words were equally intoxicating, clouding his judgment and dulling his fears.

As Plato finished his meal, Marcus leaned in closer. "Remember, Plato, our agreement is for the greater good. Sometimes, sacrifices must be made for the sake of progress. Now, let us go see Socrates."

Plato nodded, feeling a mix of relief and lingering doubt. The senator's promises echoed in his mind, intertwining with the taste of the sykites, making him feel both reassured and uneasy. He followed Marcus out of the room, the weight of the senator's words heavy on his shoulders. The thought of facing Socrates filled him with both anticipation and dread, each step toward the jail intensifying his inner conflict.

The streets of Athens were strewn with remnants of the Hermaea festival, now just echoes of the joyous celebrations that had taken place. Colorful decorations hung limply, and the smell of stale wine and leftover food lingered in the air. Here and there, people slept off the excesses of the night before, their bodies sprawled in alleyways and doorways, oblivious to the city's shifting tides.

Senator Marcus walked beside Plato, speaking in a low, persuasive tone. "Plato, you must understand the gravity of the situation. Socrates' teachings have stirred up considerable unrest among the powerful. His refusal to conform is seen as a threat to the established order."

Plato nodded, his mind racing. "But Socrates seeks only to enlighten, to challenge us to think more deeply about our lives and our society."

"True," Marcus replied, "but enlightenment often comes at a cost. There are those who fear change and will go to great lengths to suppress it. This trial is not just about Socrates; it is about maintaining the balance of power in Athens."

As they navigated through the littered streets, Plato couldn't help but notice the contrast between the somber reality of their journey and the remnants of the festive atmosphere. The scent of stale wine and rotting food mixed with the morning air, reminding him of the

transient nature of joy and celebration. It was a stark reminder of the comforts he stood to gain if he sided with Marcus.

They passed by a group of children playing with leftover festival decorations, their laughter a faint echo of the previous day's revelry. "The people love Socrates," he said, almost to himself. "Surely they will see the injustice of this trial."

"The people's love can be fickle," Marcus warned. "In times of crisis, fear and misinformation can easily sway public opinion. That is why your role is so crucial. Your support for Socrates, if not carefully managed, could lead to further unrest."

Plato felt a pang of guilt at the senator's words. He knew Marcus was right; the power dynamics in Athens were delicate. As they approached the imposing structure of the jail, his resolve began to waver. He was caught between his loyalty to his mentor and the pragmatic realities Marcus laid before him.

The entrance to the jail was guarded by stern-looking soldiers. Marcus spoke briefly with them, and they were allowed to pass. Inside, the air was damp and cold, a stark contrast to the warmth and vibrancy of the city outside. The sound of distant, clanging metal echoed through the stone corridors, adding to the sense of foreboding.

"Remember, Plato," Marcus said, his voice taking on a more urgent tone, "this meeting is an opportunity. Socrates must understand the stakes. If he continues to defy the authorities, his fate is sealed. You might be the only one who can make him see reason."

Plato nodded, though his heart was heavy with doubt. They stopped in front of a cell door, and a guard unlocked it, allowing Plato to step inside. Marcus remained outside, his presence a reminder of the choices and sacrifices that lay ahead.

As the cell door closed behind him, Plato's eyes adjusted to the dim light. He saw Socrates sitting calmly on a wooden bench, his face serene despite the grim surroundings. The sight of his mentor brought

a rush of emotions, and Plato struggled to find his voice. He took a deep breath, steeling himself for the conversation that was about to unfold. The weight of the senator's words and the promise of a better future pressed heavily on his mind, as he prepared to convince Socrates to renounce his teachings in a desperate bid to save his life.

The cell was dimly lit by a single narrow window high above, casting a thin beam of light that danced across the stone floor. Socrates sat on a wooden bench, his hands resting calmly on his knees, his eyes closed as if in meditation. The serenity on his face contrasted sharply with the cold, damp air of the cell.

Plato hesitated at the threshold, feeling a lump form in his throat. The gravity of what he was about to do weighed heavily on him. He took a step forward, his sandals echoing against the stone floor, and the sound seemed to pull Socrates from his reverie.

"Socrates," he began, his voice trembling, "I have come to see you."

"Plato," Socrates said, his voice warm and welcoming. "I am pleased to see you, my friend. Please, sit with me."

Plato moved slowly to the bench and sat beside his mentor. For a moment, they sat in silence, the only sound being the distant clinking of chains and muffled voices from other cells. Plato struggled to find the words, his mind a tangle of conflicting emotions and the senator's manipulative advice.

"Socrates," he began, his voice barely above a whisper, "I… I came to talk to you about the trial."

Socrates opened his eyes and turned to Plato, his gaze steady and kind. "Yes, I expected as much. You look troubled, Plato. Speak freely."

Plato took a deep breath, steeling himself. "The charges against you are serious. The council… they see your teachings as a threat. Senator Marcus believes that if you renounce your philosophies, you might be spared."

Socrates smiled faintly, a look of understanding and sadness in his eyes. "And what do you believe, Plato?"

"I…" Plato hesitated, the words caught in his throat. "I believe that your life is more valuable than your words. If renouncing your teachings will save you, then isn't it worth it? You can continue to teach in secret, continue to influence and inspire. We need you, Socrates."

Socrates' smile grew, but there was a profound sorrow behind it. "Ah, Plato, you speak with the love and concern of a true friend. But tell me, what good is a life lived in dishonor? If I renounce my beliefs now, what lesson does that teach? That truth is less important than survival? That fear should guide our actions?"

Plato looked down, his hands trembling. "But they will kill you. And what will we do without you?"

Socrates placed a hand on Plato's shoulder, his touch gentle but firm. "My dear Plato, the truth is immortal. It lives on in you and in all those who seek it. My death would not end my teachings; it would only affirm them. Fear not for me, but for the state of our souls if we choose falsehood over integrity."

Tears welled up in Plato's eyes. "I don't want to lose you."

Socrates nodded, his own eyes misting over. "I know, my friend. But remember, death is but a part of life, and what we do in this life echoes in eternity. Stand strong, Plato. Let not greed or fear cloud your judgment. Stay true to the principles we hold dear."

Plato wiped his tears, feeling a mix of anguish and admiration. "I will try, Socrates. I promise I will try."

Socrates embraced him briefly, a gesture of warmth and reassurance. "That is all I can ask. Now, go. The trial awaits, and you must be strong. For yourself, and for Athens."

Plato stood, his heart heavy but his resolve somewhat steadied by Socrates' words. He nodded, unable to speak, and turned to leave the cell. As the door closed behind him, the darkness of the corridor enveloped him, but Socrates' voice lingered in his mind, a beacon of wisdom in the encroaching shadows.

Outside the cell, Senator Marcus waited, his expression unreadable. "Did you convince him?" he asked.

Plato shook his head, unable to meet Marcus's eyes. "No. He remains steadfast."

Marcus sighed, a flicker of disappointment crossing his face. "Very well. Let us proceed to the trial. Remember what we discussed, Plato. Your future depends on this."

Plato nodded numbly, the senator's words barely registering. He followed Marcus out of the jail, each step feeling heavier than the last, as the weight of the impending trial pressed down upon him.

The sun was climbing higher in the sky as Plato and Senator Marcus approached the courthouse. The remnants of the Hermaea festival were still evident, with garlands hanging from posts and bits of confetti scattered across the cobblestones. The festive atmosphere had given way to a tense, anticipatory silence as people gathered to witness the trial of Socrates.

Plato felt a knot in his stomach tighten with each step. The courthouse loomed ahead, its imposing columns casting long shadows that seemed to stretch out and engulf him. Senator Marcus walked briskly, his expression one of calculated calm.

As they neared the entrance, the sounds of murmured conversations grew louder. Citizens of Athens, from the curious to the concerned, had come to see the fate of the man who had dared to challenge the status quo. Plato could see familiar faces in the crowd—students of Socrates, friends, and even those who had often debated fiercely against him.

"Remember, Plato," Marcus said, his voice low but firm, "this trial is not just about Socrates. It is about maintaining order and ensuring the stability of Athens. Your actions today will have far-reaching consequences."

Plato nodded, though his mind was a whirl of doubt and fear. As they entered the courthouse, the air grew heavier, the walls seeming to close in around him. The interior was grand, with high ceilings and rows of benches already filled with spectators. At the front, a raised platform held the seats for the judges and the accused.

They took their places, and Plato looked around, feeling the weight of hundreds of eyes upon him. The courtroom was abuzz with whispers and hushed conversations, the tension palpable. He could see the prosecuting officials preparing their statements, their faces stern and determined.

Socrates was brought in, his demeanor calm and composed, despite the gravity of the situation. He was placed in the center of the room, a solitary figure standing against the might of the Athenian legal system. Plato's heart ached at the sight of his mentor, knowing what was at stake.

The judges entered, and a hush fell over the room. The lead judge, a man with a commanding presence, called the court to order. "We are here to judge the case against Socrates of Athens, accused of corrupting the youth and impiety against the gods of the city. Let the trial commence."

The prosecutor stood and began his opening statement, outlining the charges against Socrates in meticulous detail. He spoke of the dangers of Socrates' teachings, how they sowed discord and threatened the fabric of society. His words were sharp and accusatory, painting Socrates as a dangerous subversive.

Plato's hands clenched into fists as he listened, the injustice of the situation burning within him. He wanted to shout out, to defend his mentor, but he knew that any outburst could be detrimental. Instead, he took deep breaths, trying to steady his nerves.

When it was time for the defense, Socrates stood with a quiet dignity. "I stand before you not to beg for my life, but to speak the truth as I see it. My entire life has been dedicated to questioning and seeking wisdom. If that is a crime, then I am guilty. But I ask you to consider whether the pursuit of truth and knowledge is truly a threat to our city, or whether it is, in fact, its greatest strength."

His words were powerful, resonating through the courtroom. The spectators listened intently, many nodding in agreement. Plato felt a surge of pride and sorrow, knowing that Socrates would not compromise his principles, no matter the cost.

As the trial progressed, witnesses were called, and evidence was presented. The tension in the room continued to build, each argument and counterargument adding to the weight of the moment. Plato watched, his heart heavy with a mix of hope and despair.

Then, unexpectedly, the prosecutor called upon a witness: Senator Marcus. Plato's heart sank as Marcus took the stand, a confident and authoritative figure.

"Senator Marcus," the prosecutor began, "you have had recent conversations with Plato, one of Socrates' closest students. Can you tell the court what Plato confided in you?"

Marcus nodded solemnly. "Plato expressed to me his concerns about Socrates' teachings. He admitted that Socrates' ideas might indeed be dangerous and that, in private, he has tried to convince Socrates to renounce his teachings to avoid causing further unrest."

Plato's blood ran cold. The words were twisted but not entirely false. He had spoken of the dangers as a hypothetical, in a moment of weakness and confusion, not as an admission of guilt. Yet, Marcus presented them as a damning confession.

"Plato," the lead judge called, "do you confirm what Senator Marcus has stated?"

Plato stood, his legs trembling. "I… I did express concerns, but only because I feared for Socrates' safety, not because I believed him guilty. I sought to protect him, not to condemn him."

The prosecutor seized upon Plato's hesitation. "So you admit that even you, his most devoted student, saw the potential danger in his

teachings? Your words confirm that Socrates' influence is indeed corruptive."

The courtroom murmured, and Plato felt the weight of his own words being used against him. He sat down, his heart pounding, realizing too late the extent of Marcus' betrayal.

The judges called for final statements. Socrates stood, his voice calm and unwavering. "I accept the verdict of this court. If my search for truth and wisdom is deemed a crime, then I shall face my punishment with dignity. But remember this: true wisdom comes from understanding our own ignorance, and no verdict can change that fundamental truth."

The lead judge nodded and announced the sentence. "Socrates of Athens, you have been found guilty. You are hereby sentenced to renounce your teachings or face death by hemlock."

A tense silence filled the courtroom. Socrates stepped forward, his expression resolute. "I will not renounce my teachings. To do so would be to betray everything I have stood for. I choose death."

Gasps and murmurs rippled through the courtroom. Plato felt a wave of despair wash over him as he watched his mentor make the ultimate sacrifice.

Socrates turned to address the court one final time. "I do not fear death, for it is but a transition to another state. I fear only the abandonment of truth and virtue. Let my death be a testament to the enduring power of integrity and the relentless pursuit of wisdom."

The judges, unmoved, signaled for the executioner. Socrates was led to a table where the cup of hemlock awaited. He took it without hesitation, raising it to his lips. "To you, my friends, I say farewell. Continue to seek the truth, for it is the greatest gift we can offer to the world."

He drank the poison, his face remaining serene as he sat down, the effects of the hemlock beginning to take hold. Plato watched in horror, tears streaming down his face, as Socrates' body slowly succumbed to the poison. The courtroom was silent, the weight of the moment pressing down on everyone present.

A gasp rippled through the courtroom. Plato felt as though the ground had been pulled from beneath him. He turned to look at Socrates, who remained calm and resolute, his eyes meeting Plato's with a look of serene acceptance.

As the courtroom erupted in a mix of outrage and sorrow, Senator Marcus placed a firm hand on Plato's shoulder. "We must leave now, Plato. For your safety, it is best you come with me. There are those who might see your defense of Socrates as a threat."

As Socrates took his final breath, Plato was overcome with overwhelming grief. Senator Marcus placed a firm hand on his shoulder, urging him to leave. "We must go, Plato.

Still reeling from the trial and the twisted use of his words, Plato numbly followed Marcus out of the courthouse. The senator's grip was both reassuring and foreboding, as Plato was led away from the chaos and towards an uncertain future.

Chapter 4

Whispers of the Heart

Plato followed Senator Marcus out of the courthouse, his mind reeling from the events that had just unfolded. The streets of Athens were still scattered with remnants of the festival, now mingled with the murmurs of those who had witnessed Socrates' trial. Each step felt heavy, as if the weight of his mentor's fate had anchored him to the ground.

"Plato, we must move quickly," Marcus urged, his grip on Plato's shoulder tightening. "There are those who might see your defense of Socrates as a threat. It is no longer safe for you here."

Plato nodded numbly, his thoughts a tangled mess of grief and guilt. The senator's words barely registered as he allowed himself to be led through the winding streets. The festive decorations that had once brought joy now seemed to mock the sorrow that had befallen him.

They reached a secluded house on the outskirts of the city, where Marcus had arranged for them to stay temporarily. The door creaked open, and Plato stepped inside, the cool interior offering a brief respite from the chaos outside.

Marcus closed the door behind them, his expression serious. "We need to discuss our next steps, Plato. Your safety is paramount, and we must act quickly."

Plato sank into a chair, feeling a crushing sense of inertia. The overwhelming grief and the shock of Socrates' death left him paralyzed, unable to think clearly or make decisions. He stared blankly at the table, his mind replaying the twisted use of his words against his mentor.

"Plato, are you listening?" Marcus's voice cut through the fog of his thoughts.

Plato looked up, his eyes hollow. "Yes, I… I'm listening."

"We cannot afford to be complacent," Marcus continued. "The longer we wait, the more dangerous it becomes for you. We must leave Athens, at least until things settle down. Do you understand?"

Plato nodded again, though the idea of leaving felt like an insurmountable task. He had always been a man of action, driven by his desire for knowledge and truth. But now, faced with the enormity of the situation, he felt paralyzed by indecision.

Marcus sighed, sensing Plato's hesitation. "I know this is difficult, but inaction is not an option. We must move forward, for your sake and the sake of those who support Socrates' teachings."

Plato took a deep breath, trying to summon the resolve he had always prided himself on. "You're right," he said finally, his voice wavering. "We must leave."

The senator nodded, relieved. "Good. We'll make preparations immediately. Rest for now, but be ready to move at a moment's notice."

As Marcus left the room, Plato remained seated, the weight of his grief and the enormity of the decision before him pressing down heavily. He knew Marcus was right, but the thought of leaving everything behind, especially in such a state of turmoil, left him feeling helpless and unsure.

For a moment, he allowed himself to sink further into the chair, letting the wave of exhaustion and sorrow wash over him. He knew he couldn't afford to linger in this state of inaction, but the pull of sloth, the temptation to do nothing and let the world move around him, was strong.

Finally, with great effort, Plato forced himself to stand. He had to keep moving, for his own sake and for the legacy of Socrates. The path ahead was uncertain and fraught with danger, but he couldn't allow himself to be consumed by inactivity. He had to act, even if it meant leaving behind everything he had ever known.

Plato stood by the window, staring out at the city he had known all his life. The sun was beginning to set, casting long shadows across the rooftops. The bustling noise of Athens felt distant, as if he were standing apart from the world. His mind was a whirl of thoughts, but his body felt heavy, reluctant to move.

The senator had left him alone for a while to gather his thoughts. Plato's mind replayed the events of the trial, the twisted use of his words, and Socrates' calm acceptance of his fate. The weight of it all pressed down on him, making it hard to breathe.

He sighed deeply, trying to make sense of his feelings. He had always believed in action, in the pursuit of knowledge and truth. But now, faced with the enormity of what had happened, he felt paralyzed by indecision and guilt. Had he been too passive? Had his hesitation contributed to Socrates' fate?

Plato moved to a small table where a scroll and a quill lay waiting. He picked up the quill, intending to write down his thoughts, but his hand hovered over the parchment, unable to commit to the words. The task felt overwhelming, and he let the quill drop with a sigh.

Inaction, he thought. Sloth. He had always prided himself on being a man of principle and action, but now he was mired in doubt and hesitation. He needed to break free from this paralysis, to find a way forward. But how?

He turned his thoughts to Socrates. What would his mentor have done in this situation? Socrates had faced his fate with unwavering integrity, refusing to compromise his beliefs even in the face of death. Plato felt a surge of shame at his own inability to act.

The door creaked open, and Senator Marcus entered the room. "Plato, we need to discuss our next steps. Time is of the essence."

Plato nodded, but his movements were slow, lethargic. He forced himself to focus on Marcus's words, knowing that action was necessary, even if he felt ill-equipped to take it.

"We need to leave Athens as soon as possible," Marcus continued. "I've made arrangements for a safe passage out of the city. But we must be swift and decisive."

Plato's gaze drifted back to the parchment on the table. He knew he should be preparing, packing his belongings, and making plans for their departure. But the weight of his grief and guilt made every action feel like an insurmountable effort.

"Plato," Marcus said more firmly, "I understand your grief, but we cannot afford to be idle. The longer we stay, the greater the risk. We must act now."

Plato took a deep breath, trying to shake off the heavy cloak of inaction that had settled over him. "You're right," he said, though his voice was still tinged with hesitation. "We need to leave."

Marcus nodded, his expression a mix of relief and urgency. "I will gather some necessary provisions for you. You leave at dawn."

As the senator left to finalize the preparations, Plato remained by the table, staring at the empty parchment. He knew that he needed to overcome this paralyzing despair, to take action in honor of Socrates' legacy. Slowly, he picked up the quill once more, determined to write down his thoughts and plans for the future.

Each stroke of the quill felt like an effort, but he pushed through, driven by the memory of his mentor's unwavering resolve. As he wrote, he felt a glimmer of the old determination returning, a faint but growing light in the darkness of his grief.

Plato knew that this was only the beginning. The road ahead was fraught with uncertainty and danger, but he could not afford to be idle. He had to move forward, to honor Socrates and to continue the pursuit of truth, no matter how difficult the path.

Plato paced the small room, the weight of his thoughts making each step feel heavier than the last. He was torn between the urge to see his family and friends one last time and the pressing need to leave Athens. The fear and guilt gnawed at him, making it difficult to think clearly.

Senator Marcus returned with a satchel packed with some last minute provisions and stood in the doorway watching him closely, sensing the turmoil within Plato. He stepped forward, his voice calm but firm. "Plato, we don't have much time. The longer you stay, the greater the risk to you and your loved ones."

He stopped pacing and looked at Marcus, his eyes filled with uncertainty. "I understand, but I can't just leave without saying goodbye. My uncle, my friends... they deserve to know what's happening."

Marcus sighed, placing a reassuring hand on Plato's shoulder, his expression softening. "I know this is difficult, but you must trust me. Your uncle is aware of the situation and is helping from the background. He has agreed that it is best for you to leave, temporarily. It's for their safety, as well as yours. I understand your sentiment, Plato, I do. I will make sure the rest of your family understand, but, now, you must think about the bigger picture. Your presence here puts everyone you care about in grave danger. If the authorities suspect you are still in Athens, they might target your family and friends to get to you."

He felt a chill run down his spine. The thought of his family being endangered because of him was unbearable. "But I can't just disappear without a word. There must be some way..."

Plato's mind raced. "I …I know of a place," he said finally. "An obscure and secret cave outside of town where I can lay low for a bit. It's hidden and rarely visited. I can stay there while you negotiate and protect me."

The senator's eyes lit up with interest. "That sounds perfect. If you can stay hidden there, it will buy us the time we need to ensure your safety and handle the situation."

"But only for a few days or weeks at most, right?" Plato asked, his voice tinged with desperation. "I can't stay away forever. Athens is my home."

Marcus nodded reassuringly. "Of course. Just long enough for things to settle down. Once it's safe, you'll be able to return. I promise."

Plato took a deep breath, feeling the weight of his decision. The senator's words made sense, but the thought of leaving everything behind filled him with dread. He couldn't shake the feeling that he was in danger, and yet, that all of this was happening for some greater purpose. Could he really trust the senator? With everything happening so fast, he couldn't even trust his own thoughts. Still, he knew that staying would only put those he cared about in greater danger.

"I'll go," Plato said finally, his voice heavy with resignation. "I'll go to the cave. But please, make sure my family is safe."

Marcus squeezed his shoulder. "I give you my word, Plato. Your safety and the safety of your loved ones are my top priorities. Now, we must prepare. The sooner you leave, the better."

As Marcus left to make the arrangements, Plato tried to gather his thoughts, his mind still reeling from the whirlwind of emotions. He felt a pang of sorrow at the thought of leaving without saying goodbye, but he knew it was the right thing to do. Everything was happening so fast, it was hard to think clearly. He didn't trust his own thoughts, but he trusted that his uncle and senator Marcus knew how best to handle these matters.

The senator handed him the small satchel of provisions. "This should last you for a few days. I'll check in with you as soon as it's safe. Remember, stay hidden and trust no one but me."

Plato nodded, taking the satchel. "I will. Thank you, Marcus."

With one last look at the city he loved, Plato steeled himself for the journey ahead. The path to the cave was fraught with uncertainty, but he knew he had to move forward. The safety of his family and friends depended on it.

As he left the city under the cover of darkness, Plato couldn't shake the feeling of dread that hung over him. The senator's reassurances were comforting, but the fear of the unknown loomed large. He could only hope that the cave would provide the refuge he needed, and that, in time, he could return to Athens and rebuild what had been lost.

Plato moved swiftly through the darkened streets, the weight of his satchel pressing against his side. The city of Athens gradually fell away behind him, replaced by the quiet solitude of the countryside. The moonlight guided his path, casting long shadows and illuminating the way to the secret cave he had mentioned to Marcus.

As he walked, his mind churned with thoughts of the trial, Socrates' death, and the senator's manipulative words. Each step felt heavier, burdened by the grief and guilt that had settled deep within his heart. The sound of his sandals crunching against the gravel seemed deafening in the still night.

Eventually, the familiar landscape began to change, and Plato recognized the landmarks that signaled he was nearing the cave. The entrance was well-hidden, concealed by thick foliage and a rocky overhang. He pushed through the underbrush, feeling the rough texture of the rocks under his fingertips.

With a final effort, he stepped into the cave, the cool air inside a stark contrast to the warmth of the night outside. Plato paused, taking in the surroundings. The cave was small but spacious enough to

provide shelter and a temporary refuge. He set down his satchel and took out a small clay oil lamp, carefully lighting the wick. The soft glow of the lamp cast flickering shadows on the cavern walls, creating an intimate and secluded atmosphere.

The reality of his isolation began to sink in. The cave was silent, save for the faint echo of dripping water somewhere in the depths. Plato felt a pang of loneliness, knowing that he would be cut off from the world he had known and the people he cared about.

He spread out a blanket on the ground and sat down, his thoughts racing. The senator had assured him that this was temporary, that it was for his own safety. But the uncertainty of it all gnawed at him. Would Marcus really be able to protect him? Would his family and friends be safe?

Plato leaned back against the cool stone wall, closing his eyes. The events of the past days played over and over in his mind, a relentless cycle of doubt and regret. Everything inside of him was screaming that something wasn't right, but, he had to trust Marcus, he reminded himself. There was no other choice.

Yet, as the night wore on, a sense of unease settled over him. The solitude of the cave magnified his fears, turning every sound into a potential threat. He tried to push these thoughts away, focusing instead on the teachings of Socrates and the pursuit of truth that had always guided him.

Despite his attempts to find comfort, sleep eluded him. The cave's silence pressed in on him, amplifying his thoughts and fears. Plato knew that the days ahead would be difficult, filled with challenges he had never faced before. But he also knew that he had to remain strong, to honor the legacy of Socrates and continue the pursuit of wisdom.

With a heavy heart, he resolved to endure the isolation, to use this time to reflect and gather his strength. The path ahead was uncertain, but he would face it with the same determination that Socrates had shown in his final moments.

As dawn began to break, casting a faint light into the mouth of the cave, Plato took a deep breath and closed his eyes, finally succumbing to the exhaustion that had weighed on him. The journey ahead would be long and arduous, but he was determined to see it through.

Chapter 5

The Fall of Pride

*T*he screams of the terrified people echoed in his mind, their cries for help piercing through the chaos. The deafening sound of crashing waves filled his ears as he soared fast and high above the earth, the wind whipping past him as he flew towards an unknown destination. Below, the world was engulfed in a great and terrible flood, the water rising relentlessly, drowning everything in its path. He could see ancient temples and towering cities being swallowed by the waves, their grandeur reduced to nothing more than a memory.

In the distance, he spotted a massive central temple, its spires reaching desperately towards the sky. As he flew closer, he saw that it too was succumbing to the flood, its walls crumbling as the waves battered them. He strained to reach the temple, to save those in need, but no matter how fast he flew, it remained just out of reach. Desperation gripped him as the temple vanished beneath the water. Suddenly, he was falling, tumbling towards the water below.

As he fell, the scene shifted. He was back in the courtroom, but this time he was Socrates, staring down the center of the vial of liquid poison. The poison seemed to swirl like the crashing waves of the flood, and as he lifted the vial to his lips, the liquid engulfed him, collapsing over his entire being like a tidal wave. The voices of the prosecutors echoed around him, accusing and condemning. The twisted use of his words rang in his ears, a constant reminder of his *perceived betrayal. "Plato, you betrayed me," Socrates' voice echoed, filled with disappointment and sadness. The image of Socrates drinking the hemlock, his face serene, haunted Plato's subconscious.*

The courtroom scene shifted again, and Plato found himself on trial. The faces of the jurors were shadowy and indistinct, but their voices were sharp and accusatory. "You failed him, Plato," they hissed. "You let fear and indecision guide you."

He tried to speak in his defense, but his voice was lost in the cacophony. He felt a crushing weight on his chest, a physical manifestation of his guilt and anger. The scene shifted once more, and he was trapped in a dark, enclosed space, the walls closing in on him. His heart pounded, the suffocating weight of his guilt and anger pressing down on him.

Socrates' face appeared again, close enough to touch. "You must let go of this anger, Plato," Socrates said, his voice both gentle and stern. "It will consume you if you allow it. Remember why we seek the truth."

But the voices of the judges and the prosecutors grew louder, their accusations merging into a deafening roar. Plato felt a surge of wrath, directed at himself and at the world that had allowed such an injustice. He clenched his fists, wanting to scream, but no sound came out.

Plato woke with a start, gasping for breath. His heart raced, and the silence of the cave seemed oppressive. He sat up, wiping the sweat from his brow, and tried to steady his racing thoughts. The anger he had felt in the dream lingered, a burning ember in his chest.

He stood up and paced the cave, his frustration growing with each step. How could he have allowed himself to be manipulated? How could he have failed Socrates so completely? The questions tormented him, fueling his wrath.

Plato walked to the mouth of the cave and looked out into the dawn light. The stars were fading, and the sky was turning a pale blue.

He took a deep breath, trying to calm the storm inside him. But the anger remained, simmering beneath the surface.

Returning to the cave, Plato sat down, his mind still racing. Sleep eluded him, and he spent the rest of the morning staring into the darkness of the cave, wrestling with his thoughts. The seed of wrath had been planted, and it grew with each passing hour, threatening to consume him.

As the first light of day began to illuminate the cave, Plato felt a weariness that went beyond physical exhaustion. He knew that this anger could not be ignored; it had to be confronted and understood. The path ahead was uncertain, but he resolved to face it with the same determination that Socrates had shown in his final moments.

Plato leaned back against the cool stone wall, closing his eyes briefly. He knew he had to find a way to channel his anger into something productive, to turn his wrath into a driving force for truth and justice. But for now, the anger was raw and consuming, a constant reminder of the injustice that had befallen his mentor and the betrayal he felt from those he had trusted.

He opened his eyes and stared back into the darkness of the cave, the flickering light of the oil lamp still casting shadows on the walls. The isolation pressed down on him, amplifying his negative emotions. He felt a pang of loneliness, knowing that he was cut off from the world he had known and the people he cared about. With a heavy heart, Plato resolved to endure the isolation, to use this time to reflect and gather his strength.

As the sun continued to rise, casting a warm glow into the mouth of the cave, he took a deep breath and closed his eyes once more. He sat on the cold stone floor of the cave, the remnants of his nightmare still clinging to his consciousness. The pale morning light seeping into the cave, casting long shadows that seemed to move with a life of their own. He rubbed his eyes, trying to shake off the unsettling images

from his dreams, but the emotions they stirred remained raw and intense.

He stood up and walked to the mouth of the cave, looking out at the world beyond. The early morning air was crisp, and the sky was painted in hues of orange and pink. Birds sang their morning songs, oblivious to the turmoil that churned within him. The tranquility of the scene contrasted sharply with the storm of emotions inside him.

His mind was a whirl of thoughts and questions. How had he allowed himself to be manipulated? How could he have failed Socrates so completely? The weight of these questions pressed down on him, fueling his growing anger. He clenched his fists, feeling the heat of his wrath simmering beneath the surface.

He remembered the trial, the twisted use of his words against Socrates. His mentor's serene face as he drank the poison was seared into his memory. The sense of betrayal was overwhelming, not just from the society that condemned Socrates, but from within himself. He had spoken out of fear and confusion, and now those words had contributed to his mentor's death.

He ventured outside the cave, looking for something to eat. The physical activity provided a brief distraction from his thoughts, but the anger simmered just beneath the surface, waiting to erupt. He found some wild berries and set a small snare, hoping to catch a rabbit or another small animal. As he worked, his mind kept returning to the events that had led him here. The trial, the senator's manipulation, and his own perceived failures gnawed at him. He felt betrayed by Marcus and furious at the Athenian society that had condemned Socrates.

Plato sat by the cave entrance, staring out at the forest. He tried to meditate, to find some inner peace, but the anger kept bubbling up, interrupting his thoughts. He remembered Socrates' teachings, the lessons of seeking truth and wisdom, but they seemed distant and unreachable now. His mind was clouded with anger, making it hard to focus on anything else.

How could he have allowed himself to be so easily manipulated? How could he have failed to stand up for his beliefs when it mattered most? These questions tormented him, fueling his despair. He felt like he was drowning in his own anger, unable to find a way out.

Plato's thoughts turned to Marcus. The senator had seemed so trustworthy, so convincing. But now, in the clarity of hindsight, Plato saw the manipulation, the deceit. Marcus had used him, twisted his words, and betrayed him. But why? Surely he was mistaken, he thought. The anger towards the senator, towards himself, was like a burning coal in his chest, intensifying with each passing moment.

As the morning wore on, Plato's frustration grew. The lack of human contact amplified his negative emotions, making the cave feel more like a prison than a refuge. His thoughts circled endlessly, feeding his growing wrath. He knew he had to find a way to channel his anger, but right now, it felt like an insurmountable task.

Plato stood up and began pacing the cave, trying to release some of the pent-up energy. He picked up a stone and threw it against the wall, the impact echoing through the cave. The physical release provided a momentary relief, but the anger remained, simmering just beneath the surface.

He returned to the mouth of the cave and took a deep breath, trying to calm himself. He leaned against the cave wall, closing his eyes briefly. His anger was raw and consuming, a constant reminder of the injustice that had befallen his mentor and the betrayal he felt from those he had trusted.

As the sun climbed higher in the sky, casting a warm glow over the forest, Plato took another deep breath and opened his eyes. He would not let his anger consume him. As the morning turned into midday, the cave's shadows shortened and the forest outside came alive with the sounds of nature. Plato's mind, however, was far from peaceful. He had hoped that the tasks of survival would distract him,

but they only served to remind him of his isolation and the weight of his thoughts.

Plato checked the snare he had set earlier and found a small rabbit caught in it. The sight should have brought a sense of accomplishment, but instead, it felt hollow. He prepared the rabbit for cooking, his movements mechanical and devoid of any satisfaction. The routine tasks of survival provided no respite from the storm of emotions within him.

He built a small fire outside the cave and cooked the rabbit, the smell of roasting meat filling the air. As he ate, his mind returned to the trial and the events that had led him here. Each bite seemed to fuel his anger rather than satiate his hunger. The betrayal by Marcus, the condemnation of Socrates, and his own perceived failures all gnawed at him.

The forest around him was quiet, a stark contrast to the chaos inside his mind. The isolation intensified his feelings, turning his place of refuge into a place of confinement rather than a sanctuary. Plato tried to meditate again, to find some inner peace, but the anger kept bubbling up, interrupting his thoughts.

He sat by the fire, staring into the flames. The flickering light reminded him of the oil lamp in the cave, casting shadows that seemed to mock his turmoil. He felt trapped, not just in the cave, but in a cycle of guilt and wrath that he couldn't escape. His mind raced with thoughts of what he could have done differently, how he could have saved Socrates, and how he had been betrayed by Marcus.

As the day wore on, Plato's frustration grew. The lack of human contact continued to amplify his negative emotions, making the isolation feel unbearable. His thoughts circled endlessly, feeding his growing wrath. He stood up and began pacing the area around the cave, trying to release some of the pent-up energy. He picked up a few stones and threw them into the forest, each impact echoing through the trees. The act of throwing the stones offered a brief, cathartic release, but it did little to quell the storm within him.

Plato sat back down by the fire, his mind still racing. He tried to focus on Socrates' teachings, on the pursuit of truth and wisdom, but they seemed distant and unreachable. His anger clouded his thoughts, making it hard to concentrate on anything other than the injustice he felt.

The afternoon sun cast long shadows, and Plato felt a deep sense of despair. He was alone, cut off from the world he had known and the people he cared about. The isolation was suffocating, and the anger that burned within him made it hard to see any way forward.   H   e took a deep breath, trying to calm the storm inside him. As the day turned to evening, he felt a weariness that went beyond physical exhaustion.

He stared into the dying embers of the fire, feeling the weight of his emotions pressing down on him. As the sun dipped below the horizon, casting the forest in a dusky glow, he gathered more dry wood and built a larger fire inside the cave. The flickering flames provided some comfort against the encroaching darkness, but the day's frustrations had left him feeling raw and agitated. He reached into his satchel and pulled out a small flask of wine the senator gave him, hoping it would calm his nerves.

He took a deep drink, feeling the warmth of the wine spread through his chest. Instead of soothing him, it seemed to fuel his anger. The isolation, the betrayal, and the guilt all combined into a potent mix of emotions that threatened to overwhelm him. He stood up, his face contorted with rage, and began to yell into the emptiness of the cave.

"Why!? Why did it have to be this way?" he shouted, his voice echoing off the stone walls. The sound reverberated back at him, amplifying his sense of helplessness. He picked up a stone and hurled it into the darkness, followed by another and another. Each throw was a release of his pent-up wrath, but it did little to quell the storm within.

His mind flashed back to the courtroom, the twisted use of his words, and the serene face of Socrates as he drank the poison. The anger surged again, more intense than before. Plato grabbed the flask of wine and took another deep drink, the liquid burning his throat. He threw the empty flask against the cave wall, where it shattered with a satisfying crash.

As he sat back down by the fire, breathing heavily, he noticed the shadow of an owl on the cave wall. The bird seemed to be watching him, its eyes reflecting the firelight in an almost mocking way. "Are you here to taunt me too?" he muttered bitterly. The owl's presence was a stark reminder of his isolation and the inner turmoil he could not escape.

The firelight cast dancing shadows on the cave walls, creating a surreal and haunting atmosphere. The flickering images seemed to come alive, playing out scenes of his guilt and anger. Plato felt trapped, not just in the cave, but in a prison of his own making. His wrath had become a constant companion, a reminder of his failures and betrayals.

In a fit of rage, Plato stood up and began throwing more stones, his yells echoing through the cave. "How could I have let this happen? How could I have been so blind?" His voice broke with the intensity of his emotions. He felt a tear slip down his cheek, but he quickly brushed it away, unwilling to show any sign of weakness even to himself.

He sank back down by the fire, exhausted from his outburst. The owl's shadow remained still, a silent witness to his turmoil. Plato stared into the flames, feeling the weight of his wrath pressing down on him. The wine had done little to ease his pain; if anything, it had intensified it.

The shadows seemed to grow longer, reaching out to him, pulling him deeper into his despair. As the fire began to die down, he felt a sense of clarity start to emerge from the chaos of his emotions.

He knew that this anger could not be ignored; it had to be confronted and understood. The isolation had amplified his negative emotions, but it had also given him the space to begin grappling with them.

He took one last look at the owl's shadow, feeling a strange sense of connection to the silent bird. "I will not let this anger consume me," he whispered, more to himself than to the owl. "I will find a way to honor Socrates and continue the pursuit of wisdom."

With renewed determination, Plato settled down and sat beside the embers of the fire. As the night deepened, Plato closed his eyes, finally feeling a sense of peace. Exhausted from his outburst, Plato lay down beside the dying embers of the fire. The cave was quiet, the shadows from the firelight slowly fading into darkness. He closed his eyes, hoping for a peaceful sleep, but his mind remained restless. Eventually, he drifted into a fitful slumber, the turmoil of the day following him into his dreams.

Slowly fading from dark to light, passing in and out of consciousness, the darkness of the cave opened with the cold, calculating eyes of Senator Marcus. As Plato stared into them, he felt himself being pulled deeper, diving into the blackness of the senator's pupils. The darkness enveloped him, and the sound of crashing waves filled his ears. The senator's deceitful smile lingered in the back of his mind, a stark reminder of the betrayal.

He was soaring fast and high above the earth again, the wind whipping past him as he flew towards an unknown destination. Below, the world was being consumed in a great and terrible flood, the water rising higher and higher, drowning everything in its path. He could hear the terrorizing screams of the people, their cries for help echoing in his mind. Ancient temples and towering cities were sinking beneath the waves, their grandeur and majesty reduced to nothing more than a memory.

In the distance, he spotted the massive central temple, its spires reaching towards the sky. But as he flew closer, he saw that it too was sinking, its walls collapsing as the waves crashed against them. He tried to reach the temple, to save those in need, but no matter how fast he flew, he was just out of reach. Desperation filled him as the temple vanished beneath the water. Suddenly, he was falling, tumbling towards the water below.

As he fell, the scene shifted abruptly. He was in the courtroom again, seeing through Socrates' eyes, staring down the center of the vial of poison. The liquid swirled like crashing waves, and as he lifted it to his lips, it engulfed him, collapsing over his entire being like a tidal wave. The voices of the prosecutors echoed around him, accusing and condemning. "Plato, you betrayed me," Socrates' voice echoed, filled with disappointment and sadness.

The courtroom faded, and Plato found himself trapped in a dark, enclosed space. The walls closed in on him, the weight of his guilt and anger pressing down. He struggled to breathe, his chest tight with fear and despair. Socrates' face appeared again, close enough to touch. "You must let go of this anger, Plato," he said gently but firmly. "It will consume you if you allow it. Remember why we seek the truth."

But as Socrates' face faded, Senator Marcus' face took its place. His smile was sinister, his eyes gleaming with deceit. Blood began to pour down his face and hands, a grotesque symbol of his betrayal. The blood flowed and transformed, covering Plato's own hands. He looked down in horror, seeing his hands stained with blood, solidifying his anger and guilt. "You are complicit," the senator's voice echoed mockingly. "You failed him."

The voices of the judges and the prosecutors grew louder, their accusations merging into a deafening roar. Plato felt a surge of wrath, directed at himself, at Marcus, and at the world that had allowed such an injustice. He clenched his fists, wanting to scream, but no sound came out. The pressure built until he thought he would be crushed by it.

Suddenly, the scene shifted again. Plato was standing on a vast, empty plain, the sky above a deep, foreboding gray. Socrates stood before him, his expression calm and understanding. "Plato, you have the power to change this," he said. "But you must first conquer your own anger. Use it as a tool, not as a master."

Plato woke with a start, the cave once again silent and dark. The fire had died down to a few glowing embers, casting faint shadows on the walls. He took a deep breath, his heart still racing from the intensity of the dream. The words of Socrates echoed in his mind, a beacon of clarity amidst the chaos of his emotions.

He sat up and looked around the cave, the familiar surroundings grounding him. The nightmare had left him shaken, but it had also given him a sense of clarity. He knew now that he could not stay hidden away, consumed by his anger and guilt. He stood up and walked to the mouth of the cave. The first light of dawn was beginning to filter in, casting a soft glow over the forest. The air was cool and fresh, a stark contrast to the suffocating weight of his dreams. He took a deep breath, feeling a sense of resolve settling over him.

He knew he had to return to Athens. Hiding away in the cave would not bring him peace, nor would it honor the memory of Socrates. He had to face the senator, to tell the truth, and to continue the teachings of his mentor. It was the only way to find redemption and to fight for the justice that Socrates had believed in.

With renewed determination, Plato packed his belongings and prepared to leave. The path ahead was uncertain, but he was ready to face it. The anger was still there, simmering beneath the surface, but he would not let it control him.

The owl's shadow was now gone, and the forest seemed to welcome him with open arms. Plato took one last look at the cave, a place of both torment and revelation, and then turned to face the path ahead. As he stepped out of the cave, the sun began to rise, casting a warm glow over the landscape. Plato felt a sense of hope and purpose that had been missing for too long. With a final deep breath, Plato began his journey back to Athens, ready to confront his fears and to fight for the truth. The wrath that had once consumed him had become a driving force, a fire that would fuel his pursuit of justice and wisdom. As he embarked, he remembered the words of wisdom that had always guided him: 'The beginning is the most important part of the work.' Little did he know, this beginning would lead him to the depths of knowledge and beyond.

Chapter 6

A Gluttonous Feast

Plato walked through the darkened streets of Athens, his heart pounding with a mix of fear and determination. The city was quiet at this hour, the remnants of the previous night's festivities still evident in the deserted alleyways. He approached the senator's house, his resolve hardening with each step. He had to make things right, to find a way to honor Socrates and his teachings.

He reached the door and knocked sharply, the sound echoing in the still night. After a few moments, the door creaked open, and Senator Marcus's wary eyes met his. The senator looked both surprised and concerned, his brows furrowing as he recognized Plato.

"Plato, what are you doing here?" Marcus whispered urgently, glancing around. "It's dangerous for you to be out in the open."

"I need answers, Senator," Plato replied, his voice edged with anger. "I can't hide forever. I want to honor Socrates and continue his work, but I have to know the truth. Were you involved in his death?"

Marcus's expression hardened. "This isn't the place for such accusations, Plato. Come inside, quickly."

Plato hesitated, his suspicion growing. "Why should I trust you? You've already betrayed one of the greatest men I've ever known. How do I know you won't betray me too?"

Marcus sighed deeply, his expression a mix of reluctance and concern. "I understand your anger, Plato. But standing out here in the open isn't safe for either of us. Come inside, and we'll talk."

Reluctantly, Plato followed the senator into the house. The door closed behind them with a soft thud. The familiar surroundings brought a sense of comfort, but Plato knew that the path ahead would be fraught with challenges. He had made his decision, and he would see it through, no matter the cost.

The senator led him into a small sitting room, dimly lit by a single oil lamp. Marcus gestured for Plato to sit, his demeanor cautious. He took a seat opposite Plato, his eyes probing.

"You're taking a great risk by coming here, Plato," Marcus said quietly. "But I understand your determination. Socrates' death has left a void, and you want to honor his legacy. It's perfectly understandable."

Plato's eyes narrowed, his suspicion evident. "I want to teach, to bring education to the youth. But I can't ignore the feeling that I've been manipulated. Were you the one who betrayed Socrates? Did you use my words against him?"

Marcus's expression hardened momentarily before softening into one of concern. "Plato, I would never intentionally harm Socrates. The situation was complex, and there were many forces at play. My best guess is that someone from the tavern must have overheard us talking that night. I'm doing everything I can to make things right."

Plato's gaze remained unwavering. "I need to speak with my uncle Critaeus. He will know what really happened. Please, Senator, can you bring him here?"

Marcus's eyes flickered with something unreadable, but he nodded slowly. "I understand your need for reassurance. I will contact Critaeus and arrange for him to visit you here. But you must stay hidden and safe until then."

Plato felt a wave of conflicting emotions. "Thank you, Senator. But understand this, I will not be manipulated again."

Marcus stood, his demeanor firm but shadowed by a hint of impatience. "There is no manipulation, Plato, I'm only trying to help. Don't worry yourself with such things. For now, you need to rest. You've been through a lot, and you need to regain your strength. I'll have a room prepared for you."

Plato nodded, feeling a mixture of hope and doubt. The senator's words had reassured him, but a small part of him still harbored deep suspicion. He followed Marcus down a hallway to a modest room, furnished simply but comfortably. As he settled into the bed, he couldn't shake the feeling that there was more to the senator's motives than he was being told. But what choice did he have?

As Marcus closed the door behind him, Plato lay back and stared at the ceiling, his thoughts a whirl of confusion and determination. He resolved to keep his guard up and to seek the truth, no matter what. For now, he had to trust Marcus and hope that his uncle Critaeus would provide the answers he needed.

Plato closed his eyes, letting the exhaustion of the past days overtake him. The journey ahead was uncertain, but he was ready to face it. He would honor Socrates' legacy and fight for the truth, no matter the cost.

He awoke to the soft light of morning filtering through the small window of his room. The events of the previous night were still fresh in his mind, a mix of hope and lingering doubt. He dressed quickly and made his way to the senator's study, where Marcus had asked to meet him.

The study was a cozy room lined with shelves of scrolls and books. A large desk dominated the space, cluttered with papers and various artifacts. Marcus was already there, poring over a document. He looked up as Plato entered, a welcoming smile on his face.

"Good morning, Plato. I hope you slept well," Marcus said, gesturing for him to sit.

"As well as can be expected," Plato replied, taking a seat opposite the senator. "Thank you for taking me in. I appreciate your help."

Marcus nodded, his expression serious. "I understand the position you're in, Plato. Socrates' death has left a hole in the heart of Athens that must be filled; someone must continue his work. Who better to do it than you?"

Plato felt a swell of pride and gratitude, but also a flicker of suspicion. He pushed it aside for now, focusing on the senator's words. "I want to honor Socrates and teach the youth, but I know it's a dangerous time. What do you propose?"

Marcus leaned back in his chair, his eyes thoughtful. "You can stay here, in my home while we sort things out. It's the safest place for you right now. In the meantime, you can help educate my grandchild. He's a bright boy and could benefit greatly from your teachings."

Plato nodded, feeling a sense of purpose. "I would be honored to teach him. And what about the school? Do you think it's possible to open one?"

The senator's eyes narrowed slightly, considering. "It will take time and careful planning. The political climate is still volatile, and we must tread carefully. I will speak with my colleagues, feel out their opinions, and see if we can create a safe environment for your teachings."

Plato's heart quickened with hope. "Thank you, Senator. I'm willing to do whatever it takes to make this dream a reality."

Marcus leaned forward, his gaze intense. "I believe in your potential, Plato. But we must be cautious. I'll need to ensure that the other senators are on board, that they see the value in what you're offering. It may take some time, but with patience, I believe we can succeed."

Plato felt a surge of gratitude and relief. "I understand, and I'm grateful for your support. There's one more thing, Senator. I need to speak with my uncle Critaeus. He needs to know that I am okay; that he was right and that I am sorry. He will know the truth about what happened and can provide guidance on us moving forward."

Marcus's expression tightened briefly before he forced a reassuring smile. "Of course, Plato. Like I said last night, I will contact Critaeus and arrange for him to visit. But for now, you must stay hidden. It's crucial for your safety and for our plans."

Plato nodded, feeling reassured. "Thank you. I'll trust your judgment."

The senator stood, signaling the end of their discussion. "For now, focus on helping my grandchild. He is down the hall waiting. His education is important, and it will give you a sense of purpose while we work on the larger plan."

Plato stood as well, feeling a mix of hope and a twinge of envy. The idea of running a prestigious school, of restoring his and Socrates' honor, was intoxicating. He imagined the respect and admiration he would earn, the influence he could wield. But he pushed those thoughts aside, focusing on the task at hand.

"Thank you, Senator. I will do my best," Plato said earnestly.

Marcus placed a hand on Plato's shoulder, his expression sincere. "I know you will. Together, we can make this work. Just remember to stay cautious and patient."

As Plato left the study, he felt a renewed sense of determination. He would remain discreet, follow the senator's guidance, and work towards his dreams. But the flicker of envy remained, a reminder of the prestige and honor he sought.

He made his way to the room where the senator's grandchild was waiting, ready to begin his new role as a teacher. He stood outside the door of the room where the boy was waiting, a mixture of anticipation and nervousness coursing through him. He took a deep breath,

straightened his tunic, and knocked softly. The door opened, revealing a bright-eyed boy of about twelve years old, his face lighting up with curiosity.

"Hello, you must be Plato," the boy said, his voice eager. "Grandfather told me you would be teaching me. I'm Alexios."

Plato smiled, the boy's enthusiasm lifting his spirits. "Yes, Alexios. It's nice to meet you. Are you ready to begin?"

Alexios nodded eagerly, stepping aside to let Plato into the room. The space was filled with shelves of scrolls and clay tablets, a small desk in the corner, and a large window that let in plenty of light. Plato felt a sense of familiarity and comfort among the books and learning tools.

They began the lesson with some basic math and philosophy, Plato introducing Socrates' method of questioning and dialogue. Alexios was quick and perceptive, asking thoughtful questions that showed his genuine interest. As they worked, Plato felt a growing sense of purpose. Teaching Alexios reminded him of why he had chosen this path.

After the lesson, Alexios left to attend his other duties, and Plato was left alone in the room. He sat by the window, looking out at the bustling street below. His thoughts drifted back to the senator's proposal and the promise of a school. The idea of running such an institution filled him with both hope and envy. He imagined the prestige and honor that would come with such a position, the respect he would earn from his peers, and the influence he could wield over the youth of Athens.

But with those dreams came a sense of guilt. Was his desire to teach truly about honoring Socrates, or was it about restoring his own status and achieving personal glory? The questions tormented him, fueling his internal struggle.

Plato took a deep breath, trying to calm his racing thoughts. He knew that his intentions mattered, that his motives had to be pure if he

were to truly honor Socrates' legacy. But the allure of prestige and recognition was powerful, and he couldn't deny the envy that crept into his heart. He stood up and began to pace the room, his mind racing. He thought about the teachings of Socrates, the importance of seeking truth and wisdom. He knew that he needed to find a balance, to ensure that his ambitions did not overshadow his true purpose. He resolved to stay grounded, to focus on his role as a teacher and to trust in the senator's plan.

He remembered the senator's reassurances and the promise to contact his uncle Critaeus. That assurance had given him hope, but a small part of him still harbored doubt. He knew he had to be cautious and patient, as Marcus had advised, but the waiting was difficult. The uncertainty gnawed at him, making it hard to focus on anything else.

As the sun began to set, casting a warm glow over the city, Plato felt a sense of calm wash over him. He would remain patient and cautious, following the senator's guidance. He would work towards his dream of opening a school, but he would do it for the right reasons. He would honor Socrates' legacy and fight for the truth, no matter the cost.

With renewed determination, Plato left the room and made his way to the dining area, where the senator was waiting for him. They shared a simple meal, discussing the day's lessons and the plans for the future. Marcus reiterated the need for caution, reminding him to stay hidden and safe. He nodded, feeling a mix of gratitude and impatience. He was grateful for the senator's help, but the idea of waiting, of staying hidden, gnawed at him. He yearned for the day when he could step out into the open, teach freely, and restore his and Socrates' honor.

"Thank you, Senator. I will do as you advise," Plato replied, his voice steady despite the turmoil inside him.

Marcus nodded, a faint smile on his lips. "Good. We will take this one step at a time. Stay strong, Plato. The future holds great promise if we are patient."

As they finished their meal, Plato felt a renewed sense of hope. He would remain discreet, follow the senator's guidance, and work towards his dreams. But the flicker of doubt tinged with envy remained, a reminder of the prestige and honor he sought. They sat at the dining table, the remnants of their simple meal between them. The flickering light of the oil lamps cast long shadows on the walls, giving the room a warm, intimate glow. Marcus leaned back in his chair, his expression serious as he regarded Plato.

"Plato, we need to be very careful. The political climate is still volatile, and your presence here must remain a secret for a while longer. I've spoken to a few colleagues, but we need more time to ensure your safety and the viability of the school," Marcus said, his tone measured.

Plato nodded, understanding the gravity of the situation. "I trust your judgment, Senator. I will stay hidden and focus on teaching Alexios. But I hope the school can become a reality soon. I am eager to honor Socrates and continue his work."

Marcus gave a faint smile, though his eyes were shadowed with concern. "I know, Plato. And I promise you, I am doing everything I can to make this happen. We must be patient and strategic."

The senator's words were reassuring, but he couldn't shake a growing sense of impatience. The idea of staying hidden indefinitely gnawed at him. He longed to step out into the open, to teach freely and restore his and Socrates' honor.

"When can I speak with my uncle Critaeus? Have you heard from him?" Plato asked, his voice steady.

Marcus's expression tightened briefly before he forced a reassuring smile. "Of course, Plato. I have not yet gotten word from him. He might be away on business. My contact must be brief for now. It's crucial for your safety and for our plans. As soon as I get in touch with him I will let you know."

Plato felt a wave of relief wash over him. "Thank you, Senator. I appreciate your help."

The senator stood, signaling the end of their discussion. "For now, focus on helping my grandchild. His education is important, and it will give you a sense of purpose while we work on the larger plan."

Plato stood as well, feeling a mix of hope and a twinge of envy. "Thank you, Senator. I will do my best," he said earnestly.

Marcus placed a hand on Plato's shoulder, his expression sincere. "I know you will. Together, we can make this work. Just remember to stay cautious and patient."

As they finished their conversation, Marcus's eyes flickered to the door, and his expression grew contemplative. "There are many who would not look kindly on our plans, Plato. We must be vigilant. There's more at stake here than just a school."

Plato frowned, sensing a deeper concern in Marcus's words. "What do you mean, Senator?"

Marcus shook his head slightly, as if dismissing a troubling thought. "Just be careful, Plato. The world is not always as it seems, and trust is a precious commodity."

Plato nodded, though the senator's words left him with a lingering sense of unease. He resolved to stay focused on his teaching and to trust in Marcus's plan. But the seeds of doubt had been planted, and they would grow with time.

The evening wore on, and Plato returned to his room, his mind filled with thoughts of the future. As he lay down to sleep, he couldn't help but feel a twinge of envy for the life he once had, the freedom he had taken for granted. He closed his eyes, determined to stay strong and patient.

But as the shadows lengthened and the night deepened, a quiet sense of foreboding settled over him. He would need to be vigilant and cautious, for the path ahead was fraught with unseen dangers.

The next morning, Plato awoke with a renewed sense of purpose. He made his way to Alexios's room, ready to continue their lessons. The boy greeted him with enthusiasm, and they spent the morning immersed in philosophy and debate. Yet, beneath the surface, Plato felt the weight of his situation pressing down on him.

Days turned into weeks, and Plato's role as Alexios's teacher became routine. Marcus was often away, leaving Plato to his thoughts and his growing impatience. The senator's reassurances began to feel hollow, and Plato couldn't shake the feeling that he was being kept in the dark.

One evening, as they dined together, Marcus finally spoke of the progress he was making. "I've been speaking with several colleagues, Plato. There's interest in your school, but we must move slowly. There are many who would oppose such an endeavor."

Plato nodded, though his heart sank at the thought of more delays. "I understand, Senator. I just hope that we can move forward soon."

Marcus's eyes were sharp as he regarded Plato. "We will, Plato. But remember, patience is key. Rushing into this could jeopardize everything."

Plato forced a smile, though inside he felt a growing frustration. "Of course, Senator. I will do my best to remain patient."

As the meal ended, Marcus placed a hand on Plato's shoulder. "Trust me, Plato. We will achieve our goals, but we must be careful."

Plato nodded, though the senator's words left him with a lingering sense of unease. He resolved to stay focused on his teaching and to trust in Marcus's plan. But the seeds of doubt had been planted, and they would grow with time.

As Plato returned to his room, he couldn't help but feel a quiet sense of foreboding. The shadows of doubt and impatience loomed larger with each passing day. Plato lay down to sleep, determined to

stay strong and patient. But as he drifted off, his mind was filled with questions and uncertainties. The future was uncertain, and the pressure was building. He would need to be ready for whatever lay ahead.

Chapter 7

Web of Lies

The days dragged on, and Plato's initial optimism began to wane. He spent most of his time in the small room Marcus had provided, teaching Alexios in the mornings and spending the rest of his time alone. The isolation was suffocating, and Plato found himself growing increasingly restless and frustrated with the lack of progress and vague reassurances from Marcus. His feelings of confinement and betrayal intensified.

He had expected progress, some sign that the senator's promises were being fulfilled, but there was nothing. Marcus was often away, and when he was home, he seemed preoccupied and distant. Plato's requests to see his uncle Critaeus were met with vague assurances that only fueled his suspicion and irritation.

One morning, as Plato sat at the desk in his room, reviewing the day's lesson plan, a knock at the door interrupted his thoughts. It was one of the household servants, bringing his breakfast. The servant placed the tray on the desk and left without a word, the door closing softly behind him.

Plato stared at the tray, the food suddenly unappetizing. He felt more like a prisoner than a guest, confined to his room and cut off from the world. He missed his home, his family, and the life he had once known. The walls of his room seemed to close in on him, amplifying his sense of isolation and frustration.

As the days turned into weeks, Plato's discontent grew. He noticed a change in Alexios's behavior as well. The boy, who had once been eager and respectful, had become increasingly demanding and dismissive. It was as if he saw Plato as nothing more than a servant, someone to be ordered around and dismissed at will.

That night, as Plato sat alone in his room, the firelight danced on the walls, casting shifting shadows that reminded him once again of the stories his uncle Critaeus used to tell him as a boy. Tales of a great and ancient civilization, a people of immense wisdom and power who had perished in a cataclysmic flood. The stories had always fascinated him, and now, in the flickering light, they seemed to come alive as he fell asleep.

He had the recurring dream again. The screams of terror, the crashing waves, the city being consumed by the flood. He soared above it all, trying to reach the temple, but it was always just out of reach. The dream had haunted him for as long as he could remember, and now it seemed to call to him more urgently than ever.

Plato awoke with a start, the images of the dream still vivid in his mind. Something was calling him, pulling him towards a truth he could not yet see. He sat up, rubbing his eyes, and stared into the flickering flame. The shadows seemed to form ancient, crumbling temples, remnants of the stories his uncle had woven.

The days became monotonous. Time continued on, and Plato's discontent grew. The servants' behavior only solidified his suspicions. Meals were brought to his room without a word, and the few interactions he had with the household were curt and distant. Even Alexios's attitude had shifted. The young student, who had once shown great enthusiasm for learning, now regarded Plato with a mix of indifference and condescension.

Plato tried to maintain his composure, to focus on the lessons and the promise of the school, but the constant delays and the senator's evasiveness gnawed at him. He felt a growing sense of anger and

betrayal, wondering if Marcus had ever intended to fulfill his promises.

Plato moved through the senator's home with a growing sense of unease. He had noticed subtle changes in the way the household treated him. The servants were more distant, their eyes avoiding his as they brought his meals or cleaned his room. Even the small liberties he once had, like strolling in the courtyard, and meals with the senator were subtly withdrawn.

One afternoon, as Plato passed by the kitchen, he overheard a conversation between two of the servants. They spoke in hushed tones, but their words were clear enough.

"The senator says he's a guest, but he's treated more like a prisoner," one servant whispered.

"He hasn't left his room in weeks. It's as if he's being kept hidden away," the other replied.

Plato's heart sank. The realization that he was being confined, rather than protected, began to take hold. He continued on to his room, the weight of his thoughts pressing down on him. His pride bristled at the thought of being treated like a prisoner, a pawn in some larger game.

That evening, as he sat in his room, Plato's thoughts were consumed by the fragments of conversation he had overheard. He knew he needed more information to understand the full extent of his situation. A knock at the door interrupted his thoughts, and he found a young servant girl standing there, her eyes downcast.

"Excuse me, sir," she said softly. "I've brought your evening meal."

Plato nodded, watching her as she set the tray down. An idea formed in his mind. "Wait," he said as she turned to leave. "What is your name?"

"Elara, sir," she replied, looking up at him nervously.

"Elara, I need to ask you something important," Plato said, trying to keep his voice calm and steady. "I've heard rumors that my uncle, Critaeus, is being held under guard. Do you know anything about this?"

Elara hesitated, glancing around to make sure no one else was listening. "There have been whispers, sir," she said in a low voice. "Some of the servants say that your uncle is being kept somewhere under close watch. But I don't know where."

Plato's suspicions were confirmed. He felt a surge of anger and frustration. "Thank you, Elara," he said, his voice tense. "You've been very helpful."

As Elara left, Plato sat down heavily, the full weight of his situation pressing down on him. He was not just a guest or a political refugee; he was a prisoner, being kept in the dark about his uncle's fate and the senator's true intentions.

The next day, Plato began to observe the household more closely, looking for any signs that could confirm Elara's information. He noticed the guarded looks between the servants, the way they quickly changed the subject when he approached. The guards patrolling the grounds seemed to watch him intently as he passed, their eyes filled with suspicion. It was clear that there was a larger conspiracy at play.

Determined to find out more, Plato decided to take a risk. That night, he left his room and made his way to the servants' quarters. He found Elara and pulled her aside.

"Elara, I need to know more," he said urgently. "Anything you can tell me about my uncle or what the senator is planning."

Elara glanced around nervously before speaking. "I've heard that the senator has been meeting with important people, discussing plans that involve you and your uncle. They say your uncle is being held because he knows too much."

Plato's mind raced. "And what about me? Why am I being kept here?"

Elara hesitated. "There are rumors that the senator is using you as leverage. He wants to control you and your uncle to gain power."

Plato's anger flared. "Thank you, Elara. You've been very brave to tell me this."

As he returned to his room, Plato's mind was filled with plans. He knew he had to act quickly and decisively to uncover the full truth and find a way to free himself and his uncle from the senator's grip. The time for patience and trust had ended. The time for action had come.

Plato's unease deepened as the days passed. His interactions with the household became more strained, and he could feel the tension mounting. The change in Alexios was now complete, who had once been an eager and respectful student. Now, the boy's behavior was increasingly dismissive and condescending, reflecting the manipulative influence of his grandfather, Marcus.

During one of their lessons, Alexios interrupted Plato with a smirk. "You know, my grandfather says you're a great philosopher, but you don't seem very important now, do you? Just teaching one boy in a hidden room."

Plato's pride flared. He struggled to keep his composure, replying, "Every great philosopher starts with small steps, Alexios. Even Socrates began with a few students."

Alexios shrugged dismissively. "Well, my grandfather says you should be grateful for his help. Without him, you'd be nowhere."

Plato's pride was wounded by the boy's words. He had always seen himself as destined for greatness, as a follower of Socrates who would carry on his legacy. Being confined to a small room, teaching a single, disrespectful student, felt like a mockery of his ambitions.

The incident with Alexios was the final straw. Plato decided it was time to confront Marcus directly and demand answers. That evening, he found the senator in his study, poring over documents by the light of an oil lamp. He must be careful not to play his hand just yet. There were armed guards everywhere and the senator wielded too much power to be taken for granted. His hands trembled with a mix of anger and desperation as he stepped into the room.

"Senator, I need to know what's happening. Why am I being kept here like a prisoner? When will I see my uncle? When will the school become a reality?" Plato demanded, his voice trembling with pent-up anger and frustration.

Marcus looked up, his face shadowed in the dim light. He sighed deeply, his expression weary. "Plato, you must understand the delicate nature of our situation. These things take time. I am doing everything I can, but we must be patient."

"Patient?" Plato echoed bitterly. "I've been patient for weeks. I'm kept in this room, isolated from everyone. Even Alexios treats me like a servant now. I deserve answers, Senator."

Marcus stood up, walked over to Plato and placed a hand on his shoulder, his eyes earnest but evasive. "Trust me, Plato. We are making progress, but we must proceed carefully. For now, remain hidden. It's for your own safety."

Plato pulled away, his trust in the senator wavering. "I don't know how much longer I can do this."

Marcus's expression softened, though there was a flicker of something unreadable in his eyes. "Just a little longer, Plato. We will achieve our goals, but we must be careful."

Plato's pride flared again. "And my uncle? When will I see him?

Marcus's eyes narrowed slightly. "I have sent word to Critaeus. These things take time, Plato. You must trust me."

Trust. The word felt hollow, a fragile veneer over a chasm of doubt. Plato's patience had worn thin, and his pride could no longer tolerate the evasions and delays. "I don't know if I can, Senator. Every

day I'm here, I feel more like a prisoner and less like a philosopher. This is not what Socrates would have wanted."

Marcus's face hardened. "You must understand, Plato. We are trying to protect you. The political climate is still dangerous. Your visibility must be controlled."

Plato took a step back, his mind racing. The senator's words rang hollow, their sincerity in question. He had to find a way to break free from this suffocating confinement.

"I cannot remain hidden forever," Plato said, his voice firm. "I need to reclaim my life, my purpose. If you cannot give me answers, I will seek them myself."

Marcus stood up, his demeanor shifting from weary to authoritative. "Plato, I understand your frustration, but you must remain patient. We are closer than you think. Just a little longer. I am leaving shortly and will be back in a few days and then we can discuss this further." He dismissed.

Plato's jaw clenched, the weight of his pride and frustration pressing down on him. He knew his options were limited. He nodded curtly, not trusting himself to speak further. He turned and left the study, the door closing softly behind him.

As Plato returned to his room, he couldn't help but feel a quiet sense of foreboding. The shadows of doubt and impatience loomed larger with each passing day. He knew he had to stay vigilant and cautious, for the path ahead was fraught with unseen dangers.

That night, Plato lay in his bed, staring at the ceiling. The senator's reassurances had done little to ease his mind. The days had turned into weeks, and the isolation and evasiveness were wearing him down. He could no longer ignore the growing sense of betrayal.

He sat up, his resolve hardening. He would not stay hidden any longer. He had to take control of his destiny, to honor Socrates' legacy and find out the truth. He would confront Marcus one last time and

demand answers. If the senator refused, Plato would leave and seek out his uncle on his own.

The decision brought a sense of clarity and purpose. He knew the risks, but he also knew that staying in this limbo was no longer an option. He would face whatever challenges lay ahead with courage and determination.

As the night deepened, Plato's resolve only strengthened. The pressure had built to a breaking point, and he was ready to take action. The path ahead was uncertain, but he was determined to find the truth and reclaim his life.

With a final deep breath, Plato lay back down, his mind clear and focused. Tomorrow, he would confront Marcus again, and demand the answers he deserved. The time for patience was over. The time for action had come.

Chapter 8

Wrath Unleashed

The oppressive silence of Plato's confinement had become unbearable. Each day blended into the next, the monotony gnawing at his spirit. He felt like a caged animal, his thoughts consumed by the growing realization that his trust in Marcus had been misplaced. One evening, desperate for a change of scenery, he wandered through the halls of the senator's home.

As he approached the study, familiar voices reached his ears. Marcus and his family were engaged in a conversation. Plato hesitated, his curiosity piqued. He edged closer to the partially open door, straining to hear their words.

"I never understood why anyone respected that old fool Socrates," Marcus's voice was filled with disdain. "He was a threat to our stability, filling young minds with dangerous ideas."

Plato's heart pounded as he leaned closer, careful to remain hidden. The words stung, cutting through the thin veil of trust he had placed in the senator.

"And now we have his follower under our roof," one of Marcus's sons added, his tone mocking. "We've done well to keep him hidden. Plato's no different from his mentor—just as foolish and gullible."

Rage bubbled within Plato, but he forced himself to stay silent. The senator's family continued their conversation, oblivious to his presence.

"We did what we had to," Marcus continued. "Socrates had to be silenced. Keeping Plato under control is crucial. If he knew the truth, it would ruin us."

The cold realization washed over Plato. Elara was right. The senator had never intended to help Socrates or him. They had been using him all along, manipulating his trust for their own gain.

Plato's mind raced, the implications of Marcus's words sinking in. What truth were they hiding? His thoughts turned to his uncle Critaeus, and a sense of dread settled over him. He needed to know more, to uncover the full extent of their betrayal.

He forced himself to remain calm, stepping away from the study door. The betrayal ran deeper than he had imagined. Marcus had not only manipulated him but had also orchestrated Socrates' downfall. Plato's faith in the senator shattered, replaced by a burning desire for truth and justice.

As he made his way back to his room, the anger within him grew. He knew he couldn't stay silent any longer. The time for patience was over. He needed to act, to confront Marcus and demand answers. The shadows on the walls seemed to mock him, a constant reminder of his confinement and the lies that had kept him there.

Plato's resolve hardened. He would find out the truth, no matter the cost. The next step was clear—he needed to gather evidence, to uncover the full extent of Marcus's betrayal. It was the only way to clear his name. His thoughts turned to the senator's study, to the documents and letters that might hold the answers he sought.

That night, Plato found no solace in the dancing firelight. Instead, he lay awake, his mind racing with plans and strategies. The shadows no longer brought comfort, but a reminder of the deceit that surrounded him. He knew the path ahead would be dangerous, but he was ready to face it. For Socrates, for his uncle, and for himself, he would uncover the truth.

As dawn approached, Plato rose from his bed, determined and resolute. The time for action had come. He would no longer be a pawn in the senator's game. He would reclaim his destiny, honor Socrates' legacy, and seek justice for the betrayals that had shattered his world. The anger and betrayal Plato felt after overhearing Marcus and his family's conversation festered within him. He spent the next day in a haze of indignation, his mind a whirlwind of dark thoughts and suspicions. He knew he needed to uncover the full extent of Marcus's treachery. The answers, he believed, lay hidden within the senator's private study.

That night, when the household had settled into a deep slumber, Plato moved with silent determination. He crept through the darkened corridors, his footsteps barely making a sound on the marble floors. The house was eerily quiet, the only noise the faint rustling of the night wind outside, mingled with the clank of the metal armor of the guards standing watch.

Plato reached the study, pausing to listen for any sign of movement. Satisfied that the coast was clear, he slipped inside and closed the door behind him. The room was dimly lit by the embers of a dying fire. Shadows loomed large on the walls, giving the room an ominous feel.

He made his way to Marcus's desk, his heart pounding in his chest. Plato rifled through the papers and documents scattered across the desk, his hands trembling with a mix of fear and determination. Letters, official decrees, and personal notes filled the space, but nothing that immediately caught his eye. He opened drawers, sifting through their contents with growing urgency.

Finally, at the bottom of a stack of letters, he found what he had been looking for. A series of correspondences between Marcus and other influential figures. Plato's eyes scanned the documents, and his blood ran cold. The letters revealed a sinister plot orchestrated by Marcus to discredit and ultimately lead to the execution of Socrates. It was all there in black and white—the false charges, the bribed officials, the manipulated trial.

Plato's hands shook as he read the damning evidence. His mentor's death had been a calculated move, a cruel betrayal by someone he had once considered an ally. The realization was almost too much to bear.

But the worst was yet to come. As he delved deeper into the pile of documents, he found a letter addressed to Marcus from his uncle Critaeus. It was a desperate plea for help, dated just days before Critaeus had disappeared. The letter spoke of threats and fears, of Marcus' involvement in a conspiracy against Socrates, and begged for protection for his nephew.

Next to the letter was another document—an order for Critaeus's arrest and execution, signed by Marcus himself. Plato's heart broke as he pieced together the truth. His uncle had discovered Marcus's betrayal and had been silenced to keep the secret. The senator had not only betrayed Socrates but had also orchestrated his uncle's death.

Plato clutched the letters, his mind reeling from the revelations. Rage, sorrow, and a sense of helplessness overwhelmed him. He could barely comprehend the depth of the treachery he had uncovered. Marcus, the man who had promised to help him, had been the architect of his mentor's and his uncle's demise.

The room seemed to close in on him, the shadows mocking his pain. He stood there for what felt like an eternity, the weight of the betrayal pressing down on him. He wanted to expose the senator, but to whom? According to the documents, most of the senate was already involved. In that moment, he felt more alone and helpless than he had back in the cave. His uncle was his only ally, and now he was gone. His anger swelled up within him. Finally, he knew what he had to do. He had to confront Marcus and demand justice for Socrates and his uncle. The time for waiting and hoping was over. He would no longer be a passive victim in this cruel game.

With a deep breath, Plato gathered the incriminating documents and left the study, his resolve hardened. The senator would answer for his crimes. Plato would see to it, even if it meant risking everything.

As he returned to his room, the flickering firelight seemed to take on a more menacing tone. The once comforting shadows now felt like harbingers of the confrontation to come. Plato lay awake, clutching the letters, his mind racing with thoughts of vengeance and justice. The morning light would bring a new dawn, and with it, the beginning of the end for Marcus's deceitful reign.

The stage was set for the inevitable confrontation. Plato's heart was filled with a mix of fear and determination. He knew the risks, but he also knew that he could not back down. For Socrates, for his uncle, and for himself, he would confront Marcus and demand the truth.

The first light of dawn crept into Plato's room, casting long shadows on the walls. He hadn't slept, his mind racing with the revelations from the previous night. He clutched the incriminating letters tightly, his resolve hardening with each passing moment. It was time to confront Marcus and demand justice for Socrates and his uncle.

As the household began to stir, Plato prepared himself for the confrontation. He made his way to the dining room, where Marcus and his family were gathered for breakfast. The atmosphere was deceptively serene, but Plato's heart pounded with a mix of anger and determination.

"Marcus!" Plato's voice rang out, startling everyone at the table. He stepped forward, brandishing the letters. "I know the truth! You betrayed Socrates and had my uncle killed!"

The room fell silent, all eyes turning to Plato. Marcus's face paled, but he quickly regained his composure. "Plato, what are you talking about?" he asked, his voice steady but his eyes betraying a flicker of fear.

"Don't lie to me!" Plato shouted, slamming the letters down on the table. "I heard everything last night. You never intended to help us. You used me, kept me here like a prisoner!"

Alexios, who had been smirking at Plato's earlier outburst, looked between his grandfather and Plato, a mixture of confusion and interest on his face. "Looks like the philosopher finally figured it out," he sneered.

Plato's anger flared. "You all disgust me. Socrates was a great man, and you had him killed because he threatened your power. And my uncle—" His voice broke, raw emotion seeping through. "He trusted you, and you had him murdered."

Marcus stood, his expression hardening. "Enough, Plato. You don't know what you're talking about."

"I know more than you think," Plato retorted, his voice shaking with rage. "These letters—" He gestured to the documents on the table. "They tell the whole story. You orchestrated Socrates' death, and when my uncle found out, you had him silenced."

Marcus's silence was damning. The room's tension was palpable, the air thick with unspoken accusations. Plato's fists clenched at his sides, his knuckles white.

"I demand answers," Plato continued, his voice rising. "Why did you do it? Why did you betray him? Critaeus was your friend."

Marcus's face was a mask of controlled anger. "You think you understand the complexities of power and politics? Socrates was a threat to the stability of our city. His teachings were dangerous. Your uncle wanted him silenced. I tried to stop the trial."

"And my uncle?" Plato demanded. "What threat did he pose?"

"He knew too much," Marcus admitted, his voice cold. "He could have destroyed everything we've built, what you and I were trying to build. He hated the thought of you carrying on Socrates' legacy and opening a school. I did everything I could, but your uncle left me no choice. "

Plato's heart broke at the senator's callous admission. The man he had once trusted had turned on his own friend for the sake of power. The realization was almost too much to bear.

"You are no better than the tyrants Socrates spoke against," Plato said, his voice trembling with emotion. "You have destroyed lives for your own gain."

Marcus's eyes narrowed. "Watch your words, Plato. You are walking a dangerous path."

Plato's anger boiled over. "I will make you pay for what you've done. For Socrates, for my uncle, for the truth."

The room fell into an uneasy silence, the weight of Plato's words hanging heavily in the air. Marcus's family looked on, uncertain and fearful. The confrontation had reached a boiling point, and there was no turning back.

Plato's mind raced. He knew he had to act quickly. The letters were damning evidence, but he needed a plan to expose Marcus and seek justice. He wished he could leave, but there was no way he'd make it off of the heavily guarded property. He felt trapped and powerless, but his resolve only grew stronger.

As his gaze fell on the breakfast table, he noticed a knife among the utensils. His heart pounded as he reached for it, trying to appear nonchalant. His fingers closed around the handle, and he quickly concealed it within his robes.

Determined, Plato stood tall and walked to Alexios, the senator's grandson, who had been the most dismissive and cruel towards him. Without warning, Plato grabbed Alexios by the arm and pulled him close, the knife now pressed against the boy's throat.

The room erupted in chaos. Marcus and his family jumped to their feet, their faces pale with shock and fear.

"Plato, what are you doing?" Marcus demanded, his voice steady but with an edge of concern.

"You've left me no choice, Senator," Plato said, his voice cold and resolute. "You will confess to your crimes and face justice, or I will ensure you regret ever betraying Socrates and my uncle."

Marcus's eyes flickered with a mixture of rage and fear. "You're making a grave mistake, Plato. This will only lead to more bloodshed."

Plato's grip tightened on the knife. "The only mistake here was trusting you. Now, confess, or face the consequences."

"Plato, no!" Marcus shouted, stepping forward with his hands raised. "Put the knife down. We can talk about this."

"Talk?" Plato's voice was a mixture of desperation and rage. "You've lied to me, betrayed me, and murdered my family. There's nothing left to say."

Alexios struggled, his eyes wide with fear. "Grandfather, help me!" he cried, his voice trembling.

Plato tightened his grip, the knife's edge pressing into Alexios's skin. "Tell me the truth, Marcus. Admit everything. Or your grandson pays the price."

Marcus's composure cracked, his face contorted with a mix of fear and anger. "Plato, you don't want to do this. Let him go, and we can find another way."

"Another way?" Plato spat. "The time for talking is over. You will tell me the truth, or I swear I'll do it."

The tension in the room was palpable, the air thick with fear and desperation. Marcus's family watched in horror, their eyes darting between Plato and Marcus. The senator took a step forward, his voice shaking. "Alright, Plato. I'll tell you everything. Just let him go."

Plato's grip on the knife tightened. "Speak, or he dies."

Marcus's eyes narrowed, a flicker of something unreadable crossing his face. "You've left me no choice," he said quietly. "I did it. I orchestrated Socrates' trial. I had your uncle killed. It was all to protect my position, my family. But please, let Alexios go."

Plato's heart pounded in his chest, the confirmation of Marcus's betrayal hitting him like a physical blow. The rage and sorrow within him boiled over, his vision blurring with tears of anger and grief.

"Why?" Plato choked out. "Why did you do it?"

"Power, Plato," Marcus replied, his voice cold. "Everything I did was to maintain power. Socrates was a threat. Your uncle knew too much. It was all necessary."

Plato's mind raced, the full extent of the senator's betrayal sinking in. He glanced around the room, seeing the fear in Marcus's family's eyes, the desperation in Marcus's face. He felt the knife in his hand, the weight of his actions pressing down on him.

For a moment, he hesitated, the enormity of his next decision crashing over him. He could feel the knife pressing against Alexios's skin, the boy trembling in his grasp. The room was silent, everyone holding their breath, waiting for Plato's next move.

The firelight flickered, casting long shadows on the walls. Plato's resolve wavered, but then the memory of Socrates' calm acceptance of his fate and his uncle's desperate plea for help steeled his heart.

"Justice will be served," Plato whispered, more to himself than anyone else.

Marcus stepped forward, a look of concern tightening in his face. "Plato, make the right choice. We can find a way to resolve this."

But Plato shook his head, his eyes burning with a mixture of sadness and determination. "No, Marcus. There is no resolution here. Only justice."

Before Marcus could answer, the door behind him opened, and a group of soldiers entered, their eyes widening at the scene before them. Marcus signaled them to stay back, his gaze never leaving Plato's.

"Plato, listen to me," Marcus said calmly. "There are guards everywhere. You won't make it far if you try to escape. Let's resolve this peacefully."

Plato's grip on the knife tightened, but he knew Marcus was right. The senator's estate was heavily guarded, and any attempt to flee would likely end in his capture or worse. With a frustrated sigh, he lowered the knife. He pushed Alexios away, the boy scrambled to his grandfather's side, tears streaming down his face.

"You're making a mistake," Plato muttered, his voice filled with resignation.

"Perhaps," Marcus replied, motioning for the soldiers to stand down. "But we can still find a way out of this. The guards will escort you back to your room. I suggest you rest. We'll talk more in the morning."

Plato hesitated, his mind racing with the possibilities. Exhaustion and hopelessness settled over him like a heavy blanket. Knowing he had no other choice for now, he turned and walked back to his room, the weight of his situation pressing down on him.

Chapter 9

The Silent Betrayal

The morning after the confrontation, the house was eerily silent. Plato awoke with a sense of foreboding, the tension from the previous night still heavy in the air. He barely had time to gather his thoughts before the door to his room burst open. Armed guards stormed in, grabbing him roughly.

"Plato, you are under arrest," one of the guards announced, his voice cold and authoritative. "You will come with us."

Plato struggled, his heart pounding with fear and anger. "What is the meaning of this? On whose orders?"

The guard tightened his grip. "By order of Senator Marcus."

As they dragged him out of the house, Plato's mind raced. Marcus had betrayed him once again. The realization was like a knife to his heart. They marched him through the streets, the looks of the townspeople a mixture of pity and curiosity. Plato felt humiliated and powerless.

Thrown into a dark, damp cell, Plato was left to stew in his thoughts. The heavy iron door clanged shut behind him, sealing his fate. Hours passed, the silence broken only by the distant sounds of the city. Just as despair began to set in, the door creaked open, and Marcus stepped inside, flanked by guards.

"Plato," Marcus began, his tone almost sympathetic. "I didn't want it to come to this."

Plato glared at him, his voice filled with venom. "Spare me your lies, Marcus. You've betrayed me and everyone I cared about."

Marcus sighed, stepping closer. "You leave me no choice. Your teachings and influence are dangerous. But there is a way out for you."

"What do you mean?" Plato demanded, his anger giving way to a flicker of hope.

"Publicly denounce Socrates and his teachings," Marcus explained, his eyes cold. "Do this, and you'll be allowed to open your school. You'll live, but under my control. Refuse, and you face life in prison or death."

Plato's heart sank. The ultimatum was cruel and manipulative. He remained silent, his mind racing with the impossible choice before him.

"Think about it, Plato," Marcus continued, his voice softening slightly. "You have great potential. Don't throw it all away for a dead man's ideals."

Plato's gaze hardened. "Socrates was more than just a man. He was a beacon of truth and wisdom. You can't erase his legacy with threats."

Marcus's expression turned icy. "This is not a debate, Plato. You will denounce him, or you will suffer the consequences."

With that, Marcus signaled to the guard, who handed Plato a piece of parchment and a quill. "Take these," Marcus instructed. "You have until tomorrow morning to make your decision. Write your denouncement, and you will be spared. Refuse, and you will face the consequences."

Marcus turned and left, the door clanging shut behind him. Plato was left alone in the darkness, the weight of the decision pressing down on him. He knew what was at stake, but the thought of betraying Socrates went against everything he stood for.

As the hours dragged on, Plato's resolve wavered. The cell felt like a tomb, the silence amplifying his doubts and fears. He replayed

Marcus's words over and over in his mind, each repetition chipping away at his resolve.

Finally, as night fell, the door to his cell creaked open once more. This time, it was a guard with a small lamp, the flickering light casting eerie shadows on the walls.

"You have until morning," the guard said, his voice gruff. "Make your decision wisely."

Plato stared at the parchment and quill, the weight of his choice heavy in his hands. He knew he needed to talk to someone, to hear another voice besides the one in his head. The decision was too great to bear alone.

Word of Plato's arrest spread quickly, and soon his friends came to visit him in jail. They pleaded with the guards for a few moments with him, their desperation evident. The cold, damp cell felt even more oppressive with the knowledge that others knew of his plight.

The first to arrive was Eumenes, one of Plato's closest friends. The guard allowed him a brief visit, and Eumenes grasped Plato's hands through the bars, his eyes filled with concern.

"Plato, you must consider what Marcus is offering," Eumenes said, his voice urgent. "Denounce Socrates and live to fight another day. We need you."

Plato shook his head, the internal struggle evident on his face. "How can I betray everything Socrates stood for?"

Eumenes's grip tightened. "Think about what you could accomplish with your own school. Socrates would understand. You can continue his work in a way that won't get you killed."

Plato looked into Eumenes's eyes, seeing the fear and desperation there. His friend's words struck a chord, but the idea of betraying Socrates made his stomach turn. "I don't know if I can live with myself if I do this."

"You have to survive first," Eumenes insisted. "You can't help anyone if you're dead."

The conversation was cut short by the guard, who ushered Eumenes out. As he left, Eumenes gave Plato one last pleading look, his eyes filled with hope and fear.

The next visitor was Lysandra, the priestess from the Temple of Hermes. Her eyes were red from crying, her voice trembling with emotion. She approached the cell, her hands reaching through the bars to touch Plato's.

"Plato, please. I love you. Don't throw your life away," Lysandra whispered, her voice breaking. "Denounce Socrates, if only to stay alive."

Plato's heart ached at her words, the weight of her love and his loyalty to Socrates pulling him in opposite directions. "Lysandra, I…"

"Please, Plato," she pleaded, tears streaming down her face. "I can't lose you too. Do it for us, for our future."

Her words haunted him long after she left, her plea echoing in his mind as he sat in the dark cell, wrestling with his conscience. He felt torn between his duty to Socrates' legacy and his love for Lysandra. The weight of the decision was almost unbearable.

As the hours passed, more friends came to visit, each one echoing the same sentiments. They urged him to consider the offer, to think about the future and what he could accomplish if he stayed alive. Their words blurred together, a chorus of desperate pleas that only deepened his internal conflict.

Plato's thoughts were a tumultuous sea of regret and sorrow. The path he had chosen was fraught with danger and uncertainty, but he had made his choice. The consequences would come, but for now, he was left with his thoughts and the crushing weight of his betrayal.

As the first light of dawn crept into Plato's cell, he was no closer to a decision than he had been the night before. The emotional pleas from his friends and Lysandra echoed in his mind, mixing with the memories of Socrates' teachings and his unwavering integrity. Plato's heart was heavy, his mind a battleground of conflicting emotions.

The guard returned, opening the cell door with a grating sound that echoed in the dim corridor. "Senator Marcus is waiting," he said gruffly.

Plato rose slowly, his body stiff and aching. He followed the guard through the labyrinthine corridors, his footsteps heavy with the weight of his impending decision. They stopped outside a small room, where Marcus stood waiting, a stack of parchment and a quill on the table before him.

"Have you made your decision?" Marcus asked, his voice devoid of emotion.

Plato looked at the parchment, his heart sinking. He could feel the weight of Socrates' teachings, the wisdom and integrity that had guided him for so long. But he could also feel the crushing pressure of Marcus's ultimatum, the threat of imprisonment or death looming over him.

With a deep breath, he nodded slowly. "I will do it."

Marcus's face showed a flicker of triumph. "Very well. Write your statement."

The guard handed Plato the quill, and with trembling hands, he began to write. Each word felt like a betrayal, a dagger to his conscience. He wrote of Socrates' dangerous ideas, of the need for stability and order, each sentence tearing at his soul.

When he finished, Marcus read the statement and nodded approvingly. "Good. Tomorrow, you will read this before the gathered officials. This will ensure everyone understands your position and commitment to the new order."

Plato felt a hollow emptiness inside him, the weight of his decision crushing his spirit. He had betrayed everything he believed in, and the pain was almost unbearable.

"You will remain here for the night," Marcus said, signaling to the guard. "We will escort you to the courtyard in the morning."

The guard led Plato back to his cell, the door closing with a final, resounding thud. Alone in the darkness once more, Plato's thoughts were a tumultuous sea of regret and sorrow. He had made his decision, but the cost was higher than he could have ever imagined.

As he lay on the cold stone floor, the reality of his situation settled over him like a shroud. He had denounced Socrates, betrayed his mentor's legacy, and compromised his own principles. The morning would bring a public denouncement, but for now, he was left to wrestle with his guilt and the heavy burden of his choice.

The night was long and filled with turmoil. Plato's mind raced, replaying the events that had led him to this moment. He thought of Socrates' calm acceptance of his fate, the unwavering commitment to truth and integrity that had defined his mentor's life. Could he ever forgive himself for this betrayal?

As the hours dragged on, the flickering light from a distant torch cast eerie shadows on the cell walls, reminding Plato of the stories his uncle Critaeus used to tell him about the ancient civilization of Atlantis. The tales of pride and downfall seemed more relevant than ever. He had once believed in the power of knowledge and wisdom, but now he felt lost in a sea of compromise and deceit.

The faint sound of footsteps approaching broke his reverie. The cell door creaked open, and Marcus entered, his expression inscrutable.

"Plato, you have made a difficult choice," Marcus said, his voice surprisingly gentle. "But it is the right one. You will have the opportunity to do great things, to continue your work in a way that ensures stability and order."

Plato looked up, his eyes filled with a mix of defiance and sorrow. "At what cost, Marcus? I have betrayed everything I stand for."

Marcus sighed, stepping closer. "Sometimes, sacrifices must be made for the greater good. You will understand that in time."

Plato shook his head, the weight of his decision pressing down on him. "I don't know if I can ever accept that."

Marcus placed a hand on Plato's shoulder, a gesture meant to be reassuring but feeling more like a shackle. "You will see. Tomorrow, you will denounce Socrates publicly, and then we can begin to rebuild. Your future is still ahead of you, Plato."

With that, Marcus turned and left, the cell door closing behind him. Plato was left alone once more, his mind a storm of emotions. He had made his decision, but the consequences were far from over.

As dawn approached, the cold reality of his situation settled over him like a heavy fog. He would face the gathered officials, read the statement he had written, and publicly denounce the man who had shaped his life. The thought filled him with dread, but he knew there was no turning back.

The guard returned to escort him to the courtyard, where the officials were already gathering. Plato's heart pounded as he stepped into the open air, the sunlight blinding after the darkness of his cell. He could feel the eyes of the officials on him, the weight of their expectations pressing down on him.

Marcus stood beside the platform, his expression one of calm authority. He nodded to Plato, signaling for him to begin. With a deep breath, Plato stepped forward, the parchment trembling in his hands.

"I, Plato, hereby denounce Socrates and his teachings," he began, his voice wavering. "I acknowledge that his ideas are dangerous and disruptive to the stability of our society."

As he continued, the weight of his betrayal pressed down on him, tears filling his eyes. When he finished, the silence that followed was deafening. Marcus stepped forward, a satisfied smile on his face.

"Well done, Plato," Marcus said. "Now, for your own protection, you must understand the consequences of any further defiance."

Without warning, the guards seized Plato, dragging him to a nearby room. The atmosphere was cold and menacing, the walls echoing with the sound of his footsteps.

"What is this?" Plato demanded, fear creeping into his voice.

"Consider this a reminder of your place," Marcus replied, his tone devoid of the earlier sympathy. "A precaution to ensure you keep your word."

The guards pushed Plato to his knees, and before he could react, the first blow landed. Pain exploded through his body, and he cried out. The beating continued, each strike a reminder of his compromised principles and the betrayal he had been forced to commit.

The room spun, and Plato's vision blurred. He could hear Marcus's voice, distant and cold. "Remember this, Plato. You are nothing without my protection."

As the final blow landed, Plato's strength gave out. He collapsed to the ground, the world fading to black around him. His last thought before losing consciousness was of Socrates, and the profound sense of failure that weighed on his heart.

Act 2: Initiation

"In the heart of the storm, the seeker is forged anew, tested by trials and awakened to inner truths."

Through the fire of trials untold,
Where shadows dance and secrets hold,
A spirit tempered, strength revealed,
The path to wisdom thus unsealed.

Chapter 10

Chains of Fate

Agis had never imagined that he would end up like this, sold into slavery and forced to work on an Egyptian trade ship sailing the Mediterranean. As a Spartan soldier, he had been trained to fight and die with honor for his city-state, not to be subjected to the indignity of hard labor and mistreatment at the hands of foreigners, especially ones governed by the Persians.

It had all started twenty years earlier, fifteen years before the Peloponnesian War ended. Despite his reputation as a brave and skilled warrior, Agis had been captured by the Athenians and sold into slavery. He had been passed from owner to owner, enduring beatings and harsh treatment for years, until he had finally been sold to the Egyptian traders who now held him captive.

Once a well-trained and physically fit warrior, Agis was now old, emaciated, and weak, with his once-powerful muscles wasted away from lack of food and exercise. His skin was pale and sallow, and his eyes sunken and hollow; a mere shadow of his former self. In place of his once-proud armor and weapons were tattered rags for clothing, his hair and beard unkempt and overgrown, and his deteriorating body covered in dirt and grime. Life as a slave was miserable.

Agis, alongside many others from all over the world, was forced to work from dawn to dusk, often under the hot sun with little rest or respite. They were fed meager rations, sour meat, and given only enough water to barely sustain them through the long, grueling days. Days like today, when the unrelenting heat of the sun reflecting off the water could cook a man's skin enough to resemble the scales of a shedding snake. His lips were dry and cracked, too dehydrated to bleed. If only he could have a drink of water, he thought, then maybe he could blink his eyes without them feeling like hot sand had been poured into them.

The days went on like this for what felt like an eternity. At first, he attempted to keep track of the dates and the duration of his absence from his family and brothers in arms, but eventually, time itself yielded to an eternal cycle of inscrutable pursuit. All that he had left was kept safe, deep within the mossy shell of his former self, where he held onto the last remnants of his once-fierce Spartan spirit and determination, bestowed upon him at birth by the gods. Though dimly flickering, this inner flame kept him going through the trials of his captivity and sustained his will to survive.

The days melded together in an unending cycle of labor and suffering. Agis's body moved through the motions, but his mind often drifted back to Sparta. He thought of his family, of his brothers in arms, and of the life he had once known. His memories were a bittersweet refuge, a reminder of what he had lost and what he still longed to reclaim.

Every morning, the slaves were roused from their restless sleep before dawn. They were herded onto the deck and set to work immediately, repairing the ship, loading and unloading cargo, and performing other grueling tasks. Agis's hands were calloused and raw from handling the ropes and other equipment, and his back ached constantly from the heavy lifting. The overseers showed no mercy, driving the slaves relentlessly with harsh words and the crack of their whips.

Despite the brutal conditions, Agis clung to his Spartan training and discipline. He focused on the tasks at hand, pushing his body to its

limits and beyond. He refused to let the Egyptians see his pain or weakness. He worked quickly and efficiently, knowing that any mistake could result in severe punishment.

At night, the slaves were given a brief respite, allowed to huddle together on the deck or below it for a few hours of rest. The meager rations they received barely sustained them, but Agis made sure to eat whatever he could, knowing that he needed his strength to survive. He often shared his food with the weaker slaves, those who were too frail or sick to fend for themselves. Despite his own suffering, he couldn't turn his back on his fellow captives.

Agis's thoughts often turned to escape. He knew the ship's routines and schedules intimately, having studied them over the years. He knew the strengths and weaknesses of the overseers, their habits and patterns. He had observed the comings and goings of the Egyptian traders, noting when they were most vulnerable. He waited for an opportunity, a moment when he could make his move and break free from his chains.

But the opportunity never seemed to come. The overseers were vigilant, the ship heavily guarded. Any sign of disobedience was met with swift and brutal punishment. Agis had seen other slaves try to escape, only to be caught and subjected to the overseers' wrath. He knew that he had to be patient, to wait for the right moment.

Until then, he would endure. He would survive. He would keep the flame of his Spartan spirit alive, no matter how dim it might flicker. And he would never give up hope that one day, he would be free again.

One day, however, their routine was disrupted when a group of Athenian politicians arrived at the port where the ship was docked. The sun was setting and they were almost done for the day, offloading the final barrels of grain and olive oil to a local trader in exchange for the usual timber, spices, and perfumes. It seemed strange to Agis for such a group of wealthy Athenians to come this far from their capital.

They had come not to board a ship but to negotiate a trade deal with the Egyptians.

Agis observed from a distance, his sharp eyes noting every detail. The Athenians were finely dressed, their robes and jewelry indicating their high status. Among them was a particularly distinguished-looking man, clearly of significant importance. However, it wasn't their presence alone that caught Agis's attention. It was the mysterious and withered Athenian man who accompanied them, his body battered and bruised, dressed in torn yet once-opulent clothes. He was carried on a wooden stretcher by four slaves, his limp form suggesting severe mistreatment.

Agis's curiosity piqued as he watched the negotiations unfold. The Egyptians and Athenians haggled intensely, their voices rising and falling with the fervor of their debate. The sight of the beaten man stirred something within Agis, a mix of pity and anger. This man wasn't a soldier of war; he wasn't a criminal. He appeared too refined to be a common slave or poor. The severity of his condition suggested he had crossed paths with the wrong person in power.

After much haggling, the Egyptians finally relented and agreed to take the man aboard the ship as a prisoner and forced laborer. The Athenians paid a large sum of money for the privilege, along with what could only be a barrel of wine, Agis speculated. The thought of the rich, velvety liquid made Agis's mouth water, for he had not tasted wine since the night before his capture on the battlefield many years ago. In those days, wine flowed freely, especially after a victorious battle, but Agis had not known such glory since that fateful day, long ago.

As the transaction concluded, the Egyptian foreman barked orders at the slaves to bring the beaten man aboard. The frail and wounded Athenian was unceremoniously dropped on the deck like a sack of meat, eliciting a pained moan from his limp form. As his body hit the deck, it reminded him of the sound his son's first kill had made

when he proudly dropped it at his mother's feet after a deer hunting trip when the boy was young. Agis couldn't help but feel a pang of empathy for the stranger, despite his deep-seated hatred for Athenians.

The foreman approached Agis, a sneer on his face. "You, Spartan! This one is your responsibility now," he ordered, pointing to the unconscious man. "Make sure he doesn't die. And get back to your work. We sail at dawn."

Agis felt a mix of frustration and concern as he looked at the injured man. He hated Athenians, but he hated this foreman even more. Even more, he hated that he could not simply stand up and give this Egyptian scum a proper Spartan death and be on his way. He knew that he had to complete his task quickly while ensuring the Athenian received the care he needed. The foreman's words hung over him like a dark cloud, reminding him of the consequences of failure.

As the foreman walked away, Agis knelt beside the injured man, carefully assessing his wounds. The man was in bad shape: broken ribs, bruises covering most of his body, and signs of severe dehydration. Agis knew that without proper care, the man wouldn't survive long. Tearing a rag from his own tunic, Agis began to clean and dress the man's wounds as best as he could.

The other slaves glanced at Agis as they continued their tasks, some with pity, others with indifference. Agis worked quickly and efficiently, his hands moving with practiced precision despite the soreness and blisters. His Spartan training had included treating battle injuries, and he used that knowledge now to stabilize the man.

As Agis worked, his mind raced with questions. Who was this man? What had he done to deserve such treatment? And why had the Athenians gone to such lengths to ensure his imprisonment? The mystery surrounding the stranger gnawed at him, but he knew better than to ask too many questions. Curiosity could be dangerous in their world.

The sun dipped below the horizon, casting long shadows across the deck. The day's work was finally done, and the slaves were allowed a brief respite. Agis carefully moved the injured man to a shaded area, ensuring he was as comfortable as possible. He offered the man a small amount of water from his own ration, knowing it was a precious commodity but necessary for the man's survival.

As night fell, the sounds of the port quieted, replaced by the gentle lapping of waves against the ship's hull. Agis settled down beside the stranger, his body aching from the day's labor. Despite his exhaustion, he remained vigilant, his senses alert to any signs of danger or disturbance.

For the first time in years, Agis felt a glimmer of purpose beyond mere survival. Tending to the injured man gave him a sense of responsibility, a connection to his past as a protector and warrior. As he gazed out at the darkened horizon, he vowed to keep the man alive, not just out of duty but out of a newfound sense of kinship and defiance against their captors.

Agis had been on the receiving end of the foreman's whip before, and he knew all too well the pain it could inflict. Not that he would ever admit it out loud. The Egyptians were known for their whips' ability to separate the skin from the bone of insubordinate slaves, they took great pleasure in as much. His backside was still on the mend from the last time that he failed to properly submit to orders in a timely fashion. He couldn't afford to let that happen again. In addition to their reputation for harsh punishment, the Egyptians were also known for their strict adherence to timeliness. Agis knew that if the ship didn't leave on time, it would reflect poorly and give this poor example of a man an excuse to take his frustrations and shortcomings out on him and the rest of the crew with his godforsaken whip. So, he worked quickly, quietly and diligently, determined to get the job done and avoid the consequences of failure.

Agis felt a mix of frustration and concern as he looked at the injured man. He hated Athenians, but he hated this foreman even more. Even more, he hated that he could not simply stand up and give this Egyptian scum a proper Spartan death and be on his way. He knew that he had to complete his task quickly while ensuring the Athenian received the care he needed. The foreman's words hung over him like a dark cloud, reminding him of the consequences of failure. He grudgingly took a deep breath and focused on the task at hand. He tended to the Athenian as best he could, tearing into his sore and blistered hands even further as he ripped a rag from his tunic to carefully clean and dress his wounds. He made sure the man was as comfortable as possible, despite the unreasonable conditions on the ship.

Agis, a valiant Spartan warrior, possessed vast knowledge in all facets of warfare, including the treatment of battle injuries. Regrettably, there were no medical professionals available on the vessel, and even if there were, it appeared that the man was deemed undeserving of their assistance. Consequently, Agis was given the responsibility of caring for the ailing man, despite the absence of proper medication and equipment. To make things worse, in order to nurse him back to health to the best of his ability, Agis would be forced to surrender half of his rations of food. It was a challenging task, but he remained resolute and committed. He knew that the man's recovery was imperative, and he worked tirelessly to ensure that he received the care he needed, while still tending to the rigging as ordered.

The night air was cool, a stark contrast to the blistering heat of the day. Agis's muscles ached from the relentless labor, but he forced himself to stay awake, his eyes fixed on the unconscious Athenian. The foreman's orders had been clear: make sure the man did not die. Failure was not an option.

Agis carefully inspected the man's injuries again, noting the bruises and broken ribs. The man's breathing was shallow and labored, a sign of his severe condition. Agis knew he had to act quickly if he wanted to save him. He tore a strip of cloth from his own tunic and soaked it in water from his meager ration, gently pressing it to the man's cracked lips.

"Drink, Athenian," Agis muttered under his breath, his voice a mix of frustration and concern. "You need to survive."

The man's lips parted slightly, and he managed to swallow a few drops of water. It wasn't much, but it was a start. Agis continued to tend to the man, using what little resources he had to clean his wounds and make him as comfortable as possible.

As the hours passed, the Athenian began to stir, his eyes fluttering open briefly before closing again. He was still in a great deal of pain, but at least he was showing signs of life. Agis felt a glimmer of hope, though he knew the man had a long road to recovery ahead of him. He was determined to keep the man alive, not just because of the foreman's orders, but because he felt a strange sense of kinship with the stranger. Despite their differences, they were both victims of the same cruel fate.

As the night wore on, Agis's mind drifted back to his days in Sparta. He thought of his family, his brothers in arms, and the life he had once known. The memories were bittersweet, a reminder of what he had lost and what he still longed to reclaim. Tending to the injured man gave him a sense of purpose, a connection to his past as a protector and warrior.

Agis knew that he had to be patient, to wait for the right moment to make his move. The ship was heavily guarded, and any sign of disobedience was met with swift and brutal punishment. He had seen other slaves try to escape, only to be caught and subjected to the overseers' wrath. He couldn't afford to make the same mistake.

For now, he would endure. He would survive. He would keep the flame of his Spartan spirit alive, no matter how dim it might flicker. And he would never give up hope that one day, he would be free again.

That night was the first since being forced into slavery twenty years ago that Agis did not think about how he could kill everyone on the ship and escape back home to Sparta and finally be with his family. Or of how he could just kill himself and end his suffering and indignity in some glorious and honorably Spartan way. To be stripped of his pride, of his family and his brothers was almost unbearable. His son, who was only 13 when he was captured, would now be a man in his thirties. The thought of the boy growing up without his father devastated Agis. Who would take care of his home? Who would take care of his wife and child? Were they even still alive? These thoughts often plagued his mind, but tonight, instead, there was something about tending to the young man that stole his thoughts; his mind drifting with the distant sound of the ocean, rocking back and forth through memories of his father from when he was a boy…

Agis remembered his father, a stern but loving man who had taught him the ways of the warrior. He had learned the value of honor, duty, and strength from his father. Those lessons had sustained him through the darkest times of his captivity. Now, as he tended to the injured Athenian, he felt a renewed sense of purpose. This man needed his help, and Agis would not fail him.

The next morning, Agis was exhausted. He didn't eat much the night before and he didn't get much sleep. The Athenian moaned in agony for most of the night. Though his broken ribs were still on the mend and limited his movement, he slowly became more responsive and alert. After a significant amount of time and exertion, he was finally able to muster the strength to speak. However, in his weakened state, he could only manage to exhale a single word: "water."

Agis quickly fetched a small amount of water from his ration and helped the man drink. "Take it slow," he advised, his voice gentle but firm. "You need to regain your strength."

The Athenian nodded weakly, his eyes filled with gratitude and pain. "Thank you," he whispered, his voice barely audible.

The first week mostly went like this, as the Athenian would fall in and out of consciousness from the pain. Slowly but surely, day by day, the man began to show signs of improvement. Eventually, they were able to engage in light conversation. However, it was clear to Agis that the man was reserved and guarded, reluctant to divulge too much about himself.

Despite the man's reticence, Agis was able to learn a few things about him. It turned out that he was a philosopher - not because he had revealed this fact himself, but because of the way he spoke in his sleep. Agis overheard him mumbling words like, "aristoi," indicating a familiarity with the language and concepts of philosophy; obviously an educated man of some status, he surmised. It seemed that he was keeping his own struggles to himself, but Agis couldn't help but wonder about the thoughts and ideas that were swirling around in the philosopher's mind.

Agis hated the Athenians. If not for them and their arrogance, he might not be stuck enslaved aboard this ship and instead be back home with his family and brethren drinking beer. They thought themselves smarter than every other Greek. The thought crossed his mind more then once to simply kill the poor Athenian in his sleep, putting him out of his misery and saving himself the trouble as well as his rations. He could easily blame the death on the very wounds inflicted at the hand of his fellow statesmen from before boarding. And whoever he was, it was obvious he wouldn't be missed. The corruptions of the politicians and aristocrats of their country had seeped deep into the cracks of the Mediterranean, tainting the livelihoods of all of its peoples, free and slave alike. No country was free from the transgressions, manipulation,

and corrupt taxations of the Athenian Aristocrats these days. They boldly thought themselves above all and were desperate to keep their pompous, Athenian-boots pressed tightly on the throats of anyone who dared to tread against their arbitrary rules and beliefs. But thank the gods that Sparta dared to stand against their tyranny, ultimately winning the war. It was bad enough the Persians ruled most of the eastern Mediterranean and still hungered for more, without the added weight of Greeks fighting amongst themselves. This was probably all part of some long, Persian war game designed to destabilize the entire western Mediterranean so that they alone could control the world, as far as he could tell. Who knew what sort of terrible world this would be if the girly Athenian politicians had won. At least with Sparta, they stood a fighting chance of defending themselves if the Persians ever decided to make another grasp for power over the west. If only he could drink from the cup of victory alongside his brothers instead of being trapped as a slave aboard this rat-infested vessel.

Despite his deep-seated hatred for the Athenians, Agis felt a sense of kinship with the philosopher. He recognized the man's fighting spirit alongside his intelligence and his courage, even in the face of defeat and humiliation. And so, he tried his best to see this man not as an Athenian, but as a fellow human being who had suffered and struggled, just as he had. He would take it upon himself as an honor to his fellow Greek to be able to help the injured man, tending to his wounds and bringing him food and water when he could. It would be a few weeks yet until they made it back to Egypt, usually stopping along the way at various ports for trading. Hopefully, the Athenian would not somehow accidentally stumble and fall overboard before then… Only time and the gods could tell.

Chapter 11

Stenos

*T*he screams of terror pierced his mind, the cries for help echoing relentlessly. The sound of crashing waves and overwhelming destruction filled his senses, as he found himself lifted into the air, soaring high above the earth. The wind whipped past him, carrying him swiftly towards an unknown destination. Below, the world was engulfed in a cataclysmic flood, the water rising inexorably, drowning everything in its path. He could see ancient temples and majestic cities being swallowed by the waves, their grandeur and splendor reduced to mere memories.

In the distance, he spotted a massive central temple, its spires reaching desperately towards the sky. As he flew closer, he saw that it too was succumbing to the flood, its walls crumbling as the relentless waves battered them.

He strained to reach the temple, to save those trapped inside, but no matter how fast he flew, the distance seemed insurmountable. The temple remained just out of his grasp. Suddenly, the scene shifted. The temple disappeared, and he was falling, plummeting towards the turbulent waters below.

The sensation of falling was all-consuming, the cold water rushing up to meet him. He could feel the weight of the ocean dragging him down, the darkness closing in around him. The terror was palpable, the sense of impending doom overwhelming.

As he descended into the depths, images of Socrates and his betrayal flashed before his eyes. The courtroom, the denouncement, the beating—it all played out in vivid detail. The faces of the accusers, the disappointment in Socrates' eyes, and the smug satisfaction of Marcus all tormented him. He felt the weight of his guilt and shame pressing down on him, suffocating him as surely as the water.

The dream twisted and morphed, blending the scenes of the flood and the courtroom. The waves crashing became the jeers of the crowd, the water pulling him down mirrored by the hands dragging him away from his principles. He was caught in a maelstrom of regret and fear, unable to escape.

Just as the darkness seemed complete, a glimmer of light appeared above him. It grew brighter, piercing through the oppressive blackness. The light beckoned him, offering a chance for redemption, a way out of the nightmare.

With all his remaining strength, Plato reached for the light, desperate to break free from the torment. The light grew blinding, consuming everything around him, and then—he woke with a gasp.

He awoke with a start, the salty water of the ocean splashing through a small vent in the side of the ship onto his face and jolting him out of the nightmare that had haunted him for months. In his dreams, he had seen the world submerged in a great flood, the ancient temple sinking beneath the waves as he flew high above the earth, heading towards an unknown destination. But now, as the harsh reality of being sold into slavery set in, along with the stench of salty urine, he slowly remembered that his life was far from a dream.

He was lying below the deck of an Egyptian slave boat, sailing somewhere in the Mediterranean and surrounded by the stench of urine from the barrels that served as the ship's latrine. The memories of his former life as a student of the great Socrates came rushing back to him, and with them, the pain of his teacher's death sentence by trial. It had only been three months since his master was executed. He had always

known that speaking the truth could be dangerous, but he never thought that it would lead him to this; to the execution of his master, to a life of slavery and misery.

As he carefully sat up, he felt the rough wooden planks of the deck beneath him and the shackles around his wrists, a constant reminder of his current predicament. He could feel the salt in the air stinging his cracked lips, as he pained from dehydration. The moisture he sensed beneath him was surely a mixture of saltwater and urine. One should move from things such as this, but he thought to himself, what's the point, he'd only find himself sleeping in the same spot later this evening. It was dark down here and he yearned for sunlight. Weakened from despair and starvation, he leaned his head next to a small vent on the side of the boat next to where he sat. He could almost see the horizon, but with the boat rocking up and down so much, it was difficult to follow. He continued to stare out at the endless expanse of blue, wondering where his journey would take him and what the future held for him. Was this how he would die?

"Stenos!" He heard being shouted from behind him. He recognized the voice; an abrasive sound to his ears. Endeavoring to preserve a brief instance of serenity, he pretended to not notice the call, and continued to stare off into the horizon through the small gap.

"Stenos, I know you can hear me! Stop wasting time and get over here and help me!" He could hardly forbid the look of contempt on his face as he turned and stood. He loathed the epithet he'd been given by his comrade.

"How many times must I tell you, my name is Plato? Why must you continue to mock me, Agis?"

"Oh I know, I know; your master gave you this name because of your, breadth of stature," he mocked. "But come on, look at you, how could someone so frail and petite be called Plato?" he said with a jesting, playful inflection. "There is nothing broad about you! Why, in Sparta our women hunt boars with broader shoulders than you. The men in Athens must be very small," chuckled Agis, bellowing his amusement. "Look at my arms, they are broader than your waist, puny man! Perhaps I should be called Plato?" He exclaimed.

"Better to be small and agile like a fox, than big and lumbering like a bear," retorted Plato.

"Ha, you Athenians all think you're so clever. Come, Stenos, you will grow some meat on your shoulders after you help me row, and then we can consider a new name for you. Until then, we'll stick with, Stenos; I quite like it since it speaks to your narrow stature. Besides, I've been picking up your slack all morning while you rest your pretty little Greek eyes, and if the oars master comes over here and catches you loafing around then he will surely whip what little flesh you have left off of your bones."

It had been three weeks since being beaten within an inch of his life and being sold into slavery to the Egyptian traders. His fractured ribs, while still sore, were healing well and Agis had prescribed him daily exercise in order to accelerate the healing process.

"Stroke you scum and stop talking!" shouted the oars master as he cracked his whip in the air just above Agis' head. "The next time I won't be so kind and miss, Spartan. Stop your jabber and row! And as for you, Athenian, you've spent enough time at the latrine. Pinch it off and get back to rowing, I won't tell you again!" ordered the oars master as Plato submissively approached the bench and sat next to Agis.

As Plato grabbed the oars and began to row, his thoughts turned to how fortunate he was compared to the others rowing alongside him. Despite Agis' immense strength, which bore most of the weight, Plato was able to eke out what little strength remained in his arms by simply falling in step with Agis' movements. He was certain that Agis could discern his paltry contribution to the task. Agis was undoubtedly a brute of a man, a true Spartan warrior, but Plato was grateful that he had yet to utter a word of complaint. It was evident that Agis was not someone to cross, and so Plato exerted himself to the fullest and persevered until he could go no further. This, at least, granted him the solace of honor and a small glimmer of hope to keep pressing on.

"I don't know how you would survive without me, Stenos. I'd say that you should count yourself lucky that I am here with you. By the looks of it your body is quickly failing you under these conditions," stated Agis. "Well, they will not be getting better any time soon. Perhaps you can tell me a story while we row? Something to keep our spirits up."

"Agis, my friend," Plato spoke softly, his heart heavy with grief and despair, "I fear for both my body and my mind. I long for the unbreakable spirit that you possess, for my own spirit has faltered in the wake of my master's unjust execution."

Agis became intrigued. Plato had not revealed much about his past and the reasons behind his enslavement. Despite feeling hesitant to ask, he deemed it inappropriate to do so. Clearly, Plato was distraught and despondent regarding the matter. Agis had surmised that Plato would disclose the details at his own discretion and pace. Perhaps, now…

"I am sorry to say that my master, Socrates, was wrongly condemned to death for political motives," Plato lamented. "I deeply regret that I could not save him. Worse yet, I fear that I may have failed to make an effort due to my own concerns about being persecuted. Perhaps I should have fled Greece immediately after the trial, but I was foolish and ambitiously chose to put my trust in a known senator. After Socrates was executed, I thought it would be wise to start a new intellectual pursuit. I thought the senator could help me, but eventually, I became aware of his participation in the deaths of both my mentor and my uncle. I confronted him, and then I was arrested and beaten. Foolishly, I still believed that starting a school was my path to honor my mentor's death, and with my reputation tarnished in Athens, I trusted the government and publicly denounced

my mentor's teachings as they requested. However, I was lied to again, and the next morning, I woke up having been sold into slavery by Marcus. It was my own pride and ambition that led me down this path, and now I suffer the consequences of my actions."

Plato sighed heavily before continuing, "And as for Athens, our great city-state never fully recovered from the wars. Socrates was trying to warn us, but I would not listen. The slow decay of our democracy has given way to further political corruption, and the death of philosophy and reason is now upon us. I fear for the future of our civilization, Agis. Will we ever regain the greatness that we once had, or are we doomed to suffer in this wretched existence for all eternity?"

Agis took a thoughtful pause before responding, as he wanted to convey the weight and seriousness of the situation, and ensure that his response was respectful and carefully considered, "Respectfully, young Plato, I must disagree with your assessment of the current state of Athenian democracy. Although our victory in the war may have led to your city-state's defeat, it was not the cause of your democracy's current woes. Corruption and the decline of philosophy and reason are problems that have plagued many civilizations throughout history, and they are not unique to Athens. As a Spartan warrior, I have seen firsthand the dangers of complacency and the importance of vigilance in protecting one's way of life. I urge you and your fellow Athenians to continue striving for excellence in all areas of life, and to hold your leaders accountable to the highest standards of virtue and integrity. Only then can your democracy truly flourish and inspire future generations to come."

The boat had stopped only twice at different unknown ports since Plato first boarded the ship in shackles. Each time, hope of reaching their destination and finally getting out of the belly of the wretched ship surfaced in his heart, but each time, only wine barrels, rats, and rotten food were brought on, along with a couple of new slaves to join them in the rowing below. They were barely being fed.

The moldy scraps that they were being given would not have been fed to rats back in Athens, barely enough to sustain his body, let alone his mind. If this was how he felt, then he could only imagine how Agis must feel. Surely a man of his physique required much more in order to be sustained. Each evening they were given only one piece of moldy bread and a cup of stale, salt wine. He could sense himself drifting away from his mind, away from his center, further into an unknown abyss. A dense fog began to set in, encompassing and clouding his thoughts with a heavy blanket of nothingness. His mind, which had always provided him with a great and personal sense of pride, was fading, with only the faint memories of when his pupils used to look up to him for his wit and mental stamina. Now, in his weakened state, he was finding it hard at times to even hold on to the memory of his own name. His newly given epithet from Agis seemed more authentic and tangible than his own at this point.

"Stenos, my friend," Agis bellowed, his Spartan warrior voice ringing out, "I reckon we may be approaching a port. A trader spoke of Menouthis, if my ears do not betray me. We might finally step onto land, praise the gods!" Agis noticed Plato's feeble state. The poor fellow held onto the oars as if his life depended on it. His determination to keep rowing was admirable, and it spurred Agis to play along and row for both of them.

Plato's eyes widened at the mention of land. The thought of stepping off the ship, even if just for a brief moment, filled him with a renewed sense of hope. The endless days at sea had taken a toll on him, both physically and mentally. He clung to the possibility of seeing land again, of feeling solid ground beneath his feet.

As the ship drew closer to the port, the activity on deck intensified. Slaves and crew alike prepared for the docking, the anticipation palpable. Plato and Agis continued to row, their movements synchronized, driven by the shared hope of a momentary reprieve.

When the ship finally docked, the overseer barked orders at the slaves to prepare for unloading. Plato and Agis were among the first to be allowed on deck, their muscles aching from the relentless rowing. As they stepped onto the bustling port, the sights and sounds of the city overwhelmed them. The air was filled with the scents of exotic spices and the chatter of traders and merchants.

For a brief moment, Plato allowed himself to dream of escape, of finding a way out of this nightmare. But the reality of their situation quickly set in. The guards were vigilant, their whips a constant reminder of the consequences of disobedience.

Still, the taste of freedom, however fleeting, fueled Plato's determination. He resolved to keep fighting, to hold onto hope, no matter how dire the circumstances. He glanced at Agis, grateful for the Spartan's unwavering strength and camaraderie.

"Stay close, Stenos," Agis whispered, his voice a low rumble. "We must remain vigilant. Opportunities are rare, but they do exist. We must be ready."

Plato nodded, his resolve hardening. Together, they would face whatever challenges lay ahead. The future was uncertain, but as long as they had each other, they would endure.

As they unloaded cargo, Plato's mind wandered back to the stories his uncle Critaeus used to tell him as a child. Tales of ancient civilizations of immense wisdom and power who had perished in a cataclysmic flood. The shadows from the setting sun seemed to form ancient, crumbling temples, remnants of the stories his uncle had woven.

The brief respite at the port allowed them to gather their strength and renew their resolve. As they prepared to set sail once more, Plato and Agis knew that their journey was far from over. The days ahead would be filled with hardship and struggle, but they would face them together, united by their shared hope and determination.

The days passed with an unyielding monotony aboard the ship, the relentless toil of rowing broken only by brief moments of rest and meager sustenance. Plato's mind drifted often, caught between the physical agony of his present and the haunting memories of his past. Despite the harsh conditions, he found moments of solace in the stories he shared with Agis, their bond growing stronger with each passing day.

One evening, as the sun dipped below the horizon and the ship rocked gently on the waves, Plato and Agis sat side by side, their bodies aching from the day's labor. The sky was painted with hues of orange and pink, casting long shadows across the deck. Plato gazed out at the expanse of water, his thoughts drifting back to the tales his uncle had told him as a child.

"Agis," Plato began, his voice weary but steady, "have you ever heard about the stories of Atlantis? My uncle used to tell me that it was a city of immense wisdom and power, but that its people grew arrogant and were ultimately destroyed by a great flood."

Agis nodded, his expression contemplative. "I've heard similar tales. Every great civilization has its stories of rise and fall. Perhaps there are lessons to be learned from them."

Plato sighed, his mind heavy with the weight of his own failures and the loss of Socrates. "I fear that I have already witnessed the greatest of what life has to offer. Everything seems to be downhill from here. Sometimes, I wish for death to end this suffering."

Agis placed a reassuring hand on Plato's shoulder. "Do not lose hope, Stenos. Life is a journey, and we cannot see what lies ahead. We must endure and find strength in our hardships."

Plato enjoyed sharing these stories with Agis, recounting the rise and fall of Atlantis, and the lessons his uncle had imparted. He told Agis about his nightmares and visions. Agis listened intently, the tales providing a brief escape from the harsh reality of their situation. For a

moment, they were not slaves, but two men sharing a bond over the rich tapestry of history and legend.

As the night wore on, Plato found himself slipping into a meditative state. Despite the physical torment, he felt a strange sense of peace wash over him. He closed his eyes, focusing on his breath, allowing his mind to wander into the depths of his consciousness.

Suddenly, the familiar nightmare began to unfold once more. The screams of terror, the crashing waves, the ancient temples sinking beneath the flood—it all played out with a haunting clarity. But this time, there was something new. Amidst the chaos, a mysterious green glow appeared, illuminating the dark waters. It was a tablet, glowing with an otherworldly light, its surface inscribed with symbols that seemed to vibrate and speak without words.

The tablet called to him, drawing him closer. He reached out, desperate to grasp it, to understand its message. As his fingers brushed against the glowing surface, a surge of energy coursed through him, filling him with a profound sense of purpose and enlightenment. The tablet's message was clear: this was not the end, but a new beginning.

Plato awoke with a start, his heart pounding in his chest. The vision of the green tablet lingered in his mind, its mysterious message etched into his soul. He glanced around the dimly lit hold, the sounds of the ship creaking and the murmurs of the other slaves filling the air. Despite the oppressive conditions, he felt a renewed sense of determination.

He turned to Agis, his voice trembling with both fear and excitement. "Agis, I had another dream; another vision. This time, there was a glowing green tablet. It called to me, as if it had a message."

Agis frowned, concern etched on his face. "A green tablet? What did it say?"

Plato shook his head. "I don't know, but it felt important. It felt like… a sign."

Agis squeezed his shoulder reassuringly. "Hold on to that vision, Stenos. Let it guide you through these dark times. We will find a way out of this, together."

As the ship continued its journey across the vast expanse of the Mediterranean, Plato clung to the vision of the green tablet. It was a beacon of hope, a promise of something greater beyond the suffering. The mysterious glow and the sense of purpose it brought fueled his resolve to endure, to survive, and to seek the truth.

Plato lay back down, the vision of the green tablet still vivid in his mind. He closed his eyes, allowing the waves to rock him gently as he drifted into a fitful sleep. The future was uncertain, but for the first time in a long while, he felt a glimmer of hope.

Chapter 12

Chains of Wisdom

Plato sat hunched over in the dim hold of the ship, his eyes closed, trying to center himself amidst the chaos and stench around him. The rhythmic creaking of the ship and the distant murmurs of the other slaves were the backdrop to his turbulent thoughts. Memories of his life before slavery floated into his mind, unbidden but vivid.

He recalled the serene mornings in the agora, the discussions with Socrates, and the camaraderie with his friends. The air had been filled with the scent of blooming flowers and the sounds of birdsong. Those days seemed like a distant dream, a lifetime away from his current reality. The stark contrast between his past and present life weighed heavily on him.

In those moments of reflection, he found himself pondering the meaning of his recurring dreams and visions. The lion paw, a symbol that had haunted his sleep, now seemed to represent the death of his ego. It was as if the universe was trying to strip him of his former self, to rebuild him anew. But to what end? The visions and dreams felt like pieces of a puzzle, fragments of a larger truth that eluded him.

He suspected that these visions were part of some enlightenment process, a connection with a higher power. Yet, despite this potential for spiritual awakening, the struggles he faced were overwhelming, and were a straight contradiction to anything pleasant. The physical and mental anguish of his current life overshadowed any sense of divine purpose. He kept these thoughts to himself, sharing them with no one, not even Agis.

Plato opened his eyes and gazed at the rough wooden planks of the ship. The reality of his situation was crushing. He had lost everything he held dear—his freedom, his identity, and his mentor. His spirit felt under constant attack, and he was losing his grip on his emotions and mental well-being.

The creaking of the ship seemed to mock him, reminding him of the stability he once had. The smell of the sea, which he had once found invigorating, now only served to make him nauseous. He looked at his hands, once steady and strong, now trembling and raw from the unending labor. His body bore the scars of his ordeal, and his mind was no less wounded.

He thought back to the lessons of Socrates, who had taught him about the virtues of patience, resilience, and the pursuit of truth. These teachings had been his anchor, but now they seemed distant and intangible. The principles he had once held dear now felt like heavy chains, binding him to a past that no longer existed.

But in the darkest moments, he found comfort in the memories of Socrates. The philosopher's teachings on facing adversity with dignity, faith, and hope echoed in his mind. He also drew strength from Agis, whose unyielding spirit and camaraderie provided a beacon of support. These thoughts gave him the fortitude to endure, to face his hardships with grace and resilience.

His reflections were interrupted by the call of the overseer, demanding that the slaves return to their labor. Plato took a deep breath, steeling himself for the day's work. The oar felt heavy in his hands, but he gripped it tightly, determined to keep going.

As he rowed, his thoughts continued to wander. He remembered the warmth of the sun on his face, the sound of laughter, and the feeling of belonging. These memories were a stark contrast to the cold,

harsh reality he now faced. But they also served as a reminder of what he had once been, and what he could be again.

Plato knew that he had to hold on to these memories, to use them as a source of strength. He had to believe that there was a purpose to his suffering, that the visions and dreams were guiding him towards something greater. It was this belief that kept him going, even when everything seemed hopeless.

As the day wore on, Plato's body ached with fatigue, but his mind remained sharp. He continued to reflect on his past, searching for meaning in the chaos. The lessons of Socrates, the memories of his friends and family, and the visions that haunted his sleep all merged into a tapestry of resilience and hope.

By the time the sun began to set, casting a golden glow over the churning sea, Plato felt a renewed sense of purpose. He was still a long way from understanding the full meaning of his visions, but he knew that he could not give up. The struggles he faced were part of his journey, a path that he had to walk with courage and determination.

Plato took a moment to look out at the horizon, the endless expanse of water that symbolized both his captivity and his potential for freedom. He took a deep breath, filling his lungs with the salty air, and allowed himself a brief moment of peace.

In that moment, he made a silent vow to himself. He would endure, he would learn, and he would grow. No matter how dark the days ahead, he would hold on to the light within him. The journey was far from over, and he was determined to see it through.

The sun rose steadily, casting a harsh light on the deck of the ship as the slaves resumed their grueling work. Plato could feel the heat pressing down on him, the oppressive weight adding to his physical exhaustion. The oars felt heavier with each stroke, the salt from the sea stinging the open blisters on his hands. Every muscle in his body ached, and his mouth was dry and parched. The ration of stale bread and brackish water he had received that morning did little to sustain him.

He glanced at Agis, who seemed to bear the burden of their shared labor with stoic determination. Despite his own suffering, Plato felt a deep sense of gratitude for the Spartan. Agis had become his anchor, his source of strength. Yet, even with Agis' support, Plato's spirit was flagging.

Despair gnawed at him, a constant companion. He couldn't help but wonder if his life had any meaning left. The dreams and visions, though significant, felt distant and abstract compared to the immediate reality of his suffering. He was haunted by thoughts of death, contemplating whether it would be a release from his torment.

The ship's overseer, a burly man with a whip always at the ready, paced up and down the deck, barking orders and found enjoyment in striking any slave who faltered. The crack of the whip and the cries of pain were a constant reminder of their dire situation. Plato's hands trembled as he gripped the oar, his mind teetering on the edge of despair.

"Keep rowing, Stenos," Agis murmured, his voice low and steady. "Focus on each stroke. We have to keep going."

Plato nodded weakly, trying to draw strength from Agis' unwavering resolve. But the physical and emotional toll was immense. The blistering sun, the salt that caked his skin, and the constant threat of the overseer's whip were pushing him to his limits.

As the hours dragged on, Plato's thoughts turned inward. He remembered the teachings of Socrates, the lessons on resilience and fortitude. But in his current state, those teachings felt like a distant echo, a voice he could barely hear over the roar of his own suffering.

His mind wandered to the students he once taught, the debates they had, and the sense of purpose that had driven him. The contrast between those days and his current reality was stark. He had gone

from a respected teacher and philosopher to a nameless slave, stripped of his identity and dignity.

The sun beat down mercilessly, its relentless heat sapping the energy from Plato's already weakened body. His vision blurred, the edges of his sight tinged with black. He felt as though he were on the verge of collapse, his strength dwindling with each passing moment.

Plato's thoughts were interrupted by the sharp crack of the overseer's whip, followed by a cry of pain from one of the other slaves. He turned his head slightly, catching a glimpse of the overseer lashing out at a man who had collapsed from exhaustion. The sight filled him with a mix of fear and anger. He knew that any show of weakness would bring the same fate upon him.

He focused on the rhythm of his rowing, trying to block out the pain and the despair. Each stroke was a struggle, but he forced himself to keep going. He held on to thoughts of Socrates' teachings, the importance of enduring hardship with dignity. He thought of Agis, whose strength and determination were a lifeline in this sea of suffering.

As the sun began to set, casting a red glow over the churning sea, the overseer finally called for a halt. The slaves slumped over their oars, their bodies trembling with exhaustion. Plato leaned back, closing his eyes and taking deep, shuddering breaths.

Agis placed a hand on his shoulder, offering a silent gesture of support. "We survived another day, Stenos. Rest now. We must conserve our strength."

Plato nodded, grateful for the brief respite. He knew that the struggles would continue, that the next day would bring the same pain and suffering. But for now, he allowed himself a moment of peace, drawing strength from his memories and the bond he shared with Agis.

As night fell, the ship's hold grew quieter, the rhythmic creaking of the timbers and the gentle lapping of the waves against the hull the only sounds that filled the space. The slaves, exhausted from the day's

labor, drifted into a fitful sleep. Plato lay on the hard wooden planks, his body aching, but his mind restless. He thought of the visions and dreams that had haunted him, the green tablet that seemed to call to him.

Despite the overwhelming despair, there was a small part of him that clung to the hope that these visions held a deeper meaning. That perhaps his suffering was not in vain, that there was a greater purpose to his journey. It was this hope, fragile as it was, that kept him going.

Plato's thoughts turned once again to Socrates, to the wisdom and courage of his mentor. He vowed to honor Socrates' memory by enduring, by facing his hardships with the same dignity and strength that the philosopher had shown in his final days.

With this vow in his heart, Plato closed his eyes and allowed the gentle rocking of the ship to lull him into a restless sleep. The future was uncertain, but he would face it with all the strength he could muster.

He drifted in and out of sleep, exhausted from the day's labor. As he slowly drifted visions of the familiar nightmare of the crashing city began to seep in. The screams of terror, the overwhelming sound of destruction, the ancient temples sinking beneath the relentless waves—all of it replayed in vivid detail. Then the mysterious green glow appeared again, illuminating the dark waters. It was the strange tablet again, glowing with an otherworldly light, vibrating and pulsating as if alive.

The tablet called to him, drawing him closer. He reached out, desperate to grasp it, to understand its message. As his fingers just barely brushing against the glowing surface, followed by a surge of energy coursing through him, calling him and drawing him close.

Plato awoke with his heart pounding in his chest. The vision of the green tablet still lingering in his mind, its connection to him ran deep as if a part of his very soul. The ship was asleep, and only the sound of waves and wood creaking in the distance could be heard.

He rolled over to face Agis, who was fast asleep. This was a rarity for the ship to be so quite, he thought. He hadn't been alone with his thoughts in quite some time. Plato hesitated for a moment, then whispered, "Agis, I had the dream again. The one with the green tablet."

Agis propped himself up on one elbow, his brow furrowing in concern. "The same dream? What did you see this time?"

"There was that green tablet," Plato said, his voice tinged with awe and confusion. "It glowed with an otherworldly light and had symbols on it. Again, it felt like it was speaking to me, but without words. It was as if it was trying to tell me something important."

Agis listened intently, his expression serious. "And did it say anything this time?"

Plato shook his head, "No, not with words. It's hard to explain."

Agis responded with a reassuring look on his face, "Your answers will come soon, Stenos. Get some sleep. Your tablet may still speak to you yet."

Plato nodded, feeling a sense of comfort from Agis' words. The bond they shared had become a lifeline, a source of strength that kept him going through the darkest moments. Despite the physical and emotional torment, there was a part of him that felt more enlightened, more connected to a higher purpose.

As the night wore on, Plato found himself slipping into a meditative state. The familiar rhythm of his breath, the steady rise and fall of his chest, brought a sense of calm amidst the chaos. He focused on his breathing, allowing his mind to wander into the depths of his consciousness.

The visions and dreams, though unsettling, began to take on a new significance. They were no longer just random fragments of his mind, but pieces of a larger puzzle, guiding him towards something greater. He remembered the stories his uncle Critaeus had told him, tales of ancient wisdom and lost civilizations. The visions felt like a connection to those stories, a link to a deeper understanding of the world.

Plato's thoughts drifted back to the green tablet, its glow vivid in his mind. He could almost feel its energy, its message resonating within him. As the ship rocked gently on the waves, Plato allowed himself to embrace this newfound sense of peace. His meditation practices, combined with the visions and dreams, brought him a sense of calm that he hadn't felt in a long time. He was being refined in the fire, undergoing a spiritual purging. Despite the overwhelming despair, there was a small part of him that clung to the hope that these visions held a deeper meaning.

The next morning, the ship began its approach to the port on the Mediterranean coast of Egypt. The activity on deck intensified as the crew prepared for docking. The slaves were ordered to row harder, the overseer's whip cracking in the air as a harsh reminder of their place.

Plato and Agis strained at the oars, their muscles burning with effort. The tension on the ship was palpable, a mixture of fear and anticipation. As they neared the port, the towering structures of the city came into view, their silhouettes stark against the morning sky.

Plato squinted against the harsh sunlight, trying to make out the details of their destination. The port was bustling with activity, ships of various sizes docked alongside the busy quays. Traders and merchants moved about with purpose, their voices rising in a cacophony of haggling and orders. It was a stark contrast to the oppressive silence of the ship's hold.

The ship lurched as it maneuvered into position, throwing several slaves off balance. Shouts and cries filled the air as the crew struggled to regain control. Plato's heart raced as he gripped the oar, his mind flashing to the vision of the green tablet. Was this a sign? Was something about to happen?

Amidst the chaos, Plato caught a glimpse of the shore. The sight of land filled him with a mixture of hope and dread. As the ship finally

stabilized and the docking process continued, the sense of imminent danger lingered.

The overseer barked orders, and the slaves were herded onto the deck, their chains clinking ominously. The port was a hive of activity, with traders and guards bustling about. Plato's eyes scanned the scene, his mind racing with possibilities.

As the ship docked and the gangplank was lowered, a sudden shout from the overseer cut through the noise. "Prepare to disembark! Anyone who causes trouble will be dealt with severely!"

Plato felt a surge of fear and determination. The next step in their journey was about to begin, and he knew that the challenges ahead would be even greater. The vision of the green tablet burned in his mind, a symbol of the hope and purpose that he clung to desperately.

As he stepped onto the gangplank, the reality of his situation crashed down on him once more. But this time, there was a glimmer of something more—a sense that his journey was part of something greater, something that he had yet to fully understand.

The port of Egypt awaited, and with it, the next chapter of his life. The future was uncertain, but Plato was determined to face it with the strength and wisdom he had gained from his experiences. As he took his first steps onto the foreign soil, he steeled himself for whatever lay ahead.

The slaves were marched off the ship and onto the bustling quay. The sun was already high in the sky, casting a harsh glare on the dusty streets. The air was thick with the scents of exotic spices, mixed with the stench of sweat and labor. Plato's eyes darted around, taking in the unfamiliar surroundings. The architecture was awe-inspiring, with towering structures adorned with intricate carvings and colorful frescoes. The people wore vibrant, flowing garments, their designs unlike anything Plato had seen before.

There was something about this place that felt strangely familiar, as if it were calling to him. Plato couldn't shake the feeling that his

visions and dreams were somehow connected to Egypt. The green tablet, the crashing city—everything seemed to point him here. He had never been to this land, yet his spirit felt a pull, an inexplicable connection to this ancient and mysterious place.

Suddenly, a commotion erupted nearby. A group of traders was arguing with the ship's captain, their voices raised in anger. The argument quickly escalated, and one of the traders drew a knife, pointing it threateningly at the captain.

The overseer shouted for the slaves to be moved quickly, but the narrow street was crowded, and their progress was slow. Plato could feel the tension rising, the air crackling with the potential for violence. He glanced at Agis, who was equally alert, his muscles tensed for action.

As the argument reached its peak, a sudden shout rang out, followed by the clash of metal. The trader lunged at the captain, and chaos erupted. The crowd scattered in panic, and the slaves were caught in the midst of the turmoil. Plato felt a surge of adrenaline as he was pushed and jostled, struggling to keep his footing.

In the confusion, Agis saw an opportunity. He caught Plato's eye and nodded subtly. Without hesitation, Agis broke away from the group, darting into a side alley. Plato, trusting his friend's instinct, followed close behind.

The sounds of the fight and the shouts of the overseer faded behind them as they ran, their chains clinking with every step. The alley twisted and turned, the narrow passageways offering a maze of potential escape routes.

Their hearts pounded as they sprinted through the winding streets, the sense of freedom tantalizingly close. But the reality of their situation quickly set in. The chains on their wrists and ankles slowed them down, and the city was unfamiliar territory.

Just as they rounded a corner, they came face to face with a group of guards. The guards shouted and drew their weapons, and Plato and Agis skidded to a halt, their brief moment of hope dashed.

Plato's mind raced as he tried to think of a way out. The vision of the green tablet flashed before his eyes, a reminder of the hope and purpose that had kept him going. He took a deep breath, steeling himself for whatever came next.

The guards advanced, their expressions stern and unforgiving. Plato and Agis exchanged a glance, their resolve unbroken. They had come this far, and they would face whatever challenges lay ahead with courage and determination.

But Agis's eyes held a different kind of resolve, a fiery determination that Plato hadn't seen before. As the guards closed in, Agis gave Plato a look of understanding, a silent communication that spoke volumes. Plato's heart sank as he realized what Agis intended to do. He shook his head subtly, silently pleading with Agis to stand down, knowing they were already caught and there was no hope of success.

Agis, however, was a Spartan to his core. He would rather die valiantly in battle than be captured. With a roar, he lunged at the guards, his movements swift and fierce. The guards were momentarily taken aback, but they quickly regained their composure and countered his attack.

Plato watched in horror as Agis fought with everything he had. The clash of weapons and the shouts of the guards filled the air. Despite his valiant efforts, Agis was outnumbered and overpowered. The guards struck him down, and he fell to the ground, blood pouring from his wounds.

Plato rushed to his fallen comrade, and just as one of the guards was about to thrust a sword in his side, sealing his fate along Agis', a mysterious man appeared from the shadows. The man, dressed in the garb of an Egyptian priest, raised his hand, and the guards hesitated.

"Do not kill him," the man commanded, his voice calm and authoritative.

The guards obeyed, roughly binding Plato's hands instead. Plato's heart pounded in his chest as he looked at the mysterious man, wondering why he had been spared. He turned his gaze back to Agis, who lay on the ground, bleeding out. Their eyes met one last time, and Plato saw a flicker of pride in Agis's eyes before they closed forever. At that moment, the guards struck Plato over the head, and as he blacked out, the image of the mysterious man watching over him lingered in his mind as he lost consciousness.

Chapter 13

Hands of Fate

The sun had just risen over the ancient city of Memphis, casting a golden glow on the towering pyramids that dominated the landscape. Inside the high priest's quarters, the air was filled with the scent of incense, a calming presence that had become a daily comfort to Plato. The years had passed quietly since the day he and Agis had been arrested on the docks of Egypt. Now, nearly eight years later, Plato had settled into his role as a personal slave to the high priest.

The high priest, a man named Imhotep, was seated at a low table covered in ancient scrolls and tablets. His eyes, wise and kind, glanced up as Plato entered the room with a tray of morning tea. The bond between them had grown strong over the years, a silent understanding that transcended the boundaries of master and slave.

"Good morning, Plato," Imhotep said, his voice gentle. "I have been thinking about the day you arrived here, nearly eight years ago. Do you remember it?"

Plato nodded, placing the tray on the table. "I do, master. It was a day that changed my life forever."

Imhotep smiled, a touch of pride in his expression. "I chose you for a reason, Plato. From the moment I saw you, I sensed a great destiny within you. Your ancestor, Solon, was a remarkable man, and you carry his spirit. It is no coincidence that you are here."

Plato felt a surge of gratitude. The high priest had given him more than just a role to play; he had given him a purpose. "Thank you, master. Your guidance has been invaluable to me."

Imhotep gestured for Plato to sit. "You have learned much in these years, but there is still so much more to understand. Our priesthood is not just about rituals and ceremonies. It is about understanding the very fabric of the universe."

Plato listened intently as Imhotep began to speak of the trials and secrets of the priesthood, a world that was still largely hidden from him. He had learned to read the ancient scripts and had access to many scrolls and tablets, but the deeper mysteries were reserved for the initiated priests.

"How did you know I was related to Solon?" Plato asked, curiosity tinged with respect.

Imhotep's eyes twinkled with ancient wisdom. "Your great-grandfather, Solon, was a remarkable man and is remembered in our teachings and writings. He visited Egypt and studied with our priests. It was from us that he learned the tale of Atlantis, a story passed down through our records for thousands of years. Our records go back tens of thousands of years, and Solon was fascinated by our history. I was always intrigued with the stories of the people from the islands of the sea; of the great Greek leader who traveled to Egypt. He was known as the great Yunan. His reputation preceded him, not just as a lawgiver but as a man who chose to relinquish power rather than become a tyrant. It was unheard for a leader to sacrifice his life and office so that his people could remain free. When I saw you, I felt the same spirit in you that my ancestors sensed in him. It was as if the gods themselves had guided you to us."

Plato's heart swelled with a mix of pride and humility. He had always known of his great-grandfather's legacy, but hearing it spoken by Imhotep made it feel more real, more significant. "I hope to honor his memory, master, and to learn as much as I can from you."

Imhotep nodded, his expression thoughtful. "You are already on the right path, Plato. Remember, the journey to enlightenment is long and often difficult, but it is also rewarding. You have the heart of a seeker, and that is the most important quality."

Plato felt a deep sense of purpose settle over him. The bond he shared with Imhotep was more than just one of master and slave; it was a connection of minds and spirits, united in the pursuit of knowledge and wisdom. The priest's teachings ignited a flame within Plato. 'Education is the kindling of a flame, not the filling of a vessel,' he mused, feeling the spark of enlightenment grow stronger each day.

"Master, there is something I must tell you," Plato began, hesitating slightly. "Since I arrived in Egypt, my visions and dreams have stopped. But lately, I have been waking up to the sound of my name being called, even when no one is around. It is a woman's voice, beautiful and haunting."

Imhotep's expression grew serious. "The gods speak to us in many ways, Plato. Do not ignore these signs. They may be guiding you towards a greater understanding, a deeper truth."

Plato nodded, feeling a shiver run down his spine. The high priest's words resonated deeply within him, confirming his own suspicions. The call of the gods, the visions of the green tablet, and the legacy of Solon all pointed towards a destiny he was only beginning to comprehend.

As the morning light streamed through the windows, casting a warm glow over the ancient texts, Plato knew that his journey was far from over. He had much to learn, and the path ahead was filled with challenges. But with Imhotep's guidance and the legacy of his great-grandfather behind him, he felt ready to face whatever lay ahead.

Days in the high priest's household were structured and disciplined. Plato's mornings began with preparing Imhotep's meals and assisting with daily rituals. The afternoons were spent in the scriptorium, where he copied texts and learned the ancient languages.

Evenings were often filled with discussions with Imhotep, who shared his vast knowledge on a wide array of subjects.

The priesthood in Egypt was unlike anything Plato had known. The priests were chosen from birth and trained in the secrets of alchemy, physics, mathematics, history and sacred texts, astronomy, medicine and healing, language and writing, as well as divinity and spirituality. They understood the natural elements and wielded a form of magic that was both awe-inspiring and intimidating. Plato, though not a priest, absorbed as much as he could, his hunger for knowledge growing with each passing year.

As the years went by, Plato's daily responsibilities continued to grow, reflecting his increasing trust and competence. He became more involved in the temple's rituals and began to assist with more complex tasks. Imhotep often invited him to discussions with other priests, where he listened and learned, soaking in the wisdom shared around him.

One afternoon, while arranging offerings in the temple courtyard, Plato overheard a conversation that caught his attention. A group of priests were discussing the upcoming pyramid trials and the candidates who would be participating.

"The trials are rigorous this year," one of the priests said. "Only the most dedicated will succeed."

Another priest nodded. "Yes, but those who pass will be granted access to the Emerald Tablet. It is a rare honor."

Plato's heart raced as he listened. Could this be the emerald tablet from his dreams? Apparently, the trials were his only chance to see the Emerald Tablet, to unlock the secrets it held. He knew he wasn't ready according to the priesthood's standards, but the desire to undertake the trials burned within him.

That evening, as they sat under the stars discussing the day's lessons, Plato felt the time was right to broach the subject with Imhotep.

"Master, I overheard some of the priests speaking of the Emerald Tablet and the trials required to see it," Plato began cautiously. "Is it real?"

Imhotep looked up from his work, his eyes thoughtful. "The Emerald Tablet is more than just a legend, Plato. It is a key to understanding the very nature of existence. Few have seen it, and fewer still understand its true power."

Plato's curiosity burned brighter than ever. "I want to learn more, master. I feel… connected to it somehow."

Imhotep nodded slowly. "Perhaps in time, Plato. There is much you must learn before you can even begin to comprehend its significance."

The Emerald Tablet became a focal point for Plato, an obsession that consumed his thoughts and dreams. The visions of the green tablet and the crashing city had stopped since arriving in Egypt, but the calling felt stronger than ever. And now, he occasionally woke up to the sound of his name being called, even when no one was around. It was always the same woman's voice, beautiful and haunting, echoing in his mind.

Imhotep noticed Plato's growing interest and concern. One evening, as they sat together under the stars, he decided to address it.

"Plato, I see your fascination with the Emerald Tablet has grown," Imhotep said, breaking the silence. "It is natural to be drawn to such a powerful artifact, but I must caution you. The path to understanding it comes at a great cost. It is fraught with danger and requires great wisdom and personal sacrifice."

Plato nodded, his eyes reflecting the light of the stars. "I understand, master. I am committed to learning and preparing myself. I want to be ready when the time comes."

Imhotep placed a reassuring hand on Plato's shoulder. "You have the heart of a seeker, Plato. Continue your studies and remain patient. The knowledge will come to you when you are ready."

Plato took comfort in Imhotep's words, but his longing to see the Emerald Tablet grew stronger each day. He spent his free time poring over ancient texts, seeking any information he could find about the tablet and the trials.

As the days turned into months and the months into years, Plato's role within the temple grew. He was no longer seen merely as a slave, but as a vital part of the priesthood's daily life. He participated in rituals, prepared sacred texts, and even advised on minor matters. His bond with Imhotep deepened, their conversations ranging from the mundane to the profound.

One evening, after a particularly intense discussion about the nature of the soul, Imhotep shared a personal insight. "Plato, your great-grandfather Solon was deeply interested in our teachings. He learned much during his time here, but there was one thing he sought that he never achieved—access to the Emerald Tablet. He was not here long enough to undergo the trials, but he respected their significance."

Plato's heart swelled with pride and a renewed sense of purpose. "Master, I feel that my destiny is tied to this knowledge. I want to undertake the trials, to see the Emerald Tablet for myself."

Imhotep shook his head gently. "You are not yet ready, Plato. The priests train for decades before even attempting the trials. You have only been here eight years, and much of that time has been spent in service, not training. The trials require a deep understanding of one's self, and of our teachings, and there is still much you have not learned."

Plato felt a surge of frustration but understood the wisdom in Imhotep's words. "I will continue to learn and prepare, master. I hope one day I will be ready."

Imhotep nodded, his expression softening. "I believe you will, Plato. You have the heart of a true seeker, and that is the most important quality. Continue your studies and remain patient. In time, you may find yourself ready for the trials."

As the years continued to pass, Plato's fascination with the pyramid trials and the mysteries of the priesthood deepened. He spent long hours in the scriptorium, studying the ancient texts and deciphering the secrets of the universe. The more he learned, the more his desire to achieve enlightenment grew.

One evening, while helping Imhotep organize a collection of ancient texts, Plato found himself engrossed in the intricate details of a scroll. It spoke of the trials the priests underwent, their rigorous training, and the profound knowledge they sought. The mention of the Tablet, an artifact of immense power and wisdom, captured his attention.

"The Emerald Tablet," Plato murmured, his heart racing. "Master, is this the same tablet I overheard the priests discussing?"

Imhotep looked up from his work, his expression unreadable. "Yes, Plato. The Emerald Tablet is a key to understanding the very fabric of existence.

The Emerald Tablet continued to be a focal point for Plato, an obsession that consumed his thoughts and dreams. Although the visions of the green tablet and the crashing city had stopped since arriving in Egypt, the calling felt stronger than ever.

Imhotep sighed deeply, his eyes filled with compassion. "I admire your determination, Plato, but the trials require more than just desire. They require a deep understanding of our teachings, and there is still much you have not learned. Continue your studies and remain patient. Your time will come."

Plato nodded, feeling a mix of frustration and resolve. He knew Imhotep was right, but the longing to undertake the trials and see the Emerald Tablet was stronger than ever. He resolved to continue his studies with even greater dedication, preparing himself for the day when he might be deemed worthy.

As the night drew to a close, Plato's fascination with the Emerald Tablet and the pyramid trials consumed his thoughts. The voice of the woman calling his name echoed in his mind, a constant reminder of the destiny he felt was waiting for him. He knew that his journey was far from over and that the path ahead would be filled with challenges. But with Imhotep's guidance and the legacy of his great-grandfather behind him, he felt ready to face whatever lay ahead.

The night was still and quiet, the air heavy with anticipation. Plato's heart was filled with a mixture of fear and excitement. He knew that the path to enlightenment was fraught with danger, but he was ready to take the first step.

As he lay down to sleep, the voice called his name again, this time louder and more insistent. It was that woman's voice, clear and commanding. "Plato..."

His heart pounded in his chest. The call was undeniable, and the sense of urgency was overwhelming. Plato closed his eyes, allowing the weight of the decision to settle over him. The path was dangerous, but he could not ignore the call. He would find a way to enter the pyramids and seek the Emerald Tablet for himself. The future awaited, and with it, the answers he had long sought.

The days that followed were a blur of routine and anticipation for Plato. His duties remained the same, but his mind was consumed with thoughts of the Emerald Tablet and the pyramid trials. Every moment he could spare, he spent in quiet contemplation or studying the ancient texts, seeking any clue that might guide him.

One evening, as he finished his tasks and prepared to retire for the night, the air in his chamber felt charged with an unusual energy. He lay down on his straw mat, the cool night air gently wafting through the small window. As he closed his eyes, the familiar sensation of drifting into sleep began to wash over him.

The voice of the woman, which had been a constant whisper in his mind, returned, and had grown louder and more urgent. "Plato… Plato…" it called, resonating with a strange, otherworldly echo.

Plato's eyes snapped open, his heart racing. He looked around the darkened room, but there was no one there. He had grown accustomed to hearing the woman's voice, but tonight it felt different, more insistent. He took a deep breath and tried to calm his racing thoughts.

"Why now?" he whispered to himself, feeling a mixture of fear and excitement.

The days continued in this manner, with the voice becoming a nightly occurrence. Each time it called, the urgency seemed to increase, until one night, the voice changed. It was no longer the soft, haunting call of the woman. Instead, the deep, commanding male voice returned, filling his mind.

"Plato… come to the pyramids."

The voice was so clear and powerful that it startled him awake. Plato sat up, his heart pounding in his chest. He knew he could no longer ignore the call. The sense of urgency was overwhelming, and he felt a compulsion to act. He knew he had to go, even if it meant defying Imhotep's wishes.

The next morning, he approached Imhotep with a mixture of determination and trepidation. "Master, I need to speak with you," Plato said, his voice steady despite the turmoil inside him.

Imhotep looked up from his work, his expression calm and knowing. "What is it, Plato?"

"The dreams and the voices," Plato began, choosing his words carefully. "They have become more urgent. Last night, I heard a man's voice, commanding me to come to the pyramids."

Imhotep's eyes narrowed slightly, but he nodded for Plato to continue.

"I cannot ignore this calling any longer. I know I am not fully prepared, but I feel that I must see the Emerald Tablet for myself. Please, master, allow me to try."

Imhotep's expression hardened, his voice firm. "Plato, the path you wish to take is fraught with danger. You are not yet ready, and the trials require years of preparation. The priests train for decades before even attempting the trials. You must not undertake them without the proper training. It is too dangerous."

Plato felt a surge of frustration but knew better than to argue. "I understand, master," he said, bowing his head.

Imhotep's gaze softened, and he placed a hand on Plato's shoulder. "There is something you must understand, Plato. The trials are not like any others. The Emerald Tablet is not like any book or scroll you have ever encountered. It is like a living book with a mind of its own, connected to the past, present, and future. It is mysterious and from a different time and place. Most books are safe, but this one isn't. In reading it, you become part of the story."

Plato's eyes widened with a mix of awe and fear. "What do you mean, master?"

Imhotep sighed deeply, his eyes filled with ancient wisdom. "The tablet puts the reader into a story where they actually live the characters' lives. They see, hear, taste, and feel everything as if they are actually there. It is part of the test, and it is different for everyone. This is the hardest part of the trials, and one only gets there if they can actually make it to the tablet. Most don't get that far. It is a test just to be able to use it and figure out how to read it in order to continue the test. This is a deeply spiritual trial. It is almost impossible to prepare for, and priests spend decades trying to get ready. The experience with the tablet is ethereal and different for everyone."

Plato felt a shiver run down his spine. The path he wished to take was even more dangerous than he had imagined. "Thank you for telling me, master. I will be cautious."

Imhotep nodded, his expression serious. "Remember, Plato, the entrance to the pyramid is just a front to the interior spiritual pyramid hidden within the earth between realities, and within each of us. Each room of the pyramid is a new test and trial. If one is not centered and whole, he will succumb to his visions and emotions and die. The tablet is alive."

Plato nodded, understanding the gravity of Imhotep's words. "I will continue my studies and prepare myself as best as I can."

That night, as he lay in bed, the voice returned, louder and more insistent.

"Plato… come. Come to the pyramids."

He knew he had to act. The sense of urgency was overwhelming, and he felt a compulsion to disobey Imhotep's orders and seek out the Emerald Tablet on his own. He quietly slipped out of his chamber, the cool night air sending a shiver down his spine. The temple grounds were silent, the priests and other slaves long since retired for the night.

As he made his way to the pyramids, the massive structures loomed large in the moonlight, their ancient stones holding secrets that called to him. He felt a strange sense of familiarity, as if he had been here before, guided by an unseen hand.

When he reached the base of the pyramid, he paused, taking in the immense structure before him. The pyramids were awe-inspiring, their massive stones speaking of a power and knowledge that had stood the test of time. He felt a strange sense of familiarity, as if he had been here before, guided by an unseen hand.

As he began to climb, the voice returned, more insistent than ever. "Plato… come to the pyramids." This was the first time he had heard the voice while awake.

His resolve hardened, and he knew that there was no turning back. He would seek the Emerald Tablet, face the trials, and uncover the truths that had been calling to him for so long. The future awaited, and with it, the answers he had long sought.

As he climbed higher, the night grew darker, and the sense of urgency pressed upon him. The path was dangerous, but he felt a strange peace in his determination. He was ready to face whatever lay ahead, driven by the call of destiny.

Plato reached the entrance to the pyramid, his heart racing. The path was clear but fraught with unknown dangers. He took a deep breath and cast one last glance at the stars in the night sky. After a brief moment, he stepped forward, ready to face the trials and uncover the secrets that awaited him.

The future was uncertain, but for the first time in a long while, he felt a glimmer of hope. As he disappeared into the darkness of the pyramid, the call of the Emerald Tablet echoed in his mind, a beacon guiding him toward his destiny.

Chapter 14

The Path of Trials

Plato's heart pounded in his chest as he slipped through the narrow entrance of the pyramid. The air was cool and thick with the scent of ancient stone. He moved cautiously, his steps echoing in the vast, empty corridors. He had studied the scrolls given to him by Imhotep, but he knew they only scratched the surface of the trials that awaited him.

The passageway led him deeper into the pyramid, the darkness closing in around him. He carried a small oil lamp, its flickering flame casting eerie shadows on the walls. As he walked, he couldn't shake the feeling that he was being watched, that the very stones of the pyramid were alive and aware of his presence.

After what felt like an eternity, he reached a large chamber. The room was vast, with high ceilings and walls covered in intricate carvings and hieroglyphs. In the center of the room stood a massive stone door, covered in symbols and surrounded by various geometric shapes etched into the floor.

Plato approached the door cautiously, examining the carvings. He recognized some of the symbols from his studies, but others were entirely unfamiliar. The door seemed to pulse with a hidden energy, as if it were alive.

"This must be the first trial," he muttered to himself, his voice echoing in the empty chamber. He knew that the door would not open easily, that it required solving the riddle embedded in the carvings.

He studied the symbols carefully, his mind racing to piece together their meaning. The scrolls had mentioned the importance of mathematics, geometry and natural elements, but the exact nature of the trial was still a mystery.

"To pass through, one must understand the balance of the elements and the harmony of the universe," he recalled Imhotep's words. "Only then can the door be opened."

Plato took a deep breath, his mind sharpening with determination. He knew this was only the beginning, and that the trials would only grow more difficult from here.

He carefully traced the lines with his fingers, feeling the subtle vibrations beneath the stone. He began to see patterns emerge, connections between the shapes that were not immediately obvious. The triangles formed a larger shape, the circles intertwined to create new forms, and the squares fit together like a puzzle.

He closed his eyes, allowing his mind to visualize the solution. The shapes seemed to dance in his mind, rearranging themselves into a harmonious whole. When he opened his eyes, he saw the pattern clearly.

Plato reached out and pressed on the center of the geometric design he thought started the pattern. One after the other, he pressed each design in it's center. The stone door trembled and then began to slide open with a low rumble. He had solved the first riddle, but he knew this was only the beginning.

As he stepped through the door, he heard a grinding noise behind him. He turned to see the stone door sliding back into place, sealing him inside. Panic surged through him as he realized there was no way back. He was trapped.

The chamber he found himself in was even larger than the first, with walls covered in hieroglyphs and symbols that seemed to glow faintly in the dim light of his lamp. The air was heavy with an unearthly stillness, as if the very walls were holding their breath.

Plato's mind raced as he considered his next move. He knew he had to proceed, that turning back was no longer an option. With a final glance at the now-sealed door behind him, Plato took a deep breath to steady his racing heart. The realization that he was trapped in the pyramid heightened his senses, sharpening his focus. He turned his attention to the chamber before him, taking in the intricate carvings on the walls and the floor.

The carvings depicted a series of geometric shapes, each one interconnected with lines and symbols. Plato recognized the basic forms of triangles, circles, and squares, but their arrangement was complex and perplexing. The room seemed to pulse with a hidden energy, as if the very stones were alive and breathing.

"To find the key, I must see the unseen," he whispered, repeating a line from the scrolls. "The answer lies in the harmony of the shapes."

He carefully approached the center of the room, where a large, circular design was etched into the floor. The design was surrounded by smaller geometric shapes, each one intricately detailed. Plato knelt down, examining the carvings closely. He could see the subtle connections between the shapes, the way the lines intertwined to form a larger pattern.

He remembered the scrolls that spoke of a sacred geometry used by the ancient Egyptians. The principles of balance and proportion were crucial to their understanding of the universe. He traced the lines with his fingers, feeling the subtle vibrations beneath the stone. The shapes seemed to dance under his touch, revealing hidden patterns and connections.

As he studied the carvings, a faint memory from his studies surfaced in his mind. The ancient Egyptians believed that the universe was governed by a divine order, a harmony that could be understood through geometry and mathematics. The key to unlocking the mysteries of the pyramid lay in understanding this divine order.

Plato closed his eyes, allowing his mind to visualize the solution. The shapes seemed to dance in his mind, rearranging themselves into a harmonious whole. He saw the triangles forming a larger shape, the circles intertwining to create new forms, and the squares fitting together like a puzzle.

When he opened his eyes, he saw the pattern clearly. He reached out and pressed on the center of the geometric design. The floor beneath him trembled, and the shapes began to glow with a soft, golden light. The lines connected, forming a harmonious pattern that seemed to pulse with life.

The walls of the chamber trembled, and the stone door at the far end of the room began to slide open with a low rumble. Plato's heart swelled with relief and determination. He had solved the riddle.

As he stepped through the door, he felt a surge of energy coursing through his veins. The passageway beyond was narrow and dark, the air growing colder with each step. He held his lamp high, its flickering flame casting eerie shadows on the walls.

The passageway led him to another chamber, this one smaller and more ominous. The air was thick with the scent of earth and metal. In the center of the room stood a pedestal with four small bowls, each containing a different substance: earth, water, fire, and air.

Plato approached the pedestal cautiously, sensing the importance of the elements before him. The scrolls had mentioned the significance of the natural elements in the trials, and he knew this was the next challenge.

"To proceed, one must balance the elements and understand their true nature," he remembered Imhotep's teachings.

With a deep breath, he stepped into the new chamber, his heart still racing from the excitement and fear of solving the previous

puzzle. The room was darker than the last, the air still carried a heavy, mineral scent. The flickering light of his oil lamp cast long, shifting shadows on the walls, adding to the sense of foreboding.

Plato approached the pedestal cautiously, sensing the significance of the elements before him. The scrolls had mentioned the importance of the natural elements in the trials, and he knew this was the next challenge.

He studied the bowls, noting their positions and the symbols surrounding them. Each bowl was intricately carved, the designs hinting at the elements they contained. Plato realized that he needed to arrange the elements in a specific order, one that reflected their harmony and balance.

He carefully placed the bowl of earth at the base, symbolizing stability and foundation. The heavy, dark soil seemed to anchor the pedestal, grounding it in the physical world. Above it, he placed the bowl of water, representing fluidity and life. The clear, cool liquid rippled gently, reflecting the light of his lamp.

Next came the bowl of fire, embodying energy and transformation. The small flame danced and flickered, casting a warm glow over the pedestal. Finally, he placed the bowl of air at the top, signifying breath and spirit. The bowl was empty, but Plato could feel the presence of the element, the invisible force that gave life to all things.

As he completed the arrangement, the pedestal began to glow with a soft, golden light. The elements merged together, their energies intertwining to create a harmonious whole. The symbols on the pedestal seemed to come alive, pulsating with a hidden power.

The walls of the chamber trembled, and a hidden passageway opened before him. Plato felt a surge of triumph but knew he could not afford to relax. Each step deeper into the pyramid brought new challenges and greater risks. He steeled himself for the trials ahead,

knowing that the path to the Emerald Tablet was fraught with danger and uncertainty.

He took a deep breath and stepped through the passageway, the cool air of the new chamber brushing against his face. The corridor was narrow and winding, the walls pressing in on him as he moved forward. He could hear the faint echo of his footsteps, the sound amplifying the sense of isolation and peril.

As he ventured deeper into the pyramid, the air grew colder, the darkness more oppressive. The flickering light of his lamp seemed to struggle against the encroaching shadows, casting eerie, shifting shapes on the walls. Plato felt a chill run down his spine, the weight of the ancient structure pressing down on him.

The passageway led him to another chamber, this one larger and more imposing than the others. The walls were covered in ancient symbols and inscriptions, their meanings obscured by the passage of time. In the center of the room stood a large, ornate pedestal. On the pedestal lay a fragment of some odd tablet it seemed, glowing with an otherworldly light.

He approached the pedestal with a fragment of a glowing tablet, inscriptions shimmering on its surface. Intrigued and cautious, he reached out and touched the fragment. Instantly, a surge of energy coursed through him, and his vision blurred as he was transported into a vivid vision.

He found himself standing in a grand, ancient city that resembled Atlantis, but it was different—older and more mystical. The sky was filled with swirling colors, and a sense of immense power and knowledge permeated the air. Figures of light and energy moved around him, acknowledging his presence with serene smiles.

A voice echoed in his mind, "You seek the truth, but you hold only fragments of wisdom. Complete the trials, and you shall gain the whole."

The vision shifted, showing images of a great flood, destruction, and the fall of civilizations. Among the chaos, he saw a figure standing tall, holding the complete emerald tablet, radiating light and hope.

The vision faded, and Plato found himself back in the chamber, his hand still on the fragment. He understood now—this was a test, a glimpse of the greater knowledge that awaited him. The fragment was a piece of the puzzle, urging him to continue his quest.

With renewed determination, he left the chamber, ready to face the next trial, knowing that the path to the truth was just beginning. The passageway to the next chamber beckoned, a dark and foreboding path that promised even greater challenges. Plato took a deep breath, steeling himself for what lay ahead. With a final glance at the glowing fragment, he stepped into the darkness, ready to confront the trials that awaited him.

Plato stepped through the passageway, his heart pounding with anticipation and fear. The trials so far had tested his intellect and determination, but he knew that the challenges ahead would be even more daunting. The air grew colder as he descended further into the depths of the pyramid, the flickering flame of his lamp casting long, eerie shadows on the walls.

The narrow corridor led him to another chamber, this one even larger and more foreboding than the others. The walls were adorned with more ancient symbols and inscriptions, their meanings shrouded in mystery. In the center of the room stood another pedestal, but this one was different. It was surrounded by intricate mechanisms and levers, all interconnected in a complex arrangement.

Plato approached the pedestal cautiously, his mind racing to understand the new challenge before him. He could see that the mechanisms were part of a larger puzzle, one that required precise manipulation to solve. The room seemed to hum with a hidden energy, as if the very walls were alive and watching his every move.

"This must be the next trial," he muttered to himself, his voice echoing in the empty chamber. He knew that the puzzle before him was unlike anything he had encountered so far. It required not only intellect but also precision and patience.

He examined the mechanisms closely, noting the various symbols and shapes etched into the levers and gears. Each one seemed to represent a different element or concept, all interconnected in a delicate balance. Plato realized that he needed to manipulate the levers in a specific sequence to unlock the next passageway.

"Balance and harmony," he whispered, recalling Imhotep's teachings. "Only through understanding the interconnectedness of all things can the path be revealed."

He began to move the levers, his hands trembling with a mixture of fear and excitement. He could feel the subtle vibrations beneath his fingers, the mechanisms responding to his touch. The room seemed to come alive, the symbols glowing faintly as he manipulated the puzzle.

As he worked, he became aware of a low rumbling noise, growing louder with each movement of the levers. The walls trembled, and the air grew thick with tension. He knew that he was close to unlocking the next passageway, but he also sensed that any mistake could be disastrous.

Just as he was about to complete the sequence, the room was plunged into darkness. The flame of his lamp flickered and went out, leaving him in total blackness. Panic surged through him as he realized that he had made a mistake. The mechanisms ground to a halt, and the rumbling noise grew louder, more menacing.

He fumbled in the darkness, trying to reignite his lamp, but his hands were shaking too much to succeed. The air grew colder, and he could feel the walls closing in around him. He was trapped, unable to see or move.

The low rumbling noise turned into a deafening roar, and the floor beneath him began to tremble violently. Plato's heart raced as he

realized that the chamber was collapsing. He struggled to stay calm, to find a way out, but the darkness and noise were overwhelming.

He could hear the grinding of stone against stone, the sound of ancient mechanisms failing. The walls seemed to close in around him, the weight of the pyramid pressing down on him. Plato felt a surge of desperation, knowing that his life was in grave danger.

In the midst of the chaos, he repeated Imhotep's words to himself: "Only through understanding the interconnectedness of all things can the path be revealed." He took a deep breath, trying to calm his racing thoughts. He knew that he needed to find the balance and harmony within the mechanisms to unlock the passageway.

With a renewed sense of determination, Plato reached out in the darkness, feeling for the levers. He moved them carefully, relying on his memory and intuition to guide him. The room continued to tremble, the noise growing louder, but he focused all his energy on solving the puzzle.

As he manipulated the final lever, a faint light appeared in the distance. The mechanisms began to move again, the rumbling noise subsiding. The walls stopped trembling, and the air grew still. Plato's heart swelled with hope as he realized that he had succeeded.

But just as he was about to step forward, the floor beneath him gave way. He felt himself falling, plunging into a deep, dark pit. The light disappeared, and he was enveloped in total darkness once more. The sensation of falling seemed to last forever, his mind racing with fear and uncertainty. He had no idea where he was or what awaited him at the bottom of the pit.

As he fell, he heard the deep, commanding male voice that had haunted his dreams. "Plato… the true test begins now."

Chapter 15

Wisdom in the Darkness

Plato awoke with a sudden gasp, his body aching from the fall. He was surrounded by complete darkness, the weight of the pyramid pressing down on him. Panic surged through him as he realized he could not see anything, not even his own hand in front of his face. He reached out, feeling the cold, rough stone beneath him. His lantern was shattered, its light extinguished.

He tried to stand, but a sharp pain shot through his leg, forcing him back to the ground. He clutched his leg, feeling the warmth of blood seeping through his fingers. He had injured himself in the fall, and now he was trapped in the pitch-black depths of the pyramid, alone and wounded.

Desperation threatened to overwhelm him. He had entered the pyramid prepared to face death, but now, confronted with the reality of his situation, he realized that he wanted to live. The darkness seemed to close in around him, suffocating him with its weight. He took a deep breath, trying to steady his racing heart. He knew that panic would only make things worse.

His mind raced, trying to recall any information from the scrolls that might help him. The teachings of Imhotep and the other priests had always emphasized the importance of balance and calm in the face of adversity. Plato knew he needed to gather his thoughts and focus if he was going to survive this ordeal.

He shifted slightly, feeling the sharp pain in his leg again. He reached down and gingerly touched the injury. It was a deep gash, and it throbbed with each heartbeat. He tore a strip from his tunic and wrapped it around his leg, trying to staunch the bleeding. The darkness around him felt like a living entity, pressing in on him from all sides.

Plato lay back, staring up into the void. His thoughts drifted back to Athens, to the safety and comfort of his home, and to Socrates. He thought of the wisdom his mentor had imparted, the lessons about life, truth, and the pursuit of knowledge. He couldn't let himself die here, not when he still had so much to learn and to share.

He remembered the vision he had seen in the chamber earlier, the glimpse of a world beyond the cave of his current despair. It had shown him a path to understanding, to finding his true self. That vision had given him a purpose, a reason to survive. He clung to that vision now, letting it fuel his determination.

As he lay in the darkness, his breathing steadying, he began to notice the faintest of sounds around him. The pyramid was not silent; it was alive with the creaks and whispers of ancient stone. He listened intently, hoping to find some clue, some way to navigate this pitch-black chamber.

He moved his hands over the stone floor, feeling for any sign of a passage or opening. His fingers brushed against the familiar symbols etched into the stone. He traced the lines, trying to remember their meanings and the patterns they formed. He knew that the key to escaping this room lay in understanding the symbols and finding the hidden passage.

Despite the pain in his leg and the overwhelming darkness, Plato forced himself to focus. He had to trust in his knowledge and his ability to solve the puzzles that the pyramid presented. His life depended on it.

As he sat in the darkness, the silence around him was almost deafening. His leg throbbed with pain, and he could feel his strength waning. Despite the pain and fear, he knew he had to remain calm. Panic would only lead to mistakes, and in his current situation, any mistake could be fatal.

He closed his eyes, trying to center himself. He remembered the teachings of Imhotep and the other priests, the importance of balance and inner peace. He focused on his breathing, taking deep, measured breaths to calm his racing heart. The air was cool and damp, the scent of ancient stone filling his nostrils.

As he meditated, he began to feel a strange sensation, as if he were drifting away from his physical body. A spot in the center of his forehead began pulse. The darkness around him seemed to dissolve, replaced by a vision of light. He saw himself standing in a vast, open space, bathed in a soft, golden glow. Before him stood a massive cave, its entrance dark and foreboding.

He felt a presence beside him, a guiding force that urged him forward. He stepped into the cave, feeling the cold, damp air against his skin. As he ventured deeper, he saw shadows on the walls, flickering and shifting like phantoms. He realized that these shadows were the illusions of the world, the false beliefs and fears that kept him trapped in darkness.

The vision grew clearer, and he saw a light in the distance, a beacon that beckoned him forward. He moved towards it, feeling a sense of purpose and determination growing within him. The light grew brighter, illuminating the cave and dispelling the shadows.

He understood now that the cave was a metaphor for his own mind, the illusions and fears that kept him from seeing the truth. He needed to escape the darkness and find the light within himself. The vision gave him a glimpse of the world outside the cave, a world of clarity and understanding. He knew that he had to survive, not just for himself, but to share this newfound wisdom with others.

As he moved towards the light, he felt a surge of energy coursing through his veins. The shadows on the walls began to dissipate, replaced by images of the people and places he loved. He saw Socrates, standing tall and wise, his eyes filled with kindness and understanding. He saw Athens, its streets bustling with life and activity. He saw his family and friends, their faces filled with hope and love.

The vision gave him strength, a renewed sense of determination to overcome the challenges before him. He knew that he could not let the darkness claim him, that he had to fight for his survival. The light in the distance was a symbol of the knowledge and understanding he sought, and he would do whatever it took to reach it.

The vision began to fade, and he found himself back in the dark chamber. But now, he felt a renewed sense of purpose. He had a goal, a reason to survive. He knew that he had to escape the trials and share the wisdom he had gained with others.

He took a deep breath, steeling himself for the challenges ahead. Plato began to move, using his hands to feel his way around the chamber. The pain in his leg was still there, but he pushed it to the back of his mind. He had to focus on finding a way out, on navigating the darkness and solving the puzzles that lay ahead.

He felt the cold stone beneath his fingers, the rough texture of the ancient walls. He moved carefully, inching forward in the darkness. He knew that he had to be cautious, that any misstep could lead to disaster.

As he explored the chamber, he began to notice subtle signs and symbols etched into the stone. He traced the lines with his fingers, trying to make sense of them. He knew that these symbols held the key to his escape, that they were a part of the ancient puzzles designed to test his intellect and determination.

With a renewed sense of purpose, Plato continued to explore the chamber in the dark, his mind focused on the task at hand, his fingers tracing the ancient symbols etched into the stone walls. His mind was focused, determined to decipher the clues that would lead him to safety. The vision he had experienced filled him with a renewed sense of hope.

As he moved forward, the darkness around him seemed to shift and change. The air grew colder, and he could hear faint whispers, like the distant echoes of voices from another time. He paused, listening intently, trying to make out the words. The whispers grew louder, more distinct, and he realized that they were not just random sounds. They were guiding him, leading him towards the next part of his journey.

Plato followed the whispers, his hands feeling their way along the walls. He moved slowly, carefully, his injured leg throbbing with each step. The darkness was oppressive, but he felt a strange sense of calm. The vision had shown him the way, and he trusted in the guidance of the whispers.

As he hugged the wall and rounded a corner, he felt a sudden rush of cool air. He had found an opening, a passage that led deeper into the pyramid. The whispers grew louder, urging him forward. He stepped into the passage, his heart pounding with anticipation and fear.

The passage was narrow, the walls closing in on him as he moved deeper into the pyramid. The air was thick with the scent of ancient stone and dust. He could feel the weight of the pyramid pressing down on him, but he pressed on, driven by the vision and the whispers.

The passage led him to another chamber, this one larger and more imposing than the others. The air was cooler here, the darkness less oppressive. He could see faint glimmers of light, like stars in the night sky. He moved towards the light, his steps cautious and deliberate.

In the center of the chamber, he saw a pedestal, similar to the ones he had encountered before. On the pedestal lay a small, intricately carved object. He approached it cautiously, his heart racing.

The object seemed to glow with a faint, otherworldly light, its surface covered in mysterious symbols.

Plato reached out to touch the object, feeling a surge of energy coursing through his veins. As his fingers brushed the surface, he was once again transported into a vision. This time, the vision was more vivid, more intense. He saw himself standing on a high cliff, overlooking a vast, shimmering sea. The sky was filled with swirling colors, and the air was alive with the sound of waves crashing against the rocks below.

He felt a presence beside him, a guiding force that urged him to look deeper, to see beyond the surface of the vision. He closed his eyes, focusing on the sensations around him. He felt the warmth of the sun on his face, the cool breeze against his skin, and the solid ground beneath his feet.

As he opened his eyes, he saw a figure standing before him. It was a man, tall and imposing, his eyes filled with wisdom and understanding. The man reached out a hand, and Plato took it, feeling a sense of connection and familiarity.

The man spoke, his voice deep and resonant. "Plato, you have come far on your journey, but the trials ahead will test you in ways you cannot yet imagine. You must find the light within yourself, the strength to overcome the darkness. Only then will you be able to uncover the true knowledge you seek."

Plato nodded, his heart filled with determination. He knew that the path ahead would be difficult, but he was ready to face the challenges. The vision began to fade, and he found himself back in the chamber, the object still glowing faintly in his hand.

He understood that the vision was a guide, a glimpse of the knowledge and wisdom he sought. He had to find the strength within himself to overcome the trials and escape the darkness. The object in his hand was a key, a symbol of the path he needed to follow.

Plato examined the object more closely. He saw that it was a small, intricately carved amulet, its surface covered in symbols that matched those on the walls of the chamber. He knew that the amulet held the key to unlocking the next passageway, to finding his way out of the darkness.

He moved to the walls, tracing the symbols with his fingers, feeling the patterns and connections. As he followed the whispers, an uncanny sensation washed over him. He could somehow tell that the symbols he was tracing matched those on the amulet he carried. "These symbols… they're the same," he thought, a sense of urgency and curiosity driving him forward.

As he continued, his fingers brushed against a small indentation in the wall. He paused, his heart pounding. "Could this be the place?" he wondered. "It seems impossible, but I have to try." He carefully placed the amulet into the indentation, feeling a click as it settled into place.

The walls trembled, and the air grew still. The mechanism engaged, and he watched in awe as the symbols on the walls began to glow, and a hidden door slowly slid open, revealing a narrow passageway beyond. He stepped through the passageway, the vision of the high cliff and the shimmering sea still vivid in his mind. Plato stepped through the passageway, his heart pounding with anticipation. The vision he had experienced gave him hope, but he knew the challenges ahead would test him to his limits. The narrow corridor led him deeper into the pyramid, the air growing colder and the darkness more oppressive with each step.

The passageway opened into another chamber, this one even darker and more foreboding than the last. The air was thick with the scent of ancient stone and dust, the silence broken only by the faint echoes of his footsteps. Plato felt a chill run down his spine as he stepped into the room, the weight of the pyramid pressing down on him.

His leg throbbed with pain, a constant reminder of his injury. He could feel the rough stone beneath his hands as he moved forward, feeling his way through the darkness. The amulet he had found earlier glowed faintly, casting a dim light that barely penetrated the shadows.

He paused, trying to make sense of his surroundings. The chamber was vast, the walls hidden in darkness. He could hear faint whispers, like the distant echoes of voices from another time. He closed his eyes, focusing on the sound, trying to decipher the words.

As he listened, the whispers grew louder, more distinct. They seemed to come from all around him, surrounding him in a cocoon of sound. He felt a presence beside him, a guiding force that urged him to look deeper, to see beyond the darkness.

Plato opened his eyes, his heart racing. The darkness seemed to shift and change, the air growing colder. He felt a surge of fear, the weight of the pyramid pressing down on him. He knew that he was not alone, that there were forces at work beyond his understanding.

The whispers grew louder, more insistent. He felt the presence beside him, a guiding force that urged him to look inward, to find the light within himself. He closed his eyes, focusing on his breathing, trying to center himself.

As he moved deeper into the chamber, he heard a faint noise, like the rustling of leaves in a breeze. He paused, listening intently. The noise grew louder, more distinct, and he realized that it was not just random sounds. It was the voice of a woman, whispering his name.

"Plato," the voice called softly. "Plato, find the light within yourself."

He felt a surge of energy, the voice giving him strength. He knew that he had to keep moving, to find a way out of the darkness. The vision of the light and the voice guiding him filled him with hope and determination.

As he continued to explore the chamber, the darkness seemed to grow thicker, more oppressive. He felt the weight of the pyramid pressing down on him, the air growing colder. But he did not give up. He knew that he had to find the light within himself, to overcome the darkness and escape the trials.

He reached out, feeling for any sign of an exit. His fingers brushed against a series of symbols etched into the stone. He recognized them from the scrolls, the ancient markings that indicated a hidden passageway. He carefully traced the symbols, feeling the patterns and connections.

As he worked, the whispers grew louder, urging him on. He knew that he was close to unlocking the next passageway, to finding his way out of the darkness. Even though it was dark, he closed his eyes, controlled his breathing, and attempted to visualize the patterns in mind as he traced them with his fingers. The symbols began to glow faintly, their light illuminating the chamber.

Just as he was about to complete the sequence, he felt a sudden rush of cold air. The ground beneath him trembled, and he heard a low rumbling noise. The symbols glowed brighter, and the walls of the chamber began to close in around him.

Plato's heart raced as he realized that he was in danger. The walls were moving, closing in on him, threatening to crush him. He frantically worked to complete the sequence, his fingers moving quickly over the symbols.

The rumbling grew louder, the walls closing in faster. He felt a surge of panic, but he pushed it to the back of his mind. He had to focus, to find the balance and harmony within the symbols. Just as the walls were about to crush him, the symbols clicked into place. The ground trembled violently, and a hidden door slid open, revealing a narrow passageway.

He stepped through the passageway, the vision of the light still vivid in his mind. As he moved deeper into the passageway, a sense of

calm washed over him. Plato stepped into the darkness, his fate hanging in the balance. Each step forward was fraught with uncertainty, but he felt a renewed determination guiding him. The future was unclear, but he knew he had to continue. The passageway seemed to close in around him, the air heavy with anticipation of what awaited in the depths of the pyramid. His breathing grew shallow, and his steps faltered. The walls seemed to waver, and a wave of dizziness overcame him. The last thing he saw was the darkness pressing in, before everything went black.

Chapter 16

The Keeper of Secrets

Plato awoke to the oppressive darkness of the pyramid, his body aching and his leg throbbing with pain. The faint light from the amulet had dimmed, leaving him in near-total darkness. He felt disoriented, his sense of time and space distorted by the blackness around him. The air was thick and heavy, each breath a reminder of his precarious situation.

He took a deep breath, trying to calm his racing heart. The silence was almost deafening, broken only by the faint sound of his own breathing and the occasional drip of water echoing through the stone corridors. He pushed himself up, wincing as he put weight on his injured leg. He knew he had to keep moving, but the darkness made every step feel like a leap into the unknown.

Am I truly here? he pondered, his thoughts echoing in the silence. If this is not reality, then what is the nature of this existence?

The questions echoed in his mind, each one more unsettling than the last. He knew that his senses could deceive him, that the darkness and isolation could play tricks on his mind. But he also knew that he had to find a way out, that he had to survive the trials and reach the Emerald Tablet.

He began to move forward, his hands tracing the rough stone walls as he navigated the narrow corridor. The passage seemed to stretch on forever, the darkness swallowing everything in its path. His

injured leg made each step painful, but he pressed on, driven by a determination to find the light within himself.

As he walked, his thoughts turned inward. He remembered the teachings of Socrates, the lessons about the nature of reality and the importance of self-knowledge. He realized that in order to survive, he needed to look within himself, to find the strength and wisdom that had always been there.

The corridor seemed endless, the darkness growing more oppressive with each step. Plato felt a growing sense of despair, his fears and doubts threatening to overwhelm him. He wondered if he would ever find a way out, if he would ever see the light again.

Just as he felt his resolve weakening, he noticed a faint glow ahead of him. The light was soft and ethereal, casting long shadows on the walls. Somehow, it seemed to come from within, a guiding force that urged him forward.

He moved towards the light, his steps cautious and deliberate. The glow grew brighter with each step, illuminating the corridor and dispelling the darkness. Plato felt a strange sense of peace as he followed the light, his fears and doubts momentarily forgotten.

The passageway led him to a larger chamber, the walls adorned with intricate carvings and symbols. The air was cooler here, the darkness less oppressive. The light seemed to emanate from the very walls, casting a soft, otherworldly glow.

Plato paused, taking in his surroundings. The chamber was vast, the walls stretching up into the darkness above. He felt a sense of awe and wonder, the beauty and complexity of the carvings captivating his mind. He knew that he was not alone, that there were forces at work beyond his understanding.

As he stood there, contemplating the mysteries of the chamber, he heard a faint noise. It was the sound of footsteps, echoing through the stone corridors. Plato's heart raced, his mind filled with questions. Who could be here with him? Were they friend or foe?

He listened intently, trying to make out the direction of the sound. The footsteps grew louder, more distinct, and he realized that they were coming towards him. He felt a surge of fear, his mind racing with possibilities. But he knew that he had to stay calm, that he had to face whatever was coming.

The footsteps stopped, and Plato felt a presence beside him. He turned, his eyes scanning the darkness. There, standing in the shadows, was a figure. The light from the chamber illuminated the figure's face, revealing the kind, wise eyes of the Egyptian priest.

"Plato," the priest said softly, his voice filled with warmth and understanding. "You have come far on your journey, but the trials ahead will test you in ways you cannot yet imagine."

Plato felt a surge of relief and gratitude. The presence of the priest gave him hope, a sense of connection to the world outside the pyramid. He knew that he was not alone, that there were others who believed in him and his quest.

The priest continued, his voice gentle but firm. "You must find the light within yourself, the strength to overcome the darkness. Only then will you be able to uncover the true knowledge you seek."

Plato nodded, his heart filled with determination. He knew that the path ahead would be difficult, but he was ready to face the challenges. The vision he had experienced gave him hope, a guiding light in the darkness.

The priest smiled, his eyes filled with kindness. "Trust in your inner strength, Plato. The journey is long, but the reward is great. Remember the teachings of your old mentor Socrates, and let them guide you."

With those words, the priest faded into the darkness, leaving Plato alone. But now, he felt a renewed sense of purpose. With the light from the chamber guiding him, Plato continued his journey, his heart filled with hope and determination. The future was uncertain, but he knew that he had to keep moving forward. He would find the tablet

and unlock its secrets, no matter what the cost. The corridor was long and narrow, stretching into darkness. He took a deep breath, preparing himself for the journey ahead. The whispers from his vision still echoed in his mind, reminding him to trust in his inner strength.

As he walked, his thoughts again turned inward. The corridor seemed endless, the darkness more oppressive with each step. The air was thick and heavy again, making it difficult to breathe. His leg throbbed with pain, and he could feel the exhaustion creeping into his bones. He was hungry and thirsty, his body weakening with each passing moment.

What if the priest was right and he wasn't ready? He wondered if he would ever find a way out, if he would ever see the light of day again. The questions swirled in his mind, each one more unsettling than the last. He was becoming unable to discern reality. Was he truly here, or was this some kind of elaborate illusion? He felt a growing sense of despair, his fears and doubts threatening to overwhelm him.

But then, the soft glow of the amulet seemed to brighten, casting a gentle light on the path ahead. Plato felt a strange sense of peace, his fears momentarily forgotten. He knew that he had to trust in the light within himself, to find the strength to overcome the darkness.

The corridor stretched on, the walls closing in around him. He felt a chill run down his spine, the air growing colder with each step. The silence was almost deafening, broken only by the faint sound of his own breathing and the occasional drip of water echoing through the stone passage.

Plato's thoughts drifted to his recurring nightmare, the vision of the sinking city and the cries for help. The images were more vivid than ever, filling his mind with a sense of urgency. He remembered the woman's voice, calling him forward, urging him to find the light within himself.

He closed his eyes, focusing on the sound of her voice. "Plato," she whispered, "You must find the light within yourself. Trust in your inner strength."

The memory of her voice was enough to give him comfort, and he felt a renewed sense of determination. He knew that the path ahead would be difficult, but was he ready to face the challenges? The vision of the sinking city was a reminder of the consequences of failure, but it also gave him hope. He had to survive, not just for himself, but for the wisdom he had yet to uncover.

As he walked, the corridor seemed to narrow, the walls pressing in on him. The darkness was suffocating, but he pressed on, driven by a determination to find the light within himself. He felt the cold stone beneath his fingers, the surprisingly smooth texture of the ancient walls.

His thoughts turned to his past, to the lessons he had learned from Socrates and the teachings of the Egyptian priests. The journey was not just a physical one, but a spiritual quest for understanding and enlightenment. He continued to move forward, his mind focused on the task at hand. The corridor seemed endless, the darkness growing more oppressive with each step.

With the light from the chamber guiding him, Plato continued his journey, his heart filled with hope and determination. He moved cautiously through the next passageway, his steps guided by the faint glow of the amulet. The darkness seemed to thicken around him, each step more laborious than the last. The air grew colder, and the sense of isolation weighed heavily on him. His leg throbbed with a constant, dull pain, and he could feel the exhaustion creeping into his bones.

As he continued, he could feel his senses sharpening, every sound amplified in the silence. The echoes of his footsteps bounced off the stone walls, creating a rhythm that both comforted and unnerved him. He couldn't shake the feeling that he was being watched, that unseen eyes followed his every move.

After what felt like hours, the corridor opened into a small, dimly lit chamber, the walls adorned with intricate carvings and symbols. The air was even cooler here, the darkness depreciating; giving way to a light seemed to emanate from the very walls, casting a soft, otherworldly glow.

He paused, taking in his surroundings. The chamber was vast, the walls stretching up into the darkness above. He felt a sense of awe and wonder, the beauty and complexity of the carvings captivating his mind. He knew that he was not alone, that there were forces at work beyond his understanding.

In the center of the room, illuminated by a soft, ethereal glow, was a small wooden box. Plato approached it cautiously, his heart pounding with anticipation. He knelt down, his fingers tracing the delicate patterns on the surface of the box. The box was intricately carved with ancient symbols, each one telling a story of its own. It felt warm to the touch, as if it were alive. Taking a deep breath, he carefully lifted the lid. Inside, he found a small, illuminating cross necklace, glowing with a soft, blue light. The cross seemed to pulse with energy, casting a gentle light around the chamber.

Plato held the cross in his hand, feeling its warmth and power. He knew that this object was significant, that it held the key to his next challenge. He examined the symbols on the box and the cross, trying to decipher their meaning.

As he studied the symbols, he began to notice a pattern, a connection between the carvings on the box and the walls of the chamber. He realized that the symbols were not just decorative; they were part of a puzzle, a clue to unlocking the next passageway.

Plato focused on the cross, feeling the energy it emitted. He closed his eyes, allowing the light to fill his mind. He felt a strange sensation, as if he were being lifted off the ground. The air around him seemed to vibrate, and he realized that he was experiencing a vision.

In the vision, he saw himself standing in a vast, open space, bathed in a soft, golden glow. Before him stood a massive cave, its entrance dark and foreboding. He felt a presence beside him, a guiding force that urged him to look deeper.

He stepped into the cave, feeling the cold, damp air against his skin. As he ventured deeper, he saw shadows on the walls, flickering and shifting like phantoms. Somehow he understood that these shadows that he has been encountering were the illusions of the world, the false beliefs and fears that kept human kind trapped in darkness and disconnected from the love and light of the truth. The truth that everything; all life, is connected somehow, in a grand design created by the ultimate architect; created, not by many gods, but by the one true God, the creator of the universe. That the past, present and future were somehow all the same and interconnected. He could clearly see now that the cave was a metaphor for his own mind, the illusions and fears that also kept him from seeing the truth. He needed to escape the darkness and find the light within himself. The vision gave him a glimpse of the world outside the cave, a world of clarity and understanding and connectedness. He knew that he had to survive, not just for himself, but to share this newfound wisdom with others.

The vision grew clearer, and he saw a light in the distance, a beacon that beckoned him forward. He moved towards it, feeling a sense of purpose and determination growing within him. The light grew brighter, illuminating the cave and dispelling the shadows.

As he moved towards the light, he felt a surge of energy coursing through his veins. The shadows on the walls began to dissipate, replaced by images of the people and places he loved. He saw Socrates, standing tall and wise, his eyes filled with kindness and understanding. He saw Athens, its streets bustling with life and activity. He saw his family and friends, their faces filled with hope and love.

The vision gave him strength, hope, and a renewed sense of determination to overcome the challenges before him. He knew that he could not let the darkness claim him, that he had to fight for his survival. The light in the distance was a symbol of the knowledge and understanding he sought, and he would do whatever it took to reach it.

The vision slowly began to fade, and Plato found himself back in the dark chamber, the cross still glowing faintly in his hand. He understood that the vision was a guide, a glimpse of the knowledge and wisdom he sought. He had to find the strength within himself to overcome the trials and escape the darkness.

Plato examined the cross more closely, noticing that the symbols on it also matched those on the walls of the chamber. He realized that the cross held the key to unlocking the next passageway, to finding his way out of the darkness. He carefully traced the symbols, feeling the patterns and connections.

As he worked, the whispers grew louder, urging him on. He knew that he was close to unlocking the next passageway, to finding his way out of the darkness. The symbols began to glow faintly, their light illuminating the chamber.

With renewed determination, Plato began to decipher the symbols, realizing the cross was more than just a guide—it was a key. As he studied the intricate patterns, he noticed that the cross's shape matched a sequence of symbols on the wall. "This must be it," he thought, feeling a sense of awe.

He approached the wall, the cross held firmly in his hand. He traced the symbols carefully, noting how they seemed to align with the design of the cross. "It's almost as if it was meant to be here," he mused, a shiver running down his spine.

He found a small, cross-shaped indentation, but this time it was surrounded by a series of smaller symbols. He hesitated, then pressed the cross into the indentation. Nothing happened. He frowned, looking closer. Each symbol around the indentation was faintly glowing,

pulsing in a rhythm. "There's more to this," he realized. "It's not just about fitting the cross."

He closed his eyes, focusing on the symbols' rhythm. They seemed to echo a pattern, a sequence he needed to follow. Plato took a deep breath, pressing the cross into the indentation once more. This time, he turned it slowly, aligning it with the glowing symbols in a precise sequence.

As he completed the sequence, he felt a click. The ground trembled, and the air grew still. The symbols on the walls began to glow brighter, their light spreading like wildfire. The cross acted as a conduit, channeling the energy through the symbols.

The chamber filled with a soft, ethereal light. The hidden door slowly slid open, revealing a narrow passageway beyond. Plato stepped back, marveling at the intricate mechanism. "This is no ordinary key," he thought. "This cross is a symbol, a sign of something greater."

As he stepped through the passageway, a sense of reverence washed over him. The cross had not only opened the door but had guided him deeper into his journey, foreshadowing a greater truth yet to be revealed.

The passageway seemed to close in around him, the air heavy with anticipation. Plato took a deep breath, his heart filled with hope and determination. He moved cautiously through the newly revealed passageway, his heart pounding with a mixture of fear and anticipation. The corridor was narrow and dark, the walls pressing in on him from all sides. The light from the cross in his hand provided only a faint glow, just enough to guide his steps but not enough to dispel the oppressive darkness completely.

He could hear his own breathing, harsh and ragged, echoing off the stone walls. The air was cold and damp now, filled with the scent of ancient earth and stone. Every step felt like an eternity, the silence around him heavy and foreboding.

As he continued, he began to feel the weight of his journey pressing down on him. The pain in his leg was a constant reminder of his physical limitations, and the darkness seemed to amplify his fears and doubts. He wondered if he would ever find a way out, if he would ever see the light of day again.

His thoughts drifted to the teachings of Socrates and the wisdom of the Egyptian priests. He realized that in order to survive, he needed to confront his fears and look within himself for strength. The journey was not just a physical one, but a spiritual quest for understanding and enlightenment, he reminded himself.

Plato's mind surged with a torrent of questions. What defines reality? he mused silently. Am I truly present, or is this existence merely an elaborate illusion; a shadow of the truth? The very fact that he could not tell anymore was a marvel to him. He felt a connection to everything outside of his physical self in such a way that he knew that his physical reality, as he had known it his entire life, was but a sliver of the multifaceted reality that truly existed, permeating all life. "Reality is created by the mind; we can change our reality by changing our mind," he thought, grasping the profound truth of his newfound understanding.

As he walked, the passageway began to widen, the walls gradually pulling back to reveal a larger chamber. The air grew colder, and he could feel a faint breeze stirring the darkness. The light from the cross seemed to grow stronger, casting eerie shadows on the walls.

He paused, taking in his surroundings. The chamber was vast, the ceiling lost in darkness above. The walls were covered in intricate carvings and symbols, each one telling a story of its own. He felt a sense of awe and wonder, the beauty and complexity of the carvings captivating his mind. Plato approached them cautiously, his heart pounding with anticipation.

He ventured through the passageway, the vision of the high cliff and the shimmering sea still vivid in his mind. The corridor stretched

on, the darkness pressing in from all sides. He could feel the weight of the pyramid above him, the ancient stones watching his every move.

As he walked, he felt a strange sensation, as if the walls were closing in around him. The air grew colder, and he could hear the faint sound of whispers echoing through the darkness. He knew that he was not alone, that there were forces at work beyond his understanding.

The corridor led him to another chamber, this one even darker and more foreboding than the last. The air was thick with a sense of anticipation, the darkness almost palpable. Plato felt a surge of fear, his heart pounding in his chest.

He moved cautiously into the chamber, his eyes scanning the darkness for any sign of danger. The light from the cross was barely enough to pierce the thick blackness, and he could feel the weight of the unknown pressing down on him.

As he took another step forward, he suddenly felt the ground give way beneath him. He fell, tumbling into the darkness, his heart racing with fear. He landed hard, the impact jarring his injured leg and sending a wave of pain through his body.

He lay there for a moment, catching his breath and trying to calm his racing heart. The darkness was absolute, and he could see nothing around him. He felt a sense of panic rising, but he forced himself to stay calm.

He remembered the vision of the light, the guiding force that had led him this far. He knew that he had to trust in his inner strength, to find the light within himself. He took a deep breath, focusing on the cross and the faint glow it emitted.

As he continued to lay there, he felt a strange sensation, a warmth spreading through his body. His body was exhausted. He hadn't stopped moving since he entered the pyramid. He closed his eyes, allowing the light to fill his mind. He felt a presence beside him, a guiding force that urged him to look deeper.

The vision of the sinking city and the cries for help filled his mind once again. He saw the shadows on the walls, flickering and shifting like phantoms. He was now certain somehow that these shadows were the illusions of the world, the false beliefs and fears that kept him trapped in darkness.

He knew that he had to escape the darkness, to find the light within himself. The vision gave him a glimpse of the world outside the cave, a world of clarity and understanding. The vision began to fade, and Plato found himself back in the dark chamber, the cross still glowing faintly in his hand. He understood now that the vision was a guide, a glimpse of the knowledge and wisdom he sought. He had to find the strength within himself to overcome the trials and escape the darkness, but how?

With renewed determination, Plato got up and began to search the chamber, feeling his way through the darkness. He knew that there had to be a way out, a hidden passage or clue that would lead him forward. He felt the cold stone beneath his fingers, the smooth texture of these ancient interior walls felt like marble. His fingers traced the wall until a new passage was revealed.

As he stumbled in to the new passage, he heard a faint noise, a whispering voice calling his name. "Plato," the voice said softly. It was a man's voice this time, deep and resonant. "You must find the light within. Trust in your inner light."

The voice gave him comfort, and he felt a renewed sense of determination. The vision of the sinking city and crashing waves was a reminder of the consequences of failure, but it also gave him hope. He pressed onward, each step increasing in mass as he navigated the narrow, dark passageway. The air was thick and musty, the silence around him almost oppressive. The faint light from the cross necklace provided just enough illumination to see the rough stone walls, but it did little to dispel the overwhelming sense of isolation.

He came to a halt as the passageway ended abruptly at a solid stone wall. Plato felt a surge of frustration and fear. Had he reached a dead end? He examined the wall, feeling its cold, unyielding surface with his hands. There was no obvious way forward.

Just as despair began to creep in, he noticed a small, faintly glowing symbol near the base of the wall. It was similar to the symbols he had seen in the other chambers, intricately carved and pulsating with a soft, blue light. Plato knelt down, tracing the symbol with his fingers, feeling the energy it emitted. He could literally feel the vibration of the lines of the symbols, as if they were alive and breathing with an energy.

As he studied the symbol, he felt a strange sensation, as if the ground beneath him was shifting. The air grew colder, and the light from the cross seemed to flicker. He realized that this symbol was a clue, a key to unlocking the next part of his journey.

Plato closed his eyes, focusing on the light within himself. He felt a presence beside him, the guiding force that had helped lead him this far. The vision of the sinking city and the cries for help filled his mind once again, but this time, there was something different. He saw flashes of light and shadow, a sense of movement and energy, dancing all around him.

Somehow, he instinctively understood that the symbol was connected to gravity, to the very forces that held the pyramid together. He needed to manipulate these forces to move forward, he thought, to find the next passageway. The vision of the high cliff and the shimmering sea came back to him, a reminder of the knowledge he sought.

With renewed determination, Plato focused his thoughts on the symbol. He closed his eyes, and began to breathe rhythmically in and out. His mind was clear, his inner eyes could see only complete blackness. The cave of his inner mind somehow seemed more vast than the outer world. Then, slowly a small light began to come in to

focus, coming up from below as if it traveled up his spine to his head. The light stopped in front of him. Somehow he could see the backs of his eyes, as if he was looking out from within his own head. The light was now brighter and perfectly clear and stood strong and pulsating between the center of his head and his eyes. The light continued to pulsate, brighter and brighter.

He felt a surge of energy, his body vibrating with intensity. He could feel the vibrations of his body resonating outward for miles it felt like. Somehow, his vibrations were resonating with the pyramid and with the earth itself. The air around him seemed to shimmer, and in an instant he was engulfed in a wall of blue fire. He knew that somehow he had found the key to unlocking the next part of the trial, but how?

He reached his hand up to tough the wall of blue fire, and opened his eyes. Just as his eyes opened, his hand was placing the cross necklace into the indentation on the symbol, feeling a click as it settled into place. The ground trembled, and the air grew still. The symbol began to glow brighter, casting an eerie light around the chamber. Plato felt a strange sensation, as if he were being lifted off the ground.

Suddenly, the floor beneath him gave way, and he felt himself falling into the darkness. He tumbled through the air, his heart racing with fear. The walls of the passage seemed to blur as he fell, the light from the cross flickering wildly.

He landed harshly on a cold, stone floor, the weight of his body seemed to increased by the gravity of the pyramid, causing pain to ripple through his body in waves. He lay there for a moment, catching his breath and trying to calm his racing heart. The darkness was absolute, and he could see nothing around him except for the wall of blue light that still engulfed him.

As he lay there, he felt a strange sensation, a warmth spreading through his body. He closed his eyes, allowing the light to fill his mind. He felt a presence beside him, a guiding force that urged him to look deeper.

The vision of the sinking city and the cries for help filled his mind once again. He saw the shadows on the walls, flickering and shifting like phantoms. The shadows represented the illusions of the world—the false beliefs and fears that kept him trapped in darkness. But what did that even mean to him while he was in here, he wondered.

The vision began to fade, and Plato found himself back in the dark chamber, the cross still glowing faintly in his hand. He began to search the new chamber, feeling his way through the darkness. His eyes were open and he could no longer see the wall of blue fire, but he could somehow sense the energy all around him, vibrating with intensity. He knew that there had to be a way out, a hidden passage or clue that would lead him forward. He felt the cold stone beneath his fingers, the texture of the ancient walls that somehow felt as if they were humming with energy and life.

As he searched, he heard a faint noise, a whispering voice calling his name. "Plato," the voice said softly. It was a man's voice this time, deep and resonant. "Plato" The voice gave him comfort, and renewed his sense of resolve. The vision of the sinking city was a reminding him once again of the consequences of failure, but also reminding him of the need for faith and hope. He would face the trials, no matter what and conquer his fears, and prove himself worthy of the knowledge it held.

He moved cautiously through the chamber, his mind focused on the task at hand. He knew that he had to use his inner light, this, third eye he read about in the scrolls, to manipulate gravity and escape the chamber, but he had no idea how. The vision of the sinking city and the cries for help continued to fill his mind, but this time, there was something different. The visions were so intense that he had to close his eyes trying to balance himself. He saw flashes of different colored

lights and shadow, a sense of movement and energy rising up from deep within and swirling all around him. It was absolutely beautiful, as if the lights were entertaining him with the most dazzling display of love and unity.

With renewed determination, Plato focused his thoughts back on the trials. He felt a surge of energy, his body vibrating with intensity. The air around him seemed to shimmer, and he was engulfed in a wall of blue fire again. He knew that somehow this had to do with the key to unlocking the next part of the trial.

He closed his eyes and centered his thoughts. This time, he began to manipulate the wall of fire around him with his breathing. The wall began to pulsate with every in breath, growing larger and larger. Instinctively he widened the wall of light to the point of encasing the physical wall of the pyramid itself, to the point he could actually feel the stone with his mind within his wall of light that surrounded his body. As he concentrated, the stone wall in front of him began to shift and change. The ground beneath him trembled, and he felt himself being lifted off the floor. The air grew colder, and the light from the cross seemed to flicker.

Suddenly, the floor beneath him gave way, and he felt himself falling into the darkness once again. He tumbled through the air, his heart racing with fear. The walls of the passage seemed to blur as he fell, the light from the cross flickering wildly once again.

The falling seem to be never ending. There was no sound, no echo, and no light. All was pitch black, but somehow there was an internal glow within himself that allowed him to see his hands and body. He continued to fall for what felt like ages. A calm sense of peace engulfing him as he fell. He should be terrified, he thought, but he wasn't. He began focus his thoughts, closing his eyes once more. His breathing became his focus again, and slowly became his very center of gravity. Such a strange sensation, he thought. Strange, yet, somehow, very familiar. The wall of light began to change in to

geometric shapes. Familiar, triangular shapes at first, then in to two massive pyramids, one above and one below, slowly joining together, encircling him. The shapes were spinning faster and faster, creating a new wall of light around him. They began spinning faster and faster until they disappeared. He knew they were still there, they were just moving at such a high speed that they were no longer visible. He could see he was back in the darkness and was still falling.

He landed hard on another cold, stone floor, the impact jarred his injured leg worse than before, sending a waves of pain through his entire body. He lay there for a moment, keeping his breath and his racing heart from losing balance. The darkness was absolute, and he could see nothing around him. The threat of failure began to engulf and overtake him.

As he lay there, he felt a strange sensation, a warmth spreading through his body. He closed his eyes, allowing the light to fill his mind. He felt a presence beside him, a guiding force that urged him to look deeper. The vision of the sinking city and the cries for help filled his mind once again, but this time, there was something different. He could hear a distant whisper in the darkness.

He began to frantically search the chamber, feeling his way through the darkness. He knew that there had to be a way out, a hidden passage or clue that would lead him forward. He felt the cold stone beneath his fingers, but this time he saw no symbols and felt no way out.

As he searched in the dark, he heard a faint noise, the whispering voice calling his name. "Plato," the voice said softly. It was the woman's voice again. "You must find the light within yourself. Trust in your inner strength."

Plato found himself engulfed in pure black darkness. The light from the cross was gone, and the room seemed to have no features. It was as if he was suspended in a void, with no sense of direction or

orientation. The only light he could find was within himself when he closed his eyes.

In this profound darkness, he felt a subtle yet powerful presence. It was the energy of the pyramid, vibrating through the stone and pulsing with an ancient rhythm. Somehow, he could sense the tablet's presence, an ethereal beacon calling to him. The voice that had given him comfort and renewed determination now seemed distant, yet its message echoed in his mind.

Plato took a deep breath, steeling himself. He realized that the path to the tablet might not exist in the physical realm, but in the realm of the mind and spirit. He closed his eyes again, focusing on the inner light. The symbols from the pyramid walls glowed vividly in his mind's eye, guiding him forward.

The realization struck him like a bolt of lightning: the tablet existed only in an ethereal state, not bound by physical reality. This was the key! He had to reach it through his mind, navigating the labyrinth of his thoughts and overcoming the trials within himself.

He concentrated, allowing the energy of the pyramid to flow through him. As he did, the darkness around him seemed to lift slightly, revealing faint, shimmering outlines of the room. The path to the tablet was becoming clearer, but he knew it required more than just walking towards it. It demanded a deep connection with his inner self and an unwavering focus on the light within.

With each step he took, he could feel the ground beneath him shifting. He knew that if he failed to maintain this connection, he would fall endlessly into new chambers and shafts, repeating the trials until he figured it out. The stakes were high, but his determination was unwavering.

He moved forward, guided by the light within his mind. The energy of the pyramid grew stronger, enveloping him in a cocoon of ancient wisdom and power. He understood now that this journey was not just about reaching the tablet but about transcending his physical limitations and unlocking the secrets of his own soul.

He was surrounded by darkness, feeling the walls of the chamber close in on him. Suddenly, a whisper cut through the silence: "Merkaba." The voice echoed softly but insistently. "Merkaba."

The word stirred something within him. He recalled his studies from years ago, reading about the Egyptian concepts of "Ka" and "Ba." He remembered that the Egyptians believed in the combination of the soul and the spirit to achieve eternal life. Instinctively, he knew this voice was referring to his own inner transformation, his pyramid light body.

In ancient Egyptian belief, the ka was the life force or spiritual double, present from birth and sustained after death by offerings in tombs. The ba, on the other hand, represented a person's personality and individuality, capable of traveling between the worlds of the living and the dead. For the Egyptians, achieving immortality required the ka and ba to be preserved and reunited in the afterlife, resulting in the creation of the akh, a transfigured spirit that could exist in the presence of the gods.

As Plato focused on these concepts, he began to understand. He needed to balance his ka and ba, aligning his soul and spirit to see the path ahead. With his eyes closed and his mind centered, he could feel the presence of the tablet. It was more than a vision; it was a profound sense of knowing, a connection that transcended physical sight.

He concentrated on synchronizing his body with his breathing and the pulsating vibrations of the pyramid's lights. The light within him began to glow brighter, illuminating his path. The whispers grew louder, guiding him forward. Plato knew now that this journey was not just a physical one but a spiritual quest to unite his ka and ba, to awaken his true self.

With each step down this illumined path, the feeling of the tablet grew stronger, pulling him closer. He knew he was nearing the final

trial, the ultimate test of his enlightenment. The air around him shimmered, and he felt the energy of the pyramid enveloping him. The darkness seemed to lift slightly, revealing faint, shimmering outlines. He felt the ground beneath him shift, and the air grew colder. The light within him pulsed in harmony with the pyramid, guiding him towards the tablet. He took one final, determined step into the unknown, ready to embrace the challenges ahead and unlock the secrets of the ancient wisdom.

Chapter 17

The Emerald Revelation

Plato's heart pounded as he stepped through the narrow passageway and into the final chamber. The air was heavy with an ancient stillness, and his footsteps echoed softly off the smooth stone walls. He found himself in a solid room with four walls, all featureless and devoid of any writing or hieroglyphs. The only object in the room was a single sarcophagus made of granite, its surface exceptionally smooth and cold to the touch.

As he approached the sarcophagus, a faint, eerie glow caught his eye. Hovering above the center of the sarcophagus was the tablet. It seemed to float, suspended in mid-air, emanating a subtle light that filled the chamber with a mystical aura. Plato's breath caught in his throat as he reached out to touch it, but to his astonishment, his hands passed right through the tablet as if it were made of air.

Confusion and frustration welled up within him. He had come so far, endured so much, and now, when he was finally within reach of his goal, it seemed insubstantial, untouchable. He examined the tablet from different angles, trying to find a way to interact with it, but nothing worked. The tablet remained ethereal, just out of his grasp.

He sat on the edge of the sarcophagus, trying to calm his racing mind. On the edge of the sarcophagus, he noticed a tiny carved inscription; the Greek symbols for Alpha and Omega. "Strange," he thought to himself. The carvings were so precise, and granite, such a

hard material, it seemed inconceivable that they had been crafted by human hands. He recalled the teachings and wisdom he had absorbed over the years, both in Athens and in Egypt. He remembered the high priest's words about the tablet being more than a mere object, a living entity connected to the past, present, and future. Plato closed his eyes, taking a deep breath, and focused on the light within himself.

The room around him seemed to fade, and he felt a deep connection with the energy of the pyramid. The vibrations he sensed were not just physical but spiritual, resonating with his very soul. He realized that in order to touch the tablet, he needed to align himself with these vibrations, to become one with the living pyramid both in the physical and the ethereal realms.

Plato lay down inside the sarcophagus, feeling the cold granite against his back. He closed his eyes and entered a meditative state, focusing on his breathing and the pulsating energy around him. Slowly, he felt himself syncing with the vibrations, his body and mind attuning to the ancient rhythms of the pyramid.

As he meditated, he felt a subtle shift in the air, a sense of alignment. He opened his eyes and saw the tablet still floating above him, but this time it seemed more solid, more real. Tentatively, he reached out again, and to his amazement, his fingers brushed against its smooth surface. The tablet was now tangible, responding to his touch as if recognizing his attunement.

Plato's heart swelled with a mix of awe and determination. He knew he was on the right path, but there was still much to uncover. The journey was far from over, and the tablet held secrets that he needed to unlock. With this newfound connection, he felt a surge of confidence.

He closed his eyes once more, letting the vibrations guide him, preparing himself for the trials that would come with deciphering the mysterious tablet. The first step had been taken, but the path to true understanding was just beginning. His fingers brushed against the

smooth surface of the tablet once again, and a shiver ran down his spine. The connection was real, tangible. As he traced the edges of the tablet, faint images began to flicker across its surface, like shadows dancing in the light. He saw glimpses of the visions that had haunted him for so long—the sinking city, the towering temples, the cries for help.

Closing his eyes, Plato allowed himself to be immersed in the visions. He saw the city again, vast and magnificent, its grand structures reaching towards the heavens. The images were clearer now, more vivid, as if he were standing in the midst of the ancient metropolis. He saw people moving about, their faces a mix of fear and determination. It was as if the tablet was showing him fragments of a story that had yet to be fully revealed.

Plato's mind raced as he tried to piece together the meaning of these visions. He remembered the tales his uncle Critaeus had told him, the stories of Atlantis and the great flood that had consumed it. The images on the tablet seemed to resonate with those ancient tales, but there was something more, something deeper. It was as if the tablet was guiding him, urging him to uncover a hidden truth.

He focused on the symbols and images that appeared on the tablet, trying to decipher their meaning. The more he concentrated, the more the images seemed to align with his recurring dreams. He saw the temple from his nightmares, its walls collapsing as the waves crashed against them. He saw the people, their faces etched with despair, reaching out for help.

Plato's heart pounded as he realized that these visions were not just random images; they were connected to his own journey, his own quest for knowledge. The tablet was showing him a path, a way to understand the mysteries of the past and the secrets of the pyramid. But how could he read it? How could he unlock its secrets?

He remembered the high priest's words about the tablet being a living entity, connected to the past, present, and future. He knew that

the key to understanding it lay not just in the physical realm but in the spiritual one as well. He needed to find a way to bridge the gap between the two, to connect with the tablet on a deeper level.

Plato took a deep breath and focused on his inner light, letting the energy of the pyramid flow through him. He could feel the vibrations resonating with his very soul, guiding him towards the answers he sought. The tablet's surface seemed to shimmer with a faint glow, its symbols becoming clearer.

He tried different methods to decipher the tablet, pressing his fingers against its surface, feeling the subtle vibrations. The symbols were unfamiliar, but he recalled the ancient scrolls he had studied. They mentioned the need to 'read' the tablet by engaging all the senses, suggesting that the tablet's true message was hidden beyond mere sight. He sensed that the tablet was trying to communicate with him, but the message remained elusive. He needed something more, a way to unlock its full potential. He pondered the scrolls' teachings, realizing that a key element was still missing, one that would harmonize with the tablet's vibrations and reveal its secrets.

As he pondered this, a thought struck him. Water. He remembered reading about the ancient Egyptian belief in the power of water to reveal hidden truths. Could it be that the tablet required water to be fully read? It seemed unlikely, but in this chamber filled with ancient magic and mysteries, anything was possible.

Plato's eyes scanned the room, searching for any sign of water. There was none to be found. Frustration gnawed at him, but he refused to give up. He knew he was close, so close to uncovering the tablet's secrets. He just needed to find the missing piece, the key to unlocking its full potential.

He continued to meditate, focusing on the vibrations and the energy around him. He visualized the tablet, imagining it covered in water, the symbols becoming clear and readable. He felt a surge of energy, a connection that went beyond the physical. He knew that the answer lay within him, within his ability to connect with the pyramid's ancient power.

Plato's determination grew stronger. He would not leave this chamber without unlocking the tablet's secrets. The journey had been long and arduous, but he knew that the final revelation was within his grasp. He closed his eyes, letting the visions guide him, preparing himself for the next step in his quest.

His frustration mounted as he continued to search the chamber for water. Every corner was explored, every surface scrutinized, but the room remained stubbornly dry. The thought of being so close to understanding the tablet yet being held back by such a simple element gnawed at him. He knew he needed to think differently, to find another way to connect with the tablet's ancient wisdom.

He returned to the sarcophagus, the place where he had first felt the powerful alignment with the pyramid's energy. Lying down inside it once more, he closed his eyes and entered a deep meditative state. The cold granite beneath him was a stark contrast to the warmth he felt emanating from within. The vibrations of the pyramid resonated through his body, syncing with his breath and heartbeat.

In this meditative state, the visions returned. He saw flashes of his recurring dream, the city submerged in water, the temple collapsing. The images were clearer now, more intense, as if urging him to understand their significance. He focused on the sensations, the feelings of the dream, and suddenly, a whisper echoed in his mind: "Merkaba."

The word sent a shiver down his spine. That word, again. He remembered it from the dark corridor. It was also a term he had encountered in his studies, related to the Egyptian concepts of ka and ba. He remembered that the ka was the life force, the spiritual double, while the ba represented the personality and individuality. Somehow he must merge these two together, he thought. Could this be the key?

Plato concentrated on balancing his ka and ba, aligning his soul and spirit. He closed his eyes and focused on his breathing. As his eyes closed, he felt as if he were inside his head, looking at the back of his eyelids. It was the strangest and most wonderful sensation.

He returned his thoughts to his breathing, in through his nose, in time with his internal out-breath. After some time, lights appeared again, as if dancing in step with his breathing. He watched as the lights guided him down his spine, all the way to his tailbone, where his thoughts settled for a bit. Eventually, a great light swelled within him.

Instantly, he was turned and could see long path straight up his spine, all the way to the top of his head. It was a beautiful ladder of the most magnificent colors he had ever seen. He began to travel up his spine, passing through each of these colors one by one. First, red, then orange, then yellow, each filled with its own set of emotions and waves of light that reverberated through him as he passed.

As he passed through the yellow, he came to a beautiful green light, powerful and filled with the most loving sensation he had ever felt. It was as if he were passing through his heart and the very essence of love itself. Continuing up his spine, he encountered a wonderful shade of light blue. The light consumed his entire being, and as he passed through it, he heard the most amazing music, as if sung by a heavenly choir of angels.

From there, he continued upward to the top of his spine, where he noticed the pulsing light of a dark blue. The pulse was hypnotic, situated in what he could only determine was the center of his head. It seemed to pulse in time with the beating of not only his heart but also the breath of the pyramid and the earth itself. It was enchanting.

As he passed through this temple of blue light, tears of pure joy ran down his face. His body shook with the shared energy of the experience, giving way to an all-encompassing purple light at the crown of his head. All the colors he had just passed through seemed to flash in unison, blending together in a symphony of love and light.

The lights lowered him and turned his attention to the backs of his eyes again. Instinctively, he opened them. As he did, he felt a shift within the chamber. The energy around him intensified, the vibrations growing stronger. He focused on the light within himself, and the vision of the tablet became clearer. He could almost see it, almost touch it, but it remained just out of reach.

He took a deep breath, centering himself. In his mind's eye, he visualized the water, the element that had eluded him. He saw it flowing over the tablet, revealing its inscriptions. The thought seemed to align with the ancient wisdom he had studied. Water had the power to reveal hidden truths, to cleanse and purify.

Suddenly, the answer came to him. The sarcophagus itself was the key. It was not just a place of rest but a conduit for the pyramid's energy. He needed to use it to access another dimension, a place where he could find the water he needed. Plato focused his mind, entering a state of deep meditation, and felt himself being drawn into a different realm.

In this altered state, he saw the chamber in a new light. The walls seemed to shimmer, and he could sense the presence of water. He visualized it, felt it, and with a surge of determination, he reached out. To his amazement, he felt the cool touch of water in his hands. He brought it back with him, breaking the meditative state and returning to the physical realm.

Plato opened his eyes and saw the water in his hands, shimmering with an otherworldly glow. He quickly poured it over the tablet, and the surface began to ripple and vibrate. The inscriptions became visible, ancient symbols glowing softly under his touch. He ran his fingers over them, feeling the vibrations and starting to decipher the tablet's message.

A sense of awe and wonder filled him as he realized he was unlocking the secrets of the ancient wisdom. The connection was profound, and he felt a surge of energy flowing through him. The

journey had been arduous, but he was on the brink of a great revelation.

As he continued to read the tablet, the room around him seemed to shift. The vibrations grew stronger, and the air hummed with energy. Plato knew he was on the right path, but the challenges were far from over. The tablet held secrets that would test him to his very core. With renewed determination, he focused his thoughts on the tablet, ready to unlock its full potential. The ancient wisdom was within his grasp, and he was determined to uncover its secrets, no matter the cost.

His heart raced with excitement and fear as the inscriptions on the tablet began to reveal themselves under the shimmering water. He traced his fingers over the ancient symbols, feeling the vibrations resonate through his entire being. The symbols were intricate, telling a story that seemed to connect directly with his dreams and visions. Yet, he knew that there was still more to uncover.

He lay back in the sarcophagus, allowing the cool granite to ground him once more. Closing his eyes, he focused on the inner light and the vibrations of the pyramid. The whispers of "Merkaba" and the concepts of ka and ba filled his mind. He needed to align himself perfectly with the energies of the pyramid to fully understand the tablet.

As he meditated, the chamber seemed to shift around him. The air grew thick with energy, and the visions became more intense. He saw flashes of his recurring dream—the sinking city, the cries for help, and now, the tablet itself glowing with an ethereal light. The scenes played out in vivid detail, as if urging him to understand the deeper meaning.

He felt a powerful pull, drawing him deeper into his meditation. The energy of the pyramid enveloped him, and he sensed that he was on the brink of a great revelation. The sarcophagus was more than a resting place; it was a gateway, a conduit to another dimension. Plato focused on the vibrations, letting them guide him.

In this heightened state, he became aware of another presence. It was the same voice that had whispered "Merkaba," now guiding him through the process. He felt the alignment of his ka and ba, the union of his soul and spirit. The energy flowed through him, and he realized that he was accessing a different plane of existence.

He visualized the water again, feeling its cool touch. This time, he reached deeper into the vision, summoning the water from his mind into reality. As he did, the room around him seemed to shimmer and transform. He opened his eyes and saw the water materialize in his hands, glowing with an otherworldly light. He carefully poured it over the tablet, watching as the inscriptions became clearer.

The tablet began to vibrate more intensely, and Plato could feel its power resonating through him. He ran his fingers over the symbols, deciphering their meaning. The story they told was ancient, yet it felt intimately connected to his own journey. He saw images of Atlantis, the great flood, and the people striving to save their city.

As he read, he felt a profound connection with the past. The tablet was not just a record of history but a living entity, holding the wisdom of ages. He realized that the trials he had faced were preparing him for this moment, to unlock the secrets that had been hidden for millennia.

The room around him seemed to vibrate with the energy of the tablet. He knew he was close to uncovering its full potential, but there was still one final step. He needed to bring the physical and ethereal together, to merge his reality with the ancient wisdom contained within the tablet.

Plato took a deep breath and focused on the light within. He felt the alignment of his ka and ba, the balance of his soul and spirit. The energy flowed through him, connecting him with the pyramid and the tablet. He ran his fingers over the inscriptions, feeling the vibrations guide him.

Suddenly, the room around him shifted again. The walls seemed to close in, and the air grew heavy with energy. He felt a sense of urgency, knowing that he was on the brink of a great revelation. The tablet vibrated more intensely, and the symbols glowed brighter.

He knew that he needed to stay focused, to trust in the process. He was on the verge of unlocking the secrets of the ancient wisdom. The energy flowed through him, guiding him towards the final revelation. His fingers trembled as he traced the glowing symbols on the tablet, feeling the vibrations pulse through his entire being. The air around him hummed with energy, and the room seemed to shrink and expand in response to the tablet's power. He knew he was close to unlocking its full potential, but there was one final piece of the puzzle he had yet to understand.

He lay back in the sarcophagus, closing his eyes to focus on the inner light. The word "Merkaba" echoed in his mind, a reminder of the union of ka and ba, the spiritual and the physical. He understood now that to read the tablet, he needed to transcend his physical limitations and align completely with the energy of the pyramid.

In his meditative state, he saw the familiar visions of Atlantis, the sinking city, and the great flood. But now, there was something new—a vision of himself standing before the tablet, his body glowing with an inner light. He saw the tablet vibrating, the inscriptions clear and readable. It was a sign, a guide to what he needed to do.

The voice whispered again, guiding him. It was the woman's voice. "Plato. Align with the vibrations. Become one with the tablet." He felt a surge of determination and opened his eyes, the room still shrouded in darkness. He knew what he needed to do.

Plato sat up and focused on the tablet, feeling its energy resonate with his own. He placed his hands on the surface, feeling the vibrations grow stronger. The symbols began to shift and change, revealing more of their secrets. He closed his eyes and visualized the water, feeling it flow through him, cleansing and purifying his mind.

Suddenly, he felt a pull, a shift in the energy around him. The room seemed to tilt, and he realized that the key to unlocking the tablet was not just in the symbols, but in the very fabric of the pyramid itself. He needed to align with the vibrations, to merge his consciousness with the ancient wisdom.

He took a deep breath and let go of his fears, allowing himself to fully connect with the tablet. The vibrations grew stronger, and he felt himself being drawn into a different realm. The walls of the chamber seemed to fade away, replaced by a shimmering void of light and energy.

Plato's mind raced as he tried to comprehend what was happening. He felt himself floating, weightless, surrounded by the pulsating energy of the pyramid. He saw the tablet before him, its symbols glowing with an intense light. He reached out and touched it, feeling a surge of power flow through him.

The symbols began to rearrange themselves, forming new patterns and images. Plato realized that he was seeing not just the past, but the present and future as well, all at the same time. The tablet was showing him the path, guiding him towards his enlightenment.

He felt a sudden jolt, as if the very fabric of reality was shifting. The room around him reappeared, but it was different now. The walls seemed to shimmer with an ethereal light, and the tablet glowed with a radiant energy. Plato knew he had unlocked its secrets, but there was still one final step.

The voice whispered again, this time more urgent. "Use the water. Pour it over the tablet." Plato quickly poured the remaining water over the tablet, watching as the symbols glowed brighter. He ran his fingers over the surface, feeling the vibrations guide him.

As he read the inscriptions, the room around him began to change. The air grew thick with energy, and he felt himself being drawn into the tablet. The symbols seemed to come alive, wrapping around him and pulling him into their depths.

Plato felt a surge of fear and excitement as he was whisked away into another world. The chamber disappeared, replaced by a vibrant, detailed landscape. He saw towering temples, lush gardens, and crystal-clear waters. It was Atlantis, more real and vivid than he had ever imagined.

He looked down and realized he was in the body of a young boy, experiencing the world through his eyes. He could feel the boy's emotions and senses, as if they were his own. The connection was profound, and he knew that he was living the visions he had seen for so long.

The world around him was vibrant and alive, filled with the sounds and sights of a thriving civilization. Plato felt a sense of awe and wonder, knowing that he was witnessing the glory of Atlantis firsthand. But he also felt a sense of urgency, knowing that he needed to uncover the secrets of the tablet to find his way back.

Chapter 18

Echoes of the Heart

Plato opened his eyes to a world filled with colors and sounds he had never experienced before. He found himself in the heart of of a world, surrounded by grandiose architecture, shimmering waters, and lush gardens that stretched as far as the eye could see. The city was a marvel of advanced technology and natural beauty, an embodiment of perfection and harmony. Everywhere he looked, there were signs of a society that had mastered both science and spirituality.

In the heart of this grand city, Plato's attention was drawn to the fact he was inside someone else's body and not his. He was connected to a young boy with a presence that seemed to command attention. This was Thoth, and Plato could feel his thoughts and emotions as if they were his own. Thoth was curious, intelligent, and burdened by a sense of duty that seemed too heavy for someone so young.

Thoth was not just any boy; he was the son of Thotme, the high priest of Atlantis. The priests of Atlantis were forbidden to venture into the outer rings, their lives dedicated to the spiritual and sacred duties of the inner ring, known as the Spirit Ring. However, Thoth's curiosity about the world beyond the priestly ring grew stronger with each passing day. The strict boundaries of his life often felt suffocating, and he yearned to see the world outside, to understand the lives of those beyond the temple walls.

In Atlantis, society was organized into concentric rings, each serving a distinct purpose. The innermost ring, the Spirit Ring, was where Thoth resided, filled with temples and places of worship. Here, the priests maintained the sacred knowledge and rituals that sustained the spiritual heart of Atlantis. Beyond the Spirit Ring lay the ring of Free Citizens, a bustling area where artisans, merchants, and scholars thrived. This ring was a hub of creativity and commerce, the lifeblood of Atlantis's economy.

Encircling the Free Citizens was the ring dedicated to Science and Learning. Here, the greatest minds of Atlantis delved into the mysteries of the universe, conducting experiments and crafting innovations that pushed the boundaries of knowledge. The air was thick with the scent of alchemical brews and the hum of ancient machines, a testament to the relentless pursuit of wisdom and understanding.

The outermost ring was the Military Ring, a fortress of strength and vigilance. Soldiers trained rigorously, their discipline and prowess ensuring the protection of Atlantis from any external threats. The tensions between Atlantis and the outside world had grown, with neighboring civilizations, such as Athens, becoming increasingly hostile and covetous of Atlantis's power and knowledge.

In Atlantis, balance and harmony were the cornerstones of their advanced society. To ensure that every citizen understood the interconnectedness of their world, it was mandated that each individual spend two years living and working in each of the four rings before settling into their lifelong role. This journey through the rings began in the Spirit Ring, where they learned the sacred duties and spiritual practices that sustained the heart of Atlantis. Next, they moved to the ring of Free Citizens, immersing themselves in the vibrant life of artisans, merchants, and scholars. Their journey continued to the Science and Learning ring, where they engaged in the relentless pursuit of knowledge and innovation. Finally, they spent time in the

Military Ring, where they trained in discipline and vigilance, preparing to defend their civilization from external threats. This holistic education ensured that every Atlantean appreciated the diverse functions and values of their society, fostering a profound sense of unity and shared purpose.

However, Thoth, as the son of the high priest Thotme, was exempt from this rite of passage. He was kept within the confines of the Spirit Ring to remain pure and untainted spiritually from the world beyond. This isolation, intended to preserve his spiritual sanctity, often left him feeling rebellious and curious about the lives led in the other rings. The boundaries placed around him only fueled his desire to explore and understand the world outside the temple walls, intensifying his sense of confinement and sparking his adventurous spirit.

One night, unable to contain his yearning for exploration, Thoth sneaked out of the temple. With the moonlight guiding his path, he ventured into the outer rings of Atlantis. The thrill of discovery and the forbidden nature of his escapade made his heart race with excitement. As he moved through the rings, he marveled at the vibrant life of the Free Citizens, the innovative marvels in the Science Ring, and the disciplined strength of the Military Ring.

His journey through the rings not only fed his curiosity but also deepened his understanding of Atlantis's society. Thoth saw the interconnectedness of their world, how each ring played a crucial role in the harmony and balance of their civilization. Yet, he also sensed the underlying tensions and the potential for conflict, especially with the growing influence of the military and the political ambition to dominate the outside world.

The ancient ones had left the island two centuries ago, and Thoth believed that it was time for the segregated rings of Atlantean society to blend, fostering unity and shared wisdom. He argued passionately with his father about the old ways, but Thotme and the Dweller

insisted that Thoth was destined to uphold the spiritual future of Atlantis and the planet.

As he wandered deeper into the outer rings, Thoth knew that his actions carried significant risks, but his desire to understand and possibly change the fate of Atlantis was stronger than his fear. The knowledge he gained and the experiences he lived through this journey would shape him into the leader he was destined to become, a beacon of hope in the face of impending doom. As Thoth ventured deeper into the outer rings, he made it to the most outer ring, where the military lived. There he spotted a girl, bathed in the soft glow of the moonlight. Her laughter was a melody that drew him closer, her presence a beacon in the night. She was beautiful, with a grace that seemed to belong to another world. Plato felt Thoth's heart skip a beat, a mixture of awe and nervousness flooding his senses.

The girl noticed Thoth and smiled, her eyes twinkling with curiosity and mischief. "You shouldn't be here," she said, her voice light and teasing. "You're from the inner ring, aren't you?"

Thoth nodded, unable to find his voice. The girl extended her hand. "I'm Nerissa," she said. "And you are?"

"Thoth," he replied, finally finding his words. "I've never been out here before."

Nerissa laughed softly. "Well, Thoth, it seems we both enjoy breaking the rules," she said. "Come on, let me show you around."

As they walked together, Thoth felt a sense of freedom he had never known before. Nerissa showed him the hidden corners of the outer rings, places where the rules seemed to fade away, and life was vibrant and unrestrained. They talked about their lives, their dreams, and their fears, forming a bond that grew stronger with each passing night.

Plato could feel the deepening connection between Thoth and Nerissa, the mix of joy and fear that came with their forbidden meetings. He understood the significance of these moments, the way they shaped Thoth's view of the world and his place in it. The love that blossomed between them was a powerful force, one that would challenge the boundaries of their society and set the stage for the events to come.

Thoth and Nerissa stood under the stars, their hands entwined as they gazed out over the city of Atlantis. The future was uncertain, but in that moment, they were together, defying the rules and following their hearts.

The weeks passed, and Thoth and Nerissa's bond grew stronger. They met in secret, exploring the hidden corners of Atlantis under the cloak of night. Thoth shared stories of the temple and its secrets, while Nerissa spoke of the challenges and responsibilities of her life in the military ring. Their love blossomed, despite the societal boundaries that separated them.

One night, Thoth led Nerissa to a secluded garden within the central ring. The air was fragrant with the scent of blooming flowers, and the soft glow of bioluminescent plants cast an otherworldly light. Thoth had discovered this garden during his solitary explorations and thought it the perfect place to share something special with Nerissa.

"There's something I want to show you," Thoth whispered, taking Nerissa's hand. He led her to a small, concealed alcove where a delicate fountain bubbled with crystalline water. "This is a place where I come to think and find peace."

Nerissa smiled, touched by Thoth's willingness to share his sanctuary with her. "It's beautiful," she said, her eyes shining with affection.

Thoth reached into his robe and pulled out a small, intricately carved box. "I want you to have this," he said, opening the box to reveal a pendant shaped like the symbol of the temple. "It's a symbol of our bond, something to remind you of me when we're apart."

Nerissa took the pendant, her fingers brushing against Thoth's. "Thank you, Thoth. I'll cherish it always," she replied, her voice filled with emotion.

Thoth then took her by the hand and led her deeper into the temple, through a series of hidden passages that few knew existed. "There's something else I want to show you," he said, his voice low and filled with a sense of urgency. "It's a place that's forbidden for almost everyone, but I trust you, Nerissa. You must swear to never reveal what I am about to show you."

Nerissa looked into Thoth's eyes, her expression serious and filled with love. "I swear, Thoth. Your secret is safe with me. I will never reveal it to anyone."

They descended into the depths of the temple, the air growing cooler and more charged with energy. At the heart of the temple, they reached a chamber that seemed to hum with life. In the center of the room stood a pedestal, and upon it rested the ethereal emerald tablet, glowing with a mystical light.

"This is the Emerald Tablet," Thoth said softly, his eyes reflecting the tablet's light. "It's the heart of Atlantis, resonating with the energy of the earth and the cosmos. It's forbidden for anyone to see it, but I wanted to share this with you."

Nerissa gazed at the tablet in awe, feeling its energy pulse through her. "It's incredible," she whispered. "I can feel its power."

Thoth nodded, taking her hands in his. "The tablet is the essence of Atlantis, connecting all consciousness on this planet and beyond. Its love for us and the earth is endless and unwavering. Just as my love for you, Nerissa, is eternal and unbreakable."

They shared a tender, passionate kiss, the light of the tablet bathing them in a warm, radiant glow. The chamber seemed to come alive with their love, the energy of the tablet amplifying their connection. Thoth led her to a soft, moss-covered area beneath the

tablet, where they made love, their hearts and souls intertwined in a moment of pure bliss and unity.

Their nights together were filled with whispers and laughter, dreams and plans for a future where they could be together without fear. But as the summer waned, reality began to intrude on their idyllic world. Thoth's duties at the temple grew more demanding, and Nerissa's training intensified as tensions between Atlantis and the outside world increased.

One evening, as they sat by the fountain in the garden, Nerissa spoke of her fears. "Thoth, I worry about what will happen to us. My father is growing more insistent that I focus on my duties. The outside world beyond Atlantis is becoming more dangerous, and he wants me to be ready."

Thoth nodded, understanding her concerns. "I know, Nerissa. My father is also pressuring me to fully commit to following in his steps in the priesthood. But I don't want to lose you. I can't imagine a future without you in it."

Nerissa leaned her head against Thoth's shoulder. "Neither can I. But we have to be realistic. Our love is forbidden, and if we're discovered, it could mean severe consequences for both of us."

The weight of their situation pressed down on them, and they sat in silence, contemplating the choices before them. Eventually, they both knew what had to be done. Their love, as deep and true as it was, could not survive the rigid structures of their society.

As the summer came to an end, they shared one final, bittersweet night together in the garden. "Promise me that you'll always remember this," Nerissa said, tears glistening in her eyes. "No matter what happens, this will always be our special place."

Thoth took her hands in his, his heart aching with the knowledge of their impending separation. "I promise, Nerissa. I will never forget. You will always be in my heart."

With a heavy heart, they said their goodbyes, knowing that their paths would now diverge. Thoth would dedicate himself to the priesthood, and Nerissa would fulfill her duties in the military ring. Their love, though hidden and forbidden, would remain a cherished memory, a testament to the brief moment in time when they dared to defy the rules and follow their hearts.

Years had passed since Thoth and Nerissa had parted ways, each dedicated to their respective duties within the rings of Atlantis. Thoth had become a respected priest, revered for his wisdom and dedication, while Nerissa's place within the military ring grew more significant. Despite their separation, the love they shared remained a secret, a bittersweet memory etched into their hearts.

But fate had other plans.

One evening, as Thoth was deep in meditation within the sacred temple, a sudden commotion disrupted the calm. The usually tranquil atmosphere was replaced by the sounds of hurried footsteps and urgent whispers. Thoth opened his eyes and quickly made his way to the main chamber, where he found a group of priests gathered, their faces pale with fear.

"The military is here," one of them whispered. "They've forced their way into the temple."

Thoth's heart raced. He knew the gravity of the situation. The sacred temple was a place of peace and knowledge, protected from the power struggles of the outer rings. For the military to breach its sanctity meant that something dire was afoot.

As he approached the main entrance, he saw a group of soldiers, their expressions determined and unyielding. Leading them was General Kharon, Nerissa's uncle, whose eyes gleamed with ambition and greed.

"What is the meaning of this intrusion?" Thoth demanded, his voice steady despite the turmoil within him.

General Kharon stepped forward, his gaze cold and calculating. "We have come for the tablet," he declared. "The time has come to use its power to secure Atlantis' dominance over the world."

Thoth felt a surge of anger and fear. "The tablet is not here, but somehow I feel as if you know this already. And the tablet is not a weapon to be wielded in war," he argued. "It is a sacred artifact, meant for wisdom and enlightenment."

Kharon sneered. "Your naivety will be the downfall of Atlantis," he spat. "The outside nations, once grateful for our guidance and benevolence, now seek their independence, disrupting the harmony we've maintained. The outside world is at our doorstep, arrogantly believing they can wage war against Atlantis. The former ways of maintaining peace no longer suffice. Now, brute force is necessary. We must apply pressure, dominate, and teach them to conform—or else. Now, step aside, or we will take this temple and everything in it by force."

Thoth's mind raced. For now, the tablet was safe, hidden deep in the secret inner halls of the temple, but with the full force of the military in search, it wouldn't be safe for long. He couldn't allow the general to seize the tablet. It would mean the end of Atlantis as they knew it. As he stood his ground, he noticed Nerissa among the soldiers, her eyes wide with fear and something that looked like guilt.

Their eyes met, and Thoth's heart wavered. Had she betrayed him? The thought clawed at his mind. He couldn't be sure. She might have been coerced, or worse, she might have revealed the secrets of the temple willingly. His heart ached with the uncertainty, but there was no time for personal grievances. He had to act.

"Very well," Thoth said, his voice calm but firm. "But know this: the tablet's power is not something to be taken lightly. It will test you in ways you cannot imagine."

Kharon laughed, a harsh, grating sound. "We shall see," he said, motioning for his men to proceed.

As the soldiers advanced, Thoth retreated into the temple's inner sanctum, his mind working furiously to find a way to protect the tablet. He knew the temple's secrets better than anyone, and he intended to use that knowledge to his advantage.

He led the soldiers deeper into the temple, through winding corridors and hidden passages, hoping to buy himself some time. Finally, they reached the chamber where the tablet was kept, its presence palpable even through the heavy stone walls.

Kharon stepped forward, his eyes gleaming with triumph. "Open it," he commanded.

Thoth hesitated, then approached the chamber's entrance. He placed his hands on the stone door, feeling its ancient energy thrumming beneath his fingertips. He uttered a silent prayer, hoping that the temple's guardians would protect them.

The door slowly creaked open, revealing the tablet's chamber. The soldiers surged forward, but Thoth held up his hand, stopping them in their tracks.

"The tablet can only be read by those who are worthy," he said. "It will test your very soul. Are you prepared for that?"

Kharon sneered. "We are prepared for anything," he said, pushing past Thoth.

As the soldiers entered the chamber, Thoth took a deep breath, steeling himself for what was to come. He knew that the tablet would challenge them in ways they couldn't comprehend, and he hoped that it would be enough to protect Atlantis from the general's ambitions.

But as the soldiers approached the tablet, a strange energy filled the room. The tablet began to glow, its inscriptions coming to life with an otherworldly light. The soldiers hesitated, their bravado faltering in the face of the tablet's power.

Thoth watched, his heart pounding. He knew that this was just the beginning. The true test was yet to come, and he prayed that they would all survive it.

The air in the chamber grew thick with anticipation as the soldiers hesitated, their confidence wavering in the face of the glowing tablet. Thoth stood back, watching the scene unfold with a mix of dread and hope. He knew the tablet's power was beyond their comprehension, and he silently prayed it would protect itself from their greed.

General Kharon stepped forward, his eyes narrowed with determination. "Do not falter," he barked at his men. "This is just a trick. Take the tablet!"

The soldiers exchanged uneasy glances but obeyed their leader. They advanced towards the tablet, their steps slow and cautious. As they drew closer, the glow intensified, casting eerie shadows on the walls of the chamber. The inscriptions seemed to dance across its surface, alive with ancient energy.

Just as one of the soldiers reached out to touch the tablet, a blinding flash of light erupted from its center. The room was filled with a deafening hum, and the soldiers were thrown back, hitting the walls with bone-jarring force. They groaned in pain, their eyes wide with fear and confusion.

Thoth's heart pounded in his chest as he watched the scene unfold. The tablet's power was beyond anything he had ever witnessed. He knew he had to act quickly to protect it from falling into the wrong hands.

General Kharon struggled to his feet, his face twisted with rage. "What sorcery is this?" he demanded, glaring at Thoth.

"The tablet is not meant for those who seek power for their own gain," Thoth replied, his voice steady. "It is a sacred artifact, and it will defend itself against those who would misuse it."

Kharon eyes blazed with fury. "I will not be thwarted by a mere priest," he snarled. He drew his sword and advanced towards Thoth, his intent clear.

Thoth stood his ground, his mind racing. He had to protect the tablet at all costs, even if it meant sacrificing himself. As Kharon approached, Thoth raised his hands in a gesture of supplication.

"Stop!" he cried. "You do not understand what you are dealing with. The tablet's power is beyond your control. It will destroy you if you try to take it by force."

But Kharon was beyond reason. He lunged at Thoth, his sword aimed at the priest's heart. Thoth closed his eyes, bracing for the impact.

Just as the blade was about to strike, a figure appeared between them. Nerissa, her eyes filled with determination, stood protectively in front of Thoth.

"Uncle, please!" she pleaded. "This is not the way. The tablet's power is not meant for war. It is meant for wisdom and enlightenment. You must listen to reason."

Kharon hesitated, his sword still raised. "Nerissa, step aside," he ordered. "This is not your concern."

"It is my concern," she insisted. "I cannot let you destroy everything we hold dear. Think of Atlantis. Think of the consequences."

For a moment, it seemed as though Kharon might relent. But then his face hardened, and he shoved Nerissa aside. "You have always been too soft," he spat. "This *is* for the good of Atlantis."

As he moved to strike Thoth once more, the tablet's glow intensified again. This time, the light enveloped the entire chamber, blinding everyone within. Thoth felt a surge of energy pass through him, and he instinctively reached out towards the tablet.

In that moment, everything changed. The chamber seemed to shift and warp around him, and he was no longer standing in the temple. Instead, he found himself in a vast, otherworldly landscape, filled with swirling colors and strange, ethereal beings.

Thoth realized that the tablet had transported him to a different realm, a place where the true power of the artifact could be understood. He knew that he had to navigate this new world, to learn its secrets and protect the tablet from those who would misuse it.

As he looked around, he saw Nerissa beside him, her eyes wide with wonder and fear. "Where are we?" she whispered.

"I do not know," Thoth replied, "but we must find out. The fate of Atlantis depends on it."

Together, they began to explore the strange new world, determined to uncover the truth and protect the tablet from those who sought to wield its power for their own gain.

Thoth and Nerissa stood side by side, their eyes wide with awe and apprehension as they took in the surreal landscape around them. The air was thick with a palpable energy, and the colors that swirled around them seemed to pulse with life. The ground beneath their feet was soft and yielding, like walking on a cloud, yet it felt solid enough to support them.

"We must be in the realm of the gods," Nerissa whispered, her voice filled with a mixture of fear and reverence.

Thoth nodded, his mind racing to make sense of their new surroundings. The tablet had transported them to a place where the rules of the physical world no longer applied. Here, they were closer to the divine, and the true power of the tablet could be revealed.

As they began to walk, they noticed that the landscape seemed to shift and change around them. One moment, they were surrounded by towering crystalline structures that sparkled in the light; the next, they were walking through a dense, glowing forest where the trees seemed to hum with a deep, resonant energy.

Thoth felt a strange connection to this place, as if it were calling to him, guiding him towards something important. He glanced at Nerissa, who seemed equally entranced by their surroundings. "We must find the source of this energy," he said. "I believe it holds the key to understanding the tablet."

They continued their journey, each step taking them deeper into the heart of this otherworldly realm. The air was filled with a soft, melodic hum, like the harmonious chanting of countless ethereal beings. As they walked, they encountered beings of light and energy, who seemed to acknowledge their presence with gentle nods and serene smiles. These beings radiated a sense of wisdom and peace, their forms shimmering with a radiant glow that seemed to pulse with the very heartbeat of the universe.

In the distance, Thoth and Nerissa saw a magnificent figure, seated on a throne of pure light, surrounded by an endless multitude of luminous beings. This central figure exuded an aura of immense power and tranquility, and the beings around it sang hymns of praise, their voices merging into a celestial symphony that resonated through the entire realm. Streams of glowing mist rose like incense, carrying with them the prayers and hopes of all living beings.

The sight filled Thoth with awe and reverence. He felt a deep connection to this place, as if he were witnessing the very source of creation itself. The beings of light, like angelic guardians, moved gracefully around the throne, their faces serene and their movements filled with purpose. Thoth felt a growing sense of purpose and clarity in their presence, as if the wisdom of the ages was being imparted to him through the very fabric of this divine realm.

Ahead, they saw a grand pedestal, upon which rested a colossal, glowing emerald tablet. The tablet seemed to pulsate with an inner light, its surface covered in ancient, mystic symbols that shifted and shimmered as if alive. This was the heart of Atlantis, the sacred artifact that held the secrets of their civilization. Thoth felt an overwhelming sense of duty as he approached it, knowing that his destiny was intertwined with the fate of this tablet.

"You have been chosen," the central figure's voice echoed in Thoth's mind, reverberating with authority and compassion. "The fate of Atlantis rests in your hands. You must protect the tablet and use its power to restore balance and harmony to your world. Atlantis as you know it will be no more, but its wisdom must endure. Carry it forth and rebuild in the land of Khem."

Thoth opened his eyes, his heart pounding with the weight of the responsibility that had been placed upon him. He looked at Nerissa, who seemed to share his sense of purpose and determination.

"We must return to Atlantis," he said, his voice steady and resolute. "We have been given a great task, and we cannot fail. We must save what we can and rebuild elsewhere. God, the source of all of creation, has decreed that Atlantis is no more. Our home, as we knew it, will be lost to the depths, but its spirit and wisdom must live on. We are the stewards of this sacred knowledge, and we must carry it forward to a new dawn."

Nerissa nodded, her grip on his hand tightening. "I'm with you, Thoth. Always."

As they prepared to leave the clearing, the crystalline beings gathered around them, their serene smiles offering reassurance and support. Thoth felt a sense of calm and clarity wash over him, and he knew that they were not alone in their journey.

With the smaller tablet in hand, they began to make their way back through the shifting landscape, each step bringing them closer to their home and their destiny. The vision of the crumbling city and the desperate faces of their people fueled their determination, and they knew that they would stop at nothing to protect the wisdom and power of the tablet.

The path ahead was uncertain, and the challenges they faced were immense, but Thoth and Nerissa were ready to face whatever came their way. As they stepped back into the temple of Atlantis, they

knew that their journey was far from over, and that the true test of their courage and resolve was just beginning.

Act 3: Return

"To return is to bring back the light discovered in the darkness, to share the wisdom earned and the truths unveiled."

From realms afar, with knowledge gained,
The hero's heart by trials trained,
Returns to where the journey started,
With gifts of wisdom, strength imparted.

Chapter 19

Shadows of Betrayal

The weight of the pyramid pressed down on Plato, both physically and mentally. The darkness was absolute, and his injured leg throbbed with each step he took. His only solace was the tablet, which seemed to pulse with a faint light, guiding him through the oppressive gloom. He carefully poured water over its surface, watching as the symbols illuminated and revealed their secrets.

As the symbols glowed, Plato was drawn into another vision of Atlantis. He saw Thoth, now older and wiser, standing in a vast hall filled with Atlantean scholars and priests. The atmosphere was tense, the once harmonious society now fractured by political and spiritual turmoil. Thoth's face was a mask of determination, his mind clearly burdened by the responsibility of preserving the wisdom of his people.

Plato felt Thoth's emotions as if they were his own—fear, hope, and a deep sense of duty. The vision was vivid, every detail etched into his mind. Thoth was not alone; Nerissa stood beside him, her presence a source of strength and comfort. They were preparing for a significant challenge, one that would test their resolve and their bond.

The vision began to fade, and Plato found himself back in the dark chamber of the pyramid. He felt a renewed sense of determination. The trials he faced were not just physical; they were spiritual and emotional, mirroring the struggles of Thoth and Nerissa in Atlantis.

Plato remembered the priest's words: "There are more stages of the pyramid that you must encounter to survive." He knew he had to continue following the story and visions of Atlantis to find a way out. The tablet was his guide, its ancient wisdom the key to unlocking the secrets of the pyramid.

He took a deep breath, steeling himself for the challenges ahead. Using the light from the tablet, he examined his surroundings. The room was small and featureless, the walls smooth and unyielding. The only light came from the tablet, casting eerie shadows on the walls.

As he poured water over the tablet again, the symbols began to shift, revealing more of Thoth's story. Thoth was now leading a group of priests through a series of trials, much like the ones Plato faced. Each trial tested their knowledge, their faith, and their courage.

Plato knew he had to draw on Thoth's experiences to navigate his own trials. The first trial he faced was a maze of reflective surfaces. The reflections distorted reality, making it difficult to discern the true path. Plato remembered Thoth's teachings about reflection and illusion. He took a deep breath and focused on the tablet, using the water to reveal more of its secrets.

As the symbols glowed, Plato saw Thoth navigating a similar maze, using his knowledge and intuition to find the true path. Plato mimicked Thoth's movements, trusting in the wisdom of the ancient priest. Each step felt like an eternity, but slowly, he began to discern the correct path through the maze. The reflections that once confused him now served as guides, leading him towards the exit.

Emerging from the maze, Plato found himself in another room, this one dominated by the elements. A gust of wind nearly knocked him off his feet as he entered, and flames danced along the walls, casting flickering shadows. Pools of water dotted the floor, and the ground beneath him seemed to shift as if alive.

He remembered Thoth's teachings about balance and the elements. In Atlantis, the elements were seen as both physical forces and symbols of deeper truths. Plato knew he had to interact with each element to progress. He approached a pool of water first, using the tablet to reveal a riddle etched in the surface. Solving it required knowledge of both Atlantis' lore and Thoth's wisdom.

One by one, he faced the elements. The air brought him visions of Thoth using his mind to calm a storm. The fire required him to harness his inner strength and courage. The earth tested his resilience, grounding him and reminding him of the solidity of his purpose. Each trial left him exhausted but more determined.

Exhausted, Plato collapsed against the cool stone wall. He took the tablet and poured the last of his water onto its surface. As the symbols glowed, he was transported back to Atlantis. Thoth and Nerissa stood before him, their faces etched with determination and sorrow.

The city was in chaos. The betrayal by Nerissa's uncle had thrown Atlantis into turmoil. Thoth and Nerissa were desperately trying to hold things together, but it was clear that the situation was deteriorating rapidly. Plato could feel Thoth's pain and anger, but also his unwavering resolve to protect what remained of their world.

As the vision faded, Plato felt a renewed sense of purpose. Thoth's resolve gave him the strength to continue. He had to honor the wisdom and sacrifice of those who came before him. The chamber he was in began to shift, the walls moving to reveal a new path. The echoes of Thoth's teachings and the vision of Atlantis guided him forward. As he stepped into the next trial, the weight of his journey pressed heavily on his shoulders. He knew he was on the brink of uncovering deeper secrets within the pyramid, and he was ready to face whatever came next.

Plato's heart pounded as he realized the gravity of his situation. He took a step forward, his mind focused on the trials ahead. The echoes of Thoth's teachings and the vision of Atlantis guided him, filling him with a sense of purpose and determination. He was ready to

face whatever challenges lay ahead, determined to honor the legacy of Atlantis and the wisdom of Thoth.

As Plato stepped into the darkness, his resolve was stronger than ever. His leg throbbed with each step as he moved through the newly revealed passage. The light from the tablet cast eerie shadows on the walls, making the narrow corridor feel even more oppressive. He clutched the tablet tightly, its faint glow his only source of comfort and guidance.

As he progressed, the corridor widened into a large chamber. Plato paused, wary of what new trial awaited him. The chamber was empty except for a pedestal in the center, upon which rested a large stone bowl. He approached cautiously, noticing inscriptions on the bowl's surface. They were ancient symbols, reminiscent of those he had seen in Atlantis through his visions.

Pouring water over the tablet, Plato watched as the symbols illuminated, revealing another segment of Thoth's story. He closed his eyes and let the vision consume him, eager to draw wisdom from the past.

In the vision, Thoth stood before a council of priests. The atmosphere was tense, the weight of impending disaster hanging heavily in the air. The priests debated heatedly about the military's actions and the potential consequences of unleashing the power of the tablet. Thoth's voice was calm but firm as he argued for restraint and wisdom, urging the council to remember their duty to protect and preserve knowledge, not to wield it as a weapon.

Plato felt Thoth's frustration and determination. The vision was intense, every word and gesture etched into his mind. He saw the love for Atlantis in Thoth's eyes, the same love that drove him to protect its secrets and its people.

The vision began to fade, and Plato found himself back in the chamber. He approached the pedestal and examined the inscriptions on the bowl more closely. They were riddles, each more complex than the

last. The answers lay in the teachings of Thoth and the wisdom of Atlantis.

He took a deep breath and began to solve the riddles one by one, using the knowledge he had gained from the visions. Each correct answer seemed to resonate within the chamber, the walls vibrating with an almost musical hum. The final riddle was the most challenging, requiring him to draw on all he had learned about balance, harmony, and the unity of the elements.

As he solved the last riddle, the bowl began to fill with water, seemingly from nowhere. The water glowed with a soft, ethereal light, illuminating the chamber. Plato knew what he had to do. He poured a small amount of the water over the tablet, watching as new symbols appeared, guiding him to the next stage of his journey.

The tablet revealed another vision of Thoth, this time in a vast, dark chamber filled with intricate carvings and statues. Thoth was not alone; Nerissa was with him, her presence a beacon of hope and strength. They navigated the chamber together, solving riddles and overcoming obstacles, their bond growing stronger with each challenge.

Plato felt their emotions—their love, their fear, their determination. He knew he had to channel their strength and wisdom to overcome his own trials. The vision showed Thoth and Nerissa reaching the heart of the chamber, where they found a hidden passage leading to a place of great power and knowledge.

As the vision faded, Plato found himself back in the chamber. The pedestal had shifted, revealing a hidden passageway beneath it. He took a deep breath, his heart pounding with anticipation and fear. He entered the passageway, the light from the tablet guiding his steps. The air grew colder, and the walls seemed to close in around him. Plato's mind raced with thoughts of Thoth and Nerissa, their love and their struggles. He felt a connection to them, a bond that transcended time and space.

The passageway opened into another chamber, this one filled with an eerie, unnatural light. The walls were covered in symbols and carvings, depicting scenes of Atlantis in its glory and its downfall. Plato could feel the weight of history pressing down on him, the legacy of Atlantis and the wisdom of Thoth urging him forward.

In the center of the chamber stood another pedestal, this one adorned with a small, ornate box. Plato approached it cautiously, his heart pounding with anticipation. He opened the box, revealing a delicate crystal vial filled with a shimmering liquid. The vial seemed to pulse with energy, resonating with the vibrations of the pyramid.

He knew instinctively that this liquid was essential to his journey. He poured a small amount over the tablet, watching as the symbols glowed brighter than ever before. The tablet revealed another segment of Thoth's story, drawing Plato deeper into the vision.

Thoth and Nerissa stood on a cliff overlooking Atlantis. The city was in chaos, the military's betrayal having thrown everything into disarray. Thoth's face was etched with determination and sorrow, his heart heavy with the knowledge of what must be done to save their world.

Plato felt Thoth's pain and resolve, the weight of his duty pressing heavily on his own shoulders. The vision was intense, every detail seared into his mind. Thoth and Nerissa shared a final, lingering kiss before plunging into the heart of the chaos, determined to protect the legacy of Atlantis.

The vision faded, and Plato found himself back in the chamber. The crystal vial in his hand seemed to pulse with energy, guiding him to the next trial. He took a deep breath, his resolve stronger than ever. The path ahead was uncertain, but he was determined to see it through.

He stepped into the darkness, the light from the tablet illuminating his way. As he moved forward, the halls began to shift, the walls closing in around him. The air grew colder, and the light from the tablet seemed to dim. Plato's heart pounded with anticipation

and fear, but he pressed on, determined to honor the legacy of Atlantis and the wisdom of Thoth.

The passageway opened into a new chamber, this one filled with an intense, almost blinding light. Plato shielded his eyes, his heart pounding with anticipation. He knew he was on the brink of uncovering deeper secrets within the pyramid, and he was ready to face whatever came next.

He stepped into the newly revealed chamber, his heart pounding with a mix of anticipation and fear. The light from the tablet flickered, casting eerie shadows on the walls. The room was vast and empty, save for a large, intricately carved door at the far end. The carvings depicted scenes of ancient rituals, battles, and a mysterious figure that resembled Thoth.

He approached the door cautiously, feeling the weight of history pressing down on him. The symbols on the door seemed to come alive under the glow of the tablet, revealing a series of intricate patterns that resembled a puzzle.

As he studied the carvings, he felt a strange sensation, as if the tablet was guiding him, urging him to remember the visions he had experienced. He poured water over the tablet, watching as new symbols appeared, their meaning slowly becoming clear with each vibration. The visions of Thoth and Nerissa, their love, and their struggles filled his mind, providing the clues he needed to solve the puzzle.

Plato began to manipulate the symbols, aligning them with the knowledge he had gained from the tablet. Each correct move caused the door to vibrate slightly, a musical hum resonating through the chamber. The puzzle was complex, requiring not only intellect but also an understanding of balance and harmony.

As he worked, the vision of Thoth's final confrontation with the military grew clearer. He saw Thoth and Nerissa standing together, their hands clasped, facing a group of armed soldiers. Thoth's voice

was calm but firm as he tried to reason with the military leaders, urging them to remember the true purpose of Atlantis and the importance of preserving knowledge and wisdom.

Plato felt Thoth's frustration and determination, his love for Atlantis and his desire to protect its legacy. The vision intensified, every word and gesture etched into Plato's mind. He saw the love for Atlantis in Thoth's eyes, the same love that drove him to protect its secrets and its people.

The vision began to fade, and Plato found himself back in the chamber, the puzzle almost complete. He made the final adjustments, and the door began to glow with a soft, ethereal light. He took a deep breath and pushed it open, stepping into the next trial.

The new chamber was unlike any he had encountered before. It was filled with an otherworldly light, the walls covered in intricate carvings and symbols that seemed to pulse with energy. In the center of the room stood a large, stone pedestal, upon which rested a crystal sphere. The sphere seemed to pulse with a soft, inner light, drawing Plato closer.

He approached the pedestal cautiously, feeling a sense of awe and reverence. The sphere was smooth and cool to the touch, its surface reflecting the light from the tablet. He knew instinctively that this was another test, another step in his journey.

Plato placed the tablet on the pedestal and poured a small amount of water over it. The symbols vibrated, glowing brighter than ever before, revealing another segment of Thoth's story. He closed his eyes and let the vision consume him, eager to draw wisdom from the past.

In the vision, Thoth and Nerissa stood before the council of priests, their faces etched with determination and sorrow. The council was divided, some members arguing for the military's actions, others siding with Thoth and Nerissa. The debate was heated, the weight of impending disaster hanging heavily in the air.

Thoth's voice was calm but firm as he argued for restraint and wisdom, urging the council to remember their duty to protect and preserve knowledge, not to wield it as a weapon. His words were powerful, resonating with the core values of Atlantis.

Plato felt Thoth's frustration and determination, his love for Atlantis and his desire to protect its legacy. The vision was intense, every word and gesture etched into his mind. Thoth and Nerissa shared a final, lingering look before plunging into the heart of the chaos, determined to protect the legacy of Atlantis.

The vision began to fade, and Plato found himself back in the chamber. The crystal sphere in his hand seemed to pulse with energy, guiding him to the next trial. He took a deep breath, his resolve stronger than ever. He placed the crystal sphere back on the pedestal, watching as it began to glow with a soft, ethereal light. The walls of the chamber seemed to shift, revealing a hidden passageway beneath the pedestal. Plato took a deep breath and stepped into the passageway, the light from the tablet guiding his steps.

The air grew colder, and the walls seemed to close in around him. Plato's mind raced with thoughts of Thoth and Nerissa, their love and their struggles. He felt a connection to them, a bond that transcended time and space.

The passageway opened into another chamber, this one filled with an intense, almost blinding light. Plato shielded his eyes, his heart pounding with anticipation. He knew he was on the brink of uncovering deeper secrets within the pyramid.

Plato emerged from the passageway, stepping into a new chamber that took his breath away. This room was much different than the rest. The walls were adorned with shimmering murals depicting the history and legends of Atlantis, bathed in an ethereal light that seemed to come from nowhere and everywhere at once. In the center of the room stood a grand statue of a figure he recognized immediately—Thoth.

As Plato approached the statue, he noticed that it held a staff in one hand and an orb in the other, both emanating a soft, pulsating glow. The staff and the orb seemed to be calling to him, inviting him to discover their secrets. Plato's heart raced with a mixture of awe and anticipation. He could feel the presence of Thoth, the energy of the ancient civilization, and the weight of his own quest all converging in this moment.

He stepped closer to the statue, the light from the tablet guiding his way. The symbols on the tablet seemed to respond to the presence of the statue, glowing more brightly and revealing new patterns. Plato poured water over the tablet, watching as the symbols rearranged themselves into a new configuration. The vision began to take shape before his eyes.

In the vision, Thoth and Nerissa stood together in the heart of Atlantis, their faces etched with determination and sorrow. The city around them was in turmoil, the once-peaceful society now divided by conflict and strife. The military ring, led by Nerissa's uncle, had launched an all-out assault on the central ring, seeking to seize the power of the tablet for their own ends.

Thoth and Nerissa shared a final, lingering look before plunging into the heart of the chaos, determined to protect the legacy of Atlantis. They fought side by side, their love and loyalty to each other giving them strength. But as the battle raged on, Thoth knew that their efforts might not be enough to save their beloved city.

Plato felt Thoth's anguish and determination, his love for Nerissa and his fierce desire to protect the wisdom of Atlantis. The vision was so intense that Plato could feel the heat of the battle, hear the cries of the wounded, and taste the salt of his own sweat. He was living Thoth's memories, experiencing his struggles and his triumphs as if they were his own.

The vision began to fade, and Plato found himself back in the chamber. He looked up at the statue of Thoth, feeling a deep sense of connection and understanding. The staff and the orb in the statue's hands seemed to pulse with energy, as if waiting for him to take the next step.

Plato reached out and touched the staff, feeling a surge of power flow through him. The orb in the statue's other hand began to glow more brightly, casting a soft light over the entire chamber. The murals on the walls seemed to come alive, the scenes shifting and changing to reveal new details.

He noticed that the orb and the staff were inscribed with ancient symbols, similar to those on the tablet. He poured water over the orb, watching as the symbols glowed and rearranged themselves into a new pattern. The light from the orb grew brighter, illuminating a hidden passageway at the far end of the chamber.

Plato's heart raced with anticipation. He knew that this was the next step in his journey, the path that would lead him closer to the heart of the pyramid and the secrets it held. He took a deep breath and stepped into the passageway, the light from the orb guiding his way.

The passageway was narrow and winding, the walls closing in around him as he moved deeper into the pyramid. The air grew colder, and Plato could feel the weight of the ancient structure pressing down on him. He clutched the tablet and the orb tightly, their light his only source of comfort in the darkness.

As he walked, the vision of Thoth and Nerissa continued to play out in his mind. He saw them standing together in the midst of the battle, their love and determination shining through the chaos. He felt their pain and their hope, their fear and their courage. He knew that he was following in their footsteps, retracing their journey and uncovering the wisdom they had fought so hard to protect.

The passageway opened into a new chamber, but this one was completely dark. The only light came from the faint glow of the tablet in his hand. He could hear the sound of water dripping somewhere in the distance, the air heavy with moisture and the scent of earth.

As he moved further into the chamber, he felt a growing sense of dread. The walls were smooth and featureless, offering no clues or markings to guide him. The darkness seemed to close in around him, suffocating his thoughts and sapping his strength.

Plato closed his eyes, focusing on the light within, the inner flame that had guided him this far. He took a deep breath and entered a deep meditative state, feeling the energy of the pyramid pulsing through the stone, through the air, through his own body.

In his mind's eye, he saw the tablet glowing with a brilliant light. He reached out to it, feeling its warmth and power. The symbols began to rearrange themselves, revealing a new message, a new path forward.

He opened his eyes and looked around the chamber. The symbols on the tablet were glowing brightly, guiding him to the next step in his journey. He reached for the tablet, feeling its cool surface beneath his fingers. The symbols revealed a hidden mechanism in the floor.

Plato pressed his hand against it, feeling a click as the mechanism engaged. The floor beneath him began to shift and move, revealing a hidden passageway. He took a deep breath and stepped into the passageway, the light from the tablet guiding his way.

Suddenly, the ground beneath him gave way, and Plato was plunged into darkness once more. He tumbled down a steep, narrow shaft, the walls scraping against his skin. He landed with a hard thud on a cold, stone floor. The light from the tablet flickered and dimmed, leaving him in near-total darkness.

He realized he was in a smaller, lower chamber with no visible exits. Panic began to set in as he realized the gravity of his situation. He somehow felt less connected to the pyramid and to his inner self in here. He was trapped in the depths of the pyramid, with no way out and no idea how to proceed. The only light came from the tablet, but it

was flickering, and he struggled to center himself for the water needed to use the tablet.

Plato took a deep breath, trying to calm his racing heart. He knew that he couldn't afford to panic. He needed to find a way to escape, to continue his journey and uncover the wisdom of the pyramid. He closed his eyes, focusing on the light within, the inner flame that had guided him this far.

In the silence of the chamber, he heard the faint whisper of the inner voice, urging him to look within, to find the light in the darkness. He knew that the key to his escape lay within himself, in his ability to connect with the energy of the pyramid and the wisdom of the tablet.

Plato sat down in the center of the chamber, entering a deep meditative state. He focused on his breathing, on the rhythm of his heartbeat, on the vibrations of the pyramid around him. He could feel the energy pulsing through the stone, through the air, through his own body.

As he centered himself, he felt a shift in the energy around him. The air seemed to grow lighter, the darkness less oppressive. He reached out with his mind, connecting with the energy of the pyramid, the wisdom of the tablet, the memories of Thoth and Nerissa.

Plato opened his eyes, his heart pounding with excitement. He knew what he needed to do. He reached for the tablet, feeling its cool surface beneath his fingers. The symbols were glowing brightly, guiding him to the next step in his journey.

Just as he was about to move, the ground shifted again, and Plato felt himself falling. He landed hard, pain shooting through his leg. He looked around, realizing he was in an even smaller, darker chamber. The light from the tablet was flickering weakly, and there was no water in sight. Panic set in as he realized how dire his situation was. He was trapped, injured, and running out of options.

In the near-total darkness, the only thing he could hear was the faint, rhythmic dripping of water somewhere beyond his reach. The chamber seemed to close in on him, the air growing heavier. Plato knew he needed to find a way out, but the path was unclear, and time was running out.

Chapter 20

The Light Within

Plato awoke with a gasp, his body aching from the fall. He must have fell unconscious. The air was thick and stale, a stark contrast to the relatively fresh breeze he had felt earlier. His leg throbbed with pain, and he could barely see in the dim light provided by the tablet, now significantly dimmed. He struggled to sit up, wincing as he shifted his weight off his injured leg.

Looking around, he realized he was in a much smaller room than before. The walls were smooth and featureless, the space confined and suffocating. The only source of light was the faint glow of the tablet, which barely illuminated the darkness. There were no exits, no signs of a way out, and most troubling of all, no water. His throat was parched, his lips cracked and dry.

He attempted to recall the symbols on the tablet, but without the water to reveal them, it was futile. He felt a wave of panic rising within him. The pyramid's trials were becoming increasingly dangerous, and he was trapped in a seemingly impossible situation. He had to figure out a way to move forward, but how?

Plato closed his eyes, trying to calm his racing heart. He focused on the light within, the inner strength that had guided him this far. He had to find a solution. There had to be something he was missing, some clue or insight he hadn't yet seen. Giving up was not an option.

As he tried to steady his breathing, the pain in his leg pulsed with each heartbeat, a relentless reminder of his vulnerability. He wondered how much longer he could endure this, how much more his body and mind could take. But he had no choice but to push forward. He was determined to survive, to see this through, no matter the cost.

Slowly, he rose to his feet, using the wall for support. The darkness seemed to close in around him, and the tablet's light flickered weakly. He took a deep breath, steeling himself for the challenges ahead. He had faced trials before, both in the physical world and in his visions, and he had always found a way through. This would be no different.

With the tablet in hand, he began to feel his way around the room, searching for anything that might help him. The walls were smooth and cool to the touch, offering no clues or hints. He felt a growing sense of frustration, but he pushed it down, focusing on the task at hand.

As he moved, the tablet's glow seemed to grow slightly brighter, a small beacon of hope in the darkness. He knew that the answers he sought were within his reach, if only he could remain calm and focused. He couldn't afford to lose hope now, not when he was so close.

Step by step, he made his way around the perimeter of the room, his fingers brushing against the walls, seeking any irregularities or hidden mechanisms. The darkness was disorienting, but he kept his mind sharp, refusing to let the fear take hold.

Finally, he came to a stop in the center of the room, exhausted and disheartened. He sank to his knees, the tablet clutched tightly in his hands. He knew he couldn't give up, but he was at a loss for what to do next. He closed his eyes, seeking the inner light that had guided him before, hoping for some revelation or insight.

In the silence, he could hear the faint hum of the pyramid's vibrations, a reminder of the immense power and ancient wisdom contained within its walls. He focused on that sound, letting it soothe his troubled mind. He had come this far, and he wouldn't let despair defeat him.

Plato opened his eyes, the tablet's glow reflecting in his determined gaze. He would find a way through this trial, no matter what it took. The journey was far from over. With renewed sense of determination, he stood up once more, ready to continue his search. The answers were out there, and he would find them. He had to.

Plato's eyes fluttered open in the pitch darkness of the smaller chamber. The sense of confinement was overwhelming, and every attempt to find an exit proved futile. The walls were smooth, unyielding, and devoid of any openings. His leg throbbed with pain, a constant reminder of his precarious situation. He clutched the tablet tightly, but without water, it felt like a cold, inert slab of stone.

Frustration and fear gnawed at him. He had thought he could navigate the pyramid's trials with the wisdom he had gained, but this new room felt like a trap. The air was stifling, and he struggled to keep his panic at bay. He needed to find a way to make the tablet reveal its secrets again, but how?

Closing his eyes, Plato focused inward, trying to calm his racing thoughts. He visualized the tablet, its symbols glowing with ancient knowledge. As his breathing steadied, the familiar sensation of being pulled into the vision world enveloped him once more.

He found himself in the heart of Atlantis, back inside Thoth's body. The city was alive with activity, but there was an undercurrent of tension and danger that hadn't been there before. Thoth, now older and more burdened by his responsibilities as a priest, moved with purpose through the temple. His thoughts were troubled, and Plato could feel the weight of his concerns.

As Thoth entered a secluded chamber, he glanced around, his eyes narrowing as if sensing something. Plato felt a sudden jolt of realization—Thoth could sense him. The young priest paused, looking directly at a spot where Plato's presence seemed to be concentrated. It was a strange, ethereal connection, as if Thoth could feel Plato's spirit intertwined with his own.

"Who are you?" Thoth's voice echoed in Plato's mind, though his lips did not move. It was a silent communication, a meeting of minds across time and space.

Plato tried to respond, but he had no voice in this vision. Instead, he focused on his thoughts, willing Thoth to understand. He concentrated on projecting his presence, his intentions. Thoth's eyes widened slightly, a flicker of recognition passing through them.

"You are here to help," Thoth thought, and Plato could feel the affirmation in his own mind.

Suddenly, the vision shifted. Thoth was no longer alone in the temple chamber. Nerissa appeared, her expression troubled and fearful. "Thoth, something is happening. My uncle… he knows where the tablet is hidden."

Thoth's heart raced, and Plato could feel the surge of panic and protectiveness. The temple was supposed to be a sanctuary, a place of secrets guarded by the priests. If the military had hold of the tablet, the consequences could be catastrophic.

"We must protect it," Thoth responded, his voice firm. "We cannot let them take the tablet. It holds too much power, too much knowledge."

As Thoth and Nerissa began to devise a plan, Plato felt himself being pulled back to his own reality. The transition was abrupt, jarring him back into the suffocating darkness of the smaller chamber. The tablet in his hands glowed faintly, a reminder of the perilous connection between his trials and the vision world.

Plato realized with a start that he could influence the vision, that his presence could make a difference. But this revelation came with a heavy burden. The dangers in Thoth's world were real, and they were

intensifying. The fate of Atlantis, and perhaps his own, hung in the balance.

He needed to find a way to interact with the tablet, to use it as a guide through both the visions and his physical trials. The boundaries between reality and the vision were blurring, and he had to navigate both worlds simultaneously. As the room around him seemed to close in, Plato felt the weight of his responsibility. The trials were testing not just his intellect but his spirit and resolve.

Closing his eyes again, he focused on the symbols of the tablet, hoping to decipher a clue, a hint, anything that would guide him forward. The air grew colder, and the sensation of being watched intensified. He could almost hear the whispers of the ancient priests, feel the vibrations of the pyramid guiding him.

Plato knew he was not alone in this struggle. Thoth's story was becoming his own, their fates intertwined. As he delved deeper into the ancient knowledge, he understood that the only way to survive was to face the trials head-on, embracing the wisdom and strength he had gained.

The room remained silent and dark, but Plato's determination burned brighter than ever. He would find a way through this, for himself and for Thoth. The journey was far from over, and the stakes were higher than ever. He just had to hold on and keep pushing forward, no matter the cost.

Plato felt a shiver run down his spine as he fully re-entered the dark, stifling room. The connection with Thoth had left him shaken but also filled with a newfound determination. He knew now that his actions in the vision world could impact the physical trials he faced within the pyramid. But first, he needed to decipher the immediate challenge before him.

The room was deathly silent, the oppressive darkness pressing in on all sides. Plato strained his ears, hoping to catch any sound, any clue that might guide him. His leg throbbed painfully, reminding him

of his physical limitations. He was hurt, tired, and thirsty, with no water in sight to activate the tablet's secrets.

In the silence, he became acutely aware of his own breathing. The air was thick, almost tangible, filled with the weight of the ancient structure. It felt as if the pyramid itself was testing him, pushing him to his limits.

Plato closed his eyes, trying to summon the inner light he had relied on before. The glowing cross, a beacon of hope in the dark, seemed a distant memory. He reached out with his mind, feeling for the presence of the tablet and the energy of the pyramid. A faint whisper echoed in his thoughts, urging him forward.

With a deep breath, Plato began to crawl forward, his hands sweeping the floor for any sign of a clue. The rough stone was unyielding, but he kept moving, driven by a sense of urgency. He needed to find something, anything that would help him escape this room.

As he moved, he felt a change in the air, a subtle shift that indicated a presence. He paused, listening intently. The whispers grew louder, filling his mind with a cacophony of voices. They spoke of trials and temptations, of the need to prove his worthiness. He realized that this room was designed to test not just his physical endurance but his moral resolve.

In the midst of the whispers, one voice stood out, clear and authoritative. It was Thoth's voice, filled with a sense of purpose. "You must overcome your desires and fears," it said. "Only then can you move forward."

Plato felt a surge of determination. He knew that this trial was as much about his inner strength as it was about solving the puzzle. He closed his eyes again, focusing on the vision world. He needed to understand how to navigate both realms simultaneously.

The vision took him back to Atlantis, where Thoth stood before the temple, deep in thought. The tension in the city was palpable, with

the military presence growing stronger each day. Thoth's mind was a whirlwind of emotions—fear for his people, anger at the betrayal, and a deep sense of responsibility.

Nerissa appeared beside him, her face etched with worry. "Thoth, we must act quickly," she said, her voice trembling. "My uncle is growing more impatient. He will stop at nothing to get the tablet."

Thoth nodded, his resolve hardening. "We must protect the temple and the knowledge it holds," he replied. "We cannot let it fall into the wrong hands."

Plato felt Thoth's determination as if it were his own. He understood the gravity of the situation, the need to stand firm in the face of overwhelming odds. As the vision faded, he opened his eyes, the dark room around him taking on new meaning.

The whispers of temptation grew louder, urging him to give in to his fears, to abandon his quest. But Plato knew better. He focused on the teachings he had learned, the strength he had gained from his experiences. He could feel the tablet's energy, a guiding force that gave him hope.

With renewed purpose, he continued his search, his hands finally brushing against something smooth and cool. It was a small, ornate box, intricately carved with symbols he recognized from the tablet. He opened it carefully, revealing a vial of liquid and a note written in an ancient script.

The note spoke of the trials of the soul, of the need to remain pure and steadfast. The liquid, it explained, was a rare essence that could reveal the truth hidden within. Plato realized that this was his key to solving the next riddle. But he was torn—his parched throat and cracked lips cried out for the water. The temptation to drink it was overwhelming.

As he was about to uncork the vial, Thoth's voice echoed in his mind, clearer than ever. "Plato, remember the essence of life is within you. Do not succumb to the surface temptation."

Plato hesitated, the vial trembling in his hand. Should the vial be used on the tablet or to quench his dire thirst? The vision of Thoth appeared before him, guiding him. Thoth placed a hand over his own heart, then pointed to Plato's. The message was clear: the true power lay within him.

With a deep breath, Plato put the vial to his lips and drank. The liquid was cool and refreshing, a lifeline in the stifling darkness. As the last drop slid down his throat, he felt a surge of energy. He understood now—his blood would be the key.

He opened a small wound on his arm, letting the blood drip onto the tablet. The symbols began to glow faintly, the whispers growing louder and more coherent. He traced the symbols with his fingers, feeling the vibrations resonate through him. The connection between the tablet and the pyramid was almost tangible, a bridge between worlds.

As he deciphered the symbols, a passageway began to open, revealing a narrow tunnel leading downward. Plato hesitated for a moment, the darkness beyond seeming even more oppressive. But he knew he had no choice. He had to keep moving forward.

He entered the tunnel, the whispers guiding him deeper into the heart of the pyramid. Each step was a test of his resolve, a challenge to his spirit. These temptations had been just the beginning. The true trials lay ahead, and he had to be ready for whatever came next.

As the tunnel narrowed, Plato felt a sense of unease. The air grew colder, the darkness more impenetrable. He could sense the next challenge looming, a test that would push him to his limits. But he was determined to face it head-on, to prove his worthiness and find his way out of the pyramid.

Plato felt the chill of the tunnel's air seeping into his bones, each step growing heavier as he descended deeper into the pyramid's labyrinth. The whispers from the tablet still echoed in his mind, a mixture of ancient wisdom and dire warnings. The narrow passageway seemed to stretch endlessly, the darkness ahead a void that threatened to consume him entirely.

As he moved further, the tunnel began to widen, opening into a small chamber. The space was eerily silent, the oppressive darkness making it difficult to see anything beyond the faint glow of the tablet in his hand. His leg throbbed with pain, each movement a reminder of his fragile state. He was worse off than before, both physically and mentally drained.

Plato paused to catch his breath, the weight of the journey pressing down on him. The vision of Thoth and the trials of Atlantis lingered in his thoughts, intertwining with his own struggle. He knew that his fate and Thoth's were somehow connected, their destinies intertwined by the trials of the pyramid and the secrets of the tablet.

He closed his eyes, seeking the inner light that had guided him thus far. The whispers grew louder, more insistent, urging him to continue. He could feel the presence of Thoth, a guiding force that gave him strength. But the room seemed devoid of any exit, the walls smooth and unyielding.

In the center of the chamber, he noticed a large stone slab, its surface covered in ancient symbols. The tablet's glow illuminated the carvings, casting eerie shadows on the walls. Plato approached cautiously, his fingers tracing the intricate patterns. He could feel the energy of the pyramid pulsating through the stone, a connection to the past and the mysteries it held.

The symbols seemed to shift under his touch, the ancient language revealing fragments of wisdom and warnings. Plato's mind raced, trying to piece together the clues. He knew he needed to find a way out, but the path was not clear. The temptations had tested his resolve, but this chamber felt like a final judgment, a place where his fate would be decided.

As he studied the symbols, a sudden tremor shook the ground, the walls vibrating with a deep, resonant hum. The tablet in his hand pulsed with light, the whispers growing into a cacophony of voices. Plato staggered, struggling to keep his balance as the tremors intensified.

In the vision world, Thoth stood before the temple, the air charged with tension. The city of Atlantis was in turmoil, the military presence growing stronger each day. Thoth's heart ached with the knowledge that the secrets he had shared with Nerissa were now a threat to their very existence. He could feel Plato's presence, a guiding force that gave him hope amidst the chaos.

"Thoth," Nerissa's voice echoed, filled with fear and urgency. "We must act quickly. My uncle's forces are closing in on the temple. We need to protect the tablet."

Thoth nodded, his resolve hardening. "We will find a way," he said, determination in his eyes. "We cannot let the knowledge fall into the wrong hands."

The vision began to blur, the connection between the two worlds growing stronger. Plato felt Thoth's emotions as if they were his own, the weight of responsibility and the urgency to protect what mattered most. But the physical world demanded his attention, the tremors growing more violent.

Suddenly, the ground beneath him gave way, the stone slab cracking open to reveal a hidden passage. Plato stumbled, the tablet slipping from his grasp and clattering to the floor. The darkness swallowed him as he fell, the chamber collapsing around him. His body hit the ground hard, the impact jolting through him as he tried to regain his senses.

Pain radiated from his injured leg, the darkness pressing in from all sides. Plato's breath came in ragged gasps, the oppressive weight of

the chamber bearing down on him. He reached out blindly, searching for the tablet, but his fingers found only cold stone. The whispers had faded, leaving him in silence.

In the vision, Thoth and Nerissa raced through the temple, the sound of conflict growing louder. Plato could feel Thoth's fear and determination, the urgency to protect the sacred knowledge. But the vision began to fade, the connection slipping away as he struggled to hold on.

Darkness engulfed him, the cold of the pyramid seeping into his soul. Plato's strength waned, his consciousness slipping. The trials had pushed him to his limits, and he was left with nothing but the echoes of the past and the weight of his own failures.

As his vision darkened, he heard a faint whisper, Thoth's voice calling out to him. "Do not give up, Plato. The journey is not over."

Plato's eyes fluttered shut, the darkness consuming him. In the silence, the final whisper echoed through the chamber, a promise and a challenge. "The light within will guide you." As these words reverberated in his mind, Plato succumbed to the darkness, blacking out entirely.

Chapter 21

Temptation's Abyss

Plato awoke gasping for air, the darkness pressing in on him from all sides. His body ached terribly from the fall, and his mind struggled to remember where he was. The last thing he recalled was the cryptic whisper and the consuming blackness. As he tried to move, pain shot through his leg, forcing a groan from his lips.

He reached out, feeling for the tablet that had been his guide and his light. His fingers scraped against the cold stone floor, but there was nothing there. Panic surged through him as he crawled, searching every inch of the room. The tablet was gone, vanished without a trace. He was alone in the darkness, without the one thing that had given him hope.

Frustration and despair welled up inside him. He had come so far, endured so much, only to be left in this suffocating void. The air felt heavy, and his breaths came in ragged gasps. The thought of being trapped here forever, unable to continue the trials or help Thoth, was unbearable.

Plato slumped against the wall, his mind racing. He tried to calm himself, to think rationally, but the overwhelming sense of loss and isolation threatened to consume him. His body was weak from hunger and thirst, and the pain in his leg was a constant reminder of his vulnerability.

As he sat there, enveloped in darkness, a single thought kept repeating in his mind: "The light within will guide you." But how could he find that light when everything around him was so dark? He closed his eyes, searching for the inner strength that had brought him this far. Yet, in this moment, it seemed just out of reach, elusive and distant.

Memories of his journey flooded back, the lessons from Socrates, the wisdom he had sought. He thought of Thoth, the visions that had connected him to an ancient world filled with its own struggles and hopes. He had felt Thoth's curiosity, his defiance, his love for Nerissa. Those emotions had become a part of him, driving him forward.

But now, in the oppressive darkness, those memories seemed fragile and faint. His resolve wavered, and for the first time, he truly considered giving up. What if he was not meant to succeed? What if he had been wrong to undertake these trials? The questions gnawed at him, each one a dagger to his already weakened spirit.

Plato's breathing grew shallow as he fought against the despair threatening to overwhelm him. He had faced so much already, but this emptiness, this void, was the hardest challenge of all. His eyes burned with unshed tears as he lay back, staring into the darkness, feeling the weight of his own failure pressing down on him.

He tried to remember Imhotep's words, the guidance he had received, but they seemed distant and hollow now. The connection to Thoth and Atlantis, once so vivid, felt like a fading dream. Plato's heart ached with the realization that he might never complete his mission, never uncover the truths he had sought so desperately.

Plato lay motionless, the oppressive darkness pressing in on him from all sides. The cold stone beneath him was unyielding, and every breath felt like a laborious task. He had searched frantically for the tablet, but it was gone, vanished into the ether. The absence of its comforting presence only deepened his sense of despair.

His body ached from the injuries sustained in the trials. Every movement sent sharp pains through his limbs, and he could feel the throbbing in his head from where he had struck the ground. Hunger gnawed at his stomach, and his throat was parched, every swallow a painful reminder of his dehydration.

Plato's mind was a storm of regret and self-recrimination. He had failed Socrates, standing by as his mentor was condemned and executed. He had trusted the senator, only to be betrayed and sold into slavery. He had ignored his uncle's wisdom and had chosen the path of arrogance and pride. And now, he had disobeyed Imhotep's warning, thinking himself capable of facing the trials alone.

"Why did I come here?" he whispered into the void. "Why did I think I could do this?"

Images of Thoth and Atlantis flashed through his mind, the grandeur of the city, the love he had felt for Nerissa, the responsibilities he had carried. But now, all he could see was failure. He had wanted to help Thoth, to understand the secrets of the tablet, but he had been foolish. He had overestimated his strength and underestimated the trials.

His thoughts turned darker, spiraling into a pit of despair. What was the point of continuing? He was alone, hurt, and without the tablet. There was no way out, no light to guide him. The weight of his failures crushed him, and he felt tears of frustration and hopelessness welling up in his eyes.

The room was suffocating, the darkness so complete it felt like a physical presence. Plato closed his eyes, but it made no difference. He was trapped in a void, both physically and mentally. He could feel his spirit breaking, the resolve he had clung to slipping away.

"Why didn't I listen?" he cried out, his voice echoing back to him. "Why did I think I could do this alone?"

His body trembled with exhaustion and pain, his mind teetering on the edge of collapse. He felt utterly helpless, unable to move

forward or find a way out. The despair was overwhelming, and for the first time, he truly considered giving up.

In this moment of absolute darkness, Plato faced the reality of his situation. He was alone, trapped in the depths of the pyramid, with no way to help Thoth or himself. The burden of his past mistakes weighed heavily on him, and the future seemed bleak and unattainable.

He lay still, his mind a tangled web of despair and regret. The darkness was suffocating, and every breath felt like a struggle. Just as he was about to succumb to his hopelessness, a faint, almost imperceptible glow began to fill the room. He blinked, unsure if his eyes were playing tricks on him.

Out of the dim light, a familiar figure emerged. Imhotep, the Egyptian high priest who had warned him against undertaking the trials unprepared, stood before him. His presence was both comforting and unnerving, a beacon of wisdom and a reminder of Plato's failure.

"Plato," Imhotep's voice was gentle but firm, "I warned you of the dangers these trials posed. You were not ready."

Plato's heart sank further. "I know," he admitted, his voice barely a whisper. "I thought I could do it. I thought… I thought I was strong enough."

Imhotep nodded, his eyes full of compassion. "You are strong, Plato, but strength alone is not enough. These trials require years of preparation and understanding. They are a test of the soul, not just the body."

Plato's eyes filled with tears. "I'm trapped. I don't know what to do. I've lost the tablet, and I have no way out."

Imhotep stepped closer, his gaze intense. "There is a way out, Plato. I can show you. You do not have to continue. You can leave this place and return to your life."

The words hung in the air, a lifeline thrown to a drowning man. Plato looked up, hope flickering in his eyes. "You can show me the way out?"

Imhotep nodded. "Yes, but there is a price. You must abandon the trials and all they represent. You must give up on finding the answers you seek."

Plato's heart raced. The temptation was strong. He was exhausted, in pain, and desperate for a way out. But something inside him resisted. The cries of Thoth and the people of Atlantis echoed in his mind. He saw Nerissa's face, her eyes full of hope and love. He couldn't abandon them, not now.

"But what about Thoth? What about Atlantis?" Plato asked, his voice trembling.

Imhotep sighed. "Their fate is sealed, Plato. The trials are not just about them; they are about you and your journey. You must decide what is more important: your safety or your quest for knowledge and truth."

Plato's stomach growled loudly, a painful reminder of his physical needs. As if sensing his thoughts, Imhotep produced a small loaf of bread and a flask of water. He placed them on the ground before Plato.

"You must be hungry and thirsty," Imhotep said softly. "Take these and regain your strength. Then decide."

Plato stared at the food and water, his mouth watering and his throat aching for relief. The temptation was almost unbearable. But as he reached out, he heard the cries of Thoth and the people of Atlantis growing louder in his mind. He couldn't abandon them. He couldn't give up now.

"No," Plato said, pulling his hand back. "I can't leave. I have to see this through, for Thoth, for Atlantis, and for myself."

Imhotep's expression softened, a hint of pride in his eyes. "Very well, Plato. But remember, the trials will only get harder from here. You must find the strength within yourself to continue."

With that, Imhotep faded away, leaving Plato alone in the darkness once more. But this time, the darkness didn't feel as

oppressive. He felt a renewed sense of determination, a flicker of hope amidst the despair.

Plato closed his eyes and took a deep breath, centering himself. The path ahead was still uncertain, and the challenges would be immense, but he knew he couldn't give up. He had to continue, no matter the cost.

Plato lay in the darkness, the weight of his circumstances pressing down on him with an almost tangible force. Every part of his body ached, his mind was clouded with despair, and the absence of the tablet left him feeling utterly powerless. The silence was suffocating, amplifying his isolation and hopelessness.

He struggled to sit up, his hands shaking from exhaustion. The thought of giving up crept into his mind, whispering insidiously that he had reached his limit. The physical pain, the hunger, the thirst—they were all too much to bear. He had come so far, but now, without the tablet, he felt as if he had hit an insurmountable wall.

Plato's thoughts turned dark as he remembered all his failures: his inability to save Socrates, his naivety in trusting the senator, his disregard for his uncle's warnings. Now, in the depths of the pyramid, he was faced with his greatest failure yet—disregarding Imhotep's advice and undertaking the trials without the necessary preparation.

His breaths were shallow, his body trembling. The weight of his past mistakes bore down on him, each one a reminder of his shortcomings. He had wanted to prove himself, to find redemption, but instead, he was trapped and alone, with no way out.

A soft whisper echoed in the darkness, almost imperceptible. "The light within will guide you." The words seemed distant, like a fading memory, offering a flicker of hope. But in his current state, Plato struggled to grasp their meaning. His mind was too clouded with despair to see the light.

The image of Thoth and Atlantis flashed before his eyes, a reminder of the vision that had driven him this far. He had felt their

pain, their struggle, and their need for salvation. But now, it seemed impossible to continue. The cries of Atlantis seemed fainter, more distant, as if they too were losing hope in him.

Plato closed his eyes, trying to center himself, but all he felt was an overwhelming emptiness. The physical and mental toll of the trials had drained him of his strength and resolve. He was at his breaking point, teetering on the edge of giving up.

In the midst of his despair, the vision of Imhotep returned, not as a guiding presence but as a silent observer. The food and water lay within his reach, a constant temptation to abandon his quest and save himself. The thought was so enticing, so easy, but it would mean abandoning Thoth, Atlantis, and everything he had fought for.

The internal struggle was agonizing. Every fiber of his being screamed for relief, for a way out. But a small, stubborn part of him refused to give in. The memories of his past failures pushed him to the brink, but they also kindled a faint, flickering resolve. He couldn't let this be another failure, another regret to haunt him.

Plato's eyes filled with tears, the enormity of his situation crashing over him. He felt lost, broken, and utterly alone. The path ahead was shrouded in darkness, with no clear way forward. He had reached the lowest point of his journey, where all hope seemed lost.

The whisper echoed again, barely audible but persistent. "The light within will guide you." Plato clung to the words, not fully understanding them but drawing some small measure of comfort from them. He lay back down, the exhaustion too much to fight. The darkness enveloped him, pulling him into a fitful sleep.

Chapter 22

The Eye of the Storm

Plato awoke to an all-encompassing darkness, the kind that seemed to swallow every fragment of light and hope. His body ached with a relentless pain, and his mouth was parched, each breath a struggle. He instinctively reached out, groping for the tablet, but his fingers met only cold, unforgiving stone. The tablet was still gone.

Panic surged through him. He scrambled to his feet, ignoring the sharp protests from his injured leg, and searched the small, featureless room. His hands brushed over every surface, every corner, but the tablet had vanished.

He collapsed back onto the ground, his chest heaving with exertion and despair. How could it be gone? The tablet was his only source of light, his only guide through these trials. Without it, he was lost. Tears of frustration and hopelessness welled up in his eyes, but he forced them back. Crying would do nothing to help him now.

Memories of his time on the slave ship resurfaced, unbidden. He remembered the endless days of backbreaking labor, the cruel overseers, and the gnawing hunger that never left him. There had been days, even weeks, when food and water were scarce. Yet, through it all, he had survived. He had endured. The human spirit, he realized, was capable of enduring far more than he had thought possible.

"I can survive this," he whispered to himself, drawing strength from the memory of his past resilience. If he had endured the horrors

of the slave ship, he could endure this. His voice sounded small and fragile in the vast darkness, but it was a start. He needed to remind himself of his strength, his resilience. He could not afford to lose hope, not now.

He lay back down, his body trembling with fatigue. As he closed his eyes, he focused on his breathing, trying to calm his racing heart. In and out. Slow and steady. He needed to think, to plan. Panicking would get him nowhere. He had survived worse before, and he could survive this too.

As Plato lay in the suffocating darkness, memories of his time on the slave ship began to surface more vividly. He recalled the endless days of relentless labor, the whip's cruel sting, and the gnawing hunger that had become a constant companion. The overseers had been ruthless, their cruelty a daily reminder of his captivity. Yet, amidst the despair, he had found a way to endure. He had survived.

Plato's mind drifted to the long stretches of time when food and water had been scarce. He remembered the hollow ache in his stomach, the parched throat that seemed to burn with each breath. But even in those dire circumstances, he had discovered a strength within himself. He had learned to endure the physical pain and the mental anguish, to find solace in the small moments of reprieve.

"Fasting," he thought, the word resonating deeply within him. He recalled reading about how Egyptian priests would fast to explore their inner strength, endure temptation, deny themselves to get closer to God, and dive deeper into their bond with spirit. The practice was a means to gain profound insights and unlock the mysteries within." During those harrowing days on the ship, he had inadvertently practiced fasting, not by choice but by necessity. It had been a harsh lesson in survival, teaching him that the body could endure far more than he had ever imagined.

Now, as he lay in the darkness, the memory of those days gave him a renewed sense of determination. Fasting had been a key to his

survival then, and perhaps it held the answer now. He didn't need the tablet to guide him; he needed to rely on his inner strength, his willpower, and his ability to endure.

He focused on his breathing, drawing in slow, deep breaths. In and out. He remembered the meditation techniques he had learned from the Egyptian priests, techniques that had helped him center himself and find peace amidst chaos. If he could combine fasting with meditation, he might be able to access the visions he had experienced in his dreams, to connect with Thoth without the tablet.

As he meditated, he envisioned the vastness of the pyramid around him, the energy that pulsed through its ancient walls. He could almost feel the presence of the tablet, not as a physical object, but as a source of knowledge and power that resonated within him. The connection he sought was not external; it was within.

Plato's resolve strengthened. He knew what he needed to do. He would accept his fast and meditate, drawing on the lessons he had learned and the strength he had discovered within himself. The journey ahead was fraught with challenges, but he was ready to face them. He had survived the slave ship, and he would survive this trial as well.

With a newfound sense of purpose, Plato continued his meditation, allowing the memories of his past to guide him. The darkness around him was no longer an enemy but a companion, a reminder of the resilience that lay within. He would endure, he would overcome, and he would find his way to the light.

Plato sat in the pitch-black room, focusing on his breathing and the memories of resilience that had begun to give him hope. He closed his eyes, even though the darkness was already complete, and entered a deeper state of meditation. His hunger and thirst were intense, but he tried to push them aside, focusing on the task at hand: reconnecting with the visions he had once accessed so easily in his dreams.

He visualized the events of his dreams, the vibrant world of Atlantis, the emotions and experiences of Thoth. The more he focused, the more tangible the visions became. He could almost feel the energy of the pyramid around him, pulsating in rhythm with his heartbeat. He was on the verge of a breakthrough.

In the stillness of his meditation, he began to sense something profound. The vibrations of the pyramid seemed to resonate within him, creating a harmonic frequency that connected him to the very essence of the place. He realized that his previous reliance on the tablet had been a crutch. The true power lay within him, waiting to be unlocked through his own will and focus.

As his meditation deepened, Plato felt himself slipping into a trance-like state. His surroundings seemed to fade away, replaced by the familiar scenes of Atlantis. He was no longer an observer; he was a part of the vision, immersed in the experiences of Thoth.

Thoth was standing in a grand temple, surrounded by priests and scholars. They were discussing the mysteries of the universe, the secrets of the emerald tablet, and the power it held. Plato could feel Thoth's curiosity and determination, his desire to unlock the knowledge contained within the tablet

Suddenly, Thoth turned and looked directly at Plato. It was as if Thoth could see him, sense his presence. Plato's heart raced. This was the moment he had been waiting for, the moment when his connection to the visions would become more than just passive observation.

"Who are you?" Thoth's voice echoed in Plato's mind, clear and resonant. "Why are you here?"

Plato felt a surge of emotions—fear, excitement, and a deep sense of purpose. He focused his thoughts, trying to communicate with Thoth. "I am Plato," he responded silently, hoping Thoth could understand. "I am here to learn, to understand, and to help."

Thoth's eyes widened, and Plato could feel his shock and curiosity. "You are not of this time," Thoth said, his voice filled with wonder. "You are a spirit from another age."

Plato nodded, even though he knew Thoth couldn't see the gesture. "I have been following your journey, trying to understand the secrets of Atlantis and the emerald tablet. I need to complete these trials to survive and to find the truth."

Thoth seemed to ponder Plato's words. "Our fates are intertwined," he said finally. "The trials you face are as much yours as they are mine. We must work together to succeed."

Plato felt a renewed sense of determination. This connection with Thoth was the key to unlocking the power within him. He realized that their journeys were parallel, and by understanding and supporting each other, they could both achieve their goals.

As the vision began to fade, Plato heard Thoth's voice one last time. "Remember, Plato, the power is within you. Trust in yourself and in our connection. Together, we can overcome any obstacle."

Plato opened his eyes, the darkness of the room returning. But this time, he didn't feel alone or hopeless. He had a purpose, a mission. He knew that he could tap into the power within him to navigate the trials and find his way out.

The vision had shown him the path forward, and he was ready to embrace it, no matter the challenges that lay ahead.

Plato emerged from his meditation, feeling a profound sense of clarity and purpose. The darkness around him seemed less oppressive, and the physical pain that had been gnawing at him was now a distant sensation, overshadowed by the strength he felt within. The realization that he could communicate with Thoth, that their destinies were linked, filled him with renewed resolve.

He slowly stood up, every movement deliberate as he conserved his energy. The memories of Thoth's determination and wisdom played over and over in his mind, reinforcing his belief in their shared journey. He knew now that he could draw on the power within him to face the challenges ahead.

With his eyes closed, Plato focused on the vibrations he had sensed during his meditation. He felt the pulse of the pyramid, the subtle energy that permeated the space around him. It was as if the very structure of the pyramid was alive, responding to his presence and his intentions.

He reached out with his senses, trying to connect once more with the ethereal realm where Thoth's vision had taken place. The darkness remained, but within his mind's eye, he saw the intricate designs of the pyramid, the pathways that led deeper into its mysteries. He could almost see the emerald tablet, glowing with an inner light, calling out to him.

"The light within will guide you," he whispered to himself, echoing the words that had come to him before he blacked out. He focused on the sensation of the light within him, letting it grow stronger, illuminating his path.

Suddenly, he felt a shift in the air. The vibrations of the pyramid grew more intense, resonating with the energy he was channeling. He opened his eyes, and though the room remained dark, he could see faint outlines of the walls, a subtle glow emanating from the stone.

He took a deep breath, centering himself, and began to move forward. The walls seemed to part before him, revealing a narrow passageway that had been hidden in the shadows. He knew instinctively that this was the way forward, the path that would lead him closer to his goal.

As he walked, he felt a growing connection to Thoth, a sense of shared purpose that gave him strength. He could hear distant echoes of Thoth's voice, guiding him, encouraging him to trust in his own abilities.

The passageway twisted and turned, leading him deeper into the heart of the pyramid. The air grew cooler, and the faint glow from the walls provided just enough light to see by. He could feel the weight of

the pyramid above him, the immense power contained within its ancient stone.

Finally, he reached a small chamber, and in the center of the room, there was a shallow pool of water. It was a miracle, a gift from the pyramid itself. Plato knelt beside the pool, cupping his hands to drink. The water was cool and refreshing, rejuvenating his body and mind.

As he stood up, he felt a surge of energy, a sense of invincibility. He was ready to face whatever trials lay ahead, to complete the journey that he and Thoth had begun.

With a final look at the chamber around him, he took a deep breath and stepped forward, ready to embrace the challenges that awaited him. The light within him shone brightly, guiding his way, as he prepared to unlock the secrets of the pyramid and the mysteries of the emerald tablet.

Chapter 23

Unveiled Secrets

Plato laid in the dark, cold chamber, his body aching from the trials he had endured. The physical pain was a reminder of his struggle, but it also fueled his determination. He had found the inner strength to connect with Thoth without the tablet, and this realization filled him with a renewed sense of purpose.

He sat up slowly, wincing as his muscles protested. His throat was dry, and his stomach growled with hunger, but he pushed these discomforts aside. He remembered the long, grueling days on the slave ship, where survival had seemed impossible, yet he had endured. The memory of those hardships gave him strength now.

Plato closed his eyes and took a deep breath, centering himself. He focused on the inner light, the connection he felt with Thoth, and the wisdom he had gained from the visions. He could feel the vibrations of the pyramid resonating with his own energy, creating a harmonious rhythm that pulsed through his being.

Slowly, he stood up, using the wall for support. He was in a smaller, darker room with no visible exits and no water for the tablet. The sense of hopelessness was overwhelming, but he refused to give in to despair. He knew that the trials were not just physical but also spiritual, and he was determined to see them through.

He began to walk, feeling his way along the walls, searching for any clue or sign that might guide him forward. The darkness was

oppressive, but the light within him provided a faint glimmer of hope. He focused on that light, letting it guide his steps.

As he moved, he felt a sudden surge of energy. The connection to Thoth was growing stronger, the lines between their worlds blurring. He could sense Thoth's presence, feel his emotions, and see glimpses of his reality. The visions were becoming more vivid, more urgent.

Plato stopped and closed his eyes, allowing the connection to deepen. He saw through Thoth's eyes, felt his determination and resolve. Thoth was facing his own trials in Atlantis, preparing for a confrontation that would determine the fate of his people. The stakes were high, and Plato knew that his actions would impact Thoth's world as well.

He took a deep breath and focused on the light within him. The vibrations of the pyramid resonated with his energy, creating a harmonious rhythm that pulsed through his being. He could feel the presence of the tablet, the wisdom it held, and the power it could unleash.

With renewed determination, Plato continued to move forward. He knew that the journey ahead would be challenging, but he was ready to face whatever trials awaited him. The connection to Thoth and the inner strength he had discovered would see him through.

As he navigated the labyrinthine corridors of the pyramid, he felt a growing sense of urgency. The wisdom of the tablet was within reach, but he had to act quickly. The fate of Atlantis and his own survival depended on it.

He reached a fork in the path and paused, sensing the vibrations. The left path pulsed with a strong energy, but the right path pulsed stronger, guiding him forward. He followed it, trusting in the connection he had established with Thoth and the wisdom of the ancients.

The path led him to a small chamber, and as he entered, he felt a powerful presence. It was as though the very air hummed with energy.

He closed his eyes and focused, allowing the vibrations to guide him. The chamber was dark, but within his mind's eye, he saw the intricate designs of the pyramid, the pathways that led deeper into its mysteries.

He knelt on the cool stone floor and entered a meditative state, drawing on the inner light to guide him. The memory of Thoth's teachings, the wisdom of the ancient priesthood, filled his mind. He could see Thoth's face, sense his presence, and feel his emotions.

"The light within will guide you," he whispered, echoing the words that had given him strength. He focused on the sensation of the light, letting it grow stronger, illuminating the path forward.

Suddenly, he felt a shift in the air. The vibrations grew more intense, resonating with the energy he was channeling. He opened his eyes, and though the chamber remained dark, he could see faint outlines of symbols on the walls, a subtle glow emanating from the stone.

Plato stood up, every movement deliberate as he conserved his energy. The connection to Thoth and the inner strength he had discovered would see him through. With a final deep breath, he stepped forward to embrace the trials and unlock the secrets of the pyramid.

Plato's focus intensified as he connected deeper with Thoth's world. The visions became more vivid, and he could feel the emotional weight of the events unfolding in Atlantis. Thoth's determination and the escalating turmoil around him resonated with Plato's own struggles.

Thoth stood at the edge of the temple courtyard, staring out at the vast city of Atlantis. The skyline was dominated by the majestic spires and domes of the temples and government buildings, their grandeur a testament to the city's power and influence. But the peace that once reigned over Atlantis was now threatened by internal strife and external pressures.

The military faction, led by Nerissa's uncle, had grown increasingly bold. They sought to use the power of the temple and the secrets of the tablet to dominate not only Atlantis but also the rest of the world. Thoth knew that this lust for power would lead to disaster.

Thoth's thoughts were interrupted by a soft voice behind him. "Thoth, we need to talk." He turned to see Nerissa, her face a mixture of determination and fear. Her presence stirred a complex mix of emotions within him—love, regret, and a deep sense of duty.

"Nerissa," he said softly, exhaling as he spoke. "Yes. I need to know; how does your uncle know so much about the tablet?"

She glanced around to ensure they were alone before stepping closer. "My uncle… he knows everything you told me about the tablet, even how to enter the secret temple. I'm so sorry."

Thoth's heart sank. "How did he find out?"

Nerissa's eyes filled with tears. "He found my old diary. The one I kept when we were young and foolish, sneaking around the rings. I know I shouldn't have, but, I wrote everything in there, Thoth. About the temple, the tablet, our dreams… everything. He knows every detail."

Thoth felt a surge of anger and betrayal, but it quickly turned to resolve. "It's not your fault, Nerissa. We were just children. But now we have to stop him."

She nodded, wiping away her tears. "I came to warn you. His forces are gathered all over the city. He won't stop until he gets the tablet."

Thoth took her hand, feeling the urgency of the situation. "We need to protect the tablet. If it falls into the wrong hands, it could bring about the end of everything we hold dear."

Together, they hurried into the temple, where the high priest, Thotme, was already making preparations. "Father," Thoth called out, "we have to secure the tablet."

Thotme turned, his expression grave. "I know, my son. The military's intentions are clear, and their greed will be our downfall if we do not act swiftly."

Thoth and Nerissa joined Thotme and the other priests in a sacred chamber deep within the temple. The room was filled with ancient artifacts and scrolls, the accumulated wisdom of generations. In the center, on a raised pedestal, lay the Emerald Tablet, its surface shimmering with an otherworldly light.

Thotme placed his hands on Thoth's shoulders. "This is your trial, my son. The destiny of Atlantis rests in your hands. You must protect the tablet at all costs."

Thoth nodded, feeling the weight of his responsibility. "I will, Father."

Nerissa stepped forward. "We'll do it together. I won't let my uncle destroy everything we love."

As they prepared to defend the temple, the sounds of approaching footsteps echoed through the halls. The military forces were closing in, and the final confrontation was imminent. Thoth and Nerissa stood side by side, ready to face whatever came next.

Meanwhile, in the depths of the pyramid, Plato felt the intensity of Thoth's emotions and the impending conflict. The connection between their worlds was growing stronger, and he knew that his actions would have a profound impact on the outcome.

With a deep breath, Plato focused on the light within, drawing strength from his connection to Thoth. He could feel the vibrations of the pyramid resonating with his energy, guiding him forward. The path was clear, and he was determined to see it through to the end.

As the vision of Atlantis's impending conflict faded, Plato found himself once again in the dark chamber of the pyramid. But now, he felt a renewed sense of purpose. The trials were not just about survival; they were about sacrifice. They were about protecting the

wisdom and legacy of Atlantis. He had to succeed, not just for himself, but for Thoth and the future of humanity.

With resolve, he stood up and began to move forward, guided by the inner light and the knowledge that he was not alone in this journey. He felt the weight of the pyramid's silence around him, but his heart was alive with the intensity of Thoth's struggle. He focused on the faint light within, using it to guide his steps through the darkness. Each movement was deliberate, every breath a reminder of his resolve. He could sense that the trials were converging with the visions, their outcomes intertwined.

As Plato navigated the pyramid, Thoth's world continued to unfold vividly in his mind. The temple was under siege, and the military forces, led by Nerissa's uncle, had breached the outer defenses. The sacred chamber, where the tablet lay, became the last stronghold of those loyal to the wisdom and peace it represented.

Thoth, Nerissa, and Thotme stood their ground, the glow of the Emerald Tablet casting an ethereal light over them. The air was thick with tension as the sound of clashing swords and shouts grew nearer. Thoth felt a surge of adrenaline, his heart pounding in sync with the impending confrontation.

"Thoth, we must be ready," Thotme said, as he handed his staff to his son, his voice steady despite the chaos. "The tablet is more than just a source of power. It is a symbol of our knowledge and our duty to protect it."

Thoth nodded, gripping the staff that had been passed down through generations of priests. He glanced at Nerissa, who stood beside him with fierce determination in her eyes. "We will protect it, Father," Thoth vowed.

Nerissa's uncle, General Kharon, burst into the chamber, flanked by soldiers. His eyes locked onto the tablet with a look of greed and triumph. "The time has come to seize the power that rightfully belongs to us," he declared. "With the tablet, Atlantis will be unstoppable."

Thoth stepped forward, his voice resonating with authority. "You seek to corrupt what was meant to enlighten. The tablet is not a weapon to wield but a guide to wisdom. You will not take it."

Kharon sneered. "You are a fool, Thoth. Power is meant to be used, and you have squandered it. Stand aside, or be crushed under the weight of progress."

As the soldiers advanced, a fierce battle erupted. Thoth and Nerissa fought with a blend of skill and desperation, their movements synchronized as if they were two parts of a whole. Thotme defended the tablet with unwavering resolve, his presence a beacon of stability amidst the chaos.

Plato, deep in the heart of the pyramid, felt every strike and parry as if he were there. He realized that his actions could influence the outcome of the vision. Drawing on the connection he felt with Thoth, Plato focused his thoughts, willing strength and clarity to his ancient counterpart.

Thoth, sensing Plato's support, found a wellspring of strength within himself. He fought with renewed vigor, each strike more precise and powerful. Nerissa, too, felt the surge of energy, her movements becoming even more agile and fierce.

Amidst the battle, Kharon managed to reach the pedestal, his hands grasping for the tablet. But as he touched it, a powerful surge of energy repelled him, sending him crashing to the ground. The tablet's glow intensified, and the chamber was filled with a blinding light.

In that moment, Thoth's mind connected directly with Plato's. "The tablet knows its true guardians," Thoth thought, realizing the depth of their connection. "We are meant to protect its wisdom, not exploit it."

The vision faded, leaving Plato in the darkness of the pyramid once more. But now, he felt a profound sense of unity with Thoth. Their destinies were linked, and the trials of the pyramid were not just about physical endurance but about spiritual alignment.

With a deep breath, Plato moved forward, his steps guided by the inner light and the knowledge that he was not alone. He understood that the next phase of the trials would test not only his body but also his spirit. The convergence of his world and Thoth's was leading to a moment of reckoning, and he was ready to face it.

As he navigated the labyrinthine passages of the pyramid, the air grew colder, and the darkness seemed to deepen. Yet, within that darkness, Plato felt a spark of hope. The trials were not just obstacles; they were a path to enlightenment, a journey that would reveal the true power within him. With renewed determination, he pressed on, knowing that the trials were bringing him closer to the ultimate truth, a truth that would illuminate both his path and the destiny of Atlantis.

The air inside the pyramid grew denser as Plato continued to navigate its labyrinthine passages. The cold stone walls seemed to close in around him, and every step felt heavier than the last. Yet, driven by the newfound connection to Thoth, he pressed on, his resolve unwavering.

In the vision, the battle within the sacred chamber of Atlantis raged on. Thoth and Nerissa fought side by side, their movements synchronized in a deadly dance. The soldiers, though numerous, struggled to match their combined skill and determination. Thotme, standing near the Emerald Tablet, chanted ancient incantations, calling upon the power of the gods to protect their sacred relic.

Plato's consciousness flickered between the physical reality of the pyramid and the vivid vision of Atlantis. He could feel Thoth's every movement, every breath, as if they were his own. The bond between them had strengthened, becoming an unbreakable link that transcended time and space.

As the battle reached its climax, Thoth felt a surge of clarity. "Plato," he thought, the name resonating within his mind. "We are connected. Your strength gives me hope."

Kharon, sensing his defeat, grew desperate. He lunged towards the tablet once more, his eyes filled with a manic gleam. Thoth intercepted him, their weapons clashing with a resounding crash. "You will not take what is not yours!" Thoth shouted, his voice echoing with authority.

Kharon sneered, his face twisted with rage. "You are a fool, Thoth. Power belongs to those who seize it."

Their struggle intensified, the energy of the tablet pulsating with an otherworldly light. Thoth's determination wavered for a moment, but then he felt a surge of strength from Plato. "Together," he thought, channeling Plato's resolve.

With a final, powerful strike, Thoth disarmed Kharon, sending his weapon clattering to the floor. The soldiers, seeing their leader defeated, hesitated, their morale shattered. Nerissa stepped forward, her eyes blazing with righteous fury. "Leave now, and never return," she commanded.

Kharon, realizing his defeat, snarled but backed away, signaling his soldiers to retreat. The chamber fell silent, the tension dissipating as the soldiers filed out, leaving Thoth, Nerissa, and Thotme alone with the tablet.

Thotme approached his son, placing a hand on his shoulder. "You have done well, Thoth. The tablet is safe, for now."

Thoth nodded, but his eyes were filled with sorrow. "Father, I fear this is not the end. The threat to Atlantis grows each day."

"Yes, and my uncle will not quit." Nerissa exclaimed.

Thotme sighed, his expression grave. "You are right, my son. The forces that seek to control the tablet's power are relentless. We must prepare for what is to come."

Nerissa stepped forward, her face determined. "We will stand together, as we always have. Atlantis must be protected."

As the vision began to fade, Plato felt a profound sense of unity with Thoth and his companions. Their struggle was his struggle, their

determination fueling his own. The trials of the pyramid were not just about survival; they were about understanding and embracing the deeper connection between past and present, between different realms of existence.

Back in the pyramid, Plato's mind cleared, his purpose solidifying. He knew that the path ahead would be fraught with danger and challenges, but he was ready to face them. The convergence of his journey and Thoth's was drawing near, and the stakes had never been higher.

With a deep breath, Plato steeled himself, ready to continue his quest. The final trials awaited, and he would face them with the strength and wisdom gained from his connection to Thoth. The destiny of Atlantis and his own fate were intertwined, and he would see this journey through to the end.

As he moved forward, the air around him seemed to hum with a renewed energy. The path was illuminated not by the faint light of the tablet, but by the inner light of his newfound resolve. Plato knew that he was not alone in this struggle; the spirit of Thoth and the legacy of Atlantis guided his every step.

The trials were far from over, but Plato felt a surge of confidence. The vision had revealed the power within him, a power that would guide him through the darkness and into the light. With each step, he moved closer to the ultimate truth, a truth that would shape the future of both his world and the world of Atlantis.

And so, with his heart and mind aligned, Plato pressed on, ready to face whatever challenges lay ahead. The convergence of worlds was imminent, and the final battle for Atlantis; for truth and enlightenment had begun.

Chapter 24

The Fall of Kings

Plato's senses were a whirlwind of sensations, a mix of his reality in the pyramid and the vivid vision of Atlantis. The boundaries between the two worlds had blurred, and he could no longer distinguish where one ended and the other began. Thoth's emotions surged through him—fear, determination, and a deep sense of urgency.

In Atlantis, the city was on the brink of chaos. The once serene and orderly society was now a place of frantic activity and looming disaster. Buildings trembled, and the sky above was an ominous shade of gray. Thoth raced through the central ring, his mind focused on finding the ship and the tablet. He knew that time was running out.

"Thoth!" Nerissa's voice called out, bringing him to a halt. She was out of breath, her face etched with worry. "We need to hurry. The general's forces are closing in."

Thoth nodded, his eyes scanning the horizon. "The airship is hidden in the eastern hangar. We must get there before they do."

As they ran, Plato felt every step, every heartbeat. His connection to Thoth was stronger than ever, and he could feel the young priest's determination burning within him. The convergence of their destinies was at hand, and the stakes had never been higher.

Reaching the base of a towering structure, Thoth and Nerissa descended into a hidden passageway, leading to a vast underground hangar. The airship, sleek and advanced, lay concealed beneath layers

of protective shielding. It was an engineering marvel, a testament to the Atlanteans' technological prowess.

Thoth approached the control panel and began the activation sequence. The hangar buzzed with energy as the airship powered up, its systems coming online. The ground shook with distant explosions, a reminder of the urgency of their mission.

"We have to be quick," Thoth said, his voice steady but urgent. "The general's forces won't be far behind."

Nerissa nodded, her eyes reflecting the same determination. Together, they boarded the airship, preparing for the journey that lay ahead. As the vessel ascended, Plato felt the convergence of his own reality with Thoth's, understanding that their fates were now intertwined.

In the darkness of the pyramid, Plato's body trembled with the intensity of the vision. He knew that the trials were far from over and that the final challenges would test him to his limits. But with Thoth's determination and his own newfound resolve, he felt a glimmer of hope.

The journey had only just begun, and the convergence of their destinies would soon reach its peak. The future of both worlds depended on their success, and failure was not an option.

As the airship ascended from its hidden hangar, the sight that greeted Thoth and Nerissa was one of a city in turmoil. The once proud and majestic Atlantis was now a landscape of chaos, with buildings crumbling and fires raging across the horizon. The sky above was dark, filled with smoke and the ominous rumblings of impending disaster.

Thoth guided the airship with a steady hand, his mind racing with thoughts of the mission ahead. "We need to secure the tablet and gather the people we can save," he said, his voice resolute. "The Dweller has commanded the sinking of Atlantis. We must act swiftly."

Nerissa nodded, her eyes scanning the chaos below. "Where do we start?"

"We head to the temple," Thoth replied. "The tablet is there, and we need the wisdom it contains to guide us through this."

Plato, still deeply connected to Thoth's experiences, felt every jolt of the airship, every vibration of its engines. His heart pounded with the urgency of the moment, knowing that the survival of Atlantis's knowledge and culture rested on Thoth's shoulders.

The airship maneuvered through the city, avoiding the collapsing structures and the onslaught of the general's forces. The military had become increasingly aggressive, their desire for control leading them to desperate measures. Thoth knew that time was of the essence.

As they approached the temple, the scene was one of devastation. The once sacred grounds were now a battlefield, with soldiers clashing against the temple guards. Thoth landed the airship nearby, and they hurried towards the entrance, their path fraught with danger.

Inside the temple, Thoth's father, Thotme, stood at the altar, a look of grim determination on his face. He had been preparing for this moment, knowing that the fate of their civilization was at stake.

"Father," Thoth called out, running to his side. "We need the tablet."

Thotme nodded, his eyes filled with both pride and sorrow. "It is time, my son. The Dweller's command must be fulfilled. The knowledge must be preserved, and you must lead our people to safety."

He handed Thoth the emerald tablet, its surface glowing with a mystical light. The weight of the responsibility settled on Thoth's shoulders, but he stood tall, ready to face the challenges ahead.

"Take this," Thotme said, placing a small, intricately carved amulet in Thoth's hand. "It will guide you and protect you on your journey. Remember the teachings and stay true to our path."

With a heavy heart, Thoth accepted the amulet and turned to Nerissa. "We must gather as many as we can and get them to the airship. Our time is short."

As they moved through the temple, gathering survivors and securing the sacred artifacts and scrolls, Plato felt the depth of Thoth's resolve. He understood now that their destinies were not just intertwined but that Thoth's success was crucial for the survival of Atlantis's wisdom.

In the darkness of the pyramid, Plato's resolve strengthened. He knew that just as Thoth was fighting to save his world, he too must find a way to overcome his trials and emerge victorious. The convergence of their fates was leading them towards a climactic confrontation, and the outcome would determine the future of both their worlds.

Thoth held the amulet his father had given him tightly in his hand. It glowed faintly, a reassuring presence amidst the chaos that surrounded them. He could feel the energy coursing through it, connecting him to the legacy of his ancestors and the wisdom of the priests.

Nerissa stood beside him, her eyes wide with fear but also with determination. "What do we do now?" she whispered.

Thoth looked around the central temple, his mind racing. The military forces were closing in, their footsteps echoing through the ancient halls. They had little time.

"We need to create a diversion," Thoth said, his voice steady. "We can't let them find the airship or the tablet. We need to buy ourselves some time."

Nerissa nodded, her gaze following Thoth's. "What about the amulet? Can it help us?"

Thoth glanced down at the glowing amulet, feeling the weight of its power. "Yes, it can. The amulet can amplify our energies, but we need to be careful. It's a tool, not a weapon."

He turned to the group of survivors huddled nearby. "We need to split up. Some of us will create a diversion to draw the military away from the hangar. The rest will prepare the airship for departure. We need to be ready to leave at a moment's notice."

Thoth assigned tasks quickly, his voice filled with authority. "Nerissa, you'll lead the group creating the diversion. Use anything you can find to make noise and draw their attention. I'll stay with the others and make sure the airship is ready."

Nerissa nodded, a determined look in her eyes. "Be careful, Thoth."

Thoth squeezed her hand. "You too."

As Nerissa and her group moved out, Thoth led the remaining survivors towards the hidden hangar. The ancient mechanisms of the temple shifted and groaned as they approached, revealing the airship hidden within. It was a marvel of Atlantean engineering, sleek and powerful, its engines humming with potential.

Thoth directed the survivors to start preparing the airship, checking the systems and loading whatever supplies they could. He couldn't shake the feeling of impending danger, the sense that time was running out.

As he worked, he kept the amulet close, feeling its power resonating with his own. He knew that the next few moments would be critical. They needed to be ready to move, but they also needed to ensure that the military forces were sufficiently distracted.

Suddenly, a series of explosions echoed through the temple. Thoth looked up, his heart pounding. Nerissa and her group had succeeded in creating the diversion, but it also meant that the military would soon be converging on their location.

Thoth hurried to the control panel of the airship, his fingers flying over the controls. The engines roared to life, the airship vibrating with energy. They were almost ready.

"Everyone, get on board!" Thoth shouted, his voice carrying over the noise. The survivors rushed up the ramp, their faces etched with fear and hope.

Thoth's heart raced as he watched the hangar doors slowly open. They were so close, but they still had to get past the military forces. He could see them now, rushing towards the temple, their weapons drawn.

"We need to buy more time," Thoth muttered to himself, his mind racing. He looked at the amulet, feeling its power pulsing in his hand. "Just a little more time."

As the final survivors boarded the airship, Thoth took a deep breath. They were almost there. They just needed a few more moments. He could feel the weight of his father's legacy and the responsibility of saving his people pressing down on him.

"Hang on," Thoth whispered, his eyes fixed on the approaching soldiers. "We're almost there."

The airship engines roared to life, the vibration coursing through the entire hangar. Thoth stood at the controls, his heart pounding with a mix of fear and determination. They were so close to escaping, but he knew the real challenge was just beginning.

"Everyone on board, now!" Thoth shouted, his voice cutting through the chaos.

As the last of the survivors scrambled onto the airship, Nerissa appeared, running towards the ramp. Thoth felt a brief moment of relief, but it was quickly shattered by the sight of her uncle and the military forces closing in behind her.

"Nerissa, hurry!" Thoth urged, extending a hand to her.

Nerissa reached the ramp, but her uncle's forces were right behind her. In a split second decision, Thoth activated the airship's defense systems, hoping to create a barrier between them and the approaching soldiers. But it was too late.

Her uncle, eyes burning with ambition and rage, seized the moment of chaos. Somehow, during the commotion, he managed to sneak on board, countering their diversion with his own strategic subterfuge. With a swift motion, while Thoth was focused on Nerissa, he activated a rare device on his wrist—an advanced piece of technology from the military ring of Atlantis, capable of harnessing and briefly controlling the natural electromagnetic waves in its immediate surroundings. Instantly, an invisible force spread out from him, immobilizing Thoth in mid-stride, as if caught in an invisible snare.

As the general lunged and grabbed the tablet from Thoth's grasp, a triumphant smile spread across his face. Just as he turned, Nerissa, seeing the opportunity, aimed her weapon at the retreating general. Though she missed him, the blast struck the remnants of the device, ensuring it could not be used again.

Thoth, now released from its grasp, was dazed and struggled to his feet, his eyes blazing with renewed determination. "No!" he yelled, lunging forward as he regained control of his body, but it was too late. The soldiers swarmed around them, pushing Thoth back.

Nerissa's uncle held the tablet aloft, his voice dripping with disdain. "Did you really think you could escape with this? Your weak, just like your father was. The power of Atlantis belongs to those strong enough to wield it!"

Thoth's heart sank. The tablet, the key to everything, was now in the hands of the enemy. He looked at Nerissa, their eyes meeting in a moment of shared despair, as the general boarded his own ship with the tablet.

"We can't let him leave with it," Nerissa said, her voice trembling but resolute. "We have to do something."

Thoth nodded, his mind racing. "We need to buy time. We can't let them take off with the tablet."

As the military forces continued to advanced, Thoth and Nerissa fought desperately, but the weight of the military's forces was too much to bear on their own. Their fate was sealed and the tablet was lost. The airship's engines roared, the hangar filled with the sounds of battle. Thoth's thoughts raced back to his father's teachings, the weight of the amulet in his hand a constant reminder of the legacy he carried.

In the midst of the chaos, Thoth's father, Thotme, appeared at the edge of the hangar. His presence was a beacon of hope, but Thoth knew what it meant.

"Father, no," Thoth whispered, understanding the sacrifice that was about to be made.

Thotme stepped forward, his voice calm and resolute. "Thoth, you must go. Save the people. Save the legacy of Atlantis."

With a swift motion, Thotme conjured a shimmering barrier of energy, its radiant light momentarily halting the advance of the soldiers. Thoth felt tears sting his eyes, knowing this was the last time he would see his father.

"Go, now!" Thotme commanded, his voice echoing through the hangar.

Thoth grabbed Nerissa's hand, pulling her towards the airship. As they reached the ramp, he glanced back one last time, seeing his father standing strong against the tide of enemies.

"Father, thank you," Thoth whispered, his heart breaking.

With a final surge of determination, Thoth and Nerissa boarded the airship, the engines roaring to full power. As the ramp closed and the ship began to ascend, Thoth knew they had to find a way to reclaim the tablet and honor his father's sacrifice.

The hangar doors burst open, and the airship soared into the sky. Below them, the military forces swarmed, but Thotme's barrier held, giving them the precious moments they needed to escape.

Thoth's grip tightened on the controls, his mind focused on the task ahead. They had lost the tablet, but they hadn't lost hope. The fight was far from over, and Thoth was determined to see it through, no matter the cost.

Chapter 25

Shadows of Sacrifice

The airship hovered over a secluded part of Atlantis, its engines humming softly. Inside, the survivors were huddled together, mourning their losses and trying to come to terms with the situation. Thoth stood at the helm, his eyes scanning the horizon, his mind racing with thoughts of the tablet and the danger it posed in the general's hands.

Plato approached him, his face etched with concern. "Thoth, we need to regroup. We can't let the general keep the tablet. It's too dangerous."

Thoth nodded, his jaw clenched. "I know. But we're not ready to confront him yet. We need a plan, and we need allies."

Nerissa joined them, her expression determined. "We have to act quickly. The longer he has the tablet, the more powerful he becomes. We need to find a way to take it back."

Thoth sighed, looking around at the weary survivors. "We'll need to gather more forces. Those who are still loyal to Atlantis and willing to fight for its future."

Plato nodded. "Yes we can't do this alone. We need to find people who can help us."

Thoth spread a detailed map of Atlantis on a makeshift table inside the airship. "The general has the tablet at his stronghold. It's

heavily guarded, and he has the most advanced technology at his disposal. We can't just storm in there. We need a strategy."

Nerissa studied the map, her brow furrowed. "What if we create another diversion? Draw his forces away from the stronghold so we can at least infiltrate, take out those generators and then try to retrieve the tablet."

Thoth considered her suggestion. "It's risky, but it might work. We can split into two teams. One will create the diversion, and the other will infiltrate the stronghold."

Plato looked around at the weary survivors, their faces a mix of fear and determination. "We need to gather our strength and prepare. This will be our last chance to save Atlantis."

Thoth nodded. "We'll need to be ready for anything. The general won't give up the tablet without a fight."

As they finalized their plans, the airship continued to hover in place, hidden from the general's view. Thoth, Plato, and the others knew that the final confrontation would be their greatest challenge yet.

Nerissa placed a hand on Thoth's shoulder. "We'll get through this. We have to. For Atlantis."

Thoth took a deep breath, feeling the weight of his father's amulet around his neck. "For Atlantis."

The survivors dispersed to prepare for the upcoming confrontation, their hearts heavy with the knowledge of what was at stake. Thoth and Plato knew that the final battle would be their greatest challenge yet, but they were determined to see it through to the end.

The airship began to move, heading towards the general's stronghold. The fate of Atlantis hung in the balance, and Thoth and Plato were ready to face whatever came next.

The airship glided silently through the skies of Atlantis, heading towards the general's stronghold. Inside, Thoth and Plato gathered their allies, each one readying themselves for the battle ahead. The tension was palpable, and everyone knew the stakes.

Thoth looked over the edge of the airship, his eyes narrowing as he spotted the general's forces below. "We need to understand his plan. If we know what he's aiming for, we can anticipate his moves."

Plato nodded. "We have to figure out what he's doing with the tablet. He could be planning something catastrophic."

As they approached the stronghold, they could see the general's forces moving with precision, setting up advanced weaponry and fortifications. Thoth's heart sank as he realized the scale of the operation.

Nerissa joined them, her eyes scanning the horizon. "Look at that," she said, pointing to a massive device being assembled in the center of the stronghold. "What is that?"

Plato's eyes widened as he studied the device. "It looks like some kind of superweapon. He's using the tablet to power it."

Thoth clenched his fists. "Yes and I think he intends to use the tablet to draw energy up from the earth's core. If he activates that, it could destroy Atlantis and beyond. We have to stop him."

They watched as the general stood atop a platform, overseeing the assembly of the superweapon. His voice boomed through the loudspeakers, addressing his troops.

"With the power of the tablet, we will become unstoppable! We will crush anyone who stands in our way and ensure that Atlantis reigns supreme over all!"

Thoth's blood ran cold. "He's planning to use the tablet to harness the power of the earth's core. If he succeeds, he'll have the most powerful weapon in existence."

Plato's mind raced. "We need to find a way to disable that device. If we can disrupt its power source, we might be able to stop him."

Nerissa pointed to a series of smaller generators surrounding the main device. "Those generators are channeling the energy from the tablet. If we can take them out, it might weaken the device."

Thoth nodded. "We'll need to split up. One team will create the diversion to draw the general's forces away, while the other team targets the generators."

Plato agreed. "I'll lead the diversion team. We'll cause as much chaos as possible to give you a chance to get to those generators."

Thoth looked at the group, his expression serious. "This is it. We can't afford to fail. The fate of Atlantis depends on us."

As they finalized their plans, the airship descended closer to the ground, preparing for the mission. Thoth, Plato, and their allies steeled themselves for the upcoming battle, knowing that the next few hours would determine the future of Atlantis.

The airship landed quietly in a hidden spot, and the teams disembarked, moving swiftly and silently towards their objectives. Thoth's heart pounded as he led his team towards the generators, his father's amulet clutched tightly in his hand.

Plato and his team moved in the opposite direction, ready to create the diversion that would give Thoth a fighting chance. The general's forces were everywhere, and they knew that one wrong move could mean the end.

As they moved through the shadows, the sound of the general's voice echoed in their ears, a constant reminder of the danger they faced. Thoth's determination grew stronger with each step, knowing that they had to succeed.

Thoth and his team navigated the labyrinthine pathways leading to the generators. The stronghold was heavily guarded, but Thoth's intimate knowledge of Atlantis' infrastructure gave him an advantage. He led his group through hidden passages and shadowy corridors, avoiding detection.

"We're close," Thoth whispered, his eyes scanning the area. The hum of the generators grew louder as they approached. "Remember, our goal is to disable these generators and weaken the superweapon. Stay focused."

As they reached the first generator, Thoth motioned for his team to spread out. They moved with practiced precision, placing charges at critical points. Thoth glanced back at the airship, where Plato and the diversion team were preparing to create chaos.

On the other side of the stronghold, Plato gathered his team. "We need to make as much noise as possible," he said, his voice low but determined. "Our objective is to draw their attention away from Thoth. Ready?"

His team nodded, determination etched on their faces. With a deep breath, Plato led them out of their hiding place and into the open. They moved swiftly, setting off small explosions and creating disturbances that echoed through the stronghold.

The general's forces reacted immediately, rushing to contain the perceived threat. Plato watched as the guards mobilized, leaving their posts to deal with the diversion. He knew this was their chance.

"Let's move!" Plato shouted, leading his team further into the stronghold. They clashed with the guards, the sound of battle ringing out as they fought to keep the attention away from Thoth's mission.

Thoth heard the commotion and knew Plato's team had begun their part of the plan. He turned to his team. "Now's our chance. Set the charges and get ready to move to the next generator."

They worked quickly, the charges placed and timers set. As they moved to the next generator, Thoth's thoughts were with Plato and the others, hoping they could hold out long enough.

Reaching the second generator, Thoth and his team repeated the process, moving with practiced efficiency. The tension was palpable, every second feeling like an eternity. Thoth's mind was focused, his father's sacrifice driving him forward.

"We need to hurry," Thoth urged, the sound of distant explosions spurring them on. They finished setting the charges and moved towards the final generator.

Plato's team was holding their ground, but the odds were stacked against them. The general's forces were numerous and well-armed. Plato fought with everything he had, his mind racing as he tried to anticipate their next move.

"We need to keep pushing!" Plato shouted, rallying his team. They pressed on, their determination unwavering despite the overwhelming odds.

As the battle raged, Plato caught a glimpse of the superweapon. The device loomed ominously, its power growing as the tablet continued to feed it energy. He knew they had to buy Thoth more time.

Thoth and his team reached the final generator, their movements quick and precise. As they set the last of the charges, Thoth felt a surge of determination. They were so close.

"Once these charges go off, the superweapon will be weakened," Thoth said, his voice steady. "But we'll need to move fast to secure the tablet."

The charges were set, and Thoth signaled for his team to fall back. They moved swiftly, retracing their steps through the hidden passages. The sound of explosions grew louder, echoing through the stronghold as the charges detonated.

Thoth's heart raced as they made their way back to the rendezvous point. He knew the final confrontation was imminent, and they had to be ready.

At the rendezvous point, Plato's team regrouped with Thoth's. The relief was palpable, but they knew the battle was far from over. The general's forces were regrouping, and the superweapon, though weakened, was still a threat.

Thoth looked at Plato, his expression resolute. "We've done all we can here. Now, we need to confront the general and retrieve the tablet. This is our last chance."

Plato nodded, his eyes steely with determination. "Let's finish this."

Together, they led their teams towards the heart of the stronghold, ready for the final confrontation. The fate of Atlantis hung in the balance, and they knew that only by working together could they hope to succeed.

With the stage set and the preparations complete, the final confrontation loomed. Thoth and Plato knew the next steps would determine the fate of their world, and they steeled themselves for the battle ahead.

Thoth and Plato led their teams through the dimly lit corridors of the stronghold, their hearts pounding with anticipation. The sounds of battle echoed around them, a constant reminder of the stakes. As they approached the central chamber, where the general and his forces were stationed, Thoth felt a surge of resolve.

"This is it," Thoth said, his voice barely above a whisper. "Stay focused and remember our objective: retrieve the tablet and disable the superweapon."

Plato nodded, his face set with determination. "We've come this far. We won't let them stop us now."

They moved as one, stealthily approaching the entrance to the central chamber. Peering around the corner, Thoth saw the general standing near the superweapon, the tablet in his hands. The room was filled with guards, all on high alert.

"We need another distraction," Thoth whispered to Plato. "Something to draw their attention away from us."

Plato nodded, signaling to a few of his team members. They slipped away, preparing to create the diversion. Moments later, a series of small explosions rocked the far side of the chamber, sending the guards scrambling.

"Now!" Thoth hissed, and they surged forward, taking advantage of the chaos. They slipped into the chamber, moving swiftly towards the general.

The general turned, his eyes narrowing as he saw Thoth and Plato. "You!" he spat, holding the tablet tightly. "You think you can stop me? This power is mine!"

Thoth stepped forward, his voice calm but firm. "That tablet belongs to Atlantis, not you. You've seen the destruction it can cause. If you care at all about our people, you'll hand it over."

The general laughed, a harsh, grating sound. "You're a fool, Thoth. This power will make us invincible. With this, we can control the world, there will be no more need for fighting. The rest of the world would fall in to complete submission and we will finally have peace."

Thoth's eyes flashed with anger. "At what cost? You're willing to sacrifice everything for power. That's not the Atlantis I know."

The general sneered, raising the tablet. "You don't understand. None of you do. This is our destiny!"

Before Thoth could respond, the general activated the superweapon, the room flooding with a blinding light. The ground shook, and a deafening roar filled the air. The device began to hum, its power growing as the tablet fed it energy.

Plato shielded his eyes, shouting over the noise. "We need to disable that thing, now!"

Thoth nodded, his mind racing. They had to act fast. He signaled to his team, who sprang into action, engaging the guards and trying to reach the superweapon.

The battle was fierce, the room filled with the sounds of clashing weapons and desperate shouts. Thoth fought his way towards the general, determined to stop him. The general's eyes were wild with power, his movements erratic as he wielded the tablet.

Thoth managed to get close, lunging at the general. They grappled, the tablet slipping from the general's grasp and skidding across the floor. Both men scrambled for it, their hands closing around it at the same time.

A surge of energy coursed through Thoth, the power of the tablet almost overwhelming. He fought to maintain control, his mind racing as he tried to wrest the tablet from the general.

Plato and the others fought valiantly, holding off the guards and trying to disable the superweapon. The device continued to hum, its power growing with each passing second.

Thoth finally managed to pry the tablet from the general's hands, his strength fueled by sheer determination. He stood, holding the tablet aloft, its power crackling around him.

"Stop this, now!" Thoth shouted, his voice echoing through the chamber.

The general staggered back, his face contorted with rage. "You think you've won? This is far from over!"

Before Thoth could respond, the general lunged at him, knocking the tablet from his hands. It skidded across the floor, coming to rest near the edge of the chamber. Both men froze, eyes locked on the tablet.

In that moment of hesitation, the general's forces regrouped and managed to retrieve the tablet. They quickly retreated towards the exit of the chamber, taking the tablet with them.

Thoth's heart sank as he saw the tablet slipping away. "No!" he shouted, surging forward, but he was intercepted by a group of guards.

Plato fought his way to Thoth's side, his face grim. "We need to fall back and regroup. We're not done yet."

Thoth nodded, his eyes filled with determination. "We'll get it back. We have to."

They retreated from the chamber, the battle far from over. As they regrouped, Thoth knew they were running out of time. The final confrontation was approaching, and they had to be ready. The fate of Atlantis and the world depended on it.

In the dim light of their temporary refuge, Thoth and Plato steeled themselves for the battles ahead. The tablet was still in the hands of the general, and the stakes had never been higher. They returned to the airship, their spirits heavy with the weight of their situation. Nerissa was there, waiting anxiously for news. Thoth saw the worry etched on her face and felt a pang of guilt. He approached her, taking her hands in his.

"We'll get it back, Nerissa," he said, his voice steady despite his inner turmoil. "We have to."

Nerissa nodded, her eyes shining with determination. "I believe in you, Thoth. We'll do whatever it takes."

As they regrouped, Thoth and Plato gathered their remaining forces to discuss their next steps. The urgency of their mission pressed heavily on them; they knew they had to act quickly to prevent the general from using the tablet's power for further destruction.

"We need a new plan," Plato said, his voice firm. "The general is using the tablet to amplify his power and weaponry. We have to find a way to neutralize him and retrieve the tablet."

Thoth nodded, his mind racing with possibilities. "We need to force him into a position where he's vulnerable. Something that will disrupt his control over the tablet."

Nerissa stepped forward, her face resolute. "I can get close to him. He trusts me enough to let me near. Once I'm close enough, I'll create an opportunity for you to strike."

Thoth's heart clenched at her words. "No, Nerissa. It's too dangerous. I can't lose you too."

Nerissa's eyes softened as she looked at Thoth. "We don't have a choice, Thoth. This is bigger than us. We have to do whatever it takes to save Atlantis."

Thoth struggled with the decision, torn between his love for Nerissa and the gravity of their mission. Finally, he nodded, his eyes filled with a mixture of sorrow and determination. "All right. But be careful."

As they prepared for the final confrontation, Thoth felt a surge of resolve. They had come too far to fail now. The lives of their people, the future of Atlantis, and the balance of the world depended on their success.

Nerissa took a deep breath, her mind focused on the task ahead. She approached the general's stronghold under the guise of negotiating a truce, using the pretext of surrender to get close to him. The general, suspicious but intrigued, allowed her entry.

Inside the stronghold, the atmosphere was tense. The general eyed Nerissa warily, the tablet glowing with power in his hands. "Why have you come here?" he demanded.

Nerissa's voice was steady. "To end this conflict. We want to help, but first, there's a better way to use the tablet for what you need. I can show you, but you have to let me see the tablet."

The general smirked, holding the tablet closer. "You think you can sway me? Very well, look upon it and despair."

As he held the tablet up, Nerissa's heart pounded. She glanced subtly at Thoth and Plato, who had taken up positions outside the stronghold, ready to strike.

In a swift motion, Nerissa reached for the tablet, her fingers grazing its surface. The general's eyes widened in shock, but before he could react, she activated a hidden mechanism she had prepared—a device to disrupt the tablet's energy.

The tablet pulsed violently, causing a massive surge of energy that threw the general off balance. "Now!" Nerissa shouted, her voice echoing through the chamber.

Thoth and Plato burst in, their weapons drawn. The general, enraged and disoriented, struggled to regain control. Thoth saw his chance and charged towards the tablet, determination blazing in his eyes.

But the general was not finished. He unleashed a powerful blast that sent shockwaves through the chamber, knocking Thoth to the ground. Nerissa, seeing the general preparing for another strike, made a fateful decision.

With a fierce cry, she lunged at the general, managing to knock the tablet from his hands. It skidded across the floor, coming to rest near the edge of the chamber.

The general turned on her, his face twisted with rage. "You'll pay for that, girl!" he snarled, raising his sword.

Nerissa stood her ground, her eyes defiant. "Thoth, now!" she shouted.

Thoth, struggling to his feet, saw the tablet within reach. But as he moved towards it, the general aimed his sword at Nerissa.

In that moment, Thoth realized what she was about to do. His heart shattered as she lunged at the general, sacrificing herself to create an opening for Thoth. Her scream of pain echoed through the chamber as the general's blade struck her.

"No!" Thoth cried out, his voice raw with anguish. He reached the tablet, but before he could grasp it, the general's forces swarmed around him, pulling him away.

The general, seizing the opportunity, grabbed the tablet and retreated with his guards, leaving Thoth and Plato behind in the chaos.

Plato fought his way to Thoth's side, his face grim. "We need to fall back and regroup. We're not done yet."

Thoth nodded, tears streaming down his face as he looked at Nerissa's lifeless body. "We'll get it back. We have to."

They retreated from the chamber, the battle far from over. As they regrouped, Thoth knew they were running out of time. The final confrontation was approaching, and they had to be ready. The fate of Atlantis and the world depended on it.

In the dim light of their temporary refuge, Thoth and Plato steeled themselves for the battles ahead. The tablet was still in the hands of the general, and the stakes had never been higher.

Chapter 26

The Last Stand

Thoth knelt beside Nerissa's lifeless body, his heart heavy with grief. The chamber was quiet now, the echoes of battle fading into silence. He gently brushed a strand of hair from her face, his vision blurred by tears. The loss of Nerissa hit him hard, and he could feel the weight of the moment pressing down on him.

Plato placed a hand on Thoth's shoulder, his own sorrow reflected in his eyes. "We have to keep moving, Thoth. She gave her life for this. We can't let it be in vain."

Thoth nodded, swallowing hard. He knew Plato was right, but the pain of losing Nerissa was almost too much to bear. He took a deep breath, steeling himself. "We'll make this right," he said, his voice trembling but determined.

They retreated to their temporary refuge, where the remaining survivors awaited them. The atmosphere was tense, everyone acutely aware of the stakes. The loss of Nerissa had dampened their spirits, but it had also steeled their resolve.

Plato glanced at Thoth, his expression serious. "We need a plan. The final plan. This is our last chance to stop the general and secure the tablet."

Thoth wiped his eyes, his resolve hardening. "You're right. We can't let her sacrifice be for nothing. We'll do whatever it takes."

As they began to strategize, Plato winced in pain, clutching his side. Thoth noticed the blood seeping through Plato's fingers. "You're hurt," Thoth said, concern etching his face.

Plato looked down at the wound, a deep gash from the earlier skirmish. "I didn't realize it was this bad," he admitted, gritting his teeth against the pain. The reality of the situation hit him – he could actually be hurt in this world. This wasn't just a vision; it was real.

Thoth helped Plato sit down, quickly bandaging the wound with strips of cloth. "You need to rest," Thoth said. "You can't fight like this."

Plato shook his head, determination in his eyes. "No. I have to see this through. If we don't stop the general, it's all over. Nerissa's sacrifice… it would mean nothing."

Thoth looked at Plato, seeing the fierce resolve in his eyes. He nodded, understanding the gravity of Plato's decision. "Alright. But you need to be careful. We need you alive."

Plato managed a weak smile. "I'll do my best."

They spent the next few hours planning their final assault, each detail meticulously thought out. Plato's injury was a constant reminder of the stakes – this was no longer just a test of their resolve; it was a fight for survival.

As they prepared to move out, Thoth placed a hand on Plato's shoulder. "We'll get through this," he said, his voice filled with determination. "For Nerissa."

Plato nodded, feeling the weight of his own resolve. "For Nerissa," he echoed.

They stood, ready to face the final battle. The weight of their mission pressed down on them, but they knew they had to succeed. The fate of Atlantis – and perhaps the world – rested on their shoulders.

As the survivors regrouped in their temporary refuge, the tension in the air was palpable. Thoth and Plato gathered everyone together,

their expressions grave. The loss of Nerissa had taken a toll on them all, but it had also solidified their determination to see their mission through to the end.

Thoth unrolled a makeshift map of the stronghold, pointing to key areas. "The general has fortified his position here," he said, indicating a heavily guarded chamber near the heart of the complex. "We need to strike quickly and decisively."

Plato, still wincing from his injury, leaned in to examine the map. "We'll need a two-pronged approach," he said, his mind racing. "One team to distract and draw the guards fire, and another to infiltrate the chamber and retrieve the tablet."

Thoth nodded, his eyes scanning the faces of the survivors. "I'll lead the infiltration team. Plato, you take charge of drawing their fire. We need to be in sync for this to work."

Plato met Thoth's gaze, his resolve unwavering despite the pain. "We'll make it happen."

They quickly divided into two groups, each person knowing their role. Thoth's team would be the spearhead, moving stealthily through the stronghold's labyrinthine corridors to reach the central chamber. Plato's team would draw as many of the general's forces away as possible.

Thoth's eyes lingered on the faces of his companions, the people who had fought and bled alongside him. "We've come this far," he said, his voice steady. "We're fighting for more than just ourselves. We're fighting for the future of Atlantis, for the memory of those we've lost."

Plato stepped forward, his voice firm despite the pain. "Remember, stick to the plan. No heroics, no unnecessary risks. Our goal is to retrieve the tablet and disable the superweapon. We can do this."

As they prepared to move out, Thoth took a moment to address the group one last time. "Stay focused, stay sharp. And whatever happens, know that we did everything we could."

With that, they split into their respective teams, moving silently through the darkened corridors of the stronghold. Thoth led his team with a determined stride, his mind focused on the task at hand. Every step brought them closer to the central chamber, and to the confrontation that awaited them.

Meanwhile, Plato and his team positioned themselves at a key junction, ready to create the distraction. Plato's heart pounded in his chest, the weight of his responsibility pressing down on him. He knew they had one chance to get this right.

With a nod from Plato, the team sprang into action. Explosions rocked the far side of the stronghold, sending guards scrambling. The general's forces, caught off guard, rushed to contain the perceived threat.

Thoth and his team moved quickly, taking advantage of the chaos. They slipped through the now lightly guarded corridors, their path to the central chamber clear. Thoth's heart raced as they approached the chamber's entrance, the final confrontation mere moments away.

Inside the chamber, the general stood near the superweapon, his eyes filled with a manic gleam. The tablet was in his hands, its power crackling ominously. Thoth's breath caught in his throat as he saw the device, its energy growing with each passing second.

Thoth signaled his team to hold back, taking a deep breath to steady himself. "This is it," he whispered. "We get the tablet, or we die trying."

With a final nod to his team, Thoth stepped into the chamber, ready to face the general and the decisive battle that awaited them.

As they burst into the chamber, the general turned, his eyes blazing with madness. "You dare challenge me?" he roared. "This power is mine by right!"

Thoth stepped forward, his voice calm but filled with authority. "The tablet belongs to Atlantis, not to your ambition. Surrender it and end this madness."

The general laughed, a harsh, mirthless sound. "You think you can stop me? This power will make me invincible!"

Before Thoth could respond, the general activated the superweapon. The room was flooded with blinding light, the ground shaking violently as the device began to hum with growing intensity.

Plato shouted over the noise, "We need to disable it, now!"

Thoth nodded, signaling his team to engage the guards. They fought their way toward the superweapon, determined to reach the tablet.

The battle was brutal, the air filled with the clang of weapons and the cries of the wounded. Thoth fought his way through the melee, his eyes fixed on the general and the glowing tablet.

As Thoth reached the general, they grappled fiercely. The tablet slipped from the general's grasp, skidding across the floor. Both men lunged for it, their hands closing around it simultaneously.

A surge of energy coursed through Thoth, nearly overwhelming him. He struggled to wrest the tablet from the general's grip, his mind racing.

Plato and the others fought valiantly, holding off the guards and trying to reach the superweapon. The device continued to hum, its power growing with each passing moment.

Finally, Thoth managed to pry the tablet from the general's hands, but not without a cost. The general drew a hidden dagger and plunged it into Thoth's side. Thoth gasped in pain but held onto the tablet with all his strength.

Seeing Thoth in danger, Plato rushed to his aid. He tackled the general, wrestling him to the ground. The general fought back fiercely, and in the struggle, he managed to stab Plato in the abdomen.

Plato cried out in pain, but his grip on the general remained firm. "Get the tablet to safety!" he shouted to Thoth.

Thoth, blood seeping from his wound, staggered to his feet. He looked at Plato, seeing the determination in his eyes. With a final nod, he turned and ran, clutching the tablet.

Plato held on to the general, using the last of his strength to keep him from pursuing Thoth. The general thrashed violently, but Plato's grip was unyielding. Summoning his remaining strength, Plato drove the dagger into the general's heart as he lunged in Thoth's direction. The general's eyes widened in shock before he collapsed.

Thoth, seeing the general fall and knowing time was of the essence, rushed back to Plato. He lifted his fallen friend onto his shoulders, the weight heavy but his resolve unwavering.

"We have to go," Thoth whispered, his voice strained with effort.

Plato nodded weakly, his vision blurring. "Go… save Atlantis."

Thoth carried Plato through the corridors, the sounds of battle fading as they reached the ship. The survivors helped them aboard, their faces a mix of relief and sorrow.

As the ship ascended, Thoth laid Plato gently down, the tablet secure beside them. Plato's breath was shallow, his life slipping away.

"Thoth… you must… rebuild," Plato whispered, his eyes fixed on the horizon.

Thoth nodded, tears streaming down his face. "I will. I promise."

As the ship soared above Atlantis, Plato saw the scene from his recurring nightmare unfold before his eyes – the city sinking beneath the waves, the sky darkening with storm clouds.

They could hear the terrorizing screams of the people, their cries for help echoing in the distance. The sound of crashing waves and destruction were deafening, as they lifted in the air, soaring fast and high above the earth, the wind whipping past them as Thoth flew over the sinking city. Below, the world was being consumed in a great and terrible flood, the water rising higher and higher, drowning everything in its path. They could see the temples and towering cities sinking beneath the waves, their grandeur and majesty reduced to nothing more than a memory.

In the distance, they saw a spotted a massive central temple, its spires reaching towards the sky, but as they flew closer, they saw that it too was sinking, its walls collapsing as the waves crashed against them.

With his last breath, Plato smiled, knowing his sacrifice had not been in vain. He had stood up for what truly mattered, and in doing so, had found redemption. He died with a smile on his face.

Thoth, with the tablet secure and the survivors by his side, knew their journey was far from over. They had to reach Khem and start anew, rebuilding from the ashes of their fallen home.

As Atlantis disappeared below the horizon, Thoth steeled himself for the challenges ahead. They had the tablet, but their fight for survival and the future was just beginning.

Chapter 27

A New Dawn

Thoth and the survivors stood at the helm of the airship, peering out at the desolate landscape below. Khem, the land of their ancestors, stretched out in a vast, arid expanse. The airship descended slowly, a mechanical marvel against the backdrop of a primitive world. As they neared the ground, they could see clusters of caves and primitive shelters, home to people who had never seen such advanced technology.

The ship touched down with a soft thud, and Thoth, flanked by a few of his trusted companions, stepped out. The air was hot and dry, filled with the scent of earth and ancient dust. From the shadows of the caves, figures emerged—cave people, wielding crude weapons made of wood and stone. Their eyes were wide with fear and suspicion, their bodies tense and ready to defend their territory.

"We come in peace," Thoth called out, raising his hands to show he meant no harm. His voice echoed in the stillness, but a few of the cave people, unable to understand his words and driven by instinct, surged forward with their cudgels and spears.

Thoth remained calm, his mind racing for a solution. He glanced at the device on his wrist—a relic of Atlantis he found in the ship, capable of harnessing the power of magnetic fields. With a swift motion, he activated it. An invisible force spread out from him,

immobilizing the attackers in mid-stride. Their weapons hovered in the air, their bodies frozen as if trapped in amber.

Gasps of shock and awe rippled through the crowd of survivors. The cave people, though still immobilized, began to relax, their initial aggression dissolving into confusion and curiosity.

Thoth approached the frozen figures, his eyes filled with understanding and compassion. "You have nothing to fear from us," he said gently, his voice soothing. "We are here to help you, to share our knowledge and build a better future together."

Slowly, Thoth deactivated the device, allowing the cave people to move again. They dropped their weapons, their hostility replaced by a hesitant respect. They could sense that Thoth and his people were different, not enemies but potential allies.

Thoth turned to his companions, his resolve clear. "This is where we begin anew," he said. "Here, in this land, we will build a new civilization. One that honors the past and looks forward to a brighter future."

The survivors nodded, their spirits lifted by Thoth's unwavering leadership. Together, they had escaped the destruction of Atlantis and now stood on the threshold of a new beginning. Thoth's vision and knowledge would guide them through the challenges ahead, as they sought to transform this primitive world into a beacon of enlightenment and progress.

The cave people watched in silent awe as Thoth and his companions began to settle into the area around their landing site. Thoth understood that their initial fear and aggression stemmed from ignorance and uncertainty. To build a new civilization, he needed to earn their trust and demonstrate the value of his knowledge and technology.

Thoth approached the leader of the cave people, a burly man with a stern expression and a wary gaze. He held out his hands, palms

open, as a gesture of peace. "I am Thoth," he said slowly, enunciating each word. "We are friends."

The leader, though cautious, seemed intrigued by Thoth's calm demeanor and the strange device on his wrist. He grunted in response, gesturing for Thoth to follow him to a nearby clearing where the tribe gathered.

Thoth, accompanied by a few of his people, followed the leader to a large circle where the cave people sat, their eyes filled with curiosity and fear. He knew that words alone wouldn't bridge the gap between them; actions would speak louder.

With a nod to one of his companions, Thoth demonstrated a small piece of Atlantean technology—a portable water purifier. He took a dirty, murky bowl of water and placed it in the device. Moments later, the water was crystal clear. Thoth handed the purified water to the leader, who drank cautiously at first, then with evident relief and amazement.

The cave people murmured amongst themselves, their fear beginning to give way to wonder. Thoth took this opportunity to show them more. He produced seeds from a pouch and planted them in the ground, using a device to accelerate their growth. Within minutes, small plants sprouted, bearing fruits and vegetables.

The leader's stern expression softened as he watched the miraculous growth. He nodded approvingly at Thoth, indicating acceptance. Thoth smiled and extended his hand in a gesture of friendship. The leader hesitated for a moment before grasping Thoth's hand firmly, sealing their alliance.

Over time, Thoth and his companions worked tirelessly to teach the cave people. They demonstrated how to use simple tools, shared knowledge about agriculture, and explained basic principles of hygiene and medicine. The cave people, initially skeptical, began to see the benefits of these new ways and grew more cooperative.

One evening, as the sun set over the horizon, Thoth gathered everyone around a large fire. He began to tell them stories of Atlantis, of its grandeur and its downfall. He spoke of the lessons learned, the importance of wisdom and balance, and the need to work together for a better future.

The cave people listened intently, their faces illuminated by the flickering firelight. They could feel Thoth's sincerity and passion, and it resonated deeply within them. Slowly but surely, trust was being built.

Thoth stood before the group, his eyes reflecting the fire's glow. "We have a chance to create something extraordinary here," he said. "Together, we can build a civilization that values knowledge, harmony, and the well-being of all its people."

The leader of the cave people stepped forward, his voice filled with newfound respect. "We will follow you, Thoth," he said. "Teach us, and we will learn."

Thoth nodded, his heart swelling with hope. The foundations of trust had been laid, and a new chapter was beginning. This land, Khem, would become a beacon of progress and enlightenment, a testament to the enduring spirit of humanity.

With trust established, Thoth turned his attention to the future. Before constructing a great pyramid, he envisioned and carved a giant structure out of the bedrock, with the body of a lion and the head of a man—a structure he called a Sphinx. This magnificent edifice served both as a temple and a repository for the vast wealth of knowledge from Atlantis. The cave people, now his allies, eagerly helped clear the land and gather materials for this grand project and the subsequent construction of their new society. Thoth directed them with precision, utilizing his advanced knowledge to plan the layout of the new settlement.

With the sphinx almost complete, Thoth stood at the center of the clearing, a spot he had chosen with great care. It was the perfect location for the next structure—the foundation stone of his great pyramid. He placed his hand on the ground, feeling the energy beneath the earth. This place was special; it was destined to be the heart of a new civilization.

Gathering the people around him, Thoth began to speak. "This land, Khem, will be the birthplace of a new era. Here, we will build a society based on knowledge, wisdom, and balance. The structures we create will stand for millennia, guiding future generations."

The cave people watched as Thoth used a device to draw precise geometric patterns on the ground. These patterns would serve as the blueprint for the pyramid. He explained the significance of each line and angle, teaching them the basics of sacred geometry. The people listened attentively, their minds opening to new concepts and possibilities.

Thoth's companions, skilled artisans from Atlantis, began to shape and cut the stones. The cave people, now their apprentices, assisted in the process. Thoth moved among them, offering guidance and encouragement. He knew that the success of this endeavor depended on their unity and cooperation.

As the sun set, the first stones were laid, marking the foundation of the pyramid. Thoth stood back, observing the progress. He felt a deep sense of fulfillment. Despite the loss and destruction he had witnessed, here was a chance to create something lasting and meaningful.

That night, Thoth sat alone at the edge of the clearing, gazing up at the stars. The weight of his responsibilities pressed down on him, but he was determined to succeed. The memories of his father, Thotme, and Nerissa filled his mind, their sacrifices fueling his resolve.

Closing his eyes, Thoth entered a meditative state. He reached out with his consciousness, seeking guidance from the cosmos. He

envisioned the pyramid, not just as a physical structure, but as a beacon of light and knowledge; a container of secrets.

In his vision, he saw the future—a thriving civilization, built on the principles he held dear. He saw generations of people studying the stars, exploring the mysteries of the universe, and living in harmony with nature. The pyramid stood tall, a testament to their achievements and a symbol of hope.

Thoth opened his eyes, the vision fading but the inspiration lingering. He knew that the path ahead would be difficult, but he was ready to face the challenges. With the foundation laid, it was time to build the rest of the pyramid and, with it, the future of their new world.

The next morning, Thoth addressed the people. "We have made a great start," he said. "But there is much work to be done. Together, we will build a civilization that honors the wisdom of the past and embraces the possibilities of the future. Let us continue our journey, with courage and determination."

The people cheered, their spirits lifted by Thoth's words. They resumed their work with renewed vigor, the foundation stones a reminder of their collective effort and shared vision. As the days passed, the pyramid began to take shape, its towering presence a symbol of their unity and purpose.

Thoth knew that their journey was just beginning. The challenges they faced would test their resolve, but he was confident that they would prevail. With the foundation laid and the people's trust secured, they were on the path to creating a new civilization—one that would stand the test of time and inspire future generations.

As the pyramid began to rise, Thoth found himself spending more time in quiet reflection. Each night, after the day's work was done, he would retreat to a secluded spot overlooking the construction site. Here, he would meditate, seeking guidance from the spirits of his ancestors and the cosmos.

One night, as Thoth entered a deep meditative state, a familiar presence enveloped him. The air around him shimmered, and he felt a powerful energy surge through his body. He closed his eyes, and the world around him faded away, replaced by a vision.

In this vision, Thoth found himself standing in a vast, ethereal plane. The sky above him was a swirling tapestry of colors, and the ground beneath his feet pulsed with a gentle, rhythmic energy. He sensed that he was not alone.

A figure emerged from the shimmering light, and Thoth's heart leapt with recognition. It was Plato, looking weary but resolute. They stood facing each other, the distance between them seeming both vast and insignificant.

"Plato," Thoth said, his voice echoing in the void. "You are not dead."

Plato nodded, a faint smile playing on his lips. "I am not. I have been in a deep spiritual state, connected to you and your journey. My body remains in the pyramid, but my spirit is here."

Thoth felt a surge of relief and gratitude. "I feared I had lost you," he admitted. "Your sacrifice gave me the strength to carry on."

Plato's expression grew serious. "Our paths are intertwined, Thoth. We each have our roles to play. You must continue your mission here in Khem, and I must find my way back to the physical realm."

Thoth nodded, understanding the gravity of their situation. "What must I do?"

Plato's form shimmered as he spoke. "The foundation you have laid is just the beginning. You must build a society that values knowledge, wisdom, and compassion. The pyramid will be a beacon for future generations, guiding them towards enlightenment. Remember, Thoth, the soul takes nothing with her to the next world but her education and her culture."

Thoth felt the weight of this responsibility, but also a deep sense of purpose. "I will do my best," he promised. "But what about you? How will you return?"

Plato's eyes glowed with an inner light. "I will find my way, Thoth, as we are all called to do. The bond between us is strong, and it will guide me back. Remember, the light within us is our greatest strength."

As the vision began to fade, Thoth reached out, his hand passing through Plato's form. "Thank you, Plato," he said. "For everything."

Plato's voice echoed in the void. "And thank you, Thoth. Together, we will create a legacy that will endure."

Thoth opened his eyes, the vision dissolving around him. He was back in his secluded spot, the night air cool against his skin. He felt a renewed sense of determination and clarity. Plato was not lost; he was a part of this journey, just as Thoth was.

The next morning, Thoth gathered the people of Khem. "We are not just building a pyramid," he told them. "We are building a future. A future where knowledge and wisdom guide us. A future where we honor the past and embrace the possibilities of tomorrow."

The people listened, their eyes filled with hope and determination. They resumed their work with a renewed sense of purpose, knowing that their efforts were part of a greater vision.

As the pyramid continued to rise, Thoth kept Plato's words close to his heart. He knew that their journey was far from over, but he was ready to face whatever challenges lay ahead. With each stone they placed, they were building more than just a structure—they were building a legacy that would stand the test of time.

Thoth's vision had shown him the way, and he was determined to see it through. The light within him burned brightly, guiding him and his people towards a future filled with promise and possibility.

Thoth stood on the mound, his eyes fixed on the horizon as the first light of dawn began to creep over the land. The pyramid behind him was still a skeleton of its future grandeur, but the foundations were strong, and the determination of the people of Khem was unyielding.

He felt a sense of peace, knowing that he was fulfilling his destiny. The vision of Plato had reaffirmed his purpose, and he was ready to guide these people into a new era of enlightenment and wisdom. But there was still a lingering concern for his friend and ally.

Thoth turned and walked through the bustling worksite, his presence a beacon of calm and authority. The cave people, now his devoted followers, paused in their labor to watch him pass. He approached the edge of the construction area and found a quiet spot to sit and meditate.

Closing his eyes, Thoth reached out with his mind, seeking the connection he had felt with Plato during the vision. The air around him seemed to hum with energy, and he focused his thoughts, calling out silently to his friend.

Far away, deep within the pyramid, Plato stirred. He was disoriented, his body aching from the ordeal he had endured. The darkness was oppressive, but he felt a strange sense of warmth and light emanating from within himself. The connection to Thoth, though faint, was still there.

Plato took a deep breath, his mind reaching out across the vast distance. "Thoth, can you hear me?" he thought, hoping that the bond they shared would bridge the gap between their realities.

In his meditative state, Thoth's eyes snapped open. He heard Plato's voice, faint but unmistakable. "Plato, I hear you," he replied silently. "You are not alone."

A surge of relief washed over Plato. "I thought I had failed. But now, I understand that my journey is not over."

Thoth's voice was calm and reassuring. "We are connected, my friend. Your spirit is strong, and together, we will see this through."

Plato nodded, even though he knew Thoth couldn't see him. "What must I do?" he asked, seeking guidance.

"Find the light within you, the kingdom you seek is within" Thoth replied. "The trials you face are not just physical but spiritual. Trust in your inner strength and the knowledge we have gained."

Plato felt a renewed sense of determination. He focused on the warmth within him, the light that had guided him through the darkest moments. Slowly, he began to rise, his strength returning.

"I will find my way back," Plato thought, his resolve firm. "Thank you, Thoth."

Thoth smiled, the bond between them strengthening. "And thank you, Plato. We are creating a legacy together, one that will endure through the ages."

As the connection faded, Thoth opened his eyes, the morning light bathing the construction site in a golden glow. He stood, his heart filled with hope and purpose. The journey ahead was long, but he knew they would succeed.

Far away, Plato began to move through the darkness, his mind clear and his spirit unwavering. The pyramid's secrets awaited him, and he was ready to face whatever challenges lay ahead.

Thoth looked out over the horizon, his thoughts with his friend and the future they were building. The dawn of a new era was upon them, and he was prepared to lead the way.

In the distance, the pyramid loomed, a symbol of their determination and the light within them. The journey was far from over, but with each step, they were forging a path towards a brighter future.

Chapter 28

The Dark Ascent

Plato stood alone in the cold, pitch-black darkness of the pyramid's inner chamber. The silence was deafening, broken only by the faint echoes of his own breath. Every exhale seemed to linger in the air, a reminder of his solitary existence in this ancient, sacred space. The weight of centuries pressed upon him, the air thick with the history and secrets of a long-lost civilization. Every step he took echoed ominously, reminding him of the magnitude of the task ahead.

His heart pounded in his chest, each beat a steady drum of both fear and determination. He took a deep breath, the cold air filling his lungs and sending a shiver down his spine. The darkness was so complete that it felt almost tangible, like a heavy cloak enveloping him. The loneliness and fear began to creep into his heart, whispering doubts and fears that threatened to undermine his resolve. As the silence stretched on, he began to worry if he had failed. Questions swirled in his mind—had he done something wrong? Was he destined to die alone in the darkness? The fear started to consume him, gnawing at his confidence and filling his thoughts with dread.

Suddenly, the atmosphere shifted. The air grew colder, and shadows began to swirl around him, taking on menacing shapes. Dark, indistinct forms moved in the periphery of his vision, and whispering voices echoed through the chamber, taunting and threatening him with words he could not fully understand but felt deep within his soul. The

oppressive presence of malevolent entities grew stronger, and Plato knew this was his final trial—the ultimate test of his resolve and faith.

His hand tightened around the cross he held, its smooth surface a comforting reminder of the divine protection it symbolized. Just as he felt alone and unable to bear any more, an instinctive urge made him reach for the cross hanging around his neck. It began to shine, casting a soft, radiant light in the oppressive darkness. Renewed with divine strength, Plato knew he was no longer alone; God was always with him. Summoning all his courage and belief in the divine, Plato raised the cross high above his head. "Begone, foul spirits," he commanded, his voice steady despite the fear gnawing at him from within. The words echoed through the chamber, a beacon of light in the consuming darkness.

The shadows recoiled, hissing as if burned by an invisible flame. Their forms twisted and contorted, their attempts to consume him thwarted by the radiant power of the cross. The air around him buzzed with tension, the dark entities circling him, searching for a weakness, a moment of faltering faith. But Plato stood firm, his resolve unshaken.

With a firm voice, he began to chant a prayer of protection, invoking the divine presence to shield him. "O Divine Light, protect me from the darkness that seeks to consume. Grant me the strength to stand firm and the courage to face my fears." His words were infused with unwavering faith, a powerful incantation that resonated within the chamber's ancient walls.

The room shook as the demons retreated, their malevolent energy dissipating into the ether. The oppressive darkness lifted, replaced by a serene and radiant presence. Plato stood tall, his heart pounding but victorious. He had faced the darkness within and without, emerging stronger and more resolute.

The trial had tested his very soul, but he had prevailed. As the last remnants of the malevolent entities faded away, Plato took a deep breath, feeling the weight of the ordeal lift from his shoulders. The air was lighter now, filled with a sense of peace and anticipation for what was to come. He had conquered the darkness, and now, he was ready for whatever lay ahead in his journey toward enlightenment.

As the darkness lifted and the oppressive energy faded, the atmosphere in the chamber underwent a profound transformation. The air, once thick and suffocating, now felt light and pure. A gentle, radiant glow began to fill the room, dispelling the shadows and replacing the fear with a serene and divine presence.

Plato took a moment to steady himself, his breath slowing as the tension from his encounter with the demons gradually dissipated. The change in the room was almost palpable, as if the very fabric of reality had shifted to welcome a higher, more sacred presence. The oppressive silence was replaced by a tranquil stillness, a calm that settled deep within his soul.

In the center of the chamber, a large eye manifested above Plato. It was the Eye of Providence, the all-seeing, all-knowing symbol of divine insight and wisdom. The eye radiated a soft, luminous light, its gaze both gentle and piercing. Plato felt an overwhelming sense of awe and reverence as he beheld this divine vision.

The eye seemed to look directly into Plato's soul, seeing beyond the physical into the very essence of his being. It illuminated his deepest thoughts and intentions, revealing them with a clarity that left no room for deception or doubt. Plato felt exposed and yet comforted, as if he were standing before the ultimate truth, stripped of all pretenses.

Overwhelmed by the presence of the divine eye, Plato fell to his knees. His heart swelled with a mixture of humility and gratitude. "Reveal to me the will of God," he prayed earnestly, his voice trembling with reverence and hope. His words echoed through the now hallowed chamber, a plea for guidance and understanding.

In response to his sincere prayer, the eye blinked and then seemed to glow even brighter. An all-encompassing bright white light

began to emanate from it, spreading throughout the chamber. The light was blinding yet warm, filling every corner of the room and enveloping Plato in its radiant embrace. It was as if the very essence of the divine had descended upon him, purifying his spirit and granting him profound clarity.

As the light surrounded him, Plato felt a deep sense of peace and calm wash over him. The anxieties and fears that had plagued him melted away, replaced by an overwhelming feeling of safety and love. He closed his eyes, allowing the light to permeate his being, cleansing him of any lingering darkness.

The experience was both humbling and elevating. Plato felt as though he were being lifted to a higher plane of existence, a place where the divine and the mortal met in perfect harmony. The light seemed to communicate with him, not in words, but in feelings and impressions, filling him with an understanding that transcended language.

Time lost its meaning as Plato remained in this state of divine illumination. He was no longer bound by the constraints of the physical world; instead, he was a part of something greater, a vast, interconnected web of divine consciousness. The light filled him with a sense of purpose and destiny, a knowing that he was exactly where he was meant to be.

Gradually, the light began to dim, returning the chamber to its previous state of gentle radiance. Plato opened his eyes, adjusting to the new, serene environment around him. The divine presence lingered, a comforting reminder of the connection he had just experienced.

Plato rose to his feet, his heart still aglow with the warmth of the divine light. He knew that the path ahead was one of continued challenges and growth, but he also knew that he was guided and protected by a higher power. With renewed faith and determination, he

prepared to face whatever trials lay ahead, confident in the knowledge that he was not alone.

As Plato's vision adjusted to the gentle radiance filling the chamber, he noticed twelve beings of light standing before him. These beings were ethereal and luminous, their forms shimmering with a celestial glow. Each one held a cross, a symbol of divine authority and protection. Their presence exuded an aura of wisdom, tranquility, and unwavering strength.

Plato was mesmerized by their appearance. The beings seemed to float slightly above the ground, their movements graceful and synchronized. They radiated an inner light that filled the room with a sense of peace and serenity, a stark contrast to the dark, oppressive atmosphere that had previously dominated the space.

The twelve beings spoke in unison, their voices harmonious and soothing, resonating deeply within Plato's soul. "Liberation awaits above," they said, their words carrying a profound sense of promise and hope. As they spoke, they pointed upwards, directing Plato's gaze to a divine staircase that began to materialize before him.

The staircase was made of shimmering light, each step appearing as if crafted from pure energy. It ascended high into the heavens, leading up to a beautiful celestial dome that seemed to hover above the pyramid. The sight was both awe-inspiring and inviting, a beacon of spiritual ascension and ultimate liberation.

Plato felt a deep sense of purpose and readiness. The trials he had faced within the pyramid had prepared him for this moment, and he knew that the staircase represented the final journey towards enlightenment and unity with the divine. The beings' guidance assured him that he was on the right path, supported and protected by higher spiritual forces.

With a renewed sense of determination, Plato approached the base of the staircase. Each step glowed with a soft, welcoming light, and as he placed his foot on the first step, he felt a surge of divine

energy coursing through him. The air around him seemed to hum with a harmonious vibration, encouraging him to continue his ascent.

Plato climbed steadily, each step bringing him closer to the celestial dome above. The journey was both physical and metaphysical, each step representing a higher level of understanding, purity, and spiritual alignment. The air grew lighter, and a gentle breeze seemed to guide him upward, whispering encouragement and reassurance.

As he ascended, Plato could feel the presence of the twelve beings around him, their light merging with his own, creating a symphony of divine energy. The staircase felt endless, yet every step was filled with a sense of progress and fulfillment. He was moving beyond the confines of the material world, entering a realm of pure spiritual essence.

Reaching the top of the staircase, Plato found himself standing before a large and beautiful golden double door. The doors were intricately designed, adorned with symbols and patterns that seemed to pulse with life. As he approached, the doors slowly opened, revealing a breathtaking view beyond.

A soft morning breeze touched his hair, bringing with it the fresh scent of dawn. Plato stepped through the doors and found himself at the very top of the pyramid. The vista before him was nothing short of magnificent. He stood overlooking Egypt, the landscape bathed in the golden light of the rising sun. The other pyramids stood majestically in the distance, silent witnesses to his journey.

Facing east, Plato welcomed the sun's warm embrace, its rays wrapping around his body like a divine benediction. He felt a profound sense of fulfillment and peace. He had completed his trials, emerged victorious, and now stood at the pinnacle of his spiritual journey, ready to embrace the new dawn and the wisdom it brought.

The twelve beings appeared around him once more, their presence a comforting reminder of the divine guidance that had led

him here. "You have ascended, Plato," they spoke in unison. "Your journey has brought you to the light. Continue to walk in the path of wisdom and truth."

Plato nodded, his heart swelling with gratitude and determination. He had faced the darkness, embraced the light, and now stood ready to fulfill his destiny. The journey was far from over, but he knew he was not alone. With the sun rising before him and the divine beings at his side, Plato stepped forward into the new day, his spirit soaring with the promise of enlightenment and the boundless possibilities that lay ahead.

As he gazed out over the landscape, the sun's rays illuminating the ancient land of Egypt, Plato felt a deep connection to the past and the future. He understood that his trials within the pyramid had prepared him for this moment, not just for his own enlightenment but for the greater good of humanity. The knowledge and wisdom he had gained were not his alone but a gift to be shared, a beacon of hope and guidance for others on their own spiritual journeys.

The morning breeze continued to caress his face, a gentle reminder of the fresh start that each new day brings. Plato stood tall, his mind clear and his heart open. He was ready to embrace his role as a teacher, a guide, and a bearer of light. The divine staircase and the celestial dome had shown him the way, and now it was his turn to lead others toward the same enlightenment.

With a final glance at the rising sun, Plato took a deep breath and stepped forward. The warmth of the sun's embrace and the support of the divine beings gave him the strength and confidence he needed. He descended the pyramid, each step filled with purpose and determination.

As Plato reached the base of the pyramid, he felt a sense of peace and calm settle over him. The landscape of Egypt stretched out before him, vibrant and full of life. He knew that his journey was just

beginning, and with the light of the rising sun guiding his way, he was prepared to face whatever challenges lay ahead.

With the divine beings watching over him and the wisdom of the ancients in his heart, Plato set forth into the new day, ready to fulfill his destiny and share the enlightenment he had gained with the world. The sun continued to rise, casting its golden light over the land, a symbol of hope, renewal, and the boundless possibilities that awaited him and all who sought the path of wisdom and truth.

Chapter 29

Legends of the Lost

Plato stood at the base of the pyramid, his body weary but his spirit renewed. The trials had tested him in ways he had never imagined, pushing him to the brink of his physical and mental limits. Yet, he had endured, drawing strength from the wisdom he had gained and the bond he had formed with Thoth.

As he stepped onto the warm sands of the Egyptian ground, Thoth was there to greet him in spirit, a serene smile on his face. "You have done well, my friend," Thoth said, his voice filled with genuine admiration. "You have proven yourself worthy of the knowledge you sought." Plato bowed his head, humbled by Thoth's words. "I could not have done it without your guidance and the lessons I have learned from you and your people."

Thoth placed a hand on Plato's shoulder, his eyes shining with a deep, unspoken understanding. "The journey we have undertaken together has changed us both. You carry with you now the wisdom of Atlantis and the spirit of Khem. Use it wisely."

As they spoke, Imhotep approached, his presence commanding and calm. "Plato," he began, his voice resonating with authority and warmth, "your perseverance and courage have been remarkable. You have faced trials that would break many and emerged stronger for it."

Plato turned to Imhotep, a deep respect in his eyes. "Thank you, master. Your teachings have been invaluable to me."

Imhotep nodded, a faint smile on his lips. "Remember, true wisdom lies not just in knowledge, but in its application. The path ahead will not be easy, but I believe you are ready for it."

The priest stepped back, raising his hands in a gesture of blessing. "May God guide your path, Plato. You have a great destiny ahead of you. You have received all that I have to give and you have served me well. You are free to go and do as you wish. Your time of service here is now complete."

With those words, Plato turned towards the river, where a small boat awaited to take him back to Athens. As he boarded, he looked back one last time at the towering pyramids, symbols of the trials he had faced and the wisdom he had gained. He knew that his journey was far from over, but he felt ready to face whatever lay ahead.

As the boat sailed down the Nile, Plato sat in quiet contemplation, reflecting on the lessons of the past decade. He thought of Thoth, of Imhotep, of the trials, and of the great responsibility that now rested on his shoulders. The sun set behind him, casting a golden glow over the river, and Plato felt a profound sense of peace and purpose.

Plato stood on the deck of the boat as it gently glided down the Nile, the serene waters reflecting the warm hues of the setting sun. The landscape around him was a tapestry of life: fishermen casting their nets, farmers tending to their fields, and children playing by the riverbanks. Each scene was a reminder of the simple, enduring beauty of the world, a stark contrast to the grandiose trials he had endured within the pyramid.

He leaned against the railing, lost in thought. The past decade felt like a lifetime. His mind drifted to the moments of despair and enlightenment, the teachings of Thoth, and the final sacrifice that had allowed him to emerge victorious. The pain of the wound he had sustained still lingered, a constant reminder of the cost of his journey.

As the boat continued its journey, Plato engaged in brief conversations with the crew. They were a mix of seasoned sailors and eager young men, each with their own stories and aspirations. One of the sailors, a grizzled man named Phaedrus, approached Plato with a curious look.

"You've been deep in thought since we left," Phaedrus remarked. "What's on your mind, traveler?"

Plato offered a faint smile. "Much has happened, and much still weighs on my mind. I've come a long way, and now I return home with a new purpose. Change is the only constant in life, and this journey has made that clearer than ever."

Phaedrus nodded, his eyes reflecting a lifetime of hard-earned wisdom. "A journey can change a man in ways he never expects. What is your purpose, if I may ask?"

Plato looked out over the water, the horizon stretching endlessly before him. "To teach, to share what I've learned. To guide others towards wisdom and understanding."

The sailor chuckled softly. "A noble cause. The world could use more teachers and fewer warriors."

As they sailed closer to the Mediterranean, the boat passed through bustling ports and small coastal towns. Each place brought a new encounter, a brief moment of connection that reaffirmed Plato's resolve. The sea air was invigorating, carrying with it the promise of new beginnings.

One evening, as the boat sailed under a sky ablaze with stars, Plato found himself sharing stories with a group of fellow passengers. There was a merchant from Phoenicia, a storyteller from Crete, and a young scholar from Cyrene. They gathered around a small fire on the deck, the flickering flames casting shadows on their faces.

The storyteller, an animated man named Lycaon, spoke of ancient myths and legends. "Have you heard the tale of Atlantis?" he asked, his eyes gleaming with excitement.

Plato smiled, a knowing look in his eyes. "I have heard many tales of Atlantis, each more wondrous than the last."

Lycaon leaned forward, his voice dropping to a conspiratorial whisper. "They say it was a land of great wisdom and power, but also of great folly. It was lost to the sea because of its hubris."

Plato nodded, his heart heavy with the memories of Thoth and the fall of Atlantis. "There is truth in those tales. Atlantis was a place of great beauty and knowledge, but it was also a place of great tragedy. There are lessons to be learned from its story."

The young scholar from Cyrene, a bright-eyed woman named Helena, looked at Plato with admiration. "You speak as though you have seen it with your own eyes."

Plato met her gaze, his expression thoughtful. "In a way, I have. The lessons of Atlantis are not just about a lost city, but about the human spirit and the pursuit of wisdom. We must remember them, lest we repeat the same mistakes."

As the boat approached the port of Athens, Plato felt a mix of emotions. The familiar skyline of his homeland came into view, evoking a sense of nostalgia and change. He had left Athens as a different man, burdened by the weight of Socrates' death and the failures of his past. Now he returned, not as a man seeking answers, but as a man carrying them.

The boat docked, and Plato stepped onto the shore, greeted by the sights and sounds of Athens. The city was both familiar and new, a place where his journey would continue in a different form. He took a deep breath, feeling the pulse of life around him.

With a heart full of purpose and a mind brimming with wisdom, Plato began his walk through the streets of Athens, ready to establish his Academy and share the knowledge he had gained. The journey was far from over, but he was prepared for whatever lay ahead.

Plato walked through the familiar streets of Athens, a city both unchanged and yet different from the one he had left behind. The

Acropolis still stood majestically against the sky, its marble columns gleaming in the sunlight. Yet, to Plato's eyes, everything carried a deeper significance. Every stone and every shadow seemed to hold a story, a lesson.

As he moved through the bustling agora, he noticed the faces of the people—some familiar, some new. The market stalls overflowed with vibrant goods, the air filled with the lively chatter of merchants and customers. But Plato's mind was set on a singular purpose. He was determined to establish a place of learning, a sanctuary of wisdom where young minds could be nurtured and guided.

He made his way to a quiet area outside the city walls. Here, the noise of the city faded, replaced by the gentle rustling of olive trees and the distant song of birds. It was the perfect spot, serene and conducive to contemplation. With the help of a few trusted friends and former students who had eagerly awaited his return, Plato began to lay the foundations of his school.

Days turned into weeks as they worked tirelessly. Plato's vision was clear: a place where philosophy, mathematics, and the arts could flourish. He wanted his students to question the world, to seek truth and understanding, just as he had done. The site slowly transformed— a courtyard here, a library there, classrooms that would soon echo with the voices of eager learners.

One morning, as the sun rose over the burgeoning academy, Plato stood back to admire their progress. His heart swelled with pride and anticipation. The Academy, as it would come to be known, was more than just a physical space. It was a symbol of hope, of the enduring quest for knowledge.

Plato walked through the new corridors, envisioning the future. He saw young men and women engaged in spirited debates, their minds alight with curiosity. He imagined the exchange of ideas, the growth of wisdom that would ripple out into the world.

In the coming days, students began to arrive. Some were drawn by the reputation of the great philosopher who had returned from distant lands; others were simply curious, eager to learn. Plato welcomed them all, sharing with them his vision and the wisdom he had gained from his trials in Egypt.

"Here, we will not merely teach facts," Plato announced to his first assembly of students. "We will teach you to think, to question, to seek truth in all things. Knowledge is not a possession to be hoarded; it is a light to be shared."

The students listened intently, their faces reflecting a mix of awe and excitement. They knew they were part of something significant, something that would change their lives and perhaps the world.

As the academy grew, Plato found himself more content than he had ever been. His journey had been long and arduous, but it had brought him to this place of fulfillment. He spent his days teaching, guiding, and learning alongside his students. Each evening, as the sun set and the shadows lengthened, he reflected on the path that had led him here.

One evening, after a particularly engaging discussion with his students, Plato walked alone through the quiet grounds of the academy. The stars were beginning to emerge, twinkling in the twilight sky. He thought of Thoth, of the wisdom shared and the sacrifices made. He felt a profound connection to those distant lands, and a sense of duty to carry forward the legacy of knowledge.

Plato knew that the academy was just the beginning. His teachings would spread, inspiring generations to come. As he looked up at the stars, he felt a deep sense of peace. He was home, and he was fulfilling his destiny. He had one last piece of closure he must complete in Athens; there was word of a familiar senator preaching in the streets of the agora.

Plato walked through the bustling streets of Athens, his thoughts deep in contemplation. The city had changed in his absence, but the essence of its spirit remained the same. As he neared the Agora, he noticed a small gathering of people listening to a man speaking passionately about philosophy and politics.

Curiosity piqued, Plato approached the group. As he got closer, his heart skipped a beat. The man speaking was none other than one of the senators who had betrayed him, now older and looking weary. The senator's once commanding presence had faded, replaced by a sense of vulnerability and regret.

The senator paused, his eyes scanning the crowd, and they locked onto Plato. A flicker of recognition passed over his face, followed by a wave of surprise and guilt. The murmurs of the crowd fell silent as the two men regarded each other.

"Plato," the senator said, his voice barely above a whisper. "You're alive."

Plato nodded, his expression calm and composed. "I am."

A tense silence enveloped the group, the air thick with unspoken emotions. The senator took a step forward, his eyes pleading. "I… I never expected to see you again. What happened to you, it was… it was wrong."

Plato remained silent, allowing the weight of the senator's words to hang in the air. The crowd watched, captivated by the unfolding drama.

Another senator, also part of the betrayal, emerged from the group. His face was etched with lines of regret. "We were misguided, Plato. We acted out of fear and ignorance. We thought we were protecting Athens, but we only caused harm. Senator Marcus is no longer with us."

Plato's gaze softened, his new-found wisdom and grace shining through. He could see the genuine remorse in their eyes, the burden of their actions weighing heavily on them. In that moment, he realized that holding onto anger and seeking revenge would only perpetuate the cycle of pain.

Plato stepped forward, the agora bustling with curious onlookers and the senators who had wronged him. He took a deep breath, the weight of his experiences lending gravity to his words.

"Friends, fellow Athenians, and esteemed senators," Plato began, his voice calm yet commanding. "I stand before you today, not as a man seeking retribution, but as one who has journeyed far and learned much. In the years that have passed, I have seen the depths of despair and the heights of wisdom. I have witnessed the folly of pride and the strength of humility.

"It is easy to be led astray by the allure of power and the comfort of ignorance. But it is in the crucible of adversity that true character is forged. The teachings of Socrates have shown us that the unexamined life is not worth living. It is our duty, not just to ourselves but to our society, to seek the truth, to question, and to learn. He who wishes to serve his country must have not only the power to think but the will to act."

"I forgive you, for in your actions, I have found my purpose. I have come to understand that it is through the challenges we face that we grow stronger and wiser. But forgiveness is not an end; it is a beginning."

"Today, I invite you all to join me in this new beginning. I am establishing a school, not far from here, where all who are willing to learn and to think critically for themselves are welcome. A place where the teachings of Socrates will live on, where we will explore the mysteries of the world, and where wisdom and virtue will be our guides.

"Let us build a society that values knowledge over ignorance, virtue over vice, and wisdom over folly. Together, we can create a brighter future for Athens, a city that once again leads the world in thought and understanding.

"Come, join me in this endeavor. Let us honor Socrates by continuing his legacy, by questioning, by learning, and by striving

always to be better than we are. My school is open to all who seek the light of wisdom. Let us embark on this journey together."

Plato paused, his eyes sweeping over the crowd, seeing in their faces a mix of wonder, hope, and resolve. "Thank you," he concluded, "and may we all find the courage to seek the truth and to live lives worthy of our great city."

The agora fell into a contemplative silence, broken only by the murmurs of those inspired by his words. Plato took a moment to absorb the gravity of the moment, then turned and walked away, leaving the agora behind. The sun was setting, casting a golden hue over Athens, symbolizing both an end and a new beginning.

With each step, he felt the weight of his journey lifting, replaced by a sense of purpose and hope. He made his way through the familiar streets, now teeming with potential students and followers. As he approached the outskirts of the city, the sounds of nature and the soft rustle of leaves welcomed him back to his school, his new home. In the fading light of the setting sun, Plato's legacy was set to unfold, one story at a time.

The sun had set, and the sky above Athens was a canvas of twinkling stars. A gentle breeze rustled the leaves of the trees surrounding the campfire where Plato sat, surrounded by a group of children and a few adults, all eager to hear his tales.

The firelight cast a warm glow on Plato's face as he looked around at the expectant faces. His heart swelled with a sense of fulfillment and peace. He had come a long way from the young man who had left Athens, burdened by guilt and seeking answers. Now, he was a teacher, a guide, and a storyteller, ready to share the wisdom he had gained.

"Gather around," Plato said, his voice soothing and inviting. "Tonight, I have a story to tell you. A story of a magnificent city, far across the sea, a city called Atlantis."

The children leaned in closer, their eyes wide with wonder. The adults exchanged intrigued glances, drawn in by the promise of a legendary tale.

"Atlantis was a city like no other," Plato began, his voice rich with emotion. "It was a place of great beauty and advanced knowledge, where the people lived in harmony with nature and each other. But it was also a place of great challenges and trials, where the true nature of a person's heart was tested."

He painted vivid pictures with his words, describing the grand architecture, the intricate social structures, and the profound wisdom of the Atlanteans. He spoke of Thoth, the young boy who grew into a wise leader, and Nerissa, whose love and sacrifice left an indelible mark on his soul.

Plato's voice softened as he recounted the trials of the pyramid, the vision quests, and the ultimate sacrifices that were made. He described the heart-wrenching moment when Thoth had to choose between revenge and the future of civilization, and how that choice shaped the destiny of the world.

The children listened in rapt attention, their imaginations ignited by the tales of bravery, love, and wisdom. The adults were equally captivated, lost in the world Plato wove with his words.

"And so, Thoth and the survivors of Atlantis traveled to a new land, a place we now know as Egypt," Plato continued, his voice filled with reverence. "There, they laid the foundations of a new civilization, one built on the principles of wisdom, balance, and harmony."

He paused, looking up at the night sky, the stars reflecting in his eyes. "These stories are not just tales of the past. They are lessons for us all. They teach us about the importance of wisdom, the strength of the human spirit, and the power of sacrifice and forgiveness."

Plato's gaze returned to the group, a gentle smile on his lips. "Remember, the knowledge we gain is not just for ourselves. It is

meant to be shared, to inspire and guide others. Just as the stars light up the night sky, our wisdom can light up the world."

The children's eyes sparkled with excitement and curiosity. The adults nodded in agreement, moved by Plato's words.

As the fire crackled and the night deepened, Plato continued to share his stories, the campfire becoming a beacon of knowledge and inspiration. Under the vast expanse of the starry sky, Plato felt a profound connection to the universe, to the wisdom of the past, and to the future generations he was helping to shape.

In that moment, he knew that his journey had come full circle. He had found his purpose, and he was ready to lead others on their own journeys of discovery and enlightenment. The story of Atlantis, with its lessons and legacy, would live on through him, through his teachings, and through the hearts and minds of those who listened.

As the night wore on, the children eventually drifted off to sleep, their dreams filled with visions of the magnificent city and its wise and noble inhabitants. The adults, too, left with a renewed sense of wonder and a deeper appreciation for the wisdom that Plato had shared.

Plato remained by the fire, gazing up at the stars. He felt a deep sense of peace and fulfillment, knowing that he had not only completed his own journey but had also planted the seeds for many others to embark on their own paths of enlightenment.

And so, under the canopy of the ancient sky, Plato's legacy began to unfold, one story at a time.

As Plato's words echoed through the ages, the legend of Atlantis remained, a timeless reminder of the heights and depths of human ambition. In the end, it was not the lost city that mattered, but the eternal quest for truth and understanding that Plato had set into motion."

The End.